T-Rx:

The History of a Radical Leader

by

Michael Boylan

PWI Books

Bethesda, Maryland

Cover Illustration by Seán Boylan
Copy edited by Joanna Jensen
Proof read by Lydia Johnson

The Archē Novels

Naked Reverse

Georgia (A Trilogy)

T-Rx: The History of a Radical Leader

The Long Fall of the Ball from the Wall

Preface

Where do I begin? It is not as easy for me to write as my polished father. I have no doctorate degree in history or philosophy. My path has been an interdisciplinary degree from the University of Chicago and the Committee on Social Thought, working between English literature and the cultural rise of feminism in the 19th century in the UK. My dissertation was "The Rise of Political Feminism in Victorian English Literature." My primary text of interest was George Eliot's *Felix Holt*. And though, unlike my father, I did not spend my whole life in the academy, I did teach for a number of years at the University of Illinois at Chicago, Circle Campus.

Let me tell you how I came by this manuscript. When my mother, Rebecca Coale, died on September 9, 2009 just 12 days before her 92nd birthday I, as the only child, had to take care of things. My father, Isaiah, had died much earlier on January 28th, 1983 ten years after the Vietnam War ended—to the day. Since we are non-observant Jews, we did everything through the funeral parlor (though in each case we chose a Jewish proprietor).

The process of "taking care of things" meant that I had to *downsize*. We had only so much space in our garage. I lived at the time with my husband, Charles, in Evanston, Illinois. We had a pleasant house, but it was not overly large—considering that Charles made a decent (though not extravagant) income as an insurance broker. My mother lived in Brooklyn in a rent-controlled apartment that could only go to a relative or hit "market rates" once again. Because it seemed like a fool's errand to let such a deal go to the wind, I moved out to New York for a spell to take over the apartment and go through my mother's and father's effects. What they had was stored in the second bedroom and in a small storage locker down in the basement.

What I found were various boxes that seemed to have been put together at the intervals in which they were no longer being actively used. One pair of boxes I discovered contained my dad's life mission: to try to understand the Vietnam War in terms of the domestic protest—particularly in a figure that fascinated him, T-Rx.

To get an understanding of this, I should tell you a little more about my father, Isaiah Coale. He was born in Brooklyn, NY. His parents were non-observant Jews. His father, Maury, was a lawyer at a small firm dealing in insurance. Isaiah went to public school. He attended NYU for his B.A. (1936). He then went to Columbia Law school (like his father had done) and graduated in 1939. In 1941 he enlisted in the army and saw some combat in France. In 1947 he enrolled at Harvard in history. After receiving an M.A. and passing all his tests, he transferred to philosophy. He focused upon history and political philosophy. His dissertation was on "Collingwood and the Philosophy of History."

My father got a job at Boston University in 1954 in a special program on the Holocaust. He did primary research that led to a significant international conference on Hannah Arendt's book, *The Origins of Totalitarianism*. In 1959, he left Boston University and took a job in the philosophy department at Brooklyn College (CUNY) and was reasonably happy. Since I was seven, it was a big move for the family. But I rather liked the apartment they found and it was soon subsumed under the rent control system that provided some guarantees—especially to those paid a little less, like my father at Brooklyn College. (My mother went back to teaching at this time. She taught kindergarten at a local school she could walk to.) Life was nice and controlled—I had no siblings.

When my father retired at 64—almost 65 in July 1979 (CUNY had good retirement benefits), he then wanted to devote himself to his life-long interest in original historical research on a key political figure. My father eventually chose T-Rx, from the Vietnam era. Isiah hoped to be able to add his interest in philosophy to this historical treatment.

The way this came about began when my dad got a research grant to travel to California, specifically the University of California, Berkeley, that had a repository of manuscripts on the

Vietnam War—including the protestors. One day, he came upon a trove of letters that were all connected to T-Rx. After one week of reading (under the strict conditions of the special collections in the library), he approached the curator of the Vietnam collection with the suggestion that he, my father, wanted to focus upon this one figure for the purpose of an academic work in philosophical history. The curator agreed and microfilmed the letters and made a copy. My father had the microfilm typed out so that he could look at it without fancy devices. Once he had done this, he wanted to get secondary confirmation on various extreme claims in the manuscript.

My father then engaged in original historical research. He got permission for various sets of physical records that were in private possession. He approached individuals included in this cadre around T-Rx and was remarkably successful at getting permission to use the information—though in a couple cases he agreed to change the names of living individuals.

The cache was not complete, but it gave him a quest. In some way, he felt that it put together his entire life. I didn't understand this. My mother didn't understand this. But it made sense to him, and we honored it.

My father was near to completion of the construction of the manuscript at his death.[1] His materials were put into a trunk and kept in the storage locker in my parent's rent-controlled apartment building in Brooklyn.

It was on the occasion of my mother's death that I came upon the unfinished manuscript and my father's notes when I took the task of sorting out their personal effects. Initially, I viewed my father's incomplete project to be a duty that fell upon me to complete. But it became more than that. I took a liking to the project. It was also something to which I could devote myself.

---

[1] By "completion" I mean the setting out of the manuscript so that it all made sense to him. What was barely begun was his secondary goal of creating a scholarly apparatus that would put together his life scholarship's ambitions. Sadly, that had to be left virtually un-started.

My marriage to my husband, Charles, was getting rocky.[2] Charles was working extended hours and (as I was to discover later) had been carrying on a long-term affair with his secretary. But that was not the only long-term habit my husband possessed— he was a heavy smoker.

I got his permission to travel to New York to settle the affairs of my parents. I had planned to be away a month. But around the middle of October, I was called back to Chicago because Charles was in Rush-Presbyterian hospital. He had an advanced-stage lung cancer. He had never been one to go to the doctor. He was in bad shape. They tried an experimental surgery, but it failed. Charles died on October 31, 2009.

This created a second challenge. I had to decide how I was to handle the consolidation of two households. I officially listed my residence in Brooklyn so I could keep the rent-controlled apartment. But I was also clearing up the debris of 19 years of a failed marriage. Since I had no siblings, this process was rather within my own discretion. I decided what I would keep (very little), what I would sell (I got very little), and what I would throw (surprisingly a lot).[3]

One thing in my favor during this process was that Charles had taken out a million dollar life insurance policy on himself fifteen years before (without my knowledge). I was contacted by someone in his agency who *did* know about it. I was 59 years old. One of the settlement options was an annuity of $37,000 for the rest of my life. When I turned 62 I could get some more money from Social Security, plus a widow's benefit. With the sale of the house, I figured I'd have around $43,000 a year plus an emergency fund that would allow me to make it for the rest of my life in my parents' rent-controlled Brooklyn apartment. I felt peaceful.

---

[2] I should say that we were a childless couple. We married in 1990 and I had two miscarriages. We never tried a third time.

[3] When I use the term "throw" it should be understood that I put hardly anything in the "dump." What I mean here is that I donated it to charitable organizations that recycle these items to others in desperate need.

But then there was this manuscript of my father's. I do know a few things about the time in which this manuscript was written (having lived through it with some degree of awareness). So it is that I have taken on the task that my father all but finished. This is because I believe that it is of some value to offer to the public from the post-Nixon-Ford era. It can offer some insight into the present craziness of fighting between Republicans and Democrats—that threatens to put forward ludicrous candidates such as Donald Trump for the election next year (2016).

Perhaps I should be more forthright to my readers about the story of this manuscript so that my words will not seem as cryptic as they must now appear. My father, Isaiah Coale, set out on an ambitious philosophical/historical project. He had a theory about political leadership that he wanted to demonstrate through an examination of the political activist, T-Rx, who was murdered in Atlanta in the Vietnam era. Isiah believed this man, T-Rx (pronounced Tee-Rex) or his birth name, Nehemiah Moses, was a most unusual leader.

What I was left with was a text that had three sections. The first section was a set of letters from one of the people who came to T-Rx in San Francisco. The letters were heavily footnoted and were edited to standard English (except for a sample letter, which was left alone). I read through this text and decided that it wasn't very readable, and so I have eliminated virtually all of these footnotes and have put a little of it back into the idiom in which it was written in an effort to give it the authentic flavor that Isiah had drained from it. Except for a couple of footnotes, I have refrained from adding anything new in this area (though I have added a comment or two after my father's intent, as I understand it).

My father did not have time to do more than make some rough notes on the rest of the text. Some of these have been included (my father's footnotes I have left unsigned; all my footnotes are signed I.B.).

My father had intended that this book be the three principal primary texts, along with his own interpretations on the same through his own developing historical *theory*. But because I have not been trained in this way, but rather through literature as mentioned above, I will leave the primary texts to do the talking about the historical *situation* in which a country was engaged: a limited war [Vietnam] (and the problems in such an effort) as well as an opportunity to view some of the conundrums that women face in a male-dominated society. Beyond these general themes, I find the individual portraits interesting just for their own sake. They make for stimulating reading.

At any rate, I have viewed my job as editor to make the text even more accessible to the general public and less academic. I have tried to render the letters into something like "standard English *plus*"—meaning that I've tried to take my father's version and bridge the gap between taking away the vernacular *heart* of the discourse and making it generally grammatically correct. At times when a rather pedestrian term was used to refer to an event in progress, I've re-written the sentence using more precise language according to my understanding of the events and my father's extra-textual notes on the whole project.

It is a shame that my father's extensive monograph at the end was in no condition to be published. However, the reader should get some flavor of this in his brief introduction to the project. Besides that, the three primary texts should speak for themselves.

This is a book that I feel all people will enjoy despite their particular political persuasion. I am indebted to my father for all of his work. The lengths that he had to go in order to obtain completion for these fragments were enormous, but I feel that the effort was well worth it, though my reasons for saying so are certainly different than his would have been. And now I present my father's introduction and then the longest of the three primary texts.

Iris Brooke
New York, New York
March 13, 2015

Introduction

Quos utinam qui legent scire possint quasi invitus suseeporims scribendos, qua facilius caream stultitiac atque arrogantiae crimine, qui me dodiis interposuorim Caesaris scriptis.[4]

In many respects, I feel like the commentator who wants to protect himself from the possible charge of folly. It is, I believe, the nightmare of the historian that he may wrongly interpret the material presented to him when such events are contemporary. Indeed, it is the most difficult of tasks to understand what is happening without the distancing of a different historical perspective. Such a contrasting perspective helps us to better understand our own era within a context.

When one has either a cultural or historical distancing, he may view the event as a detached observer. Given the truth of this, one might well wonder why such projects are ever attempted at all. The truth of this is that while the latter type of historical writing may be more objective and less prone to contemporary bias, it lacks the potency of the event it is attempting to describe. Oftentimes, it is the very *spirit* of the described actions that is of most importance.

One prime example of this is Thucydides. He is close enough to events so that he does not possess the distance that

---

[4] Caesar, *The Gallic War,* ed. Dr. Rice Holmes (Oxford: Scriptorum Classicorum Bibliotheca Oxoniensis, 1914): VIII.1 "And I trust that those who will read my account will understand how unwillingly I have undertaken the task of writing the commentary. For so I might more easily free myself from the charge of foolishly and presumptively intruding myself into Caesar's writings" by Lucius Cornelius Balbus, a Spaniard from Gades who received Roman citizenship from Caesar and rose to Consul.

affords impartial comment. But because he is close to the events about which he writes, he is able to capture the *spirit of the age*. This spirit exists in the highest degree during the initial action itself at T_0 (time at moment zero). As one moves away from the action in the progression $(T_1, T_2, T_3 \ldots)$, the spirit declines sharply in intensity proportional to the numeric increase in the subscript. It is for this reason that an account at T_1 is valuable. It can capture the spirit of the event better than can be described at T_n (when n > 50).

What type of event is it that is best understood in terms of its *spirit*? This is a very difficult question to answer since all events have a spirit to them: an animating principle that constitutes felt immediacy. Such a question could consume the pages of an entire volume in itself; however, let it suffice that for the purposes of this investigation, the "spirit" of a historical event will be taken to be the set of factors which is composed of particular effects upon the acting agent(s) and those who have been connected to the initial action during a T_1 temporal reference (where T_1 is a parameter upon the scope of said action, be it a day, a week, a month, or a year).

In other words, what I'm trying to determine is the force of that initial effect in all its power as an instigator of subsequent contemporary effects. Now, some have addressed this problem via legal positivism which is rooted in behaviorism. For example, Hart and Honoré set out an example of a man (Mr. A) who throws a cigarette into the side-bracken and it catches fire and burns the forest down. In this case, Mr. A is *responsible for* the forest burning down. However, consider a second scenario. Mr. A still throws out the cigarette. It still falls into the dry bracken, but this time it is about to go out. But, lo and behold, Mr. B comes along. He sees the small fire about to go out and stops his car, gets out, takes the extra can of petrol in the boot out and pours it on the flame and surrounding area. Then the flame is renewed and burns down the forest.[5] Who is responsible for the forest burning down in this second case? Clearly in the natural order, if B had not come about, there would have been *no large forest fire*. According to

---

[5] H.L.A. Hart and A.M. Honoré, *Causation and the Law* (Oxford: Clarendon Press, 1959): 42-46.

the doctrine of *novus actus interveniens* the burden of guilt is to fall upon Mr. B.[6]

Thus emerges the doctrine of joint and several liability. This may work well enough for a principle of law, but it is woefully inadequate to describe historical causation. The behaviorists consciously exclude the communal spirit as an existing entity.[7] They cannot get beyond the *cataloging* of events (as per *The Anglo- Saxon Chronicle*). This is not *history*, but a mere documentation of events (a necessary, but not a sufficient condition for engaging in history). What is needed is an account of what these factual inputs *meant* to those involved. How did they raise or lower the *joie de vivre*?

Now all actions have a spirit in this sense, but in some the ultimate significance of the event is seen less in terms of the intensity of the reaction, but rather on the ultimate historical impact of the action.

The passage of the Fourteenth Amendment to the Constitution of the United States has had a greater effect during the last few decades than it did as an emotional issue during its passage. Conversely, the Popish Plots of the seventeenth century in England were very emotionally charged, though they have little historical significance today. There are some events which are both emotionally charged and become historically significant to later generations (that is, influencing the lives of the average person in a clear fashion). Now, obviously, the contemporary historian is better able to gauge the amount of reaction at T_1 than someone writing a century later. On the other hand, a later observer could better judge how an event gains significance (or loses it) during the succeeding years than a contemporary.

As a philosophical historian, I can declare that one may *not* know whether the event that he wishes to describe will gain historical significance or not. But if it is sufficiently interesting, then he has the duty to act as first a chronicler and record it. Then

---

[6] Hart and Honoré: 123.

[7] Gilbert Ryle, *The Concept of Mind* (London: Hutchinson & Co., 1949): 11-24.

he must also engage in the speculation of causal efficacy (given the limitations on contemporary historians).[8]

In this book, I have taken on the very difficult task of examining a phenomenon which had great intensity: the student political activity during the late 1960s. The particular incident that I wish to describe, however, is not of the intense variety. It is rather an historical event that is important because of its relation to what has preceded it.

I propose the examination of a student leader (who I feel confident will not be remembered for doing anything significant). He is an obscure individual who, I daresay, is probably not recognizable to more than three percent of the American people at this writing, just three years after his death. Such a leader, one might contend, is hardly the stuff for contemporary history, which I just argued is best done when gauging the "spirit" of a historical event. To this I can only respond that I feel in this enterprise the intense spirit of the student unrest that might be viewed through a particular case. Such an analysis of the particular will say something about the unrest of the period as a whole and also that a further purpose is served in the other function of history. Whether this work fulfills this function I will leave to the judgment of my readers. I intend to reverse the usual task of the historian of consequences and judge the effect of a tradition upon the modern event. Instead of seeing the event as having significance with regard to the future, I intend to look at the event in relation to the past. Not to say that the past is somehow affected or changed by the event at T_1, but that the way all events of this kind can be viewed has now been significantly altered so that the present *is*, in one respect, changing the past. The past is changed by the way it is viewed.

To illustrate this principle, let me cite the example of person A lying to B about q. B falsely believes q to be true, but when he learns the truth he not only changes his opinion about q, but alters his judgment of his past belief about q. B might say, "I was believing in something that was false," or "my, was I duped."

---

[8] Cf. the methodology of Christian Wolff, *Preliminary Discourse on Philosophy in General,* tr. Richard J. Blackwell (Indianapolis, IN: Bobbs-Merrill, 1963): 3-14.

An event at T_4 (the revelation of the falsity of q) affects his judgments about his opinions of T_{1-3}.

Since T_{1-3} have a residual existence during T_4 insofar as they are thought about by agents during T_4, the altering of thoughts about T_{1-3} really morphs their ontology, as they exist at T_4. At the moment of *satori*, the agent alters previous opinions and their reality to him. Thus, present events can affect past ones. It is this relationship that I wish to illustrate in the postscript to this book.[9]

The subject for such an ambitious endeavor is a student radical of the late sixties named Nehemiah Moses. He called himself T-Rx. Now, this leader is interesting to the historian because he is an anti-type of a leader. What I mean by this is that the normal model for a leader is one who unites diverse factions to wield adequate power so that he can remain a leader. The character T-Rx acted in an opposite manner and yet was very influential in the short time in which he held his rather unique position.

Perhaps before proceeding, it would be wise to outline just what I mean as the classical résumé for a leader. To accomplish this task, it seems appropriate to read what some of the great leaders of our civilization have said about the quest of gaining and keeping power.

Alexander the Great was one of the first recorded great political military leaders in Western Civilization. He was tutored by Aristotle, who ingrained in his student the principles of his metaphysics that all things are constantly becoming. Each item has potentialities that become actualized in the course of its history. Such a conception is both holistic and teleological. In fact, it is often noted that Alexander's dream of uniting Asia (partly inherited from Philip his father) was put into teleological terms of being "good" for the world. Alexander sought to create a new world capital in Baghdad (which at the time seemed to be roughly central to a universe that extended to Spain in the west and to India [Pakistan] to the east). He also thought that if all

---

[9] This postscript (an intended 50,000 word treatise on political philosophy) was never completed. (I.B.)

nationalities were to intermarry, that problems of racism would fade away. These were very far-thinking ideas.

This is not surprising since his teacher, Aristotle, held that such a metaphysical process would yield similar ideas and was acutely aware of racism because he, Aristotle, (as a Macedonian) was not allowed to be a citizen of Athens (which also meant he could not own land or vote in civic matters).

Alexander wanted to bring the world together under his rule. By the use of forced migrations and interbreeding, he believed that the world could become *one* under his beneficent leadership. I believe that every great political ruler has had some version of this dream. It *is* what makes a political man choose his line of work.

Aristotle's program: intellect, courage, self-control, and justice, this could form the foundation for a sustainable base of power which would exult the ruler as it insures his future fame. Alexander makes this point in the *Secretum Secretorum.* [10]

It is true that the attribution of this text is, in many circles, questionable, the point is wonderfully illustrated that the ruler acts from certain motives to construct something for his eternal glory. This theme repeats itself throughout the writings of great rulers and generals through the ages.

Caesar's vision of Gaul at the beginning was that of three regions, "Gaul is a whole that is divided into three parts: one is inhabited by the Belgae, another by the Aquitani, and the third by the Celts. Each is unique in language, institutions, and laws. The Gauls are marked off by the river Garonne from the Aquitani, and by the Marne and the Seine from the Belgae."[11]

---

[10] *Secretum Secretorum,* parchment codex. London. Pseudo-Aristotle; see: L. Dorez, *Les manuscripts à peintures de la bibliothèque de Lord Leicester* (Paris, 1908): 4-13; this is the first part on the nature of kingship.

[11] "Gallia est omnis divisa in partes tres, quarum unam incolunt Belgae, aliam Aquitani, tertian qui ipsorum lingua Celtae, nostra Gali appellantur. Hi omnes lingua, institutis, legibus inter se different. Gallos ab Aquintanis Garumna flumen, a Belgis Matrona et Sequana dividit." Caesar, *The Gallic War,* ed. Dr. Rice Holmes (Oxford: Scriptorum Classicorum Bibliotheca Oxoniensis, 1914): 1-4.

Caesar's purpose was to weld these areas into one province of the Roman Empire. He had to change a loose relationship of loyalty into a relationship where he could dictate as he pleased to the conquered. [12] The ruler unites and subjects his domain.

This desire to unite and become ruler over all is again echoed by that great general Napoleon Bonaparte, who claimed that a prince is born when he can project the interests of his country throughout Europe.[13]

Like all great rulers and conquerors, Napoleon felt a desire to take separate elements and combine them into a whole of some sort because he wanted to unify Europe with himself as king. The point seems clear enough that great leaders seem to have the desire to combine or unite. This principle I wish to identify as the synthetic principle. It comes from the ancient Greek word, *sunthesis*, which means uniting various factions into a single composition.

When a leader is thought of as a synthesizer, he can be thought of as one who brings large groups of people together into a country. By uniting different factions, he is able to create a base of power which will enable him to rule. The clear sense of the word denotes a combining of diverse elements just as Caesar saw Gaul as being three parts to be combined under his wise authority.

In addition to this sense of uniting and putting together, it should also be remembered that the word refers to making a contract to do something concrete. The sense of this contract is an intransitive relation between the agent and that diverse menagerie that he wishes to organize. While uniting a people, a politician makes promises to those people. These promises amount to a pledge that he will successfully bring them together and that the result will create a new oneness which will function to the mutual advantage of all.

Not only do the great figures of history fit this type, but also the ordinary holders of even the lowliest post. It is the very

---

[12] *Ibid.,* ius esse belli, ut qui vicissent eis, quos vicissent, quem ad modum vellent imperarent; item populum Romanum victis non ad alteris praescriptum, sed ad suum arbitrium imperare consuesse. (I.36).

[13] Napoleon Bonaparte, *Écrtits Personnels De Napoleon Bonaparte,* ed. Than Tulard (Paris: 1969), III. a part of a letter dated March 20, 1811.

nature of a political figure to have to deal with the "polity." It would be very difficult to imagine a leader who didn't fulfill this function, yet it is against this very type I have described that I wish to offer a counter example. It will be my contention that the sentence $\{(x) \ (Sx => Px)\}$ is false as a universal definition (where p=politician and s=having the predicate of being synthetic: so that it reads that if any person has the ability to synthesize, then he will become a politician [in the broad sense of the term]).[14]

Those who possess the *synthetic type potential*, who are also organizers, often become leaders of government or industry. However, those on the fringes of society use this (and other) skills as doppelgangers of the productive social figures. They are what I have in the past termed "anti-type leaders."[15] This anti-type, as I have long suspected, is exemplified in the radical leader Nehemiah Moses. He is what I will term an *analytic* figure. Analysis comes from the Greek word (*ana-luo*) which means breaking up, loosing, releasing, dissolution, and death. This word comes from *luo* which means to unloose, undo, put an end to, set free, loose for departure. Thus, analysis stands for loosening and breaking up. The analytical leader is not one who puts the conditions of people and ideas together, but one who breaks up groups and ideas. This sort of leader fragments continually. In short, he is an anarchist. Now, is anarchy possible? There seems to be a logical contradiction in the very notion of the analytical leader. If such a leader wishes to be against the notion of positive construction, then how can he make the "suggestion" that people divide themselves? For certainly division is one type of construction, namely the construction of "division." It would seem that because of the very definitions of the constituent terms, an analytical political leader would be impossible. This conclusion, however logical, I disagree with.

The problem rests in our definition of political leader. In the ordinary sense we think of a political leader as having certain traits such as being in or aspiring to a position of governmental

---

[14] By "broad sense" here I mean that one is a politician even if he is employed in the private sector.
[15] See I. Coale, "The Origins of the Anti-Type Leader" *History and Politics* 27.4 (1964): 1-15.

power. To do this, it has been suggested that he synthetically connect together diverse sources of power that will enable him to attain to this position. This process is necessarily a synthetic one, thus making the political leader necessarily synthetic as in the universal definition offered earlier. But it is my contention that a political leader is not what he is *because* he has these attributes, but because he stands in a certain relationship to the people whom he is thought to lead.[16]

Under this definition, it is the relationship between the people and leader that becomes the unique measurement of a political leader. X is a leader if and only if he is *considered* to be a leader. In other words, leadership is not a property of x, but a relationship between x and the domain over which he rules. It is the people who determine who will be their leader (or if not the people in the sense of a democracy, the people in the sense of those who choose the leader, i.e., the political hierarchy in a dictatorship).[17] The test of leadership then is not to ascertain whether x has certain qualities such as P, but to question those in his domain and determine whether he is thought of as a leader, or is recognized as being a *political* leader.

Since relationship is what determines leadership, it would not be inconsistent to think of anyone *becoming* a leader. For example, a primitive tribe might think that a certain stone has magical properties and therefore, they elect to make that stone their leader. The stone has not made any positive doctrine of any kind. In fact, it can make no doctrines at all (assuming that it has no actual magical properties). In the same way, an individual espousing analytical principles about life and political structures may attain a position of leadership without seeking it in the ordinary fashion (which we have agreed is necessarily a synthetic venture). In such a case, his presentation can be consistent with his position.

What remains to be seen is whether his position can be consistent with the scheme of breaking up (the analytical anti-

---

[16] I. Coale, "Polity and Leadership" *Journal of Political Philosophy* 4.2 (1970): 44-54.

[17] I consider monarchies to be either benevolent (and thereby sensitive to popular sentiment) or dictatorial (as described above).

leader). This is because it doesn't seem to allow any construction. It is meant to be liberating because it is a form of examination: criticism of specific policies or criticism of the very foundations of society. But how can this liberation occur? Certainly, if an analytical leader, like T-Rx, advocated analytical positions he would contradict himself, because the very act of speaking for something ("I am against z, therefore, I support y") involves a construction. The consistent analytic leader may admit no synthetic properties. But is this possible?

These seeming contradictions can be solved by Collingwood's notion of historical imagination. Under this account, history is not a science on the model of the physical sciences, but is firmly grounded in the humanities. The competent historian must surmount these contradictions by re-constructing history through an imaginative re-enactment.[18] *This book aspires to do just that.*

Let us look at an example: T-Rx is only known to have made one public statement of policy: "Revolution begins at birth." The baby wants to escape its mother and at the same time avoid entrance into the world.[19]

Now certainly, this seems like an analytical-type statement at best. The speaker is asserting that the creative act of life itself (which, since it involves a construction, is synthetic) is not embraced by the revolutionary. Yet, at the same time, he says that it *is* revolutionary. This is a bald contradiction.

The very first action that people can possibly make (unless embryos are considered to be people) isn't made until they are well into the development process as children. The baby *doesn't try* to burst into the world, which would involve a synthetic action. Nor does he attempt to retreat into the womb, which, again, would constitute synthesis. No, the baby *wants* to do neither. Does this mean that the baby is a passive agent? No. True to the definition of analysis, it is striving towards freedom. It wants to escape its mother, yet this attempt at freedom does not involve a voluntary action, and is thus not synthetic.

---

[18] R.G. Collingwood, *The Idea of History* (Oxford: Oxford University Press, 1946).

[19] *New York Times,* "T-Rx's 'Manifesto'" (August 21, 1970): A-16.

Here, it seems, is a complete statement of the analytic position, and yet may we properly call this a *position*? Certainly if this position were espoused as a doctrine of a movement, the action could properly be called synthetic. That is, if x advocates "Revolution begins at birth," etc. (as T-Rx actually did)[20] then x is advocating something: namely a proposition which purports analytic doctrines. But the process of x's avowal constitutes a synthetic action.

Now, some may call this last action an illegitimate move. They may say that the requirements for a totally analytic leader are impossible to meet and that some synthetic action is essential. The way to solve this apparent dilemma is to lower the bar to Aristotle's *epi to polu* (for the most part). Thus, the question would become, "What would matter according to this position is whether, on the whole, the individual x brings about a greater sympathy for *analytic* feeling than *synthetic* feeling?"

Another escape might be to claim that this last reprisal is merely a statement about the nature of the English language as being structured as subject-transitive verb-object in its construction, and says nothing about the substantive claim of analytic feeling. Both of these arguments have been espoused by supporters of T-Rx, but one of the most effective defenses of the position consistent with its philosophy was offered by T-Rx himself to a reporter of the San Francisco Herald:[21]

Herald: Is it true that you are an anarchist?
T-Rx: What's an anarchist?
Herald: It's one who espouses the overthrow of the government.
T-Rx: Is that what an anarchist is?
Herald: Yes, and I think you are one. Will you agree to this label?
T-Rx: (no answer, he tightens his facial muscles, scratches his head and blows his nose)
Herald: Haven't you, in fact, told people to overthrow the government?
T-Rx: Have you ever heard me say that?

---

[20] *Ibid.*

[21] *San Francisco Herald,* "Interview with T-Rx" (September 8, 1969): C-1.

Herald: No, but I do have a quotation here from *Time Magazine* which says that you believe revolution begins at birth. Did you not say these words?

T-Rx: (no answer as T-Rx takes off his shoes and puts them atop his head).

There is no proper response to self-referential questions such as these. Thus, none is given. The respondent must be careful not to make any gesture that might be taken as a response even though nothing had been said—including the tightening of the facial muscles, blowing of the nose, and putting shoes atop one's head (since these are also responses).

Much more can and will be said about this question with reference to the following data, but before leaving the question entirely, it should be noted that the statement, "Revolution begins at birth. . ." is descriptive and not prescriptive. That is, T-Rx isn't saying that revolution *ought* to begin at birth for some set of reasons, but that it *does* begin there. He is making some sort of statement about the Human Condition with regard to liberty and Man's natural relationship to regulations and society in general. Man is always aiming at freedom, though not necessarily through his actions.

In a recent publication, Isaiah Berlin contrasts two forms of liberty: positive (the ability to do such and such) and negative (the state of not being constrained). [22] It seems to me that T-Rx conflates these so that we should not take too seriously the theory behind his protest movement. It is incoherent. I plan to discuss this further in the postscript.[23]

What is to follow are three files that constitute all the substantive primary data available on T-Rx. He has been written about in several popular news magazines, but excluding the quotation already given, this material is highly unsatisfactory as it is based upon unreliable hearsay. I have collected data from three

---

[22] Isaiah Berlin, "Two Concepts of Liberty" in *Four Essays on Liberty* (Oxford: Oxford University Press, 1958).

[23] Of course, the post-script was never completed in publishable form. (I.B.)

people close to T-Rx in order to get a more accurate picture of just what he was intending.

I began with general background material that I was able to obtain from the special collections department of the library at the University of California at Berkeley. They were very generous to me and I acknowledge their great kindness here.

This first trove gave me the landscape for the primary historical sources I knew I needed to approach.

When I approached these individuals for this book, they were all forthcoming to supply additional information. The opening set of letters obtained from Fred Abrams and Larry Cohen was not available for permission, but according to a recent Supreme Court filing, all that is needed by way of consent is permission from one party, be it a transcript of a telephone call or a personal letter. Mr. Abrams kept copies of all his correspondence with Larry, both to and from. These letters give a close view of one member of the group who got along well with T-Rx.

The second item, a diary from "Mary Taylor," was obtained with no little difficulty. I received permission from the family so long as I changed her name and any clear identifying information.

Finally, the questioning deposition of Duvall "Mad Dog" Jackson was obtained through a confidential source in the Atlanta Police Department, which prompted an official request from the Freedom of Information Act.

I have suggested some of the significance that these writings hold with regard to my theory and the career of Nehemiah Moses. More will be suggested in the post script, but these suggestions will be by no means exhaustive, and I expect that others will have more to say about the issues raised by this investigation.

By and large, the first set of letters has been heavily edited, leaving out irrelevant data and offering a coherent translation of the street talk of Larry Cohen into Standard English. I have left the first letter untouched to offer a sample of the unrestrained scribbling of this fellow (which I have footnoted for clarity). Occasionally I have made a note when certain assertions are contrary to other facts that I have discovered and documented in my investigation. I have also made brief comments after each of the sections concerning clarity and transition. It is my hope that the studious reader will be able to fill in the details that I have left out while reading the primary data and compare his conclusions with my own at the end of this work.

Isaiah Coale
Professor Emeritus
History
New York University

Part One: The Letters of Larry Cohen

Preface

There are many interesting ways in which these letters illustrate the attitudes that I have outlined in my introduction, and which I will further expound upon in the post script. For now, a few things can be said about these letters and what, as a group, they represent. Since T-Rx has no corpus of written material, the only picture that we can get is what others saw. We see T-Rx through other's eyes and therefore must understand that each one of these partial portraits has its particular biases. Larry, for example, at first greatly admired T-Rx, but later grew disenchanted. I think that the reasons for this disenchantment are what is most interesting in these letters.

In the beginning, naïve Larry saw his mentor as some kind of man who could alter the present condition of political events in the United States. Remember, Larry had just witnessed a very traumatic event: the unfortunate incarceration and murder of his friend, Mike. The status quo seemed to be inadequate to the task of providing a reasonably just society. Larry chose an alternate society that he saw as offering him possibilities that the larger culture couldn't.

The hub of this alternate picture was Nehemiah Moses. He made things work. Without his charismatic appeal, nothing would exist in this other world. Events built up until Rx's triumphant entry into San Francisco during the extremely successful peace march on July 4, 1969. Rx meant peace. He would usher in a new age of peace and prosperity (or so Larry and his comrades believed). All would prosper under this future monarch of tranquility.

But what his followers did not foresee was that this prince of peace was the amalgamation of contradiction. A political ruler has to create factions and organize certain of these factions so that he has a base of power. But T-Rx was not a faction creator. He did not wish to ascend to heights of political power. In fact, he showed his strength of sovereignty by abnegation of such temptations when the regal cries of other voices raised highest. Caesar refused the throne thrice only to finally accept it. Nehemiah Moses would never accept power for it wasn't in his nature to do so.

By not creating factions and organizing them into power bases, T-Rx frustrated his followers who wanted to implant their ideas for change upon the rest of society. If the time was ripe for change, and it is easy to see how students within the turbulent sixties would believe that the time was opportune, then they saw this leader as the one to do it. T-Rx must lead the change. The March in San Francisco illustrated his greatness and the propriety of their choice. But much to their surprise, T-Rx wanted none of their grand schemes. He was not after extending his personal dominion. Such ideas were contrary to what he felt, and he was a man true to his convictions. What he did do in response was simply what he had done all along, i.e., to live in the dynamic contradictions of laws and anarchy.

This reaction made his followers very unhappy. They required a sign that the new age was coming. They were impatient when T-Rx didn't appear to be willing to bring it in. This impatience translated to anger, which was quickly directed at T-Rx himself. This, perhaps, says something about the nature of people—or at least of young, passionate people. They want to be led. They demand a leader who will tell them how to achieve greatness and actualize their dreams. The leader stimulates their hopes and in return they will do anything for him. T-Rx violated this dictum. He offered no hope. He stimulated no dreams and some of his followers reacted with either hate or utter apathy (e.g., Mary and Alf) which caused others like Larry and Marcia to desert. (Mad Dog may be thought of as being between these two categories.) Larry no longer saw the larger society as meaningless and the alternate group as salutary. He began working and seeing others from a new point of view. They weren't as bad as he had remembered.

The episode with Mike began to take on a new place in his consciousness. It became the exception rather than the rule of the larger society. This new conviction led Larry to seek his old ties once his remedy no longer fulfilled its promise. T-Rx did not satisfy the expectations that Larry had, so he sought another alternative. This indicates that Larry did not really change. He was at the same level of consciousness when he left T-Rx as when he came to him. None of the "lessons" of Moses were heeded, and so his followers went astray.

This seemed to be true of all of the followers, except Mad Dog. He was the only one who changed—but what happened to him? He was destroyed by a society that seeks to survive by certain rules and impersonally extinguishes anyone who dares to alter or radically disseminate it.

This also will be dealt with later, but what is interesting to note at this time is how T-Rx's own followers mirrored the attitude of society. Such a leader as T-Rx is received in only one way by our culture: with contempt and homicidal fury. Such reactions tell us much about ourselves and what we hold to be "good" in our lives. To what ends do we devote ourselves? Are they worthy? What can such a man as T-Rx teach us about ourselves? These are some of the questions that the life of this man may help us answer—or at least put us in the direction of answering.

—Isaiah Coale

Coda to Introduction

My father, I believe, has rather blown up the significance of this man T-Rx and the entire Larry Cohen episode. It seems clear that during the late sixties there was a great cultural change which was brought on in part by the Vietnam War. During wartime, it is always easier for changes to come about because the usual inhibitors are temporarily in abeyance because of the unusual conditions. Men leave women to fight and the women either pine away or seek other men.

In a limited war, no one wants to deploy and be left without a female companion when he comes home. Since only a few go (unlike WWII), the warriors can feel very discriminated against and the ones at home live in constant fear that they will be soon called by the draft to fill the ranks of the civilian army. In our own experience in Vietnam, this proved to be the case, as many young people did all that they could to avoid being sent to fight for a cause that wasn't clearly in the national interest.

The mainstream society seemed to be caught in some predicament that was very disadvantageous to their personal happiness. Why should one person go and not another? Why should Frank be the only one in the neighborhood to go? Why should only college kids be exempt? What about poor people who can't afford to go to college? They began to feel very discriminated against. The army seemed to some to be a racial plot aimed at killing blacks, Mexicans, Native Americans, and anyone not fortunate enough to be among the chosen for a 1-S (student) deferment.

In an all-out war, virtually everyone serves and so no one feels put upon (at least not to the same extent). Things are consequently more stable than in limited war. I say all this not as an academic authority (indeed, I have none of the impressive academic credentials of my father) but as a person who lived through the period in question with some degree of sensitivity. I believe that the context of the historical situation tells more about the story of T-Rx than any theory of a new type of leader. Now, it is possible that I don't understand all of what my father is trying to say, and perhaps if he had lived to write his postscript, things would have been crystal clear. But from my vantage point, this story, particularly that of Larry Cohen, says more about an atmosphere that existed in the United States than about any significant political figure. Who was T-Rx anyway? He was really just a small activist leader who had one "big day" during the San Francisco Peace March of 1969. He commanded no large following and his actions do not affect us today. Why, then, is his story important?

I think it shows one case study, only. Any conclusions that might be drawn from this episode must relate to specific examples involved. It constitutes limited inductive reasoning, which might prove nothing since the data is so limited. But perhaps it can say something about what *can* happen to a society that tries to continue in an unpopular way. When there is nothing essential in the struggle, and when the people at home are affluent, then such limited struggles exact a tremendous price in weakening the moral fiber of the society's citizens as it submits its young people to the permanent scarring of an unjust society.[24] Any and all tensions and problematic institutions during such a time will be torn apart, though nothing will fill the resulting void.

Sometimes this can lead to significant change, but most likely it affords the opportunity for powerful people to increase their stranglehold on the citizenry of a nation and slowly strangle it to death.
(I.B.)

The Letters of Larry Cohen[25]

San Francisco
September 15, 1968

---

[24] Even though the United States has moved to a volunteer army after the Vietnam War, there are still these scars. I am thinking of those sent to Iraq to quash so-called *weapons of mass destruction* that proved not to be there. Either there is a hidden reason for this military escapade that will be unearthed by future historians or it's another instance of using the young men (and now women, too) for combat based upon scurrilous justifications. (I.B.)

[25] For most of these letters it has been necessary to edit them so that they read according to some kind of standard English. However, I recognize that much of the flavor of what is being said may be lost in such translation and that the translator has great power to interpret what he has before him. Recognizing this difficulty, I still believe that the nature of this slang language is such as it will be unintelligible in a few years. In the interests of appeasing both sides (the ones who demand the original words, as well as those who would appreciate a readable text), I have tried to leave in some irregularities while standardizing the bulk of the material. This first letter has been left untouched as an example of the illiterate nature of this material. Footnotes have been provided for explanation.

Larry Cohen to Fred Abrams

Dear Fred,

I'll bet that you're sorry you didn't come down, eh? Things are really groovy.[26] I've seen some real far-out crap[27] down here that I really want to lay on you.[28] I mean, people in Eugene talk about San Francisco, but nothing that they've said can really compare to really being here. I mean it.

This afternoon at lunch we met this really far-out cat[29] calling himself Mad Dog Jackson. He's a tall, skinny black dude[30] and thinks he's really something else. [31] I'll tell you.

Well, anyway, he sold us a lid and some tickets to a rock concert and told us some of the really tough places to check out.[32] Me and Mike are really waiting to dig it,[33] 'cause we've been down here for five days and this is the first action that we've gotten.[34]We only have enough money for another week saved up, so we figure to get in all the action we can before heading back to old Oregon.

How are the Ducks doing?[35] I figure a trip to the Rose Bowl isn't out of the question—well at least they ought to beat the Huskies. Food down here is real expensive so we only eat one meal

---

[26] Interesting and enjoyable.

[27] Bizarre or non-ordinary experience.

[28] "Tell to you."

[29] A Unique and personable individual

[30] A black man whose self-image is strong and confident.

[31] A positive comment set in the superlative.

[32] This is meant to be advice on pleasurable places to frequent.

[33] This phrase indicates the state of anticipation for a future pleasurable event.

[34] "Action" refers to social encounters generally including popular music, drugs, and people looking for someone who might engage in consensual sex.

[35]The "Ducks" refers to the mascot of the University of Oregon in Eugene. This was the intermediate place of interest between San Francisco and Seattle. The Rose Bowl is a college football game which (at the time) featured the winner of the Pacific-8 (west coast universities) and the Big-10 (mid-west universities). It was considered to be the highlight of the football season for those interested in football in those two conferences.

a day outside of a taco for lunch. I told Mike that I didn't think we had enough money to make the lid,[36] but he wanted to get some action so I said all right. I mean, what the hell, we've only got two weeks so why not get some cheap thrills. Tell Janet that I'm fine here and in a nice place and that I'm not seeing any other women (I'm really not). In a lot of ways I dread the thought of coming back to school, and then on the other hand, it can be a real bummer[37] sitting in your hotel room with nothing to do except eat chocolate and play cards (they're real strict about being old enough to buy booze here, and wouldn't accept my phony I.D.). Take care of yourself you old snake.

L. Cohen

Outer Space
[September 16, 1968]
Larry Cohen to Fred Abrams

Fred—

I mean I really had some really bizarre experiences since I wrote you yesterday afternoon. I mean I haven't written you in a whole week and then here's two right in a row. At any cost, I just had to get this down on paper so that I could believe it myself. Last night at the concert they had the Grateful Dead[38] and we were really getting into some tunes [39] when a man behind me and Mike says, "Hey put down them glasses." Mike had some opera glasses because it's hard to see when you are a ways away, especially with

---

[36] "Making a lid" means having enough money to purchase a plastic sandwich bag filled with marijuana.

[37] "Bummer" refers to an un-pleasurable recreational drug experience.

[38] A popular singing group out of San Francisco. The devotees of this group called themselves "deadheads"—a reference to the drug culture.

[39] "Tunes" is a synonym for "songs."

all that smoke in the place—they let you toke[40] right there on the floor!

Well anyway, you know Mike, he doesn't like anyone telling him what to do and especially some short pimply fellow like the guy that was behind us. Mike put down the glasses, but I could see that he was really mad and he was thinking the situation over for himself. He wanted to use his glasses, but he wasn't sure just how far he'd go to defend his right to view the stage. The decision didn't take too long as Mike promptly put his glasses up again.

Now, I must tell you in all honesty those glasses were not blocking anyone's view of the concert. It's far from me to ever condone anyone violating someone else's freedom, even Mike's! But the glasses were doing no harm. Still, I was just waiting for the hand to hit Mike's shoulder again and tell him to put them down. I was afraid because I know that when Mike gets mad sometimes he can cause a scene—like the time in front of the movie theater when Jack Carlson tried to get cuts from Kathy-Jo, and Mike was sore because he'd asked Kathy-Jo out for a date the next weekend and she said she couldn't (though Mike really thought it was because Jack was really beating his time).[41] Anyway, that was when Mike got into a fight and cracked Carlson's jaw.

I didn't want to get into another one like that, especially since Mike was carrying our hotel key!

Well, anyway, like I had expected, this hand comes and lays itself on Mike's shoulder, not in a defiant way, or in a hostile, pugnacious fashion, but slowly and deliberately. There was something about the way that he moved his hand that made me especially uneasy, because I had expected him to grab Mike the way people do at football games when they don't like the language of that someone in front of them. No, this fellow moves his hand so calmly and assuredly as if he knew something that we didn't. . . .

---

[40] "Toke" refers to the act of inhaling marijuana smoke and holding in the lungs before exhaling. This action sets forth the drug transfer via the areoles.
[41]"Beating his time" refers to some man trying to date some other man's girlfriend.

I don't know, it's hard to draw conclusions, but I knew what Mike's response would be. Mike had been sitting there waiting for that hand. Probably he thought it would be a hand like the ones we're used to at football games, as I said, maybe that's why he jumped so when the hand touched his shoulder. Mike was anticipating that hand for the longest duration of time before the hand touched him. Therefore, the hand didn't startle him because in every way Mike was prepared for it, or rather he was prepared for what he had expected it to be: a rough jostling as one feels during those autumn spectacles. Instead, what Mike felt was the soft, assured hand of a cold-blooded maniac (for who else would have such a queer smile on his face as if he was enjoying what was about to happen). I saw this smile out of the corner of my eye as I sat there trying to watch Mike and this character at the same time, not wanting to take my eyes off Mike and also at the same time feeling—though I'm ashamed to admit it—a dread that maybe this lunatic might do something to me as well if I showed too great of interest in what was happening.

This is a disconcerting feeling to say the least, for Mike is a buddy, though not as close as you are, Fred. Still, I don't like to think that I'd desert a buddy when he needed me. I know I wouldn't. How could I? But still I have to admit that I was scared, and that I looked at both Mike and this stranger, who sat behind Mike, out of the corner of my eye, which I tried to hide—not wanting anyone to see what I was doing. Almost affecting the status of simply a disinterested bystander who might have heard some commotion, but who wouldn't interfere in what was about to happen.

Then the hand touched Mike's shoulder and I could see Mike jump. His eyes flashed at me and I could tell that he was afraid. What he was frightened of, I'm not sure. Perhaps it was the manner of the hand (as I've suggested before), or maybe he saw that I was scared since I wasn't involving myself in what was happening. He wasn't imploring my help, I know that, because if he did I would have given it. I wouldn't let a friend down who needed me, you know that much of me, Fred.

It couldn't have been an appeal for help, because I would have recognized that and responded accordingly. No, there was something else that occasioned that look. Perhaps it was the strange city, but I suspect that Mike knew somehow, even before he saw it, that the stranger was pulling a knife. It was a long, thin stiletto that opened in almost complete silence; at least, it was undetectable above the singing at the concert.

Mike spun around half-startled and half-alert (though he had toked a bit) as the other held the knife in front of him and in a slow, confident voice declared, "Now you know, I'm a little tired of you. I told you to put those things down, and you just wouldn't listen, would you? Now I want you to give me those glasses or this knife goes into your stomach."

The man's voice was so slow and calm, as if he was asking for a glass of water or something mundane of that nature instead of threatening to kill Mike. I'll never forget that voice, it was so unnatural. How could a voice saying such terrible things remain so calm? Why was there a slight smirk on the man's face indicating that if he had the chance, he would fully enjoy putting the knife into Mike's body? My only conclusion was that this man was mentally ill and that he knew no fear because his life. . . . I don't know, but that voice was unafraid.

"Hey, Man, what's with you?" returned Mike. His voice was unsteady and I could tell that he was afraid of the man and wondered as to his sanity as well. Mike was trying to bear down for the confrontation; trying to sober up, which wasn't an easy proposition no matter how much adrenalin one has flowing.

The stranger didn't respond but stretched out his free hand for the glasses. Mike's eyes were riveted on the crazy man. He didn't look at me. He didn't ask for help from anyone.

Mike started to hand his glasses to this fellow, thinking probably that there was little that he could do in such a situation except give in. After all, glasses cost five or ten dollars and a knife wound would be more costly than that, which is what he'd face if he got into a fight with this guy. I think that if the confrontation had just been one of fists that it is possible that Mike would have taken this bully on, but as it was there wasn't any way that he could have hoped to overcome this fellow.

Mike stretched out his hand with the glasses. As he did, the other man grabbed his arm and pulled Mike's body towards him with a terrific violence. I started. The whole thing happened so fast. I would have moved to Mike's aid, except that another fellow three seats down had lunged over several people and wrestled the man with the knife to the ground. I fully expected to see an usher coming over to stop the commotion or at least to call a policeman. I didn't know why there wasn't a policeman there. They are never there when you need them.

But I don't think that it is unreasonable to expect that a disturbance be halted and that adequate protection be given to viewers of a concert. Whether one should be able to expect it or not, still this man had grabbed Mike and then it looked as if he was going to knife him, when this other fellow leaped to Mike's aid and wrestled the man with the knife to the cement tier. There flashed something metallic from the shirt of the rescuer. I couldn't see it at first, but I sensed it was a gun. The rescuer had knocked the knife free from his captive, who he held by the neck with one hand while he jammed the pistol into his stomach with the other. The words that he spoke weren't very clear, but it was something like, "Get out of here, fascist," or "Stay clear, fascist." At any rate, it was short and to the point and the other scrambled up and left in a hurry as soon as he was released. I looked around and was amazed: the police were nowhere.

"Hey man, thanks," said Mike as the other got up.

"Yeah," replied the man.

"I'll get to you after the concert," said Mike as the other returned to his seat.

The other didn't reply, but made his way deftly back to his seat. I watched him for a while, as his long curly hair would bounce about his head forming little ringlets of black motion that kept time to the sensual pulsing of the bass guitar.

Soon, however, Mike and I lit up a joint and were into the serenity of the music. You wouldn't believe it, Fred, but there are no cops to hassle you about smoking dope here in S.F. It's just free and easy. Everything was relaxed as we listened to the music free from interference from blue piggies.[42]

After the compulsory five encores or so, the concert ended and I started to head for the exit when Mike tugged at my arm.

"Over here, we got to find that dude."

---

[42]"Blue piggies" refers to the police: they are dressed in blue and often called "pigs" because of the way they treated young people with long hair. They also look like pigs when dressed with their gas masks.

I had forgotten all about our friend as the warm intoxication of the environment was programing me for a slow trip back to our hotel, but Mike seemed determined, and so I decided to go along as sometimes no resistance is the path that is the most pleasant in the short run.

"Say, buddy," yelled Mike.

The fellow didn't hear Mike and he kept on walking.

"Say," yelled Mike again.

Several people turned around, but none of them was the one that we desired to hear the urgent salutation. I felt rather nauseous myself as all the moving about was too disorienting for me at that moment, but when Mike gets his mind set on something then there is no trying to make him do otherwise.

So there we were in this tremendous crowd with Mike yelling for this fellow, and him not listening, and Mike dragging me around under and over everyone who didn't like all the confusion after just having been mesmerized by some melodious tunes. There I was feeling more and more like retching over the concrete steps over which I was so unceremoniously being dragged. It was as if I were some sort of inanimate object to which I have no physical resemblance. Various visions of sacks filled with sundry items flashed into my mind as I toyed with the resolution of pretending I was the contents of such a sack being bounced up the dirty steps stained with years of tobacco juice, food, and other possible commodities of refuge. And there I was in the process, bumping into people who were so startled by it all themselves that they excused themselves to us.

Now I would have been more polite to these people and perhaps offered them various types of explanations if: 1. I knew why we were rushing about, and 2. If I didn't feel that at any moment I would lose control of my precious stomach and promptly spill the contents of my last six hours of gormandizing.

This process seemed interminable, when finally there was a release. I mean Mike let me go. Apparently that fellow was either within range or completely out of range. Mike must have reasoned that either he could go faster without me or that if the other person was close, there was no way that I would get lost from that short of distance. But perhaps this was an overestimation on his part about my safety for distances greater than twelve inches. For in the particular condition that I was in at that moment I was about ready to black out.

Well, I reacted to this release in a completely understandable manner for the way that I was feeling: I lost my momentum and having none of my own was jostled by the gentle crowd into a vacant row of seats where the movement of my body carried me toward an arm rest, which I became convinced would not be a comfortable companion for my chin that was soon approaching some sort of rendezvous with the night fairy.

Through an extremely deft move, I avoided hitting my chin. Instead, my chin was deflected by the elbow carrying me into the backs of the seats in front. It was then that I had the opportunity to rest and my physical discomfort relieved itself, and I quickly drifted into the most marvelous of sleeps, which lasted some measurable duration, though I was in no condition to judge its length in mathematical units.

Now I know what you must be thinking right now, Fred. You don't approve and you're blaming yourself for not coming with me when I had asked you to so that I might have had someone to curb my weaker impulses and not have let myself go the way that I did. You're saying, "Why didn't I quit my job a week early?"—not even a week early (for your job really ended a week ago, the same as mine did). But you took on that extra week because you wanted the extra pay. You are thinking, what good is the extra pay when my good buddy is lying there on the dirty cement sleeping? And I'm here sitting on my fat wallet enjoying the pleasures of the permissive, affluent society's tunnel of material delights as I earn my perverse extra week's money that can only serve to separate me further from the true and meaningful aspects of living while my dear loved one sits in cold vulnerability which I could have sheltered him from if only I could have been there.

I know that those thoughts are going through your mind, but let me tell you right now, Fred, to put all those thoughts out of your mind. I have to get on by myself.

My father's been telling me that for years (and it's why he keeps giving me all those brochures on the military—join the army and see the world, especially the spectacular rice paddies of South Vietnam, one of the globe's seven wonders).

I understand, or so I have been told—that is by my father, again and again and. . . and it's true. What happened to me was my fault entirely and in no way do I hold you responsible. But let me return to my commentary.

I was lying on the cement when my repose was interrupted as I felt myself being lifted up by someone (probably an usher) and carried over the shoulder out of the seasoned atmosphere of the amphitheater into the refreshing ether of the San Francisco night. I was deposited on my back onto the grass at which point I felt able to get up and try to locate Mike. The back of my head pounded and my joints felt achy. I didn't try to move quickly, but at that moment any movement was painful. So I lifted myself up with the help of a nearby seedling as I was determined that I would find my lost comrade, and failing that, return to the hotel and try and talk them into giving me another key.

I had no sooner begun my trek than I was stopped by a familiar voice.

"Hey Larry. Larry, come here you dog. What are you doing dragging yourself around like that. You look like a dog. Get over here."

Mike's voice was pleasant to hear. I didn't mind him calling me a dog, even though, as you well remember, that name has painful memories for me—still I was uplifted by his nasal voice calling me. I don't mind telling you, Fred, that I had been feeling very frightened before I heard that voice. I don't know why, for I knew the way back to the hotel and San Francisco isn't exactly the most dangerous place in the world. But being alone as I was—I can't put my finger on it, but there was something that I didn't realize until I heard the voice of Mike calling me. It was as if that voice let me understand what had just transpired. While I was in the amphitheater and lying on the grass I didn't know what I felt except sensations and sharp pain, but when I heard that voice, I suddenly realized that I had been feeling something else, too. I had been in dread of something. Maybe it was being alone, or perhaps something else?

I'm not very good at drawing conclusions, but I know that Mike's voice illumined the events that had just transpired so that I now knew more about them than when I had been initially experiencing them.

I couldn't respond to Mike, but just turned my head slightly so that I could be sure that it was really the old pugilist or just an apparition that my state of mind had conjured up.

I turned my eyes to the direction I had perceived that the sound had originated. All was true. Mike was really there.

"Hey, Partner, I thought that I lost you. Where have you been?" As Mike approached, I noticed that he wasn't alone. There was another figure with him. It was the fellow that had helped him in the concert.

"Oh yeah," said Mike, realizing that I noticed he wasn't alone, "I want you to meet the fellow who helped me out in the concert. His name is Rex."

"T-Rx," corrected the stranger.

"That's right, Tree Rex." The other stood behind Mike almost as if he cultivated the shadows. His eyes were the feature that struck me. The sockets seemed inordinately large because his cheek bones were low and pronounced while his forehead almost made a ridge above his eyebrows. He looked like one of those cavemen that we see on those charts tracing the evolution of man. If he only had stood in the light, his appearance might have occasioned me to laugh or at least break into a smile, but as it was, I merely cleared my throat, for I didn't understand the feeling that I had when I looked at him silently in the darkness.

"Say, you look as if you've had a spill or something. How did you do that? Your face is all swollen. Did you get into a fight?" I looked down and sighed. How little Mike understood of me. The only thing that he could think of when someone looked bruised was that he'd been in a scrape. That's more his style, but these words didn't bother me. I wanted to get out of the area as the whole situation was beginning to have an unpleasant connotation to me. One thing only kept me there: the other fellow, Rex. Or rather to be more specific, it was the odd feeling that I sensed. It was a feeling that didn't seem to be entirely of my making but had some existence of its own apart from me. It was as if some real aura or power emanated from this figure. I was merely sensing it in the same manner as one hears a sound. Anyway, Rex offered to take us to a party. We got to talking a bit after the concert. I wanted to tell him how much I appreciated what he'd done for me, for us. . . . Well, then he suddenly invited us to a bash of some sort.

Mike turned his head toward Rex for confirmation of his story, which Rex supplied with a sort of nod of his head, though it wasn't really a nod but almost a faint bow that carried with it a silent elegance. My own head was still sore but I didn't need any convincing to agree to go along with this fellow to the party or wherever.

We walked down the hill to the street and hopped a cable car, standing on the outside. There were lots of people inside. We only traveled a few blocks before dropping off. We didn't pay a fare. We walked a while until we passed a bar that really looked as if it were an exciting place, with girls and shouting and loud music. Rex turned inside this place and my heart began beating faster (for it was the first real "bar" that I had been in, outside of the small town places that are in Eugene, or the bar that Mike and I tried at the bus station after we had gotten to our vacation wonderland).

Rex walked briskly through the place and didn't look around, so naturally we resolved not to gawk either—though I caught glimpses of women who were topless. This pleasant sight naturally inclined me to linger, but we were following Rex. I also noticed that Mike, too, was looking around a little as we lagged slightly behind the fast moving Rex, who either wasn't interested or was disgusted by the whole thing. Perhaps he has seen it all so many times that the entire enterprise is now boring, though I could not really understand such a state of sophistication.

We went through the bar and out into the alley in back. I heard a growling and saw a German shepherd that looked as if it might jump right for the throat if it hadn't been restrained by a chain. Still, the sensation of that man-trained killer made me more than slightly agitated, so I began to question whether I really wanted to undertake the perilous expedition that we were attempting. Nothing seemed to rattle our leader, which is the reason I just kept going on. He was so resolute in his step. There was no questioning him. His sureness made me feel ashamed, though thinking back on it, I think that there were plenty of reasons for me to be suspicious.

We walked through the alley for twenty or thirty yards and then descended down a stairwell as Rex opened a subterranean door and we followed. I thought I saw the scurrying black rodents that made a high squeaking sound. The experience made me shiver.

Now you know that I'm not afraid of animals in general, but I've heard about how rabies are so common among rats and that they are the most diseased animal species in the lower 48. I felt an almost symbolic terror because of the scurrying little varmints.

After moving down a corridor that had little light, we approached a stairway that was covered with an old, torn carpet. Rex stopped at the foot of the stairs.

"After you," said Rex in a chivalrous tone as he bowed and swept his right arm for us to continue. "We're going to the third floor."

I didn't like the idea of going up these stairs, at first. A creeping anxiety entered my mind about what might happen to us. Perhaps this Rex was a robber and was out to get us? I instinctively reached for my wallet and found it gone.

I had had seventy two dollars in that wallet, plus my return bus ticket! This made me become frantic. Was it really all gone? Could I have simply put it somewhere else? I quickly searched my person, not really caring whether I looked ridiculous or not. I wanted my money. Mike started climbing the stairs. I didn't have my wallet. Could it have fallen out as we had been walking since the amphitheater? Should I go back and search for it? Something had to be done. I couldn't get by without that money.

"What's the matter?" intoned Rex. "Lose your wallet?"

What a question. How did he know? Perhaps it was obvious from the way I was searching my person, but still the question came out of nowhere and startled me so that I couldn't respond the way that I would have liked to have answered him.

"Yes, I must have lost it at the amphitheater." My words came out as if they were being uttered by someone else. They weren't my words, or I didn't want someone else butting into my business. Why should he know whether I had my wallet or not? For all I knew, he might have taken it and now was only *inquiring* so that he might shift the blame or suspicion away from him. Or perhaps he *was about to* take Mike's money too, and this was it: our end in a dark staircase away from everyone. We might not be found for days.

I don't mind admitting to you that I had extreme apprehensions about the entire situation. My mind was confused and I was on edge so that when I heard his voice declare in a firm tone, "Here!" I jumped.

I thought that he was going to kill us or do some sort of mischief to us, but instead he had in his hand some money. "It's only five, but I don't have much. Maybe it will help."

What was he doing? He was supposed to be robbing us, not giving us money. Suddenly my suspicions about this Rex vanished and were replaced by euphoria of closeness for the compassion of his gesture. I couldn't say anything nor did I take the money.

"Take it. Somebody probably took your money when that goon was making a fuss tonight."

His voice was calm and relaxed. The action seemed spontaneous. I took the bill at his directive and stuffed it into my pocket. When we reached the third floor, Rex was anxious for the first time to go to the proposed party. We heard the music and a door was open, which we took as evidence of a party.

Inside, the atmosphere was thick with the odor of pot and hashish. The lights were low and there was a scrolling lighted sign that said, "Cocaine: *It's the Real Thing.*" Suddenly we were on our own. Rex had gone off to another part of the party while we were still surveying the scene. Within just moments, as I was just about to ask Mike about how he liked the place, a girl, who couldn't have been more than sixteen, came up to Mike and asked him if he wanted to see her undersea garden.

I was left alone.

Like my natural self, I gravitated to the corner of the room and sat down cross-legged. I observed that the composition of the party was that of several small groups. The room wasn't large, but there was a door that people occasionally went through, so I imagined that there was more to the party than I was just seeing at that moment.

The whole situation began to filter around in my head as I was trying to sort things out for myself. Then someone passed me a joint. I had had quite enough that night and didn't care for any more, so I declined it.

After this innocuous action, I was greeted almost immediately by a fellow who had tripped over something and fell down right in front of me. Remembering my old spotting techniques from high school gym, I tried to break his fall and only succeeded in protecting his head, which might have hit the floor with some force. The fellow lay in front of me for a time, so I began again to sort out what exactly was happening to me.

"Hey," said a voice of someone, which, because of a tug on my leg, I understood to be directed to me.

I looked down at the fellow on the floor who was trying to get up. Because of the darkness and the smoke, I really hadn't seen this fellow's face before. But then I saw that he was a guy no older than myself. He had a young face that was rather feminine.

"Hey," he repeated, "what do you think of Hesse?"

"You mean Herman Hesse, the writer?" I asked.

"Yeah, *Steppenwolf* and all that."

"I really don't know," I said truthfully, as I've never read the thing. I know that you have a copy and have been trying to get me to read it for quite a while, but you know I've never gotten around to it. However, my answer didn't seem of very great importance as the fellow who had put it to me seemed to disappear as soon as he had appeared—not really waiting for an answer. The smoke was now really getting to me. It was quite thick and all I could think about was the assembly we had at school about the effects of air pollution.

It's a very strange thing. I occasionally smoke and when I do the thought of vapor entering my lungs doesn't seem to bother me; however, when put into a situation where I don't want to inhale the exhaust of someone else, then I feel quite resentful at those instigators of the offensive fumes. As I was in the midst of this indignation, another fellow came over to me. He was a black man a few years older than me.

"Hey, what are you doing?" he asked.

"Fine," I answered, as I supposed this was the correct answer for this question that I took to be equivalent to "how are you?"

"I don't think I've seen you before," the other responded as he came and sat down next to me. There was some suspicion in his voice and I felt that he really didn't want to talk to me except that any outsider might be dangerous—perhaps a narcotics agent or something, so they must be investigated for the safety of the group. He must have been the security man of the party, I surmised.

"That's probably true. I've only been in town a short while."

"How'd you happen to show up here?"

His questions were a little irritating to me. I didn't like being excluded from a party, but I didn't care for his conception of inclusion either. I would have just as soon sat in peace with my private reflections rather than have to answer questions as if he was my principal.

"I came with a friend."

"Oh yeah, do I know your friend?"

I almost responded, "What is it to you, buddy?—" but I didn't. Perhaps his large frame made me reconsider this rash repartee, but I decided that the best way to get him off me was to answer his concern about my credentials for being there and put an end to the entire interrogation.

"I don't know, the fellow we came with was named Tee-Rex."

"T-Rx! T-Rx brought you?"

"Yes, do you know him?"

"Know him, why he's just about one of the biggest names around, that is, among some of us who are *out of things*, as it were."

"Out of things?"

"Counter culture, all that crap, you know."

"Oh I see," I replied, though I didn't really have much of an idea of what he was talking about. One hears about counter-culture all the time on the television, and in the papers, but when someone next to you claims that he is a member of one such group, then suddenly he realizes that everything that had been heard concerning the identity of the group is now only buzzing incoherence. It does nothing to illumine just what they are talking about. Did he mean that he was living in a commune? Or was a member of a loosely-knit gang? Or even some subversive organization? I had no idea what he meant. But I was certain about one thing: that our guide, Tee-Rex, was some kind of leader. When I realized this, everything that had happened from the concert onwards seemed to sharpen into a clarity that it hadn't had when I had first seen this fellow and his shadowy form. I had pondered on his identity. Nothing seemed to capture him. Now I could see him as a leader. The manner in which he had dispatched the man in the concert, the way that he had won Mike completely over to his side, and the facility that he brought us to this party of counter-culture friends or followers of his: all of this seemed to be consistent with what this man was now telling me. The conclusions seemed sound.

"Listen, how long have you known Trek?"

"'Trek'?"

"T-Rx—you know it's so hard to call him by his given name because of that vowel crap."

I tilted my head.

"You know. They say that you've got to have vowels to pronounce a word."

I nodded, but I wasn't so sure what this was all about.

"So if you can't say 'T-Rx' you come up with an alternative: Trek. So, some of us refer to him as Trek. Sticking a vowel in there makes it easier."

Imagine, this fellow is not only a counter-culture leader, but he even has a cult name which has no vowels in it (if I understood this fellow correctly). What was the purpose of that? Didn't they know that every name has to have a vowel in order for it to be a word? Instead of Tee-Rex, I suppose his name must be T-Rx?[43]

"Just tonight, we met him at the concert."

"Concert?" said the other in surprise. But before I could tell him which one I meant, he seemed to realize himself, "Did you go and see the Dead?"[44]

"Yes."

"Did you buy your ticket from a tall, skinny black dude?"

All of this seemed to be too coincidental. How could he have known who had sold me my ticket? I didn't like that. I felt that someone knew more about *me* than I did about *him*.

"I really don't remember much about him," I stammered. I hoped my lie was not overly apparent, but I didn't want to continue answering questions until I could be sure about what was happening. I needed to get my bearings, so I determined that I

---

[43] It is obvious that Mr. Cohen never went through Bar Mitzvah or he would know that Orthodox, Conservative, and Reformed Jews refer to the Master of the Universe as G-d or Y-hw-h, יהוה (in Hebrew). I wonder whether T-Rx comes out of this tradition? If so, it seems rather like religious heresy. IB.

[44] "The Dead" seems to refer to "The Grateful Dead" (see note: 38).

would avoid answering this staccato of rapid queries until I was more in control.

"Wait, I'll get him. Hey, this is interesting. Imagine, you came with Trek."

He got up and left, and I welcomed the respite so that I could gather my resources. But before I could reflect on what had just happened, the slithering fellow who had asked me about Hesse rose up from where he had been asleep (I had supposed) on the floor next to me (I hadn't observed his behavior during the Inquisition, such was my rattled state of mind). The fellow came over next to me and declared in a slurring voice, "The passion and the prose."

I didn't answer, but merely knitted my brow.

He placed his hand on my shoulder. "That's all there is— just passion and prose—prose and passion: a duality."

The fellow, or rather the slime (for he was slimy and he slithered everywhere he went) seemed rather happy about his statement and let out a loud sigh and smiled, but then almost as quickly he clutched my shoulder again and looked at me, trying to decide whether I understood. I felt obliged to nod my head and smile.

"That's all there is," he repeated.

"Fine," I replied. "I enjoy passionate prose."

Now, I was only trying to reassure this slime with my response. I hadn't wanted to make any sort of reply to him, but I did feel that the poor slime deserved something—even a slime has feelings. However good my intentions, the slime merely let out a groan of pain and melted down again into a puddle on the floor muttering, "No, no, passionate prose, passionate prose cannot be both together: Hesse, Hesse, no, no, no."

I didn't understand what was troubling him. I wished that I had read the book so that I might comprehend what he was referring to. Perhaps I will pick it up at the library when I get home.

I was in a room full of people but I felt as if I were standing solitary in a bubble.

Then the black guy re-emerged to his full presence, gesturing to his right, "Is this the guy?"

I turned around and was surprised to see the man who had sold us the tickets. He was a tall black guy with a medium 'fro.

"I think so," I said with a little reluctance. Everything was happening so quickly that I didn't really grasp the connection of one event to another. Then another fellow with a broad chest came over to the ticket seller and the slime again melted away.

The ticket seller chimed in, "Yeah, I remember this one. You were with another guy, weren't you?" As he made his query he smiled broadly. His teeth were very bright.

"Yeah, that's right. Right now I don't know where he is exactly. Last time I saw him he was looking at some aquarium or something?"

"Aquarium? Then he didn't come with you?"

"No, I mean yes. He came, but then he went off with some girl."

"With a girl, eh? Why didn't you say so?" The man who sold us the tickets laughed and looked to his friend. "Aquarium, eh? Where did you pick up this one? He's really crazy."

I didn't know whether to take this as a compliment or an insult, as in some circles crazy refers merely to being original, while in others it carries the denotation that it has in society at large.

Then the ticket seller stretched out his hand for me to shake. "My name's Duvall Jackson. But my friends call me Mad Dog."

I shook his hand. The name 'Mad Dog' seemed hardly to fit this rather tall, slender looking man. It would have been a much more appropriate epithet for the man who had sat next to me at the concert and jammered. That man's broad chest had convinced me that he was not a man to get into an altercation with.

"My name is Larry. Larry Cohen."

"Oh, Jewish, eh?" asked Mad Dog.

"Not really. I mean, my family is Reformed, but I'm nothing really."

"Do you speak Jewish?" asked Mad Dog again, but his friend started laughing and pretended to hit Mad Dog in the shoulder.

"Let him alone, Mad Dog."

"No I want to know. I want to know if he can speak Jewish."

This was a rather uncomfortable position to be in for me. I didn't want to answer his question, but then I didn't want to test the epithet "Mad Dog" either.

Besides, I was rather curious about T-Rx. I wanted to learn more about him.

"Not much. I was never a very good student."

"See, I *told you* he could," said Mad Dog, jumping from the floor. The other reached into his pocket and pulled out a dollar and handed it to Mad Dog. Apparently they had found time to wager, and I hadn't even detected it.

"Hey, I got to catch you later," said Mad Dog as he hopped away, happy at his winnings. I turned to watch Mad Dog disappear into the micro-mass of humanity which constituted this gathering—whatever you choose to call it.

"Is he always like that?" I asked, feeling a sudden affinity for the broad-chested man who had lost a dollar.

"No, only when he laughs."

"What's your name, anyway?" I asked. I had no real interest in the man I was talking to, but I did want to know more about T-Rx.

"My name's 'Marshall,' but I like to be called 'Prophet,' because I think that I have ESP. You know what I mean? I can predict things that happen sometimes."

"Well, Prophet, tell me more about T-Rx."

The Prophet smiled and we sat back into two gray bean bag chairs that were waiting for us on the floor. It was just about this time that the slime made a reappearance, but I adamantly didn't want to see him at the moment, so every time he surfaced, I would push him down with my hand. The Prophet spoke as if his head were especially detached from his body and he affected an "other-worldly" quality to his voice. I simply listened, while the slime oozed up and down making repeated appearances, each of which required that I put my hand on his head and push him back into the murky pool from where he had come.

The Prophet was a good storyteller. His images glistened in shiny concrete visuals, which he brought forward to embellish his upbeat paean.

It seemed that T-Rx was an activist of the early sixties. The Prophet didn't know *where* Rx started his activity, but he apparently made the stops with the Southern Christian Leadership

Conference and with the Student Nonviolent Coordinating Committee through Birmingham, Baton Rouge, Little Rock, and Selma.

The Prophet spent most of his time talking about Selma and the Edmund Pettus Bridge, for apparently it was there that Trek made his first publicized act of resistance. He was hobbling at the time because his right leg had been chewed by a dog in Birmingham, but still he managed to come to the aid of several of his comrades who were being beaten up by the police. One of them was Mad Dog. As the story goes, Mad Dog was unconscious on the cement with a policeman still clubbing him when Trek came and broke the policeman's arm. Several of the people with T-Rx carried Mad Dog away and Rx started off to help another when he caught a bullet in the shoulder. He was arrested or something, but in the mass of detainees, there was not a good enough case to hold them and so they were let go. Mad Dog recovered and has been following T-Rx ever since. According to the Prophet, T-Rx has no regard for his personal safety and would do anything to help his comrades. It seemed obvious to me that this figure had a small following of true believers and a larger admiration from society—though I had never heard of him before.

I lay in bed that night, listening to Mike snore (he stumbled back to me of his own accord). Mike had been very intoxicated so I decided that it would be best to depart. I thought of T-Rx and what he stood for, and wondered if we'd ever meet again.

All the best again,
Larry

[Editor's note: there is no record of T-Rx or Nehemiah Moses ever being arrested in Selma, nor is there any record of him being treated at any of the major hospitals in the city for a gunshot wound. There is a listing for Marcia McCrae, girlfriend of Jackson, as a volunteer at a free lunch civil rights food station; however, there is no evidence that Jackson even knew McCrae before 1967. No other associate of T-Rx was recorded as being in attendance at Selma.]

San Francisco
Sept. 18, 1968
Larry Cohen to Rebecca Cohen

Dear Mom,

Here's the letter that I promised you I'd send. I'm coming home tomorrow with Mike. We're hitchhiking up the coast, so hopefully I'll be back about a day after I start out. I know that you don't approve of hitchhiking, but there is a real necessity as I had some money stolen last week. Mike has lent me some to eat and all, but because I had to borrow from him, we didn't have enough for bus tickets. Besides, we will be coming up with a guy who really knows how to hitch, named Pierce. He lives in Seattle and so he will have a little farther to go than we will, but he has done it many times so there will be no problem.

We're both fine here and have enjoyed ourselves, especially the last few days. Hope you and Dad are fine. Also, say hi to Dave.

Love,
Larry

San Francisco
9/18/68
Larry Cohen to T-Rx

This is just to tell you that I enjoyed meeting you and that I want you to know that if you ever need me for anything that you should send me a letter or something to Eugene, Oregon—I'm in the phone book—Larry Cohen.

[*Editor's Note: This missile was never sent, but was found in the possession of Larry's effects as collected by Fred Abrams; see appendix #1. I. Coale*][45]

---

[45] My father never completed the appendix. (I.B.)

Eugene, Oregon
Sept. 21 1968
Fred Abrams to Larry Cohen

Dear Larry,

The reason I haven't been by to see you is that I'm in the hospital. Funny thing, eh? I guess I have a rather bad case of viral pneumonia. I read your letters from San Francisco with interest. It seems that you had an opportunity to meet some of the seamier people who inhabit the city. I'm happy that you didn't lose more than your money, as big cities can be very dangerous. Did you get a chance to see the art museum or hear the symphony? They're both rather good, I am told.

As far as school work goes, I have plenty to do, but it isn't the same as being able to attend classes. I sit here in bed for a seeming eternity with nothing to do as I can't have any visitors. I must stay quiet. However, this type of treatment is liable to make me "stir crazy." I'm a person who likes to be on the move, as you know, and I haven't had so much forced quiet in ages.

If you could find the time to write me another letter like your one of September 16? (15+1)? I would appreciate it. All the jokes that people make about hospital food are based on fact. That's about all I have to say for now, as one can't create something out of nothing--or so I'm told, unless I were Andy Warhol and I wrote a picture about how the nurses come and go. And here I am: horizontal—at least I'm still above ground.

The conversation in the ward is essentially nothing, too. Not much to look forward to (though I have to admit that a can of tomato soup wouldn't be bad). Stay with it, my friend.
Yours,
F.A.

San Francisco
September 27, 1968
Larry Cohen to Fred Abrams

Dear Fred,

Sorry to hear that you are in the hospital. You haven't really missed much in school as the opening of the year is always such a boring event that it's a wonder that more students don't fall asleep or get sick from the stupidity of it all. Besides, you were always a capable student and never really needed the added benefit of our sagacious teachers anyway.

I suppose that if you want a letter that is somewhat of a diversion, I'll have to go back to my stories about San Francisco, since it's the only real excitement that I've had since I hit that triple in the Little League play-offs when I was eleven. Anyway, I think that I have told you about meeting this T-Rx, and how he took us to that weird party. That night, I kept having dreams about the slime and the Prophet. One would arise from a murky swamp and hiss at me and the other would descend from the low cypress trees and threaten me. Not especially a pleasant vision.

Mike slept like a person in his inebriated condition might be expected (Mike never was one for surprises). When it was morning, I just sat up in bed thinking about what had happened. I was fixing my mind on the different things that had happened to me in an attempt to focus on some of the events. I wasn't trying to draw any conclusions—I'm never any good at that, but I was concerned about gaining a sense of all the various impressions of the previous evening as I tried to arrange the fragmentary memories into some sort of frame.

When Mike and I went out to breakfast, we found our usual place to eat was closed and so we ventured towards another place to eat. As we were walking around, who should we meet but Mad Dog. I called out to him, as he was one of the few people that we knew in the city. At first he didn't recognize us, but then he smiled and came over to us.

"Hi, how are you doing?" he asked.

"Good," I responded.

"Who's your friend?" asked Mad Dog. I'm sure that Mike didn't appreciate this because he recognized Mad Dog as the man who had sold us the tickets and naturally expected that recognition to be reciprocal. I sensed a coldness come over Mike, and so I endeavored to be particularly ingratiating to Mad Dog so that Mike might not give the impression that we weren't friendly.

"This is Mike, you sold him tickets for the concert."

"The 'Dead'?"

"Yo!"

"Well, you're a good man. Are you a friend of young lad, here?"

Mad Dog had forgotten my name, but that was natural, as well, for he'd only met me late at night during a party. An individual meets many people at a party, so he can't be expected to remember every name. I didn't mind reminding him. But before I had the chance he said, "You two are friends of T-Rx, aren't you?" "That's right," said Mike, who felt that he was more a friend of Trek than I was since it was his person that the fabled leader had rescued the night previous. "We met him at the concert."

"Well, then," began Mad Dog in a different tone, "this *is* a pleasure. Where are you two going?"

"We thought we'd get a bite to eat," I said. I waited a moment for Mike to talk, in case he wanted to respond, but suddenly he became reserved again and decided that if there was any talking to be done, he'd leave the task to me.

"I know a dandy place to get rolls and coffee for a quarter," said Mad Dog.

So we left with Mad Dog in the lead, followed by myself and Mike begrudgingly tagging along. Our walk wasn't a long one. Two blocks later we found a wood-framed establishment that had a 5x5-foot plate-glass window that sported the name of the place in lemon yellow letters: Dashiell Slept Here! In a moment, we were sliding atop shiny red plastic seat coverings into a booth while Mad Dog yelled our order to a little bald-headed man with thick black glasses behind the counter.

"So what you guys doing here?" asked Mad Dog when he had positioned himself across from us. The white, gold-speckled Formica table top was being cleaned by a busboy. The unused menus were sitting tall in a stainless steel rack that sat against the painted brick wall.

I wasn't sure what he meant by his question--whether he was referring to the lunch counter or our location in San Francisco? But fortunately for me, at that moment I was relieved from the obligation of responding to this inquiry by the entrance of T-Rx himself into the greasy spoon.

He smiled slightly at seeing Mad Dog and us and nodded his head towards the little man behind the counter.

I think I should say something about the smile of Trek. His mouth at most times was stretched as if he were facially communicating some level of sarcasm. Amidst the smile, he barely raised the right side of his mouth in a sort of quick tick. This gave a level of ambiguity so that one could not tell whether he was being serious in his critique or merely ironic with his smile. It gave me a deep uneasiness about him—an uneasiness that I hadn't experienced the night before when he presented himself from the shadows.

"I see you've met my friends," said T-Rx to Mad Dog as he slid into our booth next to him.

I was rather pleased that the important fellow had remembered us. I could observe that Mike was visibly pleased as well. I think he had felt somewhat *dissed* by the presence of Mad Dog alone. But when T-Rx made his appearance, things changed noticeably as the locus of power shifted. This new locus was one which was acceptable to Mike, as he'd have to be an ungrateful wretch not to pay some deference to a man who had most certainly saved him the night before from an unpleasant confrontation (at the very least) and possibly serious bodily injury.

"I was just asking them where they're from," said Mad Dog.

"Why don't you ask them their names? A name is more important than place of origin. After all, one can alter one's history as history is an ongoing process, but a name denotes who you are. A person's moniker is *that* which symbolically represents him."

This made Mike laugh. T-Rx shifted his eyes in a somber reprimand for this insolent disrespect for such a serious idea. Then T-Rx made a sound: it was the noise that air makes when you suck with your teeth together. Mike didn't notice, however, as he looked over to me, trying to elicit a response. I didn't know what to do, for I could see that to laugh as Mike wanted would displease T-Rx, and probably Mad Dog as well. This was something that I didn't want to do.

On the other hand, it *was* rather humorous and didn't have any buildup in the conversation. What does one say when confronted with a statement that a person is synonymous with his name? What does it mean to be a 'Larry'? Is it different than a 'Lawrence'?

How does a 'Fred' differ from a 'Mike' (not the persons, but the names)? And if names *do* designate people, then how is it that other Larrys aren't the same as I am? Why is there a difference? The very process by which a name is given is one in which some symbol (to use Trek's phrase) is attached, in many cases before the child is even born. My parents had named me soon after they were married, a full five years before I was born. How could they have made an appropriate label for me?

I read in school that many Native American nations gave *temporary* names at birth and then *permanent* names upon becoming an adult. These permanent names were meant to reflect the character of the new adult member of the community. This makes some more sense than the way we do it in the U.S. of A.

And what about *last* names? It's nobody's fault that they have some particular surname. The whole thing seemed utterly ridiculous and I wanted to laugh with Mike. The statement deserved to be laughed at, I felt— but I wasn't sure. Perhaps there was something that I had overlooked in my hasty observation that would make me seem like a fool if I showed myself either way.

I wanted to be uncommitted, but this choice wasn't open to me. I was being called upon to act. Mike's eyes were looking at me to see what I would do, so I looked over to the counter as if to be impatient about our coffee and rolls.

I wanted to back Mike up, or make some sort of stand one way or another. I wanted to do something, but I didn't. I turned my head back to the group, but then I chickened out. I didn't decide to be a coward; I just was. More precisely, my head just turned automatically. But I was still thinking.

Mike turned to me but then I was looking in another direction. There was no intermediate stage: Mike turned and then my vision was on the greasy counter—it was like a "jump-cut" in the movies, from one scene to another. No, it wasn't really like that, but I don't know any other way to describe it.

"How do you spell your name?" asked Mad Dog to Mike.
Mike was still looking at me. My head was turned, but I could feel his gaze on my soul.

"M-I-K-E." The voice was subdued, though not serious.

"Did you choose that name?" asked T-Rx.

Mike turned to the other. "What are you talking about?"

"Your name, who gave it to you?"

"What kind of question is that? Who gave you your name? Who gives anyone his name?" Mike's reply showed that he couldn't believe that the topic was really about to be pursued on a serious level. At first it was a joke and could be laughed at, but then all was serious, and this disparity between what was *expected* and what was *felt* made for a tense scene.

"Your mother?" asked Mad Dog.

"Sure my mother, and father, too."

"Well, that's an acceptable answer. Probably a common response," said Rx. "But the truth is that there are few of us who don't modify our lives in some way. For instance, many people have nicknames, or familiar names which aren't on their birth certificates, but are names which they come to be known by through the years. Thomas becomes Tommy for a little boy and Tom during high school. As the man changes, so does his name. It's a common enough process."

Trek's voice took on a tone that was in accord to the smile I had seen earlier. I didn't know just how to take him. Mike and I both listened (mainly out of respect), but soon we both felt a little fidgety. Whether this was due to what Rx was saying or not, I couldn't say.

"Now, there are those who pronounce their names slightly differently than most people do, putting accents on syllables that aren't often recognized as such—Lyn-don' becomes Lyn'-don and Jeff'-errr-son can be Jef-fer'sson or Jeff-or-son'. There are connotative reasons for these changes, but I insist that the manner in which one pronounces his name can be very important to him.

"The man who pronounces his name 'Smythe' doesn't like it being referred to as 'Smith.' The first man who insists on the long 'i' gives his name an English aristocratic tone, very unique and dignified. While 'Smith' is a common name. It refers to a common laborer and has *democratic* as opposed to *monarchical* flavor.

"I can't imagine a working class man insisting that his name was Smythe, unless he was like that D'Urberville in the novel who sought to rise above his station on the trappings of a name." This last remark was delivered with a wry sarcasm, which I at first thought was directed at that type of man, but then I became in doubt about that interpretation as the sound, D'Urberville, echoed in my mind. Perhaps he was talking about us, or maybe himself? I didn't know. There was no way that I could know; this agitated me. "Inflection of a name means something. The manner in which one pronounces his name makes that name unique. Now the obvious cases you might say are now clear, but what about the people like Jones who simply seem to pronounce their name with the same tonal distinctions as in Tom Jones. Though even here regional accents are common and come from the same family, so there aren't any other outside factors to make a spurious change. Thus, some may say that the pronunciation comes from outside ourselves and is not an indication of personal character at all.

"To this charge I contend there are differences in the intensity in which the name is spoken. One might pronounce it very forcefully and another very weakly. Or one declaims with pitch differences that would indicate the complicated relationship that one felt with the symbol that represents him: the label to the world. In the event (which I don't believe possible) that two people had accents, intensity, pitch, rhythm, spelling, and any other intonations exactly the same, I would contend that the one who was pronouncing his name in the said manner *first* was an idol to the second who was trying to emulate the first (this is excluding impersonators who are either entertainers or criminals). Such emulation would say equally as much about the other as if he had derived a new way of pronouncing his name. Imitation (as it's so rare) would constitute a form of uniqueness and thus offer a vehicle for the scientist of naming to make his judgment."

The food came, and Mike devoured his donut. Then he dumped a few tablespoons worth of sugar into his coffee. He didn't like the conversation, and I could tell that he wished to be somewhere else—walking in Golden Gate Park or feeding the pigeons—anything but to listen to some half-baked idea about why people use the names that they do.

However, my opinion was quite the opposite. After that last speech I began to feel that this T-Rx really knew something about people. He knew their hearts. I felt that he was making this speech to us for a desired effect. He knew what we were and he was trying to ferret out a reaction from us. What was puzzling to me was the reason why he was doing this.

This last question intrigued me so much that I eagerly awaited the resumption of his speech.

"Now, what I've said so far is merely descriptive and insignificant. But one must realize the general principle that is operative before he can describe how it works in application. The question is (if this is all true): why does one person use different accents, intonations, etc. than another? Is this something that one chooses to represent about his particular personality or his *conception* of that personality? Or is it something that occurs mechanically as a result of the rules of nature, so that a person has no control over this process? And if this is so, the pronunciation of a name *must necessarily* reflect the personality as shaped by his environment.

"The difference between these two approaches would greatly affect the way in which the scientist of names interprets his data. It is at this point that the scientist must put forward a hypothesis and either test it himself or rely on work already done by others. All science rests on such hypotheses. The system follows consistently from a postulate or group of initial postulates, but this says nothing about the soundness of the system, especially when there is controversy over that initial point."

I must admit that I was getting in over my head at that point. I didn't have any idea what he was talking about, and I think Rx knew this by the way he smiled as he looked at me.

"At any rate, this theory accounts for the hypothesis by offering a system of analysis and then interpreting the results as if both alternatives were operative. We can say something assuming free choice and then assuming no choice.

"The analysis takes into account the fronting motion of the rhythm etc. of vowels and consonants. Obviously, accents and the like have much to do with whether one 'fronts' a *u* or pronounces it as a 'back vowel.'

"The same holds true with the fricatives. There is a standard, but this standard is useless in our examinations of particulars.

"Now, you know that vowels have open sounds, and back vowels like a, o, and u tend to lengthen words and give them long open sounds that have certain connotative values. Simplifying things somewhat, the scientist of names knows that there is a different emotive value in the words 'load' and 'lewd.' The first is more pleasant sounding and the second harsher and more unpleasant."

It was at this point that I felt obliged to interject, "Excuse me, Mr. T-Rx, but I don't really follow you. You're giving too much jargon that I don't understand."

"It's really quite simple. You remember the high Gothic and Old English palatal umlaut? And the process of raising and fronting?"

"No," I said, "I've never heard of it."

"Hum, well, then perhaps it won't do too much good going through this even through analogy. But if you're interested, I could jot down a few articles that you could read and then you could study up on the subject and come back with the vocabulary."

"I don't think that I could handle it even with the vocabulary," I said.

"The process is really very simple, once you get within the conceptual framework," he replied. Trek seemed interested in converting me to his ideas about language and such. He was even kind enough to write it all down in the little spiral notebook I keep in my side pocket. (Otherwise, I could have never remembered all these terms.) But to tell you the truth, I don't feel easy around libraries. They are so quiet and unnatural: all those books that are worshipped as if they were deities. The only people I know that like libraries are zombies who move about in their deadness, hour after hour, in completion of a series of meaningless tasks or research.

Though I don't care for libraries, and I know that you don't either, Fred, I was still interested in this theory that I obtained in a simplified version from Mad Dog later. He said that he didn't understand any of it either, but that somehow it amounted to counting vowels and consonants. If you had too many vowels you were romantically inclined (I confess that I don't know if he was talking about love or something else, because I didn't think he was talking about 'boy meets girl') and if you were endowed with lots of consonants without those open vowels, you were more discerning and scientific.

Also certain names 'go out' when you say them (I suppose he's talking about that back and front business) and certain ones 'go in.' It's better to be full of consonants and go in, like T-Rx's own name which starts being pronounced in the front of the mouth with the 't' and moves down and back with the 'r'-and further back with the 'x.' Mad Dog was sketchy about the reason that this is good, but it connects to something about interior being superior to exterior. . . the man of the interior is supposed to be better than the opposite. I don't know why, but that's just the way that he put it. Other names go out, and if they have more vowels they become more sonorous and therefore worse on the scale of externality. I know that I probably have a few things mixed up, but that's all I understand.

'Larry' is a bad name because the 'y' is a front vowel and my name comes out, but on the other hand I have more consonants than vowels (3 to 2) so that's a balancing factor, I suppose. 'Mike' has it bad both ways, too many vowels and it comes out. 'Fred,' stays near the front, and has more consonants, so I suppose you'd be a middle man of some sort.

I don't know whether I believe any of this, but it's interesting to go through the various names that you know and determine whether they go out or in and if they have consonants or vowels in excess or balance. To test it yourself, just think about what part of your mouth the sound is being made and feel which way the sound goes—T-Rx goes back and Mike stays at the front and goes out. I'll write you more tomorrow (about what goes on) and all that,

Larry

San Francisco
October 1, 1968
Larry Cohen to Fred Abrams

Dear Fred (though Fredrick goes in more and has more consonants),

After our lecture about philology we left with neither Mike nor myself understanding anything about Trek's theory, or anything else for that matter as we were pretty confused. One thing that I knew was that Mike was somewhat uncomfortable. On the one hand, he must have felt as if he should have been friendlier to Trek (in return for Trek's assistance the other night). On the other hand, he felt a little put off by the tone of the lecture that was delivered to us, for no one wants to hear a speech that sounds like school just days before we are due back to that "prison."

When one is on vacation, he likes to take it easy. As Mike says, "Keep off my back with the books/ I'm searching for women with good looks."

That phrase says it all.

We wanted to have a good time. Of course, you know how it is, especially cooped up in the hospital there. Why, I remember when I was in the hospital to get my tonsils out. It was one miserable experience, and I was only in one day! I hope your pneumonia is improving. They say that that sort of thing can get out of hand if you're not careful.

After getting out of the little hole-in-the-wall that served coffee and rolls for a quarter, we ventured down the street with T-Rx and Mike walking together and Mad Dog and me behind. It was at this time that I had an opportunity to further question Mad Dog about the theory ('Mad Dog' goes out on 'Mad' then comes back in on 'Dog'). Suddenly we cut into an alley and walked in the back door of a supermarket.

"Pick up a bag there," directed Rx.

Mike picked up the bag and we walked over to a large bin and Rx climbed up and started handing some food down to Mad Dog, who gave it to Mike to put into his bag.

I must have had an odd expression on my face because when we got out, Mad Dog explained to me that the bin was for rejected produce and that they had just finished sorting it (which they do every morning early), after which T-Rx comes and takes what he needs.

"Why doesn't he just take welfare?" I asked.

T-Rx must have heard the question and turned around and said in an even tone,

"And do you suppose that a Vietnamese child might like some napalm for Christmas?"

I didn't understand the meaning of these words, but was enlightened by Mad Dog that Trek felt that if he accepted welfare, he would be supporting a corrupt system that was committing genocide upon the people of southeast Asia. You are either "in the system" or "out of it." That was the way that he put it. To accept welfare was to be in the system.

But what I didn't understand was how one could live in this country and not be in the system in some way. I suppose that it involves some complicated principle that I don't understand.

After that, Mike and T-Rx discussed something. But because they were a bit ahead of us, I couldn't hear—though I found out later that Rx just wanted to know whether Mike wanted to go around with them that day, and apparently Mike agreed for both of us.

We got a lift over to the courthouse, where some other people were waiting for some kind of demonstration about something that I never did figure out, but there were fifty of us or so gathered. I asked one of them what was happening.

"I don't know, I just came with a few others," he said.

I went to a girl who looked as if she was ordering some people around, and asked her what was happening.

"We're protesting," she said.

"What are we protesting?"

"Listen, don't bother me with a lot of stupid questions. I've got to organize my people."

Mad Dog was gone, and so I had no one to ask (for I wouldn't think of asking T-Rx himself). At any rate, this lasted for an hour or two when finally some police came and we were ushered outside. The people in the front were shouting and shaking their fists at the police, but I noticed that T-Rx wasn't one of them. He was standing in the middle of the group, almost passively as he flowed with the momentum and out the door.

There was something about his posture that inspired awe in me. I think that it was the strength that I felt when I looked at him, like I felt that I could do anything, and suddenly it didn't matter what we were protesting. It didn't matter. Rx was my strength and he inspired me to do anything: to overcome the most repressive and hostile force.

Sitting on the lawn outside the building I felt a part of the group even though I didn't know any of the others. It was like we shared something. A common experience perhaps, or maybe a common leader, but we were one and that feeling of unity was an inspiring happening. And felt happy to have a purpose. We were *doing* something. We weren't *watching* something on the television—about what was happening somewhere else. Instead, we were involved in something important; we were furthering the cause of justice and right.

After eating (some of the girls had made sandwiches from some variety of meats that I didn't recognize) we dispersed. Mike and I followed Rx.

"How did you like it?" asked Rx.

"Like what?" I asked.

"The sit-in."

"Was *that* a sit-in?" I asked.

"Of course it was," said Mike in a tone that indicated an impatience with someone as stupid as I was as I didn't know the meaning of common terms.

"I thought a sit-in was where you stayed for a long time," I replied.

"Larry, that was a sit-in. What did you think we were just at?" asked Mike in the same tone. I could tell that he was slightly embarrassed that he was connected with me in the presence of T-Rx, who might think less of Mike by his association with a dummy like me. Mike even started walking closer to Rx as if to exclude me, or perhaps he was pretending that I wasn't there. He wanted Rx for himself.

"Larry's *right*; the name 'sit-in' is a very indefinite word that has taken on a variety of meanings according to the contexts in which it has been used," said Rx.

"But anyone knows that was a sit-in," said Mike with an air of bravado. He wanted to ingratiate himself with Rx; however, the tactic wasn't really effective as Rx didn't let the subject drop.

"Well, obviously, I agree with you since I used the word in that context, but if you took a 'sit-in' to be only that variety of demonstration that occurred at the lunch counters of Birmingham, then what we did was something else—a semi 'stand-in,' or something like that. I don't think that there's any utility in creating a long string of expressions that indicate the same purpose. We went there to demonstrate, by our presence, a comment on state of affairs that we consider to be wrong. We acted with peaceful intentions, so therefore, I think that the term is applicable."

I felt like I had been supported by this strange leader who I had assumed was only mildly warm to me because I was a friend of Mike's and that he wouldn't have had anything to do with me if I hadn't known Mike. I had thought that he would have taken Mike's side in any dispute with me. I had been wrong.

It was decided that we would go over to a movie theater and see a flick. Apparently the last feature was just getting out, because Mad Dog told us to run into the alley, which we did without question.

There was an alley exit and when the door was opened, Mad Dog rushed in holding his and T-Rx's jackets in his hands. Some ushers appeared before Mike and I could get in, and we decided that we couldn't make it.

"What should we do now?" I asked.

"Beats me," replied Mike, who was as much amazed about the incident as I was. "Shall we wait for them?"

"A whole two hours? You've got to be kidding."

"Well, do you want to go back to the hotel?"

"And do what?" asked Mike with a look of dejection in his eyes. He was showing with his expression what I was also feeling. But I was too tense to express it. Both of us wanted to be with Rx, but didn't know what to do. We knew that it would be inexcusable to buy a ticket, when they sneaked in so craftily. There was nothing else to do in the city, and we didn't exactly relish the idea of waiting around in an alley for two hours while they watched a movie. And we didn't even consider whether it might be a double-feature, in which case the time would be more than doubled—with cartoons and all that they play at the beginning.

We were both standing there, waiting for the other to make a suggestion about what we should do to fill our time. I wanted Mike to speak first because it would be easier to deal with a proposal on the table than to offer up a new one myself. I knew that anything I could think of at that moment would be something that neither I nor Mike could possibly endorse. But on the other hand, the silence was also difficult to bear, and I fancied that I could dart down the alley at full speed (near the speed of light) and keep running until my body fell apart piece by piece from the air friction caused by the high speed at which I was moving.

I had to say something, even though Mike would reject it.

"We *could*—what do you *want* to do? We've seen the art museum already."

"If I knew what to do, I'd be long gone, buster," yelled Mike.

We were all alone, just standing there in the alley. The people from the last show had long since left the theater. It was necessary that we do something. But *what* we should do was a mystery. Our indecision made us both edgy.

Just when I felt like taking off down the alley for good, the door swung open. I could hear the squeaky hinges before I saw the metal-plated portal open. All of a sudden, as I turned around, hope rushed to me that perhaps it was Rx or Mad Dog letting us in. They knew that we'd wait around and they came to get us some seats.

But I was disappointed to see the form of an usher standing at the door.

"The movie is starting soon," said the usher. "Your friends told me to tell you to finish your smoke and come in."

Naturally, this surprised both of us, but we weren't going to show our astonishment there in the alley and give away the scenario that our comrades had begun. So we just sighed as if we were tired of having to end our little respite in the fresh air to return indoors, where we'd have to be cooped up for two hours while we watched a movie. We were escorted by the usher to where we saw Mad Dog and Rx sitting with two vacant seats next to them, with coats on them as if to reserve the places. Whether the usher was a friend of theirs or whether they actually pulled off the trick I'll never know, because no more was said about it. All that mattered was that we had seats that had been procured for us by this clever fellow, T-Rx.

The last event of the day occurred when we went to the docks to meet a shipment of seafood that was being offloaded to one of the restaurants. We helped with offload: the crates from the truck onto a pair of pallets and then into the kitchen. In return were given a small sack full of shellfish to take with us.

We went with our booty to the same room that the party had been held. It looked different in the daylight. In the room were about eight figures, minus the two that Trek had met at the party. They were already cooking over a two-burner hot plate that sat on a small shelf.

"Main course," said Rx, coming in the door.

"Did you get any meat?" asked one of them.

"Just fish," said Mad Dog.

They were cooking the vegetables that T-Rx had picked up earlier, though how they had gotten there I didn't know--perhaps someone took them back after the sit-in.

"Just plant yourself," said Mad Dog. "We'll eat in a few minutes."

You wouldn't believe it, Fred. There was a whole group of them living there. None of them had employment that I could tell, though I didn't know how they paid their rent or their expenses. At any rate, there was something attractive about their lives. They had none of the distractions that commonly affect my father and the men I know around Eugene. There was no job that they had to go to and no regulations that they were forced to obey.

It was there that I met a guy from Seattle who was returning in a couple of days to start school there. He was hitching up the coast. I paid attention just in case we didn't have enough money to make our own trip home by bus (due to the unfortunate robbery at the concert or wherever). Regardless, we decided to go with him. He called himself Captain Hook and he was trying to make it as a member of a group. During the summer, he had gotten into a music group called "Dow Jones and the Industrials" but the group couldn't get enough business to pay their expenses.

"There are lots of groups down here and the competition is fierce. You have to have a gimmick," said Hook.

I smiled at him and nodded my head. I know little about the business end of things in general. Mike wasn't paying attention.

"Look at the Beatles. They were no better musically than many other groups of their time— the Dave Clark Five for instance. But they had strange haircuts and so they became outrageous. They got their start playing music just like fifty other groups, but because of that *one break* they could start creating their own sound. You have to be willing to compromise if you gonna make it big."

There was much more said, naturally, but that's what really stuck with me: "You have to be willing to compromise." It's a strange thought, one that you certainly don't agree with, I know. You've always told me that I should stick things out and that if one follows the rules to the letter that he will eventually be recognized. Follow ideals and rules or what everyone wants you to do for a chance at the brass ring. Which do I want to do: be myself or follow some sort of script for life? I don't know. How does one make such a decision?

I tell you, Fred, I don't want to make a letter too serious, but I was upset by what I experienced in San Francisco. *Upset* is the word, because I felt that my order was overturned. Things that I took as fact were contradicted by action and word. Society progresses by the masses of people doing what they can do best: division of labor. But these people do nothing. By the other rules they should be called parasites of society: living off of what others do.

But if this is so, then why am I attracted to their way of life? Am I a parasite, too? Does this make me bad? Or is there really something to this? I have no answers, nor do I expect that there are any. Perhaps all this is just some elaborate illusion in which I have begun to believe. I don't know.

Hope that you recover soon, and that you return to school.
The best,
Larry

San Francisco
Oct. 3, 1968
Fred Abrams to Larry Cohen

Dear Larry,

I had a relapse and I was on the respirator for a few days, but now they say that I can come home, though I won't be able to attend school for some time—perhaps near the end of the fall, if all goes well. It's a strange thing how one can become ill suddenly, but the recovery takes so long. That's the way it goes, I suppose.

I enjoyed reading your letters. Your adventures were memorable and ones that I'm sure you will tell your own son someday.

Have you heard that Guy is expanding his garage this spring and will be hiring three or four new mechanics? I know how you like to work on cars and that you know some of the fellows in the shop. So that might be something you might want to look into? The mechanic's life is a good one to my way of thinking. You have short hours, lots of coffee breaks, and high pay. Besides the fact that they have a terrific fast-pitch softball team, and being in the garage you'd have a great chance of playing (which, of course, means that you'd get paid for practicing and playing some games that fall during working hours). I remember Gilbert Mooney, who didn't work more than twelve hours a week during softball season, though he got paid for forty!

Myself, I intend to continue with my studies. I only need five courses to graduate this year, so I can relax and try to get well. You haven't mentioned Janet to me. Are you two still going together? Stop over if you can. I can see visitors next week.

Yours,
Fred

Place unknown
December 12, 1968
Fragment of letter from Larry Cohen to his brother Bill

Bill,

Don't tell Mom or Dad about this letter. Can you box-up some of my things? If you can, please drop by the Tastee Diner around six. Sit in the car. I will come to you and pick up the box.

Come alone.

I don't know if I can [word indistinguishable] very well at all. Both Mike and Fred—maybe [word indistinguishable] I'm afraid I'll be next.

San Francisco
December 15, 1968
Fragment of letter from Larry Cohen to his brother Bill[46]

Bill,

---

[46] These letters were never sent but found in the effects of Larry Cohen.

I don't blame you for trying to have me picked up by the police. You probably think that I've gone off the deep end. Well maybe I have, but one thing I know is that if I go back to living in Eugene, I'll crack. Mike tried to do it their way and look what happened to him. Fred—there was no one who played it straighter than Fred—and look what it got him! I do need some things, but you will have to send them to me when I get to a safe place that can't be traced. Keep up the old spirit, Billy boy.

San Francisco
February 24, 1969
Larry Cohen to his brother Bill

Dear old Bill,

If you would be so kind, would you take my things and, except for the clothes, sell them at the penny-wise thrift shop in town and send me the money? As you know, I've withdrawn the money from my account. Also, would you please send this in care of Marcia McCrae P.O. Box 1001, San Francisco (I don't have a zip). Your cooperation is appreciated.

Eugene, Oregon
February 26, 1969
Letter from Bill Cohen to his brother Larry

Dear Lawrence,

It's needless to say how much heartache that you've caused your mother and father—and anxiety to us all. I can't say that I approve of your conduct. Your running away was imprudent; besides, it only made you seem as if you were guilty, too. I know that you claim that you weren't there. And if you weren't, that can be proved in a court of law. It's a bad way to start out in life, being a fugitive. You will be running all of your life and your punishment will be compounded.

Father called the police chief upon receipt of your last letter and he told father that if you give yourself up there in San Francisco, then they will not press charges concerning you being a fugitive from justice. That's very generous, and I suggest that you take it. They won't be that lenient for long.

It's too bad about your friend Mike. He was always one for roughhouse. Even as a lad, I can remember that he was always getting into scrapes. He should have known better than to tangle with some of those criminals in the jail; an accident was bound to happen as he's not used to dealing with such tough company. Eugene is a small town (comparatively) and your friend had never had to deal with those types before. They play rough. That's why they're in jail.

Both Philip and I went to the funeral and we were surprised to see how many people showed up.

My work is fine as tax time is approaching and we're getting most of our business now. The new laws are making things more complicated and thus more people need accountants. It's about as regular as clockwork!

I'm sorry but I will not be able to send the things that you desire. While there is still a warrant out for you, such an action on my part would constitute aiding and abetting a fugitive and would subject me to a felony and the subsequent loss of my right to practice my livelihood.

I hope that you understand.

Again, my advice to you is that you give yourself up and surrender. It's the best way. At the most, you'll serve three to six months in jail, but probably you'll get a suspended sentence—most first offenders do. Think about it. And think about how good it would feel to start life with a clean, fresh slate.

Sincerely,
William A. Cohen

Eugene, Oregon
March 13, 1969

Fred Abrams to Larry Cohen

Dear Larry,

I got your address from your brother. I hope that you receive this letter because I wanted you to know two things: first, the guy who accused you and Mike admitted that he was lying. You may remember that there were numerous witnesses who saw the fellow in the orange parka—the one that was similar to the one that Mike wore everywhere. He even had a cap like Mike did. Apparently this parka belonged to the dealer he was afraid of crossing. So he fingered Mike, who had been at the Johnson's party earlier as you had (wearing that same parka).

Well, just before sentencing he was told privately that if he would name the dealer that he'd get a year knocked off of his sentence. So with the prospect of only spending a year and a half instead of two and a half (plus the probability that the pusher would be spending seven or more years) he told the real story, naming the dealer and exonerating you. That means that you're free. There's no outstanding warrant on you.

The second thing that I wanted to tell you is that I'm better. I've been out of the hospital for two weeks and in another couple I'll be able to leave the house and walk around town. I know that you were very worried about me and that's why you came to see me (my parents told me). That was very kind of you, especially as you were in some danger at the time. I'll never forget that.

Unfortunately, I'll have to take classes this summer if I want to be able to go to back to college this fall. My father has been talking to some of the people at the college and they told him that because of my unusual circumstances, I might be able to get a certificate of admission pending my high school diploma in June. That would make me eligible for some scholarships that I want to get.

I wondered whether you might be with the same group of people that you met last fall before school? I can see why you might never want to show your face back here again, but in case you do, remember that I'd be anxious to see you and would help in any way that I can (if you need a place to stay or something). Write me if you get the time.

—Your friend, Fred

San Francisco
March 23, 1969
Larry Cohen to Fred Abrams

Dear Fred,

It was nice to get your letter. I just got it two days ago as I was in San Diego with the fellow that I told you about, Ron Adair, who we call Captain Hook. He was the guy that hitched to Eugene with me last summer before school. He's from West Seattle and is always talking about what an interesting place Seattle is. Sometimes I wonder why he's not in Seattle if it is really such a good town.

Marcia gave me your letter, which got to her by our circuitous mail route. Some of the incidents that you mention are painful to remember. It takes a crisis to bring out the worst in people, but I did want to straighten you out about a few things.

First, Mike was at the party and I wasn't (though I did go to a McDonalds at the time when the party had broken up and the groups had hovered around the same spot). That is, most of the people who had been at the party were also at McDonalds, so it was a natural mistake for someone to make. It's a real post-party hangout in Eugene. I left when the partygoers invaded the place. Secondly, Mike was with those guys who were dropping acid and mescaline. He had come in his parents' car, which was parked in the lot behind. He had left his coat in the car, or so he told me. He had bought some grass and was going to get the money (which he used to put in his glove compartment). That's when the cops came in for the raid. I don't know how he completely evaded the net that they put around the place. But he did.

It was then that I heard some commotion from his car and decided that there was trouble still left in the glove compartment. I was outside. I'd just started walking home after trying to decide whether I was going to make one last try with Janet or not. I decided that she wasn't worth it so I just started strolling home. Mike picked me up and we drove to the Safeway parking lot where Mike told me everything. It was in the parking lot that Mary-Jean Watson saw us together. The time was just right for a circumstantial connection. Mike was driving me home when we saw some patrol cars in front of his house, so I told Mike that maybe he ought to figure out an alibi: say that he was with me the entire night or something (little did I know that I was suspected too). "You can use me as an alibi." I said those words.

I asked Mike if he was holding anything (drugs) and he said he had a little grass, so I advised him to toss it, which he did. We went to my house, but Mike didn't want to stay. His excuse was that my house would be the next place they'd try, so he made arrangements to meet me behind the college stadium the next evening at six.

The police did come to our house next. They didn't want me (yet) but they asked for Mike, and I told them that there must be some mistake and that we had been at the drive-in and that Mike had gone home early (I didn't complete my story because I could tell that they wouldn't be persuaded). I also figured that anything I might say would only implicate me somehow. I saw then that by giving Mike an alibi, I was making myself a suspect too, so I didn't say too much.

But I left open the possibility that Mike could have gone back to the drug party. That feeling isn't a pleasant one. To feel that one must not say something to help a friend because to do so would not only fail to help the friend, but would also hurt himself is not a good feeling. I can't determine how much of my decision was controlled by self-interest. . . it's impossible to say. But what is clear is that I *did* feel something. I didn't want to get myself into trouble. When it came right down to it, I wanted to save myself. Such an emotion made me feel like an animal. I hated myself for feeling it, but I did.

"So you weren't with him *all* night?" asked the officer.

"No sir, not all the night. Like I said, he went to a party and met me at the drive-in and then we went around a little. Mike left me a couple hours ago."

The words came so easily—even though I was fighting them. So what, if they wouldn't help Mike? I had been by myself. I didn't want them to think I had been at the party, too. There was nothing to prove that I wasn't. I knew that if I weren't careful that instead of believing me, they'd think that they had another suspect—me.

"You didn't see him again?" asked the officer.

"No sir," I said, not knowing about snoopy Mary-Jean. I had cooked my own goose. I should have included something about riding around with Mike, but that would look too suspicious. I wanted to help Mike, I really did. At the bottom of it all I would have sacrificed for him--at least I think, hope, that I would have. However, what was on my mind at the time was that there was no sense in two going down.

"Thank you, sorry to have troubled you," said the policeman, though I could tell that he felt he had a new detail that he didn't have before. I didn't like the look in his eye. He was going to get me, I decided that night in bed. As I tossed about, I heard the words "you can use me for an alibi—use me, use me, use me." The words just kept ringing in my mind. There was a collision between what I said and what I did.

Then I started thinking about Mike and what *he* should do. If he stays away, they're going to think he's guilty for sure. Perhaps they only wanted to question him as they had questioned me? On the other side, if they had a warrant out for him, surely he could beat the rap as they couldn't have any evidence implicating him. I decided that I would advise Mike to turn himself in. I had to split.

"That's crazy," said Mike the next night.

"Well that's all they did to me."

"But you weren't there."

"How can they prove anything? You said that nobody saw you," I replied.

"I know, but that hasn't stopped them from jailing people before. Who says that they need evidence?"

"C'mon, this isn't the Soviet Union. We have fair trials here."

"Yeah," he replied. I don't know if there was a note of sarcasm in his response or not. It was a weak, muffled reply, uncharacteristic of the boisterous fellow who I knew. Mike was scared; he didn't know what to do.

As I think back on it, I'm not sure why I sounded so positive to Mike. I didn't have any information that really supported my claims. There was nothing. I don't think that I wanted him taken in so that there could be no suspicion about myself. I didn't have any feelings like that that I can remember, but they say that sometimes we desire things that we don't consciously admit. It is the fear of that: of unconsciously wanting Mike put away so that I wouldn't be under "fire."

I suppose this is what worries me the most. This fear causes some sort of guilt within me. In one way I do blame myself. And yet, on the other hand, I don't because I didn't *want* him to go to down. I wasn't choosing him over me; it was more complicated than that. I can't explain it very well, because I don't understand it myself.

All I know is that I have terrible fears whenever I think about it. Whenever I get on the subject, some powerful surging takes over. I become extremely nervous so that I don't know what to do or where to go. My breathing increases to short, quick breaths so that I feel that I will blackout. I reach for some furniture to steady me.

I am faced with the clashing of a thousand alternatives: decisions and revisions that I have made before, but which within a minute are overtaken and rearranged into new patterns that suddenly transform into the same old pictures once again. But this time the montage is different in that just moments before an arrangement of images becomes newly connected to another meaning which made the composite different. I don't know *why,* but it was.

The change is there, but what is the significance? It is nothing more than itself. I see the movement as change, but perhaps it is simply random movement. It goes towards nothing and becomes nothing except vague shapes that I see as something, but because they are vague, they can be something else too.

So while the time for decisions and such is being reversed in a moment, I become suddenly tranquil, as if nothing of it all mattered to me. The shifting and the lack of solid identity were nothing at all. It is at these times that I become most worried that I'm losing my mind. But what do I know of such things?

They are only the romantic musings of some adolescent who's had a few bad breaks, right? Of course I'm not going to kill myself. What could be more silly?

"Have you gone by my house?" asked Mike in a stiff, quiet tone. I remember his making a fist with his right hand and with his left he made a cup. Then the cup surrounded the fist--restraining the threat.

"No," I said. "I just have been thinking all day, I guess. Trying to put together all of what you told me last night. It's like some television show or something. I mean, don't you have the inclination to act according to the script they give us?"

Mike didn't follow the drift of what I was saying and took it as seeing his situation as somehow very light.

"I've got to do something," he said in a way that let me know that he didn't want me to leave. Then Mike dropped both of his hands into his lap: no more fist and cup.

I felt very close to Mike, the big hunk who was always so dominant and slap-happy that you could never imagine him to have a problem. He simply stayed away from those sorts of things. Mike would turn everything into a joke. But perhaps not everything really *is* a joke? I can hang this on him. He needed to discriminate. It sounds like I'm judging him, but I felt the same way.

"I don't know what to advise you to do."

"I know you can't tell me what to do. If I stay away I'm free, but what good is it? If I turn myself in, I may get a record, and then I'll be branded with a felony conviction that makes me a half-citizen. Imagine being half a citizen, and I can't even vote yet!"

Suddenly I didn't put myself in Mike's place, but I began to consider what I should do to advise him. But before I could say anything, he began himself. "I don't know what I'll do, but let's not talk about it any longer. I want to relax. How about going up to the basketball court at the deserted school and playing a little ball. Then I'll decide, and you can get some supper."

I don't mind admitting that I considered what would happen if we got stopped by the police on our way or during our game, but I consented and we played.

Mike's game was a little off, but we had a good sweat. When it was over, Mike insisted that I leave. We had played over an hour, and I was exhausted, though Mike didn't look that winded. I kept waiting for him to break down in tears, but of course he didn't. It was that night that I came to see you. I didn't know that I was a wanted man at that moment. Nor did I know that Mike had turned himself in. All that I knew was that you had had your relapse and the doctors that night were not very optimistic about your chances of survival. I thought you'd probably die.

Leaving the hospital, I went back home, cutting through people's yards and entering our back door. I was in a quiet mood and came in silently, when I heard talking in the living room. I listened and heard the voice of the same policeman telling my parents that I was wanted in connection with the drug raid. My father was furious at me, while my mother was questioning the officer on what sort of evidence they had. I didn't stick around to find out, but left as silently as I had come in after grabbing a half-loaf of bread that was lying on the counter.

I slept over on the campus and went to the bank just after it opened to withdraw my money before I was known to be wanted. There was no trouble, and I found a convenient place to stay while I thought about the best way to leave town. It was in the afternoon of the second day that I heard over the diner radio the story about Mike. I know nothing more than you do, but I knew that I was leaving that night. Needless to say, I was depressed about the whole thing and gravitated to the only place that I knew: San Francisco. More in another letter.

Yours,
Larr

San Francisco
April 21, 1969
Larry Cohen to Fred Abrams

Dear Fred,

Life in S.F. has been interesting. This freedom thing is great—don't get me wrong—but there are real differences in the quality of life here than in Eugene. The pace of life isn't so fast, and I am in an environment in which, though I could be wanted by the F.B.I., I don't think that they'd find me. There are a number of SDS[47] types around here with convictions or warrants on them for arson, robbery, and murder, and no one's found out anything about

---

[47] Students for a Democratic Society: a student activist group that gained status through most of the 1960s. Then in the summer of 1969 it began to fragment until it dissolved in 1974. I.C.

them. I don't live with any of them, but they are a considerable group. The police just leave certain sections alone. I don't know why.

I live in a different place than that in which the party was held so many months ago. This building is not a condemned apartment building like the other one, but an abandoned factory building. This building is also condemned. This means a green light for squatters. But since there are no real "rooms" we have to make do by creating various temporary spaces that aren't very private. Who knows—if someone buys the place, we'll be out on our asses in a day. But we're willing to accept the risk.

So room is covered. Nada. Board is on T-Rx's model: casual labor for goods delivered. It's the barter system. No money passes hands. It's totally legal!

Some of the others in the group sell drugs, but I'm not into it. Among our members is a newcomer named Alf. He's a Brit who thinks he's tough shit. You know the type: a short guy who has an attitude problem. The people in our core group include Ron Adair (called Captain Hook), Alf McTaggart, Duvall "Mad Dog" Jackson (and his woman Marcia), Marshal, aka the "Prophet," and T-Rx.
It's a small group, but we live off of scrap vegetables (that are picked up as refuse from a couple local supermarkets) and free meat from helping unload daily shipments from a truck at this restaurant (it's cheaper for them than hiring teamsters). The store's regular employees won't do teamster work, as they support other unions. So we are it: sweat for meat. It's a fair bargain.

I don't do much during the day except read. I'm finding that I really enjoy science fiction and a new writer called Vonnegut. Occasionally we hand out leaflets for some cause, but primarily we have the days to ourselves and during the nights we hit various parties where my favorite pastime is talking with the ones there who are interested in science fiction. One fellow I met recently, a blonde, Nordic guy from British Columbia, is particularly interested in Ray Bradbury. He's created a notebook where he writes down all his thoughts on each of Bradbury's stories and novels. It isn't complete, of course, but it's a grand project. He's hoping to create a concordance for the collected works.

Outside of that life is pretty calm,
Larr

Eugene, Oregon
May 25, 1969
Fred Abrams to Larry Cohen

Dear Larry,

I don't suppose it has crossed your mind, but if you ever want to come back to Eugene there would be nothing stopping you. I heard that your parents have been writing you, but that you haven't written back. In a way, I can't blame you--the way that they showed such a lack of confidence in you. But then again, people are the way they are for a reason. They are getting on in years and feel guilt acutely.

As far as the climate here, there are jobs for the asking this summer. Money is flowing for people who want it. If you're keen on work, there's plenty of it.

I'm taking a heavy load this term, but it isn't too bad. I'm feeling fine and have been accepted at Reed College and Oregon State. I've got scholarships so that will be no problem, but there is part of me that wishes that I could just take off like you have and leave. There must be a tremendous feeling of freedom in that, which I envy. At any rate, I wish you happiness and success as always.
Fred

San Francisco
June 1, 1969
Larry Cohen to Fred Abrams

Dear Fred,

Not much had been going on except for what I had described to you in the last letter (save that we changed condemned buildings).

We have been somewhat more active on the political front as spring is a better time to get the students at San Francisco State excited than at any other time. It's amazing how stupid the college officials are. They consider the students to be a mass of idealistic souls who want to improve things and create a better world. But actually everyone does it because it's an exciting experience. I think there is perhaps even something sexual in defying a large institution. I know that sounds dumb, but I've heard it from Rx, and I think that there's something to it.

Most of them are just a bunch of kids who want to be left alone. They aren't worried about philosophy, but just want a chance to have sex in peace without interference.

I think that working with these types is very boring and I never go except when it is necessary (such as maximum support maneuvers). What I wanted to tell you about, though, was the appearance of a new force in our group. Her name is Mary. She just arrived a week ago. She's from Edina, Minnesota, which I take to be a suburb near Minneapolis. There is something that bothers me about her that I can't put my finger on. She is very good looking, yet tries to keep everyone at bay.

Anyway, we were up at the north end of the city, handing out literature with some "state kids"[48] when this curious conversation took place.

Mary is a medium height young lady in her early twenties. She's thin (with more "legs" than "body"). She had been sitting on a bench outside our place. She had taken out a hairbrush and was taking out the snarls from her waist-length straight blonde hair. Her face revealed her intense concentration when a short guy in denims and a tie-dyed t-shirt walked over and stood in front of her. At first she shut her eyes, hoping he'd go away. But when she opened them again he was right in front of her, staring.

"How long have you been going to school?" she asked.

"This is my second year," said the fellow, thrusting his hands into his jean pockets.

"I went a couple years to Macalester," said Mary.

"Where's that?"

---

[48] "State kids" appears to be young people who attend San Francisco State University. (IB)

"Minnesota."

"Must be cold there," he said, sitting down next to her.

"Well, it's not as warm as it is here," she said as she got up to hand some literature to someone who was passing on the sidewalk. After doing her duty, she sat down very close to the fellow and as she did so she brushed her hip against his side.

He reacted accordingly and almost dropped his pile of pamphlets.

After that he was anxious to stay close to her, but at the same time she became more distant.

"Have you ever been up to the campus?" he asked.

"Yes, I've been there once, but it was dark. The guy I was with wasn't interested in giving me a tour at the time."

I know how he took that. He felt that she was inviting him to make his bid for her, but what I didn't know then was that Mary could turn it on or off at a moment's notice. The action was just out of some bad movie, but in real life, such things are not corny, because no one knows what's going to happen next.

One is always afraid to read a "communication" wrongly and be thought of as a shark. But I felt that there was no doubt what she was telling him with her behavior.

"How would you like to go up with me tonight and I'll show you some of the *ins* and *outs* of the campus?" His proposition was bold, but I wasn't surprised.

"Are you sure that's all you want to show me?" she asked with a wry smile.

"Well, it's a big campus, and there's a lot that I may be able to get into during your tour which you haven't seen before." His tone was too artificially confident.

"There isn't anything, I'm afraid, that you could show me that I haven't seen," she said with a sigh. "My last tour was quite thorough. Besides—" she began in an almost mocking tone as she smiled, "I hear that the campus is somewhat dangerous, and I'm not sure that you're big enough to be out at night."

I wasn't sure of her intention. But I could tell that the fellow was humiliated, especially knowing that someone else (me) had witnessed what had just happened.

I felt sorry for him, and yet, I suppose, he got what was coming to him. There must have been certain protocols, I surmised, and he didn't understand the rules of engagement.

Later, Mary said to me when we were walking back (we didn't have money for a bus): "Are all the state guys that conventional?"

"Conventional?" I repeated, for I couldn't understand why he was *conventional*.

"You know," she clarified, "so concerned with all the things that students in the fifties were concerned with: cars, money, girls. . . ."

"I think that everyone is concerned with those things," I replied.

"Oh Larr," she laughed (people call me Larr now, it's Rx's name for me). "You know what I mean. The concerned student of now is much more *politically* oriented. We are a generation of people that care more about what happens to our society and the disadvantaged than our own paltry troubles. The kids of the fifties were so materialistic and concerned only with their own welfare without giving a damn about the rest of the world."

"Yes, I see what you mean," I said, though I thought that either she was saying something that was over my head, or something that was such a stupid commonplace that I could have heard it from one of the tv network news announcers. She had such a confidence about her that contrasted to my own insecurity that I didn't reply. There is something powerful about her. She knows what she wants and she knows how to apply herself to get it. I felt as if I should be respectful to her so as not to make her an enemy and later regret such an action.

Fred, I'm happy to hear about your school. I don't think that I'll be coming back to Eugene. I like it here. I work only a few hours a day and live comfortably. Rx got me a library card and now I'm reading a book by Jules Verne called *Journey to the Center of the Earth*.
Yours,
Larr

San Francisco
June 18, 1969
Larry Cohen to Fred Abrams

Dear Fred,

I just had to write you as some interesting things that have been happening around here and I just had to tell someone about them. First, there's going to be a demonstration against the war in Vietnam on July Fourth that we hope will draw a million people. It will be bigger than the April march.[49] You know it isn't the policy around here to get excited about organizing anything. We make up our minds to go to something or not, kind of spontaneously; but this is different. All sorts of groups from everywhere have come by and have been working out tactics. I guess that Rx knows lots of small groups like us and some big ones as well that he is representing. It's very strange--I mean, if I had such a position I would feel very good. I mean the power and all, but it seems to affect Trek in the opposite way, that is, he's very quiet and seems depressed about something. I asked Mad Dog about it.

"The man's just tired," replied Mad Dog.

"But why? This should be a big break for him. I mean, all those people. I've heard about how he likes to change things and fight corruption and wrong wherever he finds it. Well, here's an excellent channel for him to do it."

"What do you mean?"

"Well, lots of people gravitate to power, right?" The other just nodded his head in a noncommittal way as if he wanted to hear all of what I had to say before answering me. "The more people he gets to march, the greater his power and the more power that is his, the easier it will be for him to effect change since politics in this country is run by blocks of power."

Mad Dog didn't answer right away. He looked down to his folded hands and started breathing through his mouth. "T-Rx doesn't need the numbers. He's gotten them before. Two years ago, he was on the line for a big protest here and he was on-line with people from New York City.[50] He's been there and done that." Then Mad Dog pulled off the red bandana that he wore on the top of his head and wiped his brow. Then he re-tied it while clearing his throat. "T-Rx doesn't want power." The voice was soft and unlike his normal voice. I didn't understand it.

---

[49] April 5-6 in San Francisco; it drew an estimated 10,000 people. (IC).

[50] April 15, 1967 the estimated crowd was 60,000 and in NYC it was double that. (IC)

"He doesn't want power?" I repeated. "But why not? Doesn't he mean those things about fighting injustice and all?"

"He means it. But it's not about *him*. It never has been," he said, looking slowly up from his hands.

"Then why? I don't understand."

"He's an agitator. He wants to be the spark that starts a fire. But the people are the ones who will have to make it all happen." The answer was firm this time, as if some resolution had been reached by the speaker.

"But he'll never change anything unless he does something really big right now," I said.

"No way, José." Mad Dog smiled and looked me in the eye and repeated, "No way," as if that phrase had some esoteric meaning— or maybe he was quoting Rx. I don't know. What I do know is that he changed the subject—not as if he had anything to hide, or couldn't answer, but as if the subject had been fully discussed and that there was no more that could be said and to try would only be a useless exercise in our leisurely routine. He's an unusual man, Trek, but I'm convinced that he's unhappy in his role as leader of all these people.

I can remember his attitude on a typical day when we'd get up and eat. Trek would ask, "What do you want to do today? There's a jail trial of a guy who's innocent we could go to, or a strike of grape workers we could support, or maybe a flagrant case of job discrimination somewhere. . . . If nothing else works out, we could always go to a school and protest the War somehow (leaflets, or personal testimony, petitions—anything)." Then we would all talk it over and we'd do something—though sometimes it would just be something as stupid as splitting up and going our separate ways that day.

There was never any pressure on any of us to do what anybody else wanted to do just because the others wanted to do it. Rx was very good that way: he let us do whatever we wanted (though there were times when I wished he'd just come out and tell me what he wanted me to do). Sometimes, I wouldn't feel like doing anything and I'd just go down to the bay and watch small boats and gulls flying around. I could sit there for hours and let my mind drift over what was out there. I'd go over my life as it was (every detail) and what it had been.

There are times when I wish I could have only two hours of living a day and the rest of the time to think over what had happened in those two hours. It makes the time living more intense and full. When I don't think, I feel like there is never time enough to do the things that I want to do. Life becomes crammed with spirits that threaten me and jostle that little pouch of good feelings that I keep somewhere under my navel (in concert with my beer belly).

T-Rx never liked schedules, though he actually does things quite regularly. Still, he has never espoused the regulated life. It is my opinion that it didn't really matter to Rx whether someone wants to do things at the same time of the day or not. But then, he has never been one to espouse a particular position as absolutely true for everyone.

For example, I remember one day everyone was talking about how stupid the middle class is that follows baseball (supporting the Giants or the new Oakland A's) when Rx pounded on the table after taking a beer out of the refrigerator (Rx never drinks beer). "What's wrong with baseball?" he asked.

Captain Hook, who had been delivering his harangue, looked dumbfounded at him and tried to summarize his arguments, but he was confused. "Well, it is a sport that is financed by the capitalists for the entertainment of the middle class so that they don't have to think about the hard realities that exist for the suppressed classes of the United States. I mean look, every day, people go hungry, undergo racism, or are kidnapped to go to war. Money could change all that. Instead, there's a big chunk of this money that the fat wads spend on tickets that should be spent for the oppressed classes—that's what I'm trying to say. What social good is there in hitting a little white ball?"

"And I suppose that you object to people washing the feet of someone with oil because the money spent on precious oils could have better been used to feed the poor?" Rx's tone was almost *otherworldly*—I didn't understand it, but we all laughed. "Might it be an outlet against racism?" put the Prophet.

"Yes, it's a truly American pastime buying hot dogs at the game—I suppose you're going to tell me that you have season tickets or something," returned Captain Hook with a wry smile, looking at Trek.

"Was Babe Ruth a middle class bourgeoisie? Or how about Jackie Robinson?

In fact, I'd wager that most of the ball players were from disadvantaged homes, at least from the twenties onwards. And look at the morality of the sport compared to football and basketball.

"Instead of the army concept that you have in most team sports that emphasize contact and fast action, in baseball there is slow movement and attention to skill. I'd say that if Johnson or Nixon played baseball we'd probably be in a better position today."

"C'mon Rx. I've never seen you play ball, and when was the last time you've ever gone to a game?" Alf was joining in on behalf of Captain Hook, though he generally didn't agree with him.

"I've never been to a professional game. Do you want to buy me a ticket?"

"Never been to a game and yet you're telling us that baseball is the cure for all of our social ills?"

"I never said anything of the sort, [A]lf (Rx frequently called Alf simply 'lf,' eliminating the 'A'—I suppose it was something to do with his vowel-consonant theory). I'm merely trying to tell you something. I'm speaking just to *you*. I'm not an orator preaching for the masses.

"If I could ever hold a steady job, it'd be as a midwife, though admittedly the demand isn't too great these days."

I didn't understand what Rx was talking about, but what made the exchange interesting to me is that the day before I had heard Trek talking about how a certain group of teenaged college students, who were helping a group of us throw rocks at the administration building of their college, were not sufficiently into the protest. Instead, those college kids were talking sports as they heaved a rock at a window. They were comparing it to a forward pass in football or a peg to home by an outfielder in baseball. Trek admonished them for not recognizing what they were *really* doing. He wanted them to get serious and forget the sports talk.

Now here is Trek, talking on two sides of the same issue in a matter of days—what did it mean? He could be simply inconsistent, or perhaps a different issue was at stake both days. I don't know. These speculations are beyond my range.

But I do like ball games. Though, considering what has been said, I'm not sure whether I should? Well, I've strayed from my topic a little, but I'll get back to that in another letter.

Yours,

Larr

San Francisco
June 26, 1969
Larry Cohen to Fred Abrams

Dear Fred,

You must be pretty busy at this time what with your summer school and all. I remember that it was just last year that we were starting our summer jobs and Mike suggested that we all go down to San Francisco at the end of the summer to see if all the stories about the town that we had heard in Eugene were true.

When I think of what has happened to us all over these twelve months, it seems incredible. Why, in just the last twelve months, I've had more happen to me than in the previous eighteen years!

Things have been changing around here as well, especially of late. As I told you, one of the changes is the proposed March on July Fourth. This, as I said in the last letter, is putting pressures on T-Rx. These pressures appear to be less than beneficial.

The other change that I didn't have time to tell you about in the last letter is the appearance of a new face around our place. Her name is Alice Gissleson (lofts of consonants). She's from Minnesota (just like Mary Taylor) and was going to some small college up in that area (I think they call it Pembroke) when she decided to come here instead. I'm not sure how much schooling she's actually had. All that I know is that she was attending a college when she dropped out.

I am not sure what I think of her yet. Sometimes she can be a little pushy. But on the other hand, she can be very nice to talk to one-on-one. In group situations, though, she often starts spouting political philosophy, kind of like Captain Hook always does, except that she seems to know what she's talking about.

One thing that I know—Mad Dog dislikes her. I don't know why, but whenever she gets into a relaxed group thing, he leaves with Marcia. I wonder how Marcia likes it now that she isn't the only girl in our group—though actually she could hardly be considered as part of the group in one respect since she spends all of her time with Mad Dog when he wants her and the remainder in her room (in our new living situation, there are two private bedrooms, with Mad Dog and Marcia having one and the other one being rotated between us on a two week basis). Alf told me that Marcia reads all day when Mad Dog isn't around. I asked him what she reads and he told me that it was mainly novels and the like. I can't understand someone spending her time reading novels (unless they are science fiction) when there is so much to think about in the city we live in. For example, there is the beautiful bay to look at. That's what I like to do.

The others don't seem to have formed an opinion about Alice, though I heard an interesting conversation while I was in the bathroom between T-Rx and our newcomer about the March.

"How many people do you think we'll get?" asked Alice, in a soft voice.

"It's difficult to say. Thousands for sure, but just how many is up to the fates—I hope that they spin us a shirt and not a carpet."

Alice laughed. "You're really a clown, you know it? I mean, here you put on this appearance of being so aesthetic and all when really you're just a great comedian making jokes about everything." Nobody really reacted except Mary, who got up and left.

"Jokes?" asked Rx in an amused tone. I was aghast at the manner in which she was addressing Rx. Nobody else in our group would have called him a clown; not even Mad Dog, who is closest to Rx.

"Yes, I've noticed that you love to make allusions to something that you feel the person with whom you are with has no knowledge of. Isn't that correct?"

"I don't know what you mean," said Rx in a semi-serious voice.

"I think that you know very well what I mean," was the retort that I expected, but I was surprised.

There was a silence.

I'm not a very good judge of human relationships, but I think that both Mary and Alice have the hots for Trek. I have entered our common area several times to find one of them in his embrace. It was obvious they had been kissing.

I don't know why, but I was furious at Mary and Alice for kissing Rx. It's not that I imagined that Rx didn't like women (because I'm sure he has had his share, though I have never personally seen him with one), but that a newcomer could just move in on him and try to possess him was somewhat disturbing. Don't get mistaken; it's not that I have a crush on Trek. I just felt that girls were moving too quickly and manipulating him.

After the most recent incident, I was obliged to sit in the bathroom for another hour before the couple left after doing whatever they did and moved into another room. Then I emerged and I noticed that Alice and Trek were acting rather strangely: sometimes they were very friendly and at others extremely distant. Two days later, I was with Mary and two State students who were protesting the building of a new road when she appeared to be getting bored.

"We aren't doing any good here," she said.

"I know," replied the other man.

"I don't mind getting sore legs if I think that I'm really doing something, but I don't exactly cherish the idea of standing around being ignored," chimed in Mary.

"You could take your clothes off," he said.

The other State student laughed, and I smiled. I thought that someone had finally put Mary in her place. I liked that. She was always making retorts meant to put people in *their* places and now she was getting a little of the same.

"I don't mind that at all; it's just that I don't like doing it for these pigs, who are nothing but a group of lousy fascists."

"Well, let's get away from the fascists," he said in a suggestive voice.

Mary had gained some initiative in her remark, but he brought the fight back to her. She was again on the defensive.

"Oh, yeah?" she said, smiling from one side of her mouth.

"What do you have in mind?"

"How about the back seat of my car?"

"What's so special about the back seat of your car?" she asked tauntingly.

"It doesn't have a steering wheel," he said, almost mocking her. He was daring her now. What had started as a simple repartee of double entendre was now a game where Mary's bohemian nature was being called into question. Was she as tough and free as she was trying to appear? The State student knew that she had recently come from Minnesota and he could also detect the hesitation in her reply. There was nothing she could do except say 'yes' or 'no.'

I felt like laughing at her but there was something inside me that was scared; maybe it was for Mary, or perhaps I was scared about the uncertainty of the whole thing.

"What time do you have?" she asked in a tone that was bravely trying to sound like the bravado of a few moments before. It was clear what she was going to do; she'd get the time and then declare that she had to be somewhere. I began to feel relieved even as the other lifted his forearm to check his watch.

"Two-thirty," he said.

"I can give you ten minutes, because I have to be somewhere. Can that suffice for you?" She had accepted the challenge, but not with courage, she was backing into it. I could tell that all of us knew that she was scared, but her determined personality and stubborn pride forced her to continue. I almost felt sorry for her. But the State fellow didn't. I could tell by his manner that he thought she was a bitch and should be taught a lesson.

I watched with some disbelief and almost shock as they walked to his car and opened the rear side door. I stopped where I was: thirty feet away, and didn't know what to do. I just stood there staring at the car when I noticed a tug at my arm—it was the other State person who was along with us. She was looking up at me with a big smile that intimated to me that she thought that it was time to pair off and that it was our turn next. I didn't like the possibility of that occurrence.

It's not that she wasn't all right to look at, though such things never really mattered to me, but I suppose it was her eagerness that bothered me. It was as if she was boiling inside for me before I had even considered that she could have such thoughts at a time such as this. My eyes went back to the car as I became sensitive that my clinging vine was wrapping herself around me and giggling at the same time. I felt like throwing her down onto the ground, but I felt that would be too cruel, so I merely tried to mildly disengage myself. But the physical effort that I expended on this score was worse than wasted, for this little climber only took my movement as evidence that I was hearing the primitive call, too. I'm a little embarrassed to state that when I tried to push her off in more direct terms I found that the vine had so entangled herself about me that I couldn't easily extricate myself.

Here I was, a man in the prime of his life, and I couldn't free myself from this little ivy who took my person to be some sort of trellis.

Then the back door was opened, and out came the State fellow buttoning his trousers, his shirt opened and flying in the breeze. I started over to the car to help her if I could. I didn't want to put her in a compromised situation and embarrass her. But I felt that she had been cruelly used, and simple compassion bid me go to her. As I moved, I heard a little squeal and I believe the little vine decided that it was our turn. Suddenly I pulled down my arm in a way that freed me. The girl didn't take the hint but continued to follow me.

Mary was in the back seat, lying on her back. She was pulling up her pants as I approached. I paused momentarily until she was through with her dressing before approaching closer. Then she noticed me. "What's the matter? Do you want some? Come in; today's Tuesday: two for the price of one." Her voice was bitter and I could sense the tension.

"We're going home now," I said quietly.

The vine was wrapping herself around me again and giggling all the more. "Don't you feel sorry for me, boy, I can take care of myself." Mary's voice was gravely.

"I know you can. It's time to go."

"See this body?" she exclaimed as she slid out of the car and came over to me, her shirt open and her pants not yet fastened. I hated the sight. I wanted to cry, to comfort her, but anything that I might do would be mistaken for some other sort of motive, so I stood where I was.

"Do you see it?" she yelled. "Do you see these?" she said lifting up her breasts and falling against me as she began sobbing, though no tears dropped from her eyes. The vine was still giggling, thinking that this was some sort of group encounter and was unbuttoning her own blouse to get in on some of the action, when I started buttoning-up Mary. I had to get her away from here.

The noise was making me nervous. There was Mary's sobbing mixed with the workman's machines and the vine's giggling. I fumbled with her blouse and began fastening her pants. Almost in direct proportion to the work I was doing to put Mary together, the vine was becoming undressed so that by the time I was through with Mary, she was wrapping herself around me in her undies. I turned my head and spoke as firmly as I could.

"I really have to go; some other time."

"Oh, I know," she giggled, not taking me seriously.

"See you later," I said as I freed myself and began walking away with Mary. Then it hit her that I was *really leaving*. She began to have a little fit; hopping up and down, calling me names. The State fellow came over to her and lifted her up and put her in the back seat. She would be happy now.

My attitude towards Mary had changed. As I sat in the bus going back, I couldn't think of anything to say. I just wanted to do something so that she might feel better. But I knew that anything I might do might be just the thing that would be more than she could stand.

When we were near our stop she turned to me and said, "Isn't there somewhere where we could go for a while? I don't feel like going back just now."

I smiled and took her arm, leading her to the exit. We got out and walked towards the Bay. It was about three quarters of a mile, but the walk would be good for us. I continued my silence until we sat down on an old dock that was in the midst of being destroyed by someone's neglect.

"What an interesting old pier," she said. "I didn't know that it was here." I felt happy that she liked one of my private places.
"You have to walk carefully, because the wood is rotting in places. Follow me." It seemed strange that I was giving Mary orders as she was the one who was always telling others what to do and how to perform their tasks. But now she wasn't Mary, but someone else: a young girl from Minnesota.

We sat down and talked for a long while. She was from a suburb of Minneapolis called Edina and her high school was one in which there was a lot of drug trafficking, which is how she started on grass. "Do you toke?" she asked me.

"No, not anymore," I said. "I don't know; I don't really like it. I never did. I suppose that the only reason I did it for a time was because I felt pressure from other people to do it, but I get afraid when I'm stoned."

"I don't like it either," she confessed.

"Why do you do it?" I asked.

"My boyfriend used to do it. He and I were very close, you know. I would have done anything that he wanted me to."

I liked talking with her. She was really a very sensitive person. It seems that she broke up with her boyfriend and the pain of it all made her quit school and come out to San Francisco. She didn't really want to live anymore, but she couldn't go through with suicide, so she drifted about.

"How do you do it?" I asked.

"Oh, you mean money?" she answered.

I hadn't *meant* money. I just wanted to know how she could continue with such a miserable existence. That life is nothing but a series of empty spaces of time when you are sitting alone watching the bay trying to sort out what has happened to you in your mind. What I wanted to know is what kind of feelings she had at these moments when a person can feel alone, tender, quick.

"I get checks from home—Oh, not big ones, my parents aren't that rich, but they have *enough*. And they've agreed to keep sending money to me until I'm married." She laughed. "They certainly don't understand anything. Their world is *so* much different than mine that they can't understand my values and think that I have to go along with their old capitalistic mores. Yes, they're W.A.S.P. all the way—White Anglo-Saxon Protestants, with all the putrid that goes with the term."

"I take it you don't like your parents," I said, not knowing exactly how to react to her.

"It's not a question of *liking* them. I suppose in their own circles they are pretty decent sorts. If I could accept the garbage that they call *values*, I suppose we'd be the best of friends. It's just that they are so closed-minded to what I believe in; it's that which is intolerable for me." Then she paused for a time. "I guess what they say is true: never trust anyone over 30."

We didn't say much more of substance. We looked out to Alcatraz and the boats moving in their purposive patterns. The sun was steady. It was only a few days after the solstice. It gave us an extra interval.

After a time, we walked back. Mary had somehow lost that vulnerability that she had displayed moments before. It was as if talking brought out some kind of soothing balm of antagonism that numbed the new sores. This made me sad, for I never like to numb my pain, but rather preferred to let the hurt have its sway for an interval in which it would consume itself and vanish.

"Hurt cannot be sustained," as Rx says, "because we're in pain all the time anyway in one sense." While in contradiction to this last statement, the realization of this principle is soothing.
"But perhaps *everything* is different than all this, we cannot say." This last statement is pure T-Rx. He will say something, undercut it, contradict it and then disclaim any ability to speak on the subject. There is something sustaining in this for me, which constitutes an entirely different attitude than Mary had when she pacified herself in my company—wishing to put troubles behind her as soon as possible so that she could get on with it.

Keep hitin' those books.
Larr
p.s. and don't hurt your knuckles!

San Francisco
July 7, 1969
Larry Cohen to Fred Abrams

Dear Fred,

Things aren't very peaceful around here. I can honestly say that for the first time since I came down here, it's unpleasant to be here. As you read in the papers, no doubt, the March came off as scheduled on July 4. What you didn't read in the rag sheet were the problems that occurred in this edifice.

It is difficult to know where to begin. Perhaps I should relay the breakfast conversation that I heard (without eavesdropping) between Mad Dog and T-Rx before the July 4th March. Marcia was at the compound and so there were just two groups of two in the restaurant, sitting at different tables. It was a cheap Chinese place that served a hearty wonton soup with crispy noodles on the side: $1.50. The white speckled Formica tables gave the place the feel of an echo chamber. There wasn't much noise, and I don't believe that they were trying to conceal what they were saying.

"I don't like her, Rx," said Mad Dog, filling his face with crispy noodles and downing it with water.

"I'm not sure that you do," said Trek, raising his voice slightly. "What do you mean?"

"Well, the way she's been after you. Don't you think we've all seen it?"

"What if she has?" replied Trek.

"Of course, that's nothing, I suppose, except that you know as well as I do that there are two types of women in the world: chicks and bitches. Mary is of the latter category. She's no good, and if you let her get close to you everything will be ruined. I say get rid of her."

"You're right, of course, about her character—and her ideas aren't like ours—but what of it? Perhaps I let her have too much of me, but things like that happen."

"Things like that happen! What is this? If you don't like someone you don't have to hand open-arm invitations to them. Once or twice is one thing, but she's been here almost a month. This could become serious."

"Hell, if it will set your mind at ease, I'll tell you something. Yesterday, I told her to go looking elsewhere when she came to me."

"What's that supposed to mean? Were you turning to Alice?" Mad Dog's tone was intense. He placed his elbows on the smooth Formica surface and inched closer to T-Rx.

"I don't know, perhaps nothing at all after what you've been telling me."

"She's a dogmatist."

"I know."

There was a long pause, in which the only sound that could be heard was McDonald (the guy I was with) sipping the hot soup so it might get cooler and Mad Dog tapping his fingers on the table.

"I've got to go," said Mad Dog, getting up suddenly.

"Say," began T-Rx as he reached out his arm to stop Mad Dog for a moment. "Thanks for coming to me like this."

"It's your neck, my friend." Mad Dog turned and left. I waited and watched Trek finish his meal. Then, almost on cue, two women (unknown to me) came in and sat at the table with him. They both wore wire-rimmed glasses and high-waist, long dresses. One dress was red with characters of some sort set out in a pattern. She was the taller of the two. Her blonde hair flowed over her shoulders. The other had on a plain kelly-green dress with a cloth belt that asserted her "empire" waist. Her medium length black hair was pulled back in a bun. They both looked intently at T-Rx. It was only another of the endless conferences that he had about the March as yet another group wanted to get into the picture.

"We wanted to know if your people want some pictures of Stalin and Marx to carry with them?" ask Ms. Green Dress. The woman's voice was smug. She began pulling back her hair on the side of her head (which was a futile task since it was already tightly arranged in her bun).

"No pictures," replied Rx calmly.

"What?" the two ladies exclaimed.

"You heard me," was his equally calm reply.

"What about Ché? Everybody loves Ché," said Ms. Red dress.

Trek shook his head.

"What are you, some kind of fascist?"

"That's exactly right. I'm another black shirt. That's me."

"If we can't bring posters, then we're not coming."

"You can bring posters, all that you want: on the War, on Civil Rights, on eliminating Poverty—but not on faction politics. This is a broad movement and we don't want to mess it up with various splinter groups getting into fights. Besides, the best effort can be made through a unified whole."

"You sound like an imperialistic pig. Are you sure that you're not one of Nixon's boys?"

"You heard how it stands. It's the only way to handle a large march like this."

"We want *our* posters."

"Then don't come."

"We've got five hundred people with us."

"That's too bad. We like to have as many as we can marching. But as it stands I think we've already got twenty thousand, so your presence won't be missed."

They got up to go and said a few nasty things to Trek before leaving, which I couldn't hear—even in the echo chamber. As the clear glass door to the restaurant swung shut, I wanted to go over to him and tell him that someone was with him.

But something held me back and told me that it wouldn't be the best time to go to him. I can't describe the anxiety that I felt in empathy for him.

Later, as I sat by the water on my pier, watching the bay, I thought about Mary, and how she had been making a play at Rx. She had beaten out Alice for his attention. Trek didn't accept Mary exactly, but then he didn't reject her either. It's a tenuous distinction to make, but it is there. T-Rx lived between the extremes. He didn't like to force someone out of our community which, in theory, was open to anyone who wanted to come and share with us. The entire mission of who we were didn't allow for the dismissal of someone from our group.

I was afraid that Mad Dog was somewhat jealous of Mary's influence with Rx. And though Mary didn't sleep at night with Rx, there was speculation that they had sexual relations at other times when no one was around (though no one had proof of it). No one had caught them with a flash from their Kodak.

T-Rx wasn't a Marxist, as is evident by his treatment of the representatives of the People's Alliance or whoever the red and green dresses represented. Trek was just as harsh with people of the other side. I remember when some high school kids came to a booth that he was manning by signing people up and making assignments for the March in Golden Gate Park the Sunday before. One pimple-faced young man with a crew cut strutted proudly forward. He was smiling broadly.

"How many people do you have?" asked Rx in a monotone.

"Maybe a hundred," said the youth proudly.

"What time can you make it?"

"How about one o'clock."

"One? Why come at all?"

"We could make it earlier, except a large portion of us have to play in a Fourth of July concert that morning."

"So you're going to play in a concert that morning, supporting the status quo and in the afternoon, you're going to defy mommy and daddy and sneak out to a demonstration with the rest of your friends, eh? Well, let me tell you something, if you want to come, fine--we'd love to have you. But for your own sakes, make a choice between the concert and the March. If we were only concerned with body counts, don't you think we'd get a sponsor and give away free beer or something to get maximum participation? Bodies don't mean a thing to us. We want commitment."

There was no response. The boy looked sadly at Rx and walked away.

These are just two examples (the red and green Marxists and the pimply-faced musician), but there are many more. T-Rx found himself in a position in which he disliked a great many people and groups because in order for him to form a cohesive unit among the dissenters, their motives had to be held up to scrutiny.

Trek didn't want anyone with radically different motives than he had.

"I have a clear idea of what I'm talking about, but I'm sure that you wouldn't understand it." This was delivered to Mary.

"What I understand is that you are antagonizing many socialist groups who would be glad to help us, except that you won't go along with a few minor points that anyone interested in the worker ought to endorse." Mary started cleaning her right four fingernails with her right thumb. She didn't look down but did it automatically.

"Tell me, what should I endorse?" T-Rx's tone was not sarcastic, but seemed to have a genuineness to it. I believed in Rx.
"Well, for one thing, the United States Government is a corrupt fascist regime that is committing war crimes far greater than the world has ever seen." Mary became animated as she talked. She was on a roll. "It is oppressing minorities at home and the working man in general throughout the country.

"To counter this, it should it nationalize industry, create a guaranteed income for all with no bogus requirements, a universal health plan, and provide for anyone's basic needs throughout his life. No one should have more than he needs to live comfortably, and the right of inheritance should be abolished." Near the end of this speech Mary, seemed to be losing steam. She started cleaning the nails of her left hand. I sensed that she was groping for specific projects that were being endorsed by the Students for Socialist Revolution or some such group of which she was a member. Trek scratched his nose in complete silence as we all waited for an answer.

"What's a fascist government?" he asked.

"Don't you know what a fascist government is?" she asked, with a manner that showed that her one year of college was very important to her own conception of herself.

"No, I don't, can you tell me or not?"

Mary laughed. "This is ridiculous."

"Can you tell me or not?"

Everyone in our compound was present, even Marcia, Alice, and the Prophet. Trek was peeling an orange now, slowly, knowingly.

"Of course I can. This is stupid." Mary got up to leave.

"If you can, why don't you enlighten me?"

Mary didn't know how to take this. She sensed that perhaps T-Rx wasn't being completely candid with her. "What do you want?" she asked.

"I want you to tell me what a fascist government is. You said that you knew, and you used it in your harangue. Now, what is it?" Trek was halfway through the orange peel.

"It's a repressive government that carries out fascist policies." Mary stood up and inhaled noisily through her mouth.

"That's not a definition," said Mad Dog. "You can't use the word you're defining in the definition."

Mary's eyes flinched at the rebuke. Mad Dog hadn't even finished high school and *he* was telling *her*, a drop-out college student, how to define a word. I wanted to laugh, but I restrained myself. The situation was tense.

"All right, it's a repressive government."

"A fascist government is a repressive government?" returned Mad Dog.

"Yes."

"Then all repressive governments are fascist?"

"Yes," she said nervously. Trek's orange was almost peeled. He kept his eyes upon his work without looking up.

"What is a repressive government?" asked Trek as he put aside the last of the orange peel.

Mary paused, not wanting to answer—she was being humiliated she thought, but she could see no way out of her situation. "One that doesn't let the people be heard."

"How are people heard?" asked Trek.

"What do you mean?"

"You just said that a repressive government is one that doesn't allow the people to be heard. Now I'm asking you what that means." Trek separated the first two sections of the orange and put them into his mouth.

"Are you going to ask me what everything means? What is this, some sort of history of words?" Mary laughed and looked around for support, but only little Alf was laughing with her.

She started to leave and then she regrouped. "It's like—when—"

"Yes?"

"When the government is able to do something that the people don't want and gets away with it."

"How does an observer determine whether the people want something?" asked Trek.

"By a vote or something."

"By vote or what other method? Do you have another method in mind?" Rx consumed two more orange sections.

"I don't know—*revolution* perhaps."

"Then a country where there are either elections or revolutions is a country where the people are happy and there is no repression and no fascism? Correct?"

Mary pulled up her hip-hugger pants. She started making various facial gestures that concluded in a positive nod of her head.

Trek put the last of the orange into his mouth and chewed it deliberately. Then he smiled for a moment before slamming his hands down upon the Formica table top. "No. This is not correct. We elected a president in 1964 who promised peace and gave us war."

Then Mad Dog chimed in. "Elections satisfy your definition of popular input, which means by your own account that we are *not* fascist because we had an election and continue to have them at regular intervals. Yet here we are in the midst of many problems—not the least of which is the War in Vietnam."

Mary notched her wide leather belt to the last belt hole. Then she looked up again. "Well, you've got to agree that the Nazis were fascists, right? Your word games aren't going to take that away. They didn't hold elections. They were brutal. They murdered the Jews." Mary smiled.

Trek licked the orange residue from his fingers and said, "But the Nazis got to power from a popular election. Thus, it isn't the existence of an election that makes a country fascist. There must be something more. It could be the murder of 6 million Jews. But then only one country in history would be fascist." Trek scratched his head. "There must be something else that fulfills your definition. What is it?"

"Well, Nazi elections weren't fair."

"Soviet elections aren't fair. Are the Soviets fascist?"

"No, the Soviets fought the Nazis. Don't you know anything about World War II?" Mary grinned as if she had checkmate.

"Perhaps you can enlighten us on World War II after you define the word 'fascist.' It cannot be the absence of unfair elections or else the Soviets would be fascist just like the Nazis. The countries of Eastern Europe and China would also be fascist. But I doubt that you'd want to say that. Thus, we're back to where we began."

Mary sighed and looked at her wrist watch. Then she shook her head. Look, I know what a fascist is: Hitler, Mussolini, Franco. But you try to twist everything I say because you think you're so *cool*. Well, I don't have time for such antics. See you later."

Then Mary turned and left. She didn't look back: one more person who wouldn't show for the March.

There have been other incidents when I noticed the mounting pressure on Trek by others in the *Movement*. He was more interested in knowing the motivation of participants. He seemed to be more of a guru than a political organizer. This made me wonder why he got into political organizing in the first place.

Later that day, Mad Dog and I were at my favorite pier looking out on San Francisco Bay. It was late afternoon.

"Why does he do it?" I asked Mad Dog. My attention was captured by a tug boat that had become disengaged from the larger vessel it was towing.

"He's an activist."

"But he hates organizations, and yet he's putting himself at the top of one."

"I disagree," returned Mad Dog. "An organization exists through time. This is a one shot thing. He's just the director of a large scene that must be just right for the proper effect."

"The proper effect?"

The point of a civil demonstration is to create turmoil with the least chance for violence that is required to make the point."
Out in the bay, a tugboat whose towline had broken took measures to replace it and once again was able to guide its freight to the pier. I kept these things in mind, but as time went on it didn't exactly turn out that way. Too bad.
Larr

San Francisco
July 8, 1969
From Larry Cohen to Fred Abrams

Dear Fred,

Here's the continuation of that long letter I began yesterday. I tell you, things are getting so bad that I think I might leave here. I never thought I'd be considering this, but I feel driven to it by conditions that are getting to be intolerable. And I'm not the only one to feel this way. One day after the March, the Prophet and Alice split the scene together. No one knows where they went.

On July second, two days before our proposed March, Mary came in to our dwelling when Rx was out, but the rest of us were around. We were in the common room sitting on our furniture—such as it was. The room was substantial. We occupied only one corner. The flooring was stained cement; the stains had probably occurred when the building (now condemned) was once a warehouse. Even though the place was condemned, it still had electricity and water (neither of which we paid for).

Mary was accompanied by Alf and two people I'd never seen. They all sat down on a couple of produce crates when Mary called over Captain Hook.

"Hook, I'd like you to meet some friends of mine, Ché and Tara."

There was a nodding of heads as Captain Hook pretended to act as if he knew what was going on.

"Comrades," began Mary, "this is our cell. Hook here is one of our supporters, aren't you?"

She was referring to the fact that Captain Hook's coffee house act was finally catching on and he was getting money for it, which he shared most generously with the group. Our entire standard of living was markedly better for his contribution.

"I don't know," said Captain Hook modestly.

"Oh, c'mon, don't be so modest, you are the principle breadwinner for our cell; don't deny it."

"Our *cell*?" said Captain Hook incredulously. We never referred to our group as a "cell". The words seemed foreign to him. I felt strange myself. What was the intent of the term? I didn't think of our community as a prison or cell.

"Anyway, comrades, Hook here is a part of a rock singing group that is doing very well these days."

"What is the name of the group?" asked Ché, setting his gaunt, delicate hand on an unused crate as if it were a hot stove.
I could tell that Hook didn't want to talk. I was upset at Mary for her behavior. Why was she doing this? What was she trying to prove?

"Ah, Captain Hook and his Kid Hookers," Hook replied to Ché in an offhand, trying to sound matter-of-fact.

"Tara, what do you think of that?" The question was posed as if there was something to make of it. Here they were discussing their opinion of someone.

"The band's name puts in mind the exploitation of women by reminding us of the contradictions of capitalism," was Mary's reply.

"Exponent of degenerate music," was Ché's reaction.

"It's not all that bad, believe me. If you can make a few bucks from the suckers, you take them, right?" said Mary.

Captain Hook was about to get up and leave, but Mary bid him to stay.

"I'm not going to sit here while you tell me that what I do is no good. You benefit from what I do. If you don't like it, don't take any of my money."

"I don't take any of the money," replied Mary. "But that's beside the point."

None of them knew, but me, where Mary *really* got her money. I knew that she got it from her father, who was a businessman. This was a stain that her friends who were sitting at the table with her would have never condoned—had they known. I knew this. I wanted to tell them, and expose this Mary—pretty little rich girl who was playing revolutionary Marxist.

"We want to make you a part of *our* group," said Ché.

"What group?" asked Captain Hook.

"Young Democrats for Liberating the United States," he replied.

"I never heard of it."

"It's part of the U.S.L.A."

"The U.S.L.A.?"

"The United States Liberation Army," said Mary. "They are a splinter group of the Capitalism Liberation Front and the Students for a Democratic Society—you've heard of them, I hope."

"Yes."

"Anyway," began Tara, picking up where Ché left off, "we are looking for young dedicated socialists who will help us overturn this war-mongering decadent society."

"You want me?" asked Hook, surprised.

"They want everybody," said Alf with a grin. Hook turned his head away in disgust from Alf. None of us had taken to the British bloke since his liaison with Mary.

"I'm not your man. I'm a decadent singer, remember?" said Hook.

"We all have to play our parts. Some of us must appear to be a part of the system so that we can bring about its collapse when the time comes," said Ché as he took off his crimson stocking cap and ran his fingers through his stringy, long black hair.

"Maybe you haven't heard, but rock music, especially the kind that I play, isn't really a part of what you might term the *establishment*. I'm counterculture," said Hook, gesturing with his hands to make his point.

"Which is precisely why *we* want *you* to belong to our organization," said Ché, putting his stocking cap back on. "You hate the War and injustice against the worker, don't you?"

"What does this have to do with anything?" queried Captain Hook.

"It means that you are one of us!" declared Tara for the first time. Tara was very small. She was perhaps five foot, one inch and maybe 90 pounds. She had short, greasy black hair. She looked as if her lineage was Filipino. She was gathering a tone of celebration. They were preaching a sermon to him, and Hook didn't know what to do. Hook was surrounded. I don't know what I would have done in the same situation, perhaps I would have given in too as he did.

I don't know, but what I do know is that I was sick with the entire thing. In some odd way, I blamed T-Rx for it all. If it wasn't for his letting Mary in and the way he was organizing the March, we wouldn't be in such a mess. He should have left well enough alone. But no, he had to come out and change things: stir things up so that all sorts of odd people were moving in and out of our place, bringing all sorts of evil influences.

Mary and Alf weren't secretive about their sleeping together. They did it in front of us all each night (since in our warehouse digs there were no longer *any* separate rooms). No taste was shown and the unseemly display is getting more than I can handle. Mary is trying to shake up our group, and I don't like it. This letter can't continue like this, but you know I'm going to keep writing, because you are the only one that I can talk to about such things.

Larr

San Francisco
July 10, 1969
Larry Cohen to Fred Abrams

Dear Fred,

My thoughts about leaving have changed, though I'm somewhat embarrassed to tell you why. The March came off all right as you probably read in the papers. We got a larger than expected group and it went peacefully.[51] I think that the leaders in Washington can't afford to ignore this overwhelming show of dissatisfaction with the War effort. What bothers me is the use of terms like "capitalism" and "oppression." I don't know what they mean exactly. In the last few days, I've heard so much about these terms that I can't really understand what they stand for, except that it is what everyone believes is wrong. The workers produce all the goods so they should get all of the money for doing it, right? I don't know, I've never taken anything in economics (social studies was never one of my best subjects, as you well might remember). But I know that the War is bad because I might have to be drafted. The local board in Oregon has listed me as 1-A, and that means that I might be called up any day to go and fight. The reception of this notification came only a couple months after my eighteenth birthday.

Trek has advised me to change my place of registration—he says that when you do that, it takes time to reclassify you and so you have bought some freedom. I hear that they are talking about some lottery system. Have they started this system yet? Do you know?

What I want to tell you about is an encounter I had with Mary. I know that I have said many things about her that are less than complimentary. I also know that deep inside of me, I despise her. But there is something compelling about her that draws me to her. She has me at her command and there is nothing that I can do about this. What a terrible admission to make, but it's true!

First I suppose I ought to explain a few things so that you'll understand some of what I'm talking about. Ever since I left Eugene, I've found a home in San Francisco where I can just *be*. I can stay in one place and not feel the kinds of pressures that I felt in Oregon. There are no parental pressures here. There are no expectations that I find some kind of job where I'd have to spend the better part of each day earning money that I didn't really need nor want.

---

[51] National Park Service estimates put the crowd between 50,000 and 65,000 people. There were no arrests due to violence.

What happens to you is that they get you into a situation where you are earning lots of money so that your bank account is growing and then they dangle all sorts of goodies in front of you so that you'll buy them with the money you have saved. But then you don't have any more money and you have to continue earning money to pay off debts that you've accumulated or to continue to support a lifestyle that is grossly inflated over what a person really needs to get by.

I didn't want to fall into that kind of financial rut. The direction was too planned. Not planned by a particular person, but by a system. And it pointed me toward *nowhere*.

I came down here seeking *somewhere*, which I admit was too idealistic, perhaps—but it is what I believe in to a great extent. I wanted an alternative or at least an opportunity to think about things (besides the obvious fact that it was the only place I knew and afforded a perfect place to hide from the parents). All that I had hoped for in San Francisco seemed to be here. I was truly happy.

But when Mary came, things were disrupted. And then there emerged this idea for a March. These two factors seemed to disrupt things just when they were settling down to something that I could enjoy. At first, as I've said before, I wasn't sure what I thought about Mary, but then she started getting close to Trek, and somehow I didn't like that. This feeling disturbed me and made me wonder why.

I couldn't get a hold of this until I chatted with Mad Dog after the March.

"She's a bitch, a white bitch," said Mad Dog.

"Why do you say that?" I asked, as it had been the first time that I had to talk about my feelings with someone else. I trusted Mad Dog, he always looked out for me, and I was confident that he wouldn't turn on me.

"Look what she's doing to the group; it's coming apart."

"I have noticed some friction around here lately, but don't you think that a good portion of that is being caused by the March?"

"Look, we've gone on marches before, plenty of them. I've been with Rx since the middle sixties and I know that neither one of us is happy unless we're doing something about this rotten society of ours. We march, and we march.

"Thus, I'm telling you that it isn't about the March. Marching is about all that you can do and maintain a balance between being inside society and being outside it."

"I don't understand what you mean, *a balance*?"

"Yes, a balance—you see, we know that to work within the system for change merely supports the system that you're trying to change. If you're unsuccessful in changing it, then you have contributed to the very thing that you've wished to alter. If you are completely outside the system you have no contact with it, and by your absence you have allowed evil and death to continue in the same way. For without your fighting against the system, you've given the evil monster more nutrition for its continued existence. Therefore, you have to continue to resist—but to resist in the right way."

"You mean, that if you do nothing, then your lack of positive action effectively means that you've contributed to the evil itself?" I smiled as Mad Dog took off his white sweat band that was already damp as beads of water were dripping down his brown forehead.

"Yes. The only thing to do is to fight it from a position that is both in and out of the system. You can't get away from evil ever, but you can fight it."

We decided to turn into our doughnut shop for some sugary fare. This seemed interesting to me. What a clear purpose for one's life: fighting evil. The position was so clear that I could do no better than to simply stay by this leader and listen to his words of wisdom. Was this what I had been looking for?

"How does Mary fit into this?" I asked as I stuffed some reject doughnut holes into my mouth.

"As you can surmise for yourself, this position of being half-in society is a delicate one. There must be a premium placed upon stability of certain essential factors since the usual means of stability can't be relied upon. One lives with death constantly and so one's principles become fashioned out of that unwelcome straggler in the group. They come and go—like Alice and the Prophet. The imperative of balance puts one into this perilous position without any assurance at all. Any principles that result come from the process itself and do not precede it. Do you understand what I mean?"

"I think so," I said, though I really didn't have much understanding of what he said at all, but merely had him repeat what he said so that I could write it down in my spiral notebook and study it later. This is what I often do, because I'm not very good at making instantaneous reactions.

"So you can see that Mary, the bitch, has ruined everything as she's tried to move him away from what we know: the balance." Mad Dog finished his reject doughnut holes as well.

"She's trying to change his lifestyle," I said in response.

"If she has her way, she'll either drive Rx into society or out of it, but there won't be any room for one of her kind with us."

I began to get an inkling of what Mad Dog was talking about, and I think that some of his views corresponded to what I had been thinking. Mary was disrupting things and ruining Trek. I didn't resent this because I was jealous, but because I admired T-Rx as we all do, and don't like seeing his unique posture harmed in any way. There are very few Treks and the destruction of one wasn't particularly appealing to me.

I began to form a hatred for Mary.

After T-Rx seemed to make a break with Mary, she began going around with Alf, a fellow who I believe has no values whatsoever. I despised Alf and Mary. I wondered why they bothered staying around. There was something almost sinister about the entire situation. This was how I was feeling until one day after we had finished the March and its disagreeable consequences.

I was sitting on my favorite pier next to the 12th piling on the right side alone, listening to the water by the bay, when who should come to me but Mary. She seemed alone, the same way that she had the day that I had brought her to this spot. On that day I had seen a part of her that I had never seen her show to anyone else.

"It's peaceful," she said as she sat down next to me. Six inches or so separated our hips.

"Hello," I said, feeling irritated to be disturbed, especially by her, but at the same time amazed at the difference in the tone of her voice and her facial expression from what I normally expected.

"I thought I might find you here," she said, but I didn't reply.

"The March really was impressive," she said. We were leaning back on our arms as our legs hung out over the pier. I began kicking my legs back and forth in the air using the pier as my fulcrum.

"One might say that," I replied, trying to imply by my tone that I wasn't supporting her. My far gaze turned to Alcatraz.

"Do you think that it will make any difference?"

"What do you mean?" I asked.

"The War, do you think that marches like this bring it any closer to an end?"

This seemed an odd question to me. I suppose I had never really considered whether the March might actually bring a quicker end to the War or not. I marched because it was organized by T-Rx. I paused and in this interval she reached over and touched my right hand with her left so that one of our two backstops were united.

"I don't know," I said, "does it matter?" There was a bitterness to my voice that was perhaps a bit excessive.

"Why do you hate me?" she asked.

"I don't hate you," I said, meaning that to hate someone is to have a strong emotion for them that I didn't want to admit to having, considering this creature before me.

"Well, then you do a pretty good imitation of hating."

"I don't know what you mean." My words were garbled. I wasn't clear headed. She was acting contrary to her usual haughty manner and that confused my sense of direction. There was a slight breeze that raised her long, straight, blonde around her head into a sort of halo.

"You've been so distant to me. More than that, I think that you've been actively hostile."

Then I turned my gaze from Alcatraz and looked right at her. "I don't like the way that you've—" I began trying to tell her all about the way that she had treated T-Rx and how at that very moment I could push her into the water, jump in and hold her head under if I thought that her feeble carcass was worth the effort and risk, which I didn't. But before I could elucidate any of these points, she interrupted me.

"—I know that there have been certain differences between me and Rx. There's bound to be between two people who have a love affair like we did for a while."

My eyes widened on the words "love affair." I felt sickened to think that she could be so brazen as to suggest that she could have ever affected Rx in such a way as to begin to label it "love." Why, all that she had to offer was sex. It was that simple: a body. Love is something else—I don't know exactly what it is but I do know that it is akin to the feeling that I have when I come down to the Bay to experience all that spreads before me. Sometimes it's pleasant and relieves me of my troubles, and at other times it is disturbing so that I want to go away. But I always come back, and it is always there.

There is an unmistakable aura to the Bay.

"And when these relationships breakup or become strained, then there can be some hard feelings on the part of all the parties involved. I don't blame Rx at all. In fact, it touches me to think that I meant, or mean so much to him that he would alter himself at our parting."

"He isn't altered," I retorted.

"But *he is*, and you can see it. I think that's why you have animosity towards me." Mary began to caress my hand which was under hers.

"Listen, you don't, you . . . you don't understand anything." I was struggling for words. It isn't easy for me sometimes to say what I really mean. Besides, she was getting me to defend a side that I didn't believe in. Sure Rx was changed. I knew it. She knew it. Everyone knew it. I couldn't deny it. But it wasn't for the reasons that she was saying. She had no control over it—or maybe she did, but it wasn't because Rx loved her. He didn't. I knew it.

"What don't I understand, Larry?" She moved closer to me so that her hip and leg were touching mine. I felt as if I wanted to cry. There were no tears, or physical welling, but all the same I was breathing heavily and I felt tight in my chest. She had control over me, and I think that she knew it.

"What do you want?" I asked.

"I want to know what's wrong," she said, putting her hand upon my shoulder.

I got up and walked to the end of the old pier. "Things are shifting around. They aren't the same." I was contradicting myself, but I didn't want to defend a position that wasn't right.

Mary got up and came up behind me, putting her arms around my waist and pulling me against her body. "And you, being one of the most sensitive persons I know, probably has an answer," she purred.

"I don't know anything. T-Rx spent all his time trying to organize a march, and you kept bringing in people who didn't want to do things *his* way. You were challenging him." I said the words, but they didn't have any effect as she twisted me around to her and touched my face.

"I don't want to split the group up. I want to strengthen it. I think that Rx has great potential. He could be a great leader. Don't you think so?"

I didn't believe her. Why was she saying this? It must be some sort of trap, I thought. Her hand was soft. I lifted it away from my face, then I felt her press her body next to mine. "Yes," I replied. But I didn't know what I was saying.

We spent several other days near the water together. She would tell me how she wanted to make Trek into a national figure that could really affect policy changes. I didn't know what to think of this. She really did seem to love Trek, and seemed to be sincere about making him great. And what would be wrong with that? He was continually trying to get something done. As a national figure, his opinions would be more important, and would influence hundreds of thousands of people. Political action in this country is measured in power which is acquired in garnering large quantities of voters. By just living around San Francisco, Trek wasn't doing anything. He needed to mobilize nationally to really get his views across.

Mary was tender. I didn't think that she could be that way. I had always suspected that she could act differently around me than others because I had been with her during a difficult time.

"You know me, Larry, nobody else knows me like you do." Those were her words. We were close.

I wanted to ask her about Alf and why she continued to sleep with him. If I was the one who knew her and who she felt closest to, then why didn't she spend her time exclusively with me? This behavior of hers bothered me, but I didn't want to press her. I don't want to ruin a good thing. She is the first girl that I have been able to become close to since Janet. I know that I ruined that with my possessiveness, and so I want to keep it easy, yet somehow that is a difficult proposition to abide with. Anyway, that's what's happening here. Keep in touch—Larr

San Francisco
July 15, 1969
Larry Cohen to Fred Abrams

Dear Fred,

I'm coming home. I'll leave soon, and should be home in a few days, depending on whether I can get a ride up the coast.
L.C.

Note left on Fred Abrams door, found July 25, 1969.

—Dropped by; you weren't home. I'm hanging out with some dudes on the campus. You can find me in the Red Eagle tonight after ten.
L.C.

Note left by Fred Abrams at the Red Eagle July 25, 1969 in care of the bar tender for Larry Cohen[52]

—Stayed until one. If you are in trouble, can I help? I'm sure that your family would be happy to see you. Are you planning a visit? I'll be at home tomorrow morning if you need anything.
Fred Abrams

Seattle
August 1, 1969
Larry Cohen to Fred Abrams

Dear Fred,

Sorry that I missed you. I haven't time to explain now. Big things are happening here that I can't tell you about. You can write me in

---

[52] These and other miscellaneous scraps were found in the notes of Fred Abrams which he donated to the University of Oregon Library Collection on the Vietnam War.

care of the Queen Anne Post Office, Mercer St. Seattle, Washington, 98117.
Larr

Seattle
August 2, 1969
Fred Abrams to Larry Cohen

Dear Larry,

I don't know how we missed each other. I got your note that day that you came over and I wasn't there, and so I made a point of staying around at the bar so I wouldn't miss you again. It was my loss, but I'm glad to hear from you. It seems to me that things are pretty rough for you lately. I don't know what to tell you. It's really impossible for me to give advice to anyone. Who am I to tell anyone else how to live his life? But I do think that you are right in trying to assess your situation and to act on your considered judgment.

My own studies have progressed well and I have only a week and a half to go until my vacation (which is about a month). I've only been to Seattle once with my Uncle when I was fourteen. It seemed like a nice city. When I was there they had just constructed the Space Needle for the World's Fair which had been a few years earlier. Don't you think that the Pacific Science Center is a great place? It is so modern in design. There is a food pavilion in which I had these waffles that were topped with strawberries and ice cream. Besides this delicacy, they had delights from all over the world. I think that you would enjoy going there. I can't remember too much else, but I'm sure you've found your way around the city and know much more about everything than I ever did.

I will have a part-time job with the post office while at school. I have a scholarship for 3/4 of my tuition and will get a loan for the remainder of it. My job should cover my living expenses and dorm fees. Dad has offered me a no interest loan of up to five hundred dollars if I need it, so I'm in very good spirits about my own prospects.

I am worried about you. I hope that none of the group that you've been with are dangerous in any way. I read in the paper about some guys in a group in Idaho who were killed when they got into a fight with some other group. I know that your group is no motorcycle gang, but sometimes tough people will prey upon groups of less aggressive types.

Just a word of caution.

This Mary seems like a very changeable girl. You say she is from Edina, Minnesota? Did you know that the suburb of Edina has one of the highest per capita incomes of any municipality in Minnesota? I have done some research on it in the *World Almanac* and in my opinion your friend might be from wealthy parents. It wouldn't surprise me if she was the owner of a sizeable bank account herself! Don't let yourself get entangled with anyone who might hurt you.

There are a lot of people (as I'm sure you know) who are always trying to take advantage of others. I hope that you will not be a victim.

Best of luck in all that you do, and I hope to hear from you soon.

Yours,

Fred

Seattle
September 10, 1969
Larry Cohen to Fred Abrams

Dear Fred,

I've started this letter several times. I seem to want to write when things aren't so good. That event that I alluded to, is going to happen soon; maybe in a month. I can't talk about it now for security reasons. . . .

I'd like to fill you in on a few things. I suppose that you were surprised to hear that I was coming home, eh? Not any more surprised than I was. As you remember, I was starting to see some of Mary, but the relationship was an odd one because we would be very close when by ourselves, but when we returned to the common area, she would fall over Alf and I would be left in the cold. At first this didn't bother me, for I felt that things would be safer for me if the others didn't know that I was being friendly to Mary (who some regard as an enemy). But then I began to get second thoughts about what I should do. I began to feel very schizoid about the whole thing. Here I was being her lover in the daytime (though not her physical lover) while at night time Alf was her mate. Everything seemed to be getting very phony.

I was out with Captain Hook when the entire issue came to a head. "You know, I don't understand you," said Hook. We were in our favorite Chinese Restaurant consuming wonton soup and egg rolls.

"What do you mean?" I asked, though I knew that he was going to say something about Mary. We had been very discreet about it at first, but now things were surfacing every so often, as I was going through this tremendous conflict that I was alluding to earlier.

"Don't give me that bad-Mary-the-socialist shit."

"What do you mean?" I asked.

"That you and her are like close—too close." Hook leaned forward onto the Formica table. He wore a silver-colored ring on his right hand. It had a ruby stone in it. I looked at the ring and a red scar on the back of the same hand. The two seemed to form a composition of some sort. Then I looked back to my accuser.

"That's ridiculous," I said. I felt the words being spoken. I had wanted to bring my relationship with Mary out in the open, but when it came right down to it, I couldn't do it.

"Is it? I've seen how you two talk these days, and it doesn't take a fool to deduct that there's something going on between you."

"You're crazy."

"I don't think so. You two have been carrying on like you had some great secret that no one else knew about. It's so obvious. Everyone knows about it."

I didn't answer. I couldn't lie about it to him. But I couldn't admit it either. There was something about Mary that I despised. No getting around it. I was for the group, and she was against it. Yet, she said that she only wanted to exalt Rx to the national position that he deserved (though to do that she needed to change the entire conception of the group as it was).

"Hey, don't get tense about this. She's an attractive woman—" Hook's words really stung. I knew that she was good looking, but I had always hated people who went for women just for their bodies (at least I had always hated such types since I had come to San Francisco). Mary and I had formed a *talking* relationship. We weren't calculating on how to get the other to bed. That wasn't the point with us.

It wasn't that I didn't find her attractive, but it wasn't the driving force between us. So that when it came to the essence of my feelings toward her, I had to admit that I was more excited about her companionship than her physical features.

"Look, she's got her plan. She wants to *do* everyone in the group. She started with Rx, who took her for a while, and then she tried to come to me, but I didn't want her."

I looked up at Captain Hook. I didn't like the inference that he was making about his being so pure as to have been able to have resisted the charms of the lovely Miss Mary. He reacted to my look and cleared his throat. "Look, I was going with a couple girls from my singing group. A man's only got so much energy, you know. Besides, she is the type that comes on too strong for me. I like *hip* people, you know: people who are interested in rock music and are into drugs. I can trust them.

"They are easy-going and don't cause any upsets. We all have one thing in common: we try and survive with as little pain as possible. That's not to say that I would do *anything* that gave me pleasure, but I have my standards: I reject hard-liner dogmatists. I also know that I need a certain amount of *work* mixed with a certain amount of *good times*.

"I hate our government as much as she does, but I'm not out to change it. Anything they put in there to replace it would be the same rot."

"Why did you march with us then?" I asked.

"Everyone was doing it. My friends were in it. It was a very exciting event, like a ball game at Candlestick Park." Hook took out a cigarette and lit it with a paper match.

When he had taken a few deep drags, he looked back at me. "We were walking along, stoned as hell and watching the other freaks who hated us or even the straight middle class families who were so sincere in their efforts to end an unjust war. The whole thing was a giant game as far as I'm concerned. We substituted grass for hot dogs, that's the only difference." Hook smiled and took another deep drag.

My own anger swirled. This guy had no true political opinions but saw the entire venture as a party or game. I looked down at the dots in the Formica and tried to find some sort of pattern. But it was a vain gesture. There was nothing.

It was then that I became aware of uneasy echoes of Hook's comment and began to question myself. Why had he marched? Why had I marched? How was I any better than—I was getting a warning. My covert behavior wasn't as swift as I had thought it to be. I was not unseen as I had thought I was. People knew that I was seeing Mary (at least, that was the opinion of Hook).

What should I do? This question tormented me. There was no clear direction for me. I had to make my own way—somehow. When Mary joined me at our group, I was less than friendly to her. That much was true.

But still I went to the same pier and sat next to the same piling, waiting for her to come and talk. I was not disappointed.

"Hi," she said, kissing me on the lips and putting her cold hand against my bare chest (my shirt was partially unbuttoned). I didn't respond. I wondered what would happen if I took her at that instant and grabbed her by the neck and threw her into the water. How many people would find out? Would any of them care? If I put rocks in her clothes she might sink to the bottom of the bay and stay there, undetected. How humorous that might be—almost like an old gangster picture! I would be little Caesar, *"now listen you guys, yeah, yeah."*

"What's the matter, darling?"

"Darling"— she had never used that word with me before. The very sounds oozed of middle class saccharin. I wanted to reply, "W*hat do you want, 'bitch'?*" But, of course, I didn't. I folded my hands in my lap instead.

She put her head on my shoulder. I remember when Janet used to do that. How I would love it when she'd snuggle up with me in the theater, showing all of our friends that she and I were a couple and that there was nothing that was going to come between us. I wore her i.d. bracelet and she wore my school ring, which had to have tape wrapped around it so that it would fit her small fingers. We did it all.

Now somehow everything was changed. Mary put her head upon my shoulder when no one was watching. There was no movie to watch to lull our senses, but only the incessant pounding of the salt water upon the old pilings.

"You're troubled, what's on your mind? Why won't you talk about it?"

"It's nothing," I said at last. The smell of the water and the green algae floating atop filled my sinuses so that I felt like a commercial on television—except that *here* there were no illusions. All was stark. There was nowhere to go, and that realization scared me.

Inside my chest I felt a rumbling that made my skin crawl. I so wanted to hold Mary and hide within her warmness, but the words of Captain Hook were still too fresh in my mind. He knew, and despised me for it. But perhaps no one else knew? Did T-Rx know? Would he have to know? Maybe he didn't.

"Hey, I know you better than that."

"Why do you sleep with Alf?"

"Wow! What brought that on?" she asked, bouncing backwards. She immediately started pulling her long hair back over her shoulder.

I don't know why I asked the question. I wasn't thinking about it, but somehow the words just spewed forth on their own accord.

"Just tell me. Don't give any of your bullshit." I looked into her blue eyes: the eyes of a pretender—but a pretender to whom I was deeply attached.

"I've never heard you talk like this Larry. I'm not sure that I like it," she replied in a tone that acted as if she were shocked. She turned away so that all I saw was her mane of blonde hair. But I knew she was only creating a cover to stall for time.

"Do you think I care? Why should I care if you like my tone? I asked you a direct question and all you can do is avoid the issue. Answer me!"

I felt my body tense, though my speech was very calm. I felt perfectly lucid. Time seemed to measure itself to me in milliseconds.

"I will not! If you're going to treat me like this, I'm going." She got up to leave, but I wasn't going to let her play that exit line so easily. I grabbed her left arm and pulled her to the deck. She came down awkwardly and seemed to stop moving—at least that was the way it appeared to me, but because time was proceeding at a different pace I could not really attest to whether she had really stopped or if that was only an apparition. Then she let out a yell of pain.

"God dammit, you've hurt my shoulder!"

It's strange that I didn't wonder if someone might have heard her cries, for I merely watched her get control of herself and sit-up. If she had thought to have cried rape or something on that line, she might have been able to get me arrested, for her blouse was torn to her bare bosom.

Mary fixed her gaze at the bay and seemed to turn time back on its normal course. She rearranged her blouse by buttoning up. Then she reached into her purse and took out a hair pin that brought together the tear and made herself modest again.

"What the hell's gotten into you?" she asked in an intense, though softer, voice.

"You run away from things and never stick around. Well, I asked you a question—darling, and I want an answer. I deserve an answer."

"You want an answer, well here it is: I sleep with Alf because he's good at sex, and I like it. How's that?" Mary smiled.

"That's no answer."

"What do you mean 'that's no answer;' what other answer is there?"

"That's what I'm asking you."

She could tell by my face that I wasn't going to be put off by her stupid *non sequiturs*. I wanted to know *why*. I'm not sure just what that meant at the time, or now thinking back on it, what it *could* have meant. It was a primitive question that sought knowledge. I had to understand something: a something that I couldn't have expressed in so many words, yet that was what I was asking her to do for me.

"You're really hooked on me, aren't you?" she asked as her voice changed.

I didn't know what to say. She was changing the subject again. I wanted to throw her on the deck again and rip off all of her clothes and leave her to her fate. I wanted to show her my power. But instead I put my arms out to her. She came to me and cried.

I no longer cared for answers, or maybe she *was* answering me; I don't know. What I do know is that no matter whatever happens to me, I will remember that moment as one in which a phony person revealed herself. I have thought about that incident a lot, trying to make myself believe that it, also, was part of her act. But I can't believe it. She was being as sincere as she knew how to be, I suppose. I might have bought it except for two previous episodes: one involving Alf and myself and the other involving Mary and T-Rx.

It should be mentioned that Alf usually was a loner. He didn't do very much with the rest of the group. He was one of those *short guys with an attitude*. Because of this he would never be a part of one group only. He would go with the drug crowd sometimes, with the drinking crowd at other times, and the women/gambling group at other times. He seemed to have no rules except to massage the pleasure center of Alf. Whereas T-Rx and Mad Dog were highly principled to their causes, Alf was akin to Mary in her chameleon behavior. Captain Hook was fiercely loyal to rock music and a particular group of drug users. Alf seemed to give allegiance to no one. About all that I know about him was that he was from England. He spoke with a British accent, and dressed in a more flamboyant manner than any of the rest of us, who generally stuck to jeans and either t-shirts or blue collared-shirts.

Alf approached me just after I had come back for lunch. I was up and going to take a walk.

"Do you mind if I walk with you?" he asked.

"Go ahead," I said, thinking that his question was stupid.

"How long have you been with the group?" he asked.

Alf had come a month or so after I had, but I preferred to keep all that a secret to him.

"A while." We started walking in the direction of Chinatown, which was a couple miles away. Alf put his hands up to his knuckles into his red pant pockets (his pants were so tight he couldn't slide more than that inside).

"I don't know how it is here in the States, I've only been her a couple of years, but where I come from it isn't considered good form to press in on another fellow's action." Alf gave me what I'm sure he took as a threatening stare.

"Another's action?" I repeated, not knowing exactly what he was talking about.

"I know you're dumb, but you can't be such an imbecile that you can't catch the drift of my meaning: you've been seeing Mary."

"*Seeing* her?" I repeated. The very tone of his accusations were such that I didn't want to engage in this discussion.

"Listen," he said, pushing me against the side of the building that we were walking past. "I don't like your attitude. You freaks can talk all that you want about *peace* and *love* and all that crap that you want to, but I was raised in a country of men and not homosexuals like you puny nothings here—I can take care of myself. Mary is a hot piece of meat and I don't intend to give her up for any sniveling feeble-minded transvestite who thinks that he will reach her 'mind.' Do you understand me or *not?*"

Alf's aggressiveness suddenly made me think of Mike. I remembered how we had encountered that lout at the concert. If I were like Mike, I would have taken the opportunity to thrash the slob right then and there. Only two things stopped me from laying him out on the sidewalk; 1. I was sick of him and didn't want any involvement with him at all, and 2. I knew that I couldn't deck him.

"Ha," I said weakly. I wanted to say something with bravado, but my defiant act became introverted and much of the sound remained in my throat.

"You don't think I will?" Alf had me against the bricks. His right hand was on my throat and I was starting to gag. All that I could think about was falling in the arena when Mike and Rx were walking around. What a long way that moment was from where I was pinned against the wall with a hand that was choking me.

Mike was such a brutal fellow, but all his impulses derived from a basic goodness.

I brought together two rough people at that instant, Mike and Alf, but there was never any comparison between the two. The Mikes of the world seem to be crushed by their own goodness, while the unprincipled Alfs thrive.

Fred, I'm sure you could make something out of these observations. I'm not very adept at putting things together. But I do know that there is something wrong in a world that allows the Alfs to exist and kill the Mikes. I wanted to stand up to Alf, the way that I had failed to stand up to evil when Mike faced *his* crises, but when Alf hit me, I slunk to the sidewalk. I didn't get up even though I could have. The punch didn't knock me out, but I didn't care to fight. Instead, I slumped into the muck of the sidewalk: tobacco juice, dog b.m. stains and urine smells that adorn the right angles where building meets street.

Alf was simple. There was nothing complicated in his message. He wanted me to leave Mary alone, because he liked sleeping with her. He didn't want any interference—even though my relationship with Mary was purely conversational. I lay on the pavement, feeling strong emotion; wanting to do something yet reveling in my inactivity.

The second incident concerns Mary and T-Rx. I heard this via Mad Dog so you should listen accordingly. This is the way Mad Dog told me how it went.

"You have a great success," said Mary.

"I have nothing."

"You're too modest. There are thousands who look to you for leadership. We could lead a successful revolt against the government if you put your mind to it."

"You're crazy," replied Rx.

"You heard the people, they were carrying *prescription* signs for your name: **Rx: For The People**."

"You put them up to that."

"Listen, you are the prescription that this country needs. Don't you know how unpopular the War is? There is a great base that could be mobilized: millions of people—and you're the man to do it. You're trusted and you have contacts everywhere."

"This is a fantasy."

"No it isn't. There is a vacuum of power. Nixon is a president who was elected with a plurality, not a majority. His power base is small. Already you can see that the two-party system is going out. Next election, McCarthy and Wallace[53] will lead successful third and fourth parties and factions will form between right and left. The situation is just as Engels described it."

---

[53] The reference is to Eugene McCarthy and George Wallace.

"Political philosophy isn't really anything substantial. I shy away from statements. Statements about statements lead to bullshit. That's why I shy away."

Mary got up and moved about the room, disturbed. "I don't know why you put on the air of buffoonery. You ARE a leader—whether you like it or not. Don't you know what has happened? You've organized a march."

"I march every day."

Mary laughed and moved over to Trek and sat down on his lap and put her arms loosely around his neck. "Yes, but you don't handle large sums of money each day. You have been supported by vested interests who aren't about to let you fall from prominence."

"No one has any control over me," said Trek.

"Don't you think so?" She kissed him lightly on the lips.

"Does the name Peter Rossi mean anything to you?"

"No."

"Well, he's somebody who has a big stake in you becoming the kind of leader who will promote his interests." Trek pulled her arms away from his neck.

"What kind of story are you giving me? These are lies."

"No, they aren't. You let me handle some of your negotiations, if you remember, and I dealt with these people."

"Who gave you the right to—" began Trek as he bounced Mary off his lap. Mary was agile and landed on her feet.

"How do you think that you could have organized a March of that size without any negative incidents? Do you think such things just fall from the skies?" Now Mary was leaning over Rx.

"I don't care who gave what to whom. No one can make me take any particular position, nor force me to be some kind of demigod. I lead a political life, but I'm not a political man. I don't want power."

Mary turned her nose up at this.

"Well, my friend, you've got it. Thousands would give anything to be in your place. Don't you know that you could be a national figure in just a matter of months?"

Trek didn't respond.

"Everything that you believe in could be accomplished."

"What do I believe in?"

Ignoring the response, she continued. "You owe it of all to us: the people who work with you, who live with you, who love you."

"Who do you love?" put Trek, scrunching up his nose.

"Don't you know that Mad Dog and Larry want you to step up and take your rightful place? They want you to be the leader that they know you are."

"So you've been talking to Larry now. Why couldn't you have left him alone?"

"He wants you to come to the meeting in Los Angeles next week. You'll disappoint a lot of people if you don't come. Big plans are being made."

"I don't care anything about big plans."

"Well, you do care for your safety. I know of certain factions who might be so mad at you that they might think of taking some revenge. They figure that they have given you *money* and manpower while you have let them down." Mary was standing over Trek with her hands on her waist and her elbows out like triangles on each side.

Rx looked down to the floor and shook his head. "Where did all this 'supposed' money come from? And where did it go? I never saw a cent of it."

"I bought two expensive ads in national magazines and we contributed to the defense fund of some important radical leaders."

Trek sighed. Then he looked up to Mary. "How much money are we talking about?"

"One hundred fifty thousand."

"But I never authorized—"

"—Yes, but the executive is responsible for what—"

"—so that's it, eh?"

"Mox nox in rem."[54]

"Is that your pig latin?"

"C'est une trap academique pour toi?"[55]

"Whatever."

---

[54] Let's get this thing moving.

[55] It's an academic trap for you—ungrammatical.

Mary laughed and tried to kiss Rx, but he got up and lit a cigarette. His fingers fumbled with the match as she approached and rubbed his chest with her fingers. "I can make you great," she said.

"You will make me dead," he replied.

"Let's screw," returned Mary.

"You can do what you like," he said, throwing down his newly lit cigarette. "I think I'm going to the fishmongers and test the comparison."

"So I'm a dead fish, am I?" she said in controlled anger.

"Are you?" he replied as he left the room.

Needless to say, Fred, this conversation didn't do much for my confidence in Mary. But, nonetheless, there still flared something within me. At times I had been very much influenced by what she had to say, but at others, like when I talked with Mad Dog, I had an entirely different picture of her.

"She's a white devil."

"I don't know what she wants to prove," I replied.

Mad Dog sat back and sipped on his beer. The bar was yellow in color due to the light that was tinted as it came through the window shades. I wanted to register my surprise at how new these shades were in comparison with the rest of the place. At times I think I felt a kinship to those shades: new orifices decorating a crumbling edifice.

"You know T-Rx isn't the most popular person with some people around."

"What do you mean?" I asked.

Mad Dog didn't usually drink, and I kind of thought that perhaps the alcohol was beginning to loosen him somewhat. I wanted to know this secret about Rx. Perhaps it wasn't ethical, but I wanted to know. "Well, you know that he has a long record of work in the South?" I finished my beer and pushed the glass to the side of the rustic wooden table.

Mad Dog lit a smoke. "There was this one time in Alabama—just an hour outside of Birmingham, that we met a group of rednecks who were carrying clubs. We were on a one-half mile demonstration for voting rights. It was toward evening and getting darker. Trek advised us to close our ranks and pick up stones or anything that we could use to avoid being slaughtered. The police weren't anywhere. You know, on most of the demonstrations the police were right on us from the start, baiting us and trying to provoke something so that they could get an excuse for crushing one of us 'uppity niggers.' But now, just when in the sight of one of their rednecks they might have been welcome, they weren't in sight." Mad Dog took another long sip of beer and a shot of rum. "I was there with him, and you know that he had helped me out of a few jams earlier. Well, I was frightened then. We had gotten it before, and each time after you get the hell knocked out of you, the body is less inclined to let the same happen to it again. It's a self-preservation mechanism." He paused.

"Yes," I said to let him know that I was with him. He leaned forward in his chair and put his hand on my arm as if to steady himself and opened his mouth as if to talk and then stopped. He lifted his glass and rushed in some more rum. I wanted to help, but there was nothing that could be done. The memory was closing in on him.

"Closing in just like a circle contracting around us. Just like a circle, except for a street lamp which broke the continuity. I don't mind telling you that I was more frightened than I have ever been in my life. Something like that freezes you—" He paused. The man in front of me, normally a tough person who keeps everyone at an arm's distance, was letting me become close to him. I wanted to do something but what could I do?

"There was nothing to do but stand there, and wait. I turned my head and I saw that Trek was smiling. It wasn't a nervous smile, but a smile like one has when he is faced with some paltry feat. I could tell that he didn't see the group facing us as any threat. Even though we were isolated and a small group against superior numbers who were armed with clubs and baseball bats, while we only held pebbles, Rx wasn't afraid: he was smiling." Mad Dog's voice took on an eerie quality that disturbed me.

"I thought he was crazy, but then he yelled, 'let's keep on moving, brothers and sisters, there isn't anything out there that can harm us.' The words were so contrary to what we saw, and yet there is something about that man that when he says something, you believe him. We saw the group, but he told us that they couldn't hurt us. I don't know if we even considered whether he was speaking on the same terms that we were thinking; namely, physical hurt. But still we continued, together, walking cautiously, but following Trek's lead."

Mad Dog's voice was now inspired. He had a glazed look to his eyes, and his hand no longer gripped the glasses of booze. I felt the sentiment rising within me too, as I pictured the scene.

"The group of us was following T-Rx, who led us in a phalanx towards one point in the circle that trapped us. When he got to the point where he could walk no further, Rx stopped and asked if he might pass through. The man blocking the way didn't say anything, but swung his bat from where he was holding it on his side and struck T-Rx on the shoulder with a dull thud that sent T-Rx sprawling onto the dirt road. Nobody stirred. There was no noise except the sound of Rx rolling in the dirt and the man who hit him was breathing heavily.

"Trek put his hand to his shoulder and rubbed it with his free hand. Then he looked up at the man who had struck him and smiled. Rx was only a few feet away from the thug who had struck him. The attacker was only a young person like ourselves. Rx shook his head and slowly lifted himself up.

"We were all watching. No one moved or said a word. Everyone wanted to see what would happen next.

"Rx pulled himself up slowly, but even as he was doing this the boy swung again, this time aiming for Rx's head. Trek was turned three quarters away from the lad, and so it was coming at his blind side. Nothing could be more unfair than hitting a man when he was down, who wasn't armed, and was turned away, but this brute was swinging with all his might at Rx's head with such force that it would have surely shattered his skull had he not ducked. The boy missed and lost his balance slightly as the bat had such force. Rx was up in an instant and he grabbed the shoulder of the man and pulled him down to the ground while simultaneously bringing up his knee so that the attacker's head hit the rising knee. T-Rx brought both hands down onto the back of the boy's neck in one fluid motion so that the other hit the ground in just moments after the two forceful blows.

"The guy with the bat didn't move; he lay there as blood began to trickle out of the side of his mouth. That was all that was necessary. That moment of silence was broken as all the members of the mob came down on us with a fury.

"But though one of their number was injured, they didn't fight with any more fervor than we did, as T-Rx seemed to have inspired us. The fighting was vicious and was soon over; it was only a few minutes as people began to disperse and run away. There were no police. Trek and I, armed with a stick, headed towards the main street of town." There was a long silence.

A fly buzzed overhead and alighted on Mad Dog's head, but he didn't brush it away.

"They took us in, naturally, after we reported the incident to the police.

"'It would look better for us to report it ourselves,' said Rx to me. But it seems that the fellow that was killed was the son of a powerful business man, who wanted all the demonstrators to pay for what had been done.'"

Mad Dog finished his drinks and pushed the glasses aside. Then he looked me right in the eye. "Now I'm sure, to this day, that Trek didn't kill that guy. He might have knocked him out, or given him a concussion, but the blow wasn't sufficient to kill someone. But it seems the scum was indeed dead. It's my opinion that he was killed by someone in his own group who wanted to get rid of him for some reason that we are ignorant about—in any case, this guy wanted our hides for it, even though the man started the violence."

I shook my head in disbelief at the story, though I knew from my own experience that the law can be asinine and is so clumsy that innocent people can get ground up in the process.

"The sheriff didn't have any way for us to remain safe within his little berg, so he told us that he knew that it wasn't our fault, and that if he held us over for a trial or hearing, there was a good possibility that we might get lynched or murdered.

"The rail thin man, with a high pitched voice and sails for ears, was in his early thirties. We represented trouble for him with a capital 'T.' If we went down, there would be an investigation and he'd probably lose his job for not protecting us. Therefore, he told us to keep quiet within our cell and when it was well past midnight he'd set us free.

"There were five of us in jail and when we were released we all hiked out to the state highway and got a ride on a truck going to Mobile."

Then Mad Dog blew his nose and cleared his throat. He looked over toward the door. I didn't know whether the story was finished. I waited for some kind of sign, but didn't get any so I signaled the barmaid to get us fresh drinks. Mad Dog lit another smoke.

"That's why we left the South. That guy, the businessman, was after Rx. He hired someone to kill him, since he was a known figure in the Movement at the time."

The drinks came. We each took a sip.

"'Freedom Marchers' they called us at the beginning. But we lost our freedom walking for others."

"So that's when you left?"

"Trek didn't want to leave. He'd just as soon have been killed, I think. But coincidentally, it was the time when Dr. King was moving his efforts up North, and the whole energy that had been given to the South was waning, so the circumstances were right for us to change as well."

"And this guy who was hired to kill T-Rx?"

"I don't know what happened to him. Maybe it was all in my head? I don't know. But we were followed for a long time in Alabama. But when we left, so did our tail. Maybe it was the F.B.I.? I don't know. If it was, they saved our butts."

The two of us lifted our glasses and touched them together to mark our prayer of thanksgiving.

"So that's why you don't want Rx getting involved with large public movements like the peace march," I said, making what I thought was a proper deduction.

"That's part of it. But get me straight: though I don't think that anyone is trying to kill T-Rx now, I do think that he doesn't fit well with traditional racist, gun-toting, Bible-thumping America." Mad Dog stopped. He ground out his smoke and he began rubbing his hands together. Then he looked up again, "I also don't want him to get involved with some of the elements who are operating under the cover of radicalism. There are bad dudes out there who pretend to be a part of the Movement when they are really John Birch Nazis."

"What do you mean?"

Mad Dog leaned forward. "There are two sorts of bad guys: the first would like to go undercover to *stop* the Movement. The second sort would like to exploit the Movement for money and power."

"I don't understand."

"The first are the John Birch Society and fellow travelers of the same. They'd like nothing better than to dispense with the so-called leaders of the Movement. The second are in the business of making money: local entrepreneurs and the mob, are two examples of groups out to make money through drug sales and loan sharking. And there is a third group who are some political fanatics who would love to establish themselves in some kind of power position on the Left, and will do anything they can to put themselves in such a place. All it takes are a few hundred suckers, and they can do anything they want, and gain considerable *influence* as a result. There are too many factions involved for the wrong reasons."

I was very uneasy. I eagerly slurped down my drink, but it didn't do any good. Here I was with Mad Dog, who sat before me feeling the weight of his close friend's anxiety at being threatened. My feeling was of a different nature. I had guilt of being partly responsible, through my seemingly innocent conversations Mary. They may have not been so *innocent*. Maybe she was working for one of the three groups that Mad Dog was describing?

I didn't want Rx hurt.

Mad Dog slumped to the table. The alcohol was taking its effect. I imagined T-Rx slumped before me instead, and I felt a tremendous pressure that I could not abide. I went to the lavatory. (Unsigned)

Seattle
September 21, 1969
Larry Cohen to Fred Abrams

Dear Fred,

I ran out of paper on my last letter. It takes me awhile to write you such lengthy letters as I do, but I have to get some of these things out for my own sake. I trust you.

Still, untold is the reason why I left San Francisco. For some time, I couldn't face my possible complicity in a plot to hurt Trek (through Mary). It is still difficult to think about, but here it is. When I got back with Mad Dog, I went to my bed to read the newspaper. Mad Dog was asleep and besides us, the place was vacant.

Then a few hours later Mary came in, and she was laughing and alone—no Alf. She noticed that I was the only one there (Mad Dog was hidden by a partition). Her manner was loud as if she had been drinking. I didn't want to deal with someone else who had been drinking because just then I was so depressed. From the time that Mad Dog had gotten into his story, I had harbored this intense hatred of Mary. The very sound of her name made me clench my fists in rage. But when she came in, somehow all that I could feel was fear. I was afraid she would come over to me and make me change my mind that I had so resolutely decided just minutes before.

I cannot express to you the feeling that I had when I heard her talking. All of my life in Eugene, my parents had painted a world that was inhospitable and threatened to carry away people whenever they stopped striving to survive. I knew that they were born in the Great Depression and knew first-hand great hardship, but still, I felt that the picture was slightly old-fashioned. I mean, with all the government welfare programs, no one would ever starve to death. And there was so much money in our country that I felt that a person with simple tastes could get on without any interference. This sanguine picture was getting marred by my involvement with Mary. And then I felt the friction through the tension forming within this group (that I had once felt was the haven of peace). Events were interfering with each other constantly! That's why I came home.

But then I discovered that sometimes you can't any longer *come home*. That option was lost for me. I wanted tranquility. Why couldn't I be left alone to go about freely? All I wanted to do was exist without constant disturbance. But this didn't seem possible.

That's why I left Eugene, thinking that the world there offered the worst possible outcome.

My paradise in the sun was beginning to show signs of being no better. All the things that I believed in as a child were now being debunked. The Movement was filled with guns and money just like the War and the rest of this gangster-ridden society. My idol, T-Rx, was a man who was being threatened with going public again, which would certainly mean his demise. A man can't resurface when he has so many enemies. And yet, it was Mary who was pressing him to do it! Mary—my Mary, who could be such a wonderful person when she sat with me on "my" dock as I would ponder the mysteries of San Francisco Bay and engage in conversation. This same Mary was trying to destroy one of the greatest people I've ever known. I loved Mary, but I felt more than love for Rx: I felt awe.

This tension was unbearable, as you can well imagine. I didn't like the situation at all. The only thing I could do was either renounced Trek or Mary. They were at odds and I couldn't have both of them. Naturally, there was no effort required for this decision: T-Rx came before anyone. I made my decision.

I got up and walked around our space. It was pretty vacant—only Mad Dog, Mary, and me. Then I returned to my cot.

"Larry," said Mary, who saw me sitting on my pallet. I didn't respond, but watched her as she made her approach. Her blouse was three-quarters unbuttoned so that her bra-less chest would periodically display her breasts to me as she bounced forward.

"What an awful day I've had, Larry," she said, sitting next to me on my cot. I wondered if Mad Dog was awake? Would he hear what was going on? Of course not—he had been drinking and he was fast asleep. There was no possibility that he could hear what she was saying. Besides, there was some distance between where we were and where he was sleeping.

"You haven't been around for a while," I said.

"I know," she said in a loving voice. "I've been neglecting my Larry, haven't I?" She lifted her hand and touched my face. This was not the response that I was trying to elicit. I didn't want her to refer to our personal relationship, especially when I had decided that she was the cause for all the evil that was befalling T-Rx. "Is it true that you were the one who suggested the July 4th March to Rx?" Mad Dog hadn't mentioned this, but I had to know. The thought came upon me immediately.

"What are you talking about, Lawrence?" Her voice was soft and alluring. I felt a revulsion at her seductive manner which was so deceitful. She would do it with anyone anytime, why should her easy manner be attractive to me? Jan had been such a good woman to me. I had been her first and she mine. What was I lowering myself to do?

"The March, dammit, you know what I'm talking about. Whose idea was it?" I was talking much too loud. What if Mad Dog should wake because of my yelling and come out to find Mary sitting on my bed with me? I'd have to leave. I could never face him or anyone again.

"Why are you concerned with some silly old march, Larry, dear?"

The line could have come out of an old movie. Was the whole world some kind of poorly written script? Why were people so predictable, and all their actions so ordinary? I am real. I expect that others will be also, but when I experience someone acting according to a role that is so conventional, I wonder whether they are anything but comic book characters. Perhaps I only see them as such, or maybe they really are that way because they can't be anything else, or maybe they imitate the models that they see—not knowing that the models are only illusions?

I don't know; such speculation is beyond me. The only thing that I know is the experience of being depressed at the unoriginal way that she approached me. How many hundreds of men have heard the plastic sentiments of Marilyn Monroe from the lips of imitation wannabes? How many take the cue to become Rock Hudson, Clark Gable, or whoever is in fashion to model his role? That's the way we've seen it done in the movies. Ergo, that's the way life *really is* out there.

What a distressing thought for someone who believes in a reality not based in Hollywood. How many seek to live the clichés: "Come with me to the Casbah, we will make beautiful music together"?

The words in my head filled me with horror. I tried to make a joke, imitating Tallulah Bankhead, "*Darling* I don't know what I want, *nobody* does!"

Mary responded with a high-pitched partial laugh. I'm not sure she recognized the quotation or whether she believed me or whether she thought I was serious about our plastic romantic situation. She reacted by stroking my cheek and then kissing me on the lips.

"Mary, Mary quite contrary—" was my response, pulling back.

"Larry, Larry, lies with Mary," she returned, laughing. She loved it. I was depressed. The joke was the real thing. For Mary *the real thing* was nothing more than a series of lines delivered with a certain pace and timing. They were commonplace, used over and over to express the same saccharin sentiment. How I hated all of it. How I longed to be back in high school, parking with Janet behind the large statue. Things were pure then: straight forward, plain dealing. While now, I didn't understand anything that was happening.

She kissed me again and touched my shoulder under my shirt. I pulled her to me and rolled on top of her. That wasn't right. She must be on top of me. She soon righted herself and took the role of the aggressor. Mad Dog was asleep, or listening to what was happening. I didn't know which. At any moment someone might come past my Masonite half-wall that gave us a little privacy and see us, but quickly these thoughts drifted from my mind. Gradually Mary morphed into Janet and how I missed her.

Sept. 22

You can guess what happened. I was sick about it. I let it happen. I could have stopped it, but I didn't act. I had no courage to do what I felt to be right. It's strange that I didn't feel a great sense of revulsion after it was over. I was kind of numb. I got up, got dressed, put my things into a backpack, and took a walk. I didn't have many things, a few paperbacks, magazines, two changes of clothes, and a toothbrush. All these seemed as parts of my body, parts that had let me down.

I wasn't angry with myself, but I felt sad. I had no strength to do anything. So I walked and found myself near the center of town and trying to thumb a ride. What I was doing and why I was doing it never occurred to me. I was tired and could not trust myself to think, but I knew that I had to keep moving. That was certain. In my mind there was a kind of peaceful feeling that made me want to sleep. Despite the fatigue I kept walking and thumbing with little luck until I was near the freeway. It was a long walk, but I planted myself on the on-ramp, determined not to move until I got a ride. It was only an hour before I got into a van headed for Eureka. The driver was a guy like myself who asked where I was from and I told him. He said that he liked Oregon and how there were too many people in California and all that.

Soon I was asleep in a baseball diamond just a mile or so off the freeway. I got a postcard to write you. That's about it. Except that when I finally arrived, I decided that I hadn't gone anywhere and that I was farther away from where I wanted to go than before I left. What would happen to T-Rx? I wanted to do something as I felt sort of responsible, but what could I do in Eugene?

I was only there a day or so on the outskirts when I came to see you. I was waiting for you when I met Marcia in the bar.

"What are you doing here?" I asked.

"We're going up to Seattle," she said.

"Seattle?"

"T-Rx has something he wants to do. Do you want to come along?"

"I don't understand. What are you doing here?"

"I went north with Hook who's trying to get us some place to stay. I thought I'd stop in Eugene and find you."

"But how did—"

"I had the address of your friend, Fred Abrams, and went to his house to ask him if he had any news of you, but found all the information that I needed in the note that you left him."

"But why did you—"

"Never mind. Both Trek and Mad Dog were sorry to see you go, you know. You are a favorite of theirs. They are happy that you left though, because it showed them that things were rotten where they were and that they had to move. You showed them the way."

I felt confused. How could my meaningless action show anything to anyone? I didn't like it. My action had only one meaning: no meaning. I didn't think about purpose. I came to Eugene because, because—I don't know why.

"Why don't we get out of here," she suggested.

I was led out of the bar and down the road. Marcia put her arm lovingly around my waist. There was no longer anything in my mind that was coherent. I needed some time by myself.

"We can get a place to sleep over at the University," she said. "Hook put me on to some people before he left."

We walked a very long ways without talking. I didn't know what to say and was trying to organize my thoughts. All that I could think of was working on cars with Jan looking on. You know, she thought that I could open up a garage someday. She used to talk about how we would settle down just outside of town and that we could go camping two or three times a month. She loved fishing and I remember a few exciting trips that we took. Somehow everything pure and right seemed to spin about the recollected image of her. I was a body, empty of value, walking aimlessly in a world that didn't care about anything except existing. I thought about a short story I read about a man who committed suicide because he thought the world was without meaning. At the time I thought the story was stupid. (I think that you pointed out to me much of the literary reasons for this, which I don't know from a donkey's ass.) I just didn't like it and felt it was trite. But now the story seemed to be a poignant story about the true nature of everything. How wonderful it would be to commit that ultimate act. But how could I hope to do that, when I couldn't even turn Mary down? I couldn't even control my body. I gave in to her one-step-at-a-time, and soon it was over.

We got to the sorority house. Some girl was away and we had her room. I was so self-absorbed that I hadn't really been thinking that I was with Marcia, someone that I didn't know very well (none of us did except Mad Dog), until we sat down in a chair and she brought me a beer. The room was constructed for two people. There were also two functional desks and two small closets. It was just the venue for collegial roommates.

I sat down on one of the beds and Marcia sat next to me. I turned and really looked at her for the first time that evening.

"We've never gotten to talk much," I said.

"No, though I feel as if I know you. Mad Dog talks a lot about you." Marcia wore her hair in very well-kept cornrows.

"He does?"

"Yes. He was afraid that you might leave us for good. I tried to persuade him that you'd come back, but he had the silly idea that you were disgusted by him just before you left. It seems he got drunk with you and made a *spectacle*?"

"A spectacle?" I answered. Marcia had beautiful skin, though she wasn't a *come on*. Physically she was very attractive; her soft brown skin and sympathetic kindness calmed me.

"That's what he called it. I wasn't there, of course, but I found him asleep when I got off of work at six. He'd already had a few. I took off. But later, I found out that he left for the bar at ten with you so that must have meant that he got into it a bit."

"He had a few drinks, but he didn't make a spectacle."

"I'm glad you said that, I'll tell him. He'll appreciate that. You know he thinks quite a bit of you."

I didn't know what to say. I didn't like someone talking about me. I preferred talking about someone or something else.
"Well, I like him too, as well as Rx, of course."

"Yes, it seems the three of you hit it off very well. You know that Mad Dog is concerned about Trek."

"I know. It has something to do with his getting too much publicity so that some of his enemies might get at him."

"That's not all. That bitch, Mary, has gotten Rx involved with some loans from some criminals who are trying to get some power within the Movement. It seems that she accepted quite a bit of money in Trek's name and threw it away. Now, they are after Trek to pay it back."

"Why don't they press Mary?" The very sound of her name was difficult, but with Marcia, things seemed in a form of reality I could deal with.

"It seems that Mary's gotten some power of her own among the Worker's Liberation Front and that she has a lot of muscle to counteract the other element."

"This other element, is it Mafia or something?"

"I don't think it's that big. I'm not sure exactly, but I think it's more local than that. At any rate, you can see that T-Rx is experiencing pressure from several fronts."

As she talked, I couldn't help being attracted to her beautiful shape. I'm not using the word "figure" because that implies the curvature of the hips compared to the stomach, but rather, I was taken by the undulations of her entire body which were visible through the thin shirt and jeans that she had on. It was an abstract assessment. I liked Mad Dog too much to ever try anything with her.

"What can we do?" I asked, not knowing exactly what I was doing or saying. I reached for her hand. It was warm and soft to the touch.

"I don't know. Mad Dog thought that you might have some ideas. He always has had a great deal of respect for your judgment."

I felt ashamed of myself. Judgment! Me having judgment—why, I couldn't control myself when it was the most important time to do so—how could I be said to have any self-control? But control wasn't the issue; it was judgment. But one implies the other, doesn't it?

"I'm a weak man," I confessed. She turned to me and lifted her hand to my cheek. Her fingers were soft and glided over my skin, just skimming over the last layer of cells so that only they could transmit by the gentle motions a thrill of excitement. I began to become confused.

The crime that she was committing was the theft of my heart, which she had instantly commandeered. Marcia was always the silent one. She never took part in any of the discussions. She was a loner, like myself. I could understand just how she felt when everyone was talking and you want to listen, for that's all you can do—the others are putting out too much energy. If you say something suddenly, at best it may not be heard, but at worst, everyone will turn and screw up their faces into grotesque masques of disgust: —what is he saying —that's nonsense —oh shut up shut up SHUT UP WILL YOU? I won't stop. I have as much right as anyone to—but no, I will wait for the right moment. I prefer that. I wouldn't want to do anything else.

Besides, the listener is the one who can observe. When you are always a part of something, you can't always see what is happening. How can you, since one can't look at anyone else except in a mirror (and we all know what a joke that is). I suppose that is what attracted me to Rx. He could sit in a group, be the leader, and not participate at all. He could organize and yet be as outside of everything as I was. The two states were in opposition somehow, and yet, that is where he was. Mad Dog and Marcia were like me, observers. Mary was an activist. T-Rx was in the middle.

As Marcia hugged me, I felt her bosom press against my chest. I knew that I wanted her and felt the same sensation from my sensitivity to her, but we stopped and looked in each other's faces.

"I don't think of you as weak and neither do the men."

By "the men," she was referring to Trek and Mad Dog. I had never known that they liked me or thought of me as being in the inner circle. I had always thought that I was in the outermost circle, the lowest echelon—along with Alf, Mary, or Captain Hook. I would have thought they were much higher than I was. In fact, (though I didn't think of it in units until just now as I write this) I had unconsciously assumed that the primary reason that Mad Dog was against Mary was that she was getting closer to T-Rx than he wanted, and so felt a jealousy. But if Mary wasn't there, then what was his (Mad Dog's) real motivation? If I'm in the inner circle, then why didn't I feel like it? Why didn't someone tell me so that I could act like it?

"Marcia—" I began, but I couldn't finish my sentence. How trite I was. I wouldn't go on acting according to some kind of script. I pulled away suddenly and walked to the mirror.

"What's the matter?" I could hear her saying, but she said nothing.

"I need a smoke," I said absently, then turned around and walked back to her. I couldn't resist the allure of her charms. I stroked her hair; she seemed so beautiful to me now. All that I could say was, "Marcia."

The person who stood in front of me was a woman I had never gotten to know. She was the keeper of a secret that excited me. I couldn't believe that they thought so highly of me. Her loving fingers had brought life back to me. I wanted to respond, but when I touched her, I felt that somehow I was being inauthentic.

I so wanted every caress to be right. I didn't want to just touch her and make out. What I really wanted was for everything to be all right. *Truth* was what I sought, yet, somehow it was alluding me. She inspired the desire for it, but yet in her was not the fulfillment I sought. My feeling was strong that she was my guide to somewhere else, and that I should not mistake the guide for the destination. And my destination was not with her.

Her eyes looked into mine. We still sat facing each other: myself on a chair now and she on the bed.

"Where can I find it?" I asked my guide.

"Find what?" she said as she leaned forward and put her fingers on my cheek again and pulled me over to the bed. I came to her.

"Perhaps it's over here," she said with a smile.

I knew it wasn't. Every instinct inside me told me that it wasn't so. And yet there was something within me that at that moment so wanted to be with her. It was a desire to submit to her warm embrace and to lose myself in a sensual escape. The bedspread near the pillow was stained and ugly. I turned to her.

"Marcia," I began, "why do we live?"

She smiled and laughed, "I like you, Larr."

Very few people call me that. I devised the name to coincide with T-Rx s theory of language. The name goes from the front to the back, becoming lost in the larynx. But she didn't understand my question, though by calling me 'Larr' she had indirectly spoken to something that I had been thinking about, unconsciously perhaps—I don't know, who knows what he is thinking about? We have certain fixations, which we only interpret later as a reconstruction of data.

She kissed me lightly on the lips. I knew that she was waiting to see what I'd do, but I didn't know. I was completely lost. I had this fixation and wasn't sure what it was but only that kissing Marcia wouldn't fulfill its desire.

I drew away from her and held her face in my hands. "You are a very kind person for coming. There are things that you have given me that have helped." My words began smoothly, but were now faltering. "Things that, well, it's difficult to express clearly—I don't know all about it myself."

She understood. I know that she did by the look that she gave me. But still, I had to make certain that more of my thought would be communicated to her. "I need to be close to you right now, but I don't want things to get too complicated." There was a pause and I ended saying, "I need to think things out."

Send me a note when you can,
Larr

Seattle
November 12, 1969
Larry Cohen to Fred Abrams

Dear Fred,

It's been awhile since I've heard from you. I trust that you are well and finding college as wonderful as you hoped that it would be. I know that you are the kind of person who can be a success at whatever you want, if only the breaks go your way. Perhaps someday I will go back to school. I don't think I'm material for university (4 year), but here in Washington they have what they call community colleges (2 year) that offer courses in a wide variety of areas and are much less demanding than 4-year colleges. I don't think I'd ever go for any kind of degree, but it might be interesting to go back and take a course in history or something.

I've been holding off talking to you about the project that we've been planning. The reason for this is that it is illegal, and that I wouldn't want to put you into a compromising position. It seems that soon I will be able to talk about it with you. We have been planning for quite a while, and soon it will happen.

What I can talk to you about are the meetings that are spent planning this project and an interesting conversation that I had with T-Rx. Concerning the meetings, it seems that Trek has wielded a coalition of splinter groups together for a project that may drastically affect the sentiment of those backing the Vietnam War.

These groups are from 25 persons to 100, depending on which groups are invited to a particular meeting and what portion of the group attends.

The reason that it takes so long to do anything is that before any action is taken at this level, all the factions have to have a say in *what* they believe should be done and *where* it should be done. Also, it seems that there must be clear reasons for acting in the way that they propose. I know this sounds rather garbled, but let me relate to you part of one meeting so that you can see for yourself.

A: I propose that we take Odegaard prisoner (Charles Odegaard is the president of the University of Washington).

B: And do what?

A: Make them stop the War.

B: And what makes you think that they'd do that?

A: Do you think that they'd let the head of a large university die? Think of the political leverage we'd have. He's an important person.

B: Look, even if you took Nixon hostage, you couldn't get them to stop the War. It's bigger than that.

C: B's right, the only way that we can stop the War is by a revolution.

D: Yes, revolution!

(Several others cheer for this response.)

B: I wasn't talking about revolution. (Great noise and confusion follow. B has to shout to be heard). It's no good.

C: Revolution! Yes! Revolution! Now!

(Crowd begins chanting: 'Yes, Revolution NOW!')

B: You dumb bastards, how far do you think we'd get with a revolution? They'd kill us with tanks, we wouldn't last an hour! (A sudden calm takes over as the chanting stops.)

B: An overt revolution is absurd. Remember what the Ruskies did in Czechoslovakia? No, what we need are isolated incidents of violence coupled with legitimate pressure through demonstration and confrontations with authorities. This is the answer. We must destroy the institutions of this country slowly by eroding the phony ethic on which they were constructed.

A: What are you talking about? Erode the ethic?

B: Family and organized religion are the two solidifying factors that middle-America falls back upon. If we can attack those, I think that the climate of this country will be one in which change can be brought about.

D: But that could take years!

B: So what? If we are dedicated to the overthrow of this system, we have to be prepared to wait. It takes time. In my organization, we have been working on implementing these objectives. It's the only sure way.

C: But we want change *now*. We don't want to wait. *Change now, it's too late; we won't wait!*

(Intermittent chanting of *Change now, it's too late; we won't wait!*)

B: You all are a collection of morons. If you want to carry on with a group cheering section, then maybe you should go to the Huskies games. Such public displays of adolescent emotion are sickening. You'll never achieve anything right away. This country took two hundred years to build, you aren't going to be able to change it, pull it down in one glorious demonstration.

E: Who says we're interested in pulling it down? We want to stop the War.

(There was a general grumble of agreement.)

B: Oh, is that all that you want, oh? In that case perhaps you should resume your tantrums and wild gyrations. That's the only way that you'll ever do anything. And when we win or lose that cause (and hundreds of thousands of men have died), then you'll all be happy. You'll cut your hair, get married, and have a nice green lawn. What a pretty picture. You'll let this leviathan in Washington continue its corrupt ways until it gets us into another war, or leeches your life out of you in some other way.

Yes, you can have it all: your radical chic and all the conventional comforts and modern conveniences. But as for me, I'll keep trying to destroy the institutions of this rotten country until it kills me. You all make me nauseous.

(B leaves in disgust and there is general murmuring as a resolution is voted upon as to whether there should be a discussion of what B said or if the proposed defacement of First Avenue movie houses should be considered. The latter proposal wins the day.)

For all their talk about the evils of democracy, these meetings usually are run rather loosely—not according to Robert's Rules of Order. Trek says that the meetings are a joke, but that for all their faults, they are all that we have to work with.

I was surprised at how many people in Seattle knew Trek or knew of him. I suppose that many Seattleites have been to San Francisco at some time or other so that is how they knew him or of him. It is my opinion that T-Rx isn't widely known outside of his regional area.

Nothing gets done at these meetings. Everyone argues about what are the *goals* and how to achieve them. This makes things chaotic. The only time there is any order is when a leader like T-Rx shows up for the meeting. This order only displays itself on the force of his personality. Then there is no rancorous discussion, only a somnolent stillness as fifty or so mesmerized faces absorb the messages of true wisdom that comes forth from this living oracle.

These groups are nothing except people who, on the one hand love to argue with closed eyes, and then on the other, blindly obey some figure who tells them what to do. They have left their parents and denounce them, but crave some substitute authority figure. Leaders like T-Rx fulfill the order.

I have thought a lot about Rx recently. We've found another "Nob Hill" to live on in Seattle. Here they call it Queen Anne Hill, overlooking the Space Needle on one side, and Seattle Pacific College on the other. Also, I'm only a half-hour walk away from the Sound. The water is beautiful and has a different effect upon me than the Bay. I hike down First Avenue (another First Avenue) to Mercer Street and down a bank of steps and I'm there. It's a long beach with a railroad that runs through it. I can sit on the rocks or throw stones into the water. There is something more natural about sitting on rocks rather than on a condemned pier. I brought Rx with me one day after having breakfast at Ozies (a small greasy spoon near the post office). I had been here (in Washington) for a while, but hadn't done much talking to anyone. There was a larger group living in the house where we were, but there was less activity among us. We did little to no demonstrating: it was just folk drifting in and out. I don't know how the bills were paid. I didn't ask.

Anyway, Rx and I were walking together, alone for the first time in a long while. I thought I noticed a smile on his face, but I couldn't be sure.

"How do you like it?" I asked.

"Seattle?" he responded.

"I don't know, just everything is different: the city, the people, your new life."

"It will pass," he said as he inhaled audibly. It was a strange habit that Trek had that confused me. Mad Dog connected it to Trek's consonant theory. By inhaling he was able to internalize all that he had put out into the world. It was also a way of bringing back any evil that he may have occasioned in his life so that it was *pulled out* of his victims and came home again.

It will pass. This comment had me confused. What did he mean? Was it that all was passable? Or mediocre? Or perhaps he meant that his life would pass, or time would pass—in time this too will pass. I considered it impertinent to ask him what he meant, so I moved on to something else.

"Things are quite different than they were in California."

"The language always changes."

"I mean, the groups that we used to have aren't the same."

"Did you know, Larr, that gemination[56] and Common Germanic palatal umlauts were instrumental in the change from Germanic to West Germanic?"

"C'mon Rx, you know I don't know anything about language. I'm trying to describe to you the differences between our life in San Francisco and here."

"I know, and I want you to know why the final dental and alveolar consonants combinations became assimilated between the fifth and ninth centuries. I'm describing something to you."

I laughed. Then Trek took out a little notebook that he always carried with him and wrote it down (otherwise I wouldn't have remembered it). It must be some kind of joke that I didn't get.

"Changes often happen," Rx began once we got to the water. "No one knows why they happen, but the change itself can be mechanically described. I think that is a more honest approach, don't you? It's a joke to pretend that we know the 'why' of anything, so what's the use of pretending? Explanations of that sort fall into political traps of imagined cause and effect. What can be described is a series of non-contiguous actions that exert a force upon some object in a given medium."

---

[56] "Gemination" is a term from linguistics. It refers to consonant elongation when a consonant is given longer expression than a short consonant. It is separate from consonant stress. Here, as elsewhere, T-Rx seems to have studied linguistics at the post-high school level.

I didn't know what he was talking about. And the only way I could remember what he said was to jot it down in my own spiral notebook that I kept handy.

His words were preciously cryptic to me. T-Rx had great learning. If only he had gone to graduate school, I'm sure that he could have been a professor or something.

"Are you going to go along with the—" I began.

"I don't know. Do you think we should?"

It was the first time that Rx had ever asked me my opinion on anything. I felt flattered. "I suppose you're right," I began. "But I think that they are more happy discussing policy than actually doing something that might make a meaningful difference. They denounce capitalism while living off the income of their wealthy parents. They eschew the materialism of the middle class while buying expensive stereo equipment and spending huge amounts of money on drugs. Nothing is different."

I wanted to talk to Rx about some of the things that Marcia had told me, but I didn't know how to phrase it. Discussion with Trek was always difficult for I never knew how to take him. Just when I might feel at ease, then he would talk in a way that would lose me—like some high falutin' theory, and I would feel as if he were mocking me.

The man was so intelligent that he had every right to mock a dullard like myself, but that doesn't alleviate the acute discomfort that I felt when ridiculed. But perhaps he wasn't ridiculing me, but merely assuming that I was smarter than I really was, in which case my silence was only confirming him. I turned my gaze again to Puget Sound and the various boats. There were far more private water vessels in Elliot Bay than there were in San Francisco Bay (which was mostly commercial). They've told me that there are more boat owners (as a percentage of the population) in Seattle than in any other city, save for Hong Kong.

"Yes," I replied again to his original question.

"About San Francisco?" put Trek.

"Yes," I said

"Why did you leave? Things were so nice for you there."

"I couldn't take certain dynamics: the hypocrisy of the *true believers*." Good. It was said very indirectly, but the question was out. He had brought me to it. Now the burden of discussion was on him. I waited for some comment on the history of the English language, while hoping beyond expectation that he might tell me something of the pressures that he was subject to and how his life was a haunted one. I wanted to know about the man in the South, who wanted him dead (Mad Dog's story). And I wanted to know about the local loan sharks who were after T-Rx because of Mary's mishandling of funds. I waited. I wanted to tell him, but I couldn't do it on my own.

T-Rx smiled, slyly, I thought. Then he shoved his hands into his pockets. The only noise was the water lapping up against the rocks.

I would have to be the one to break the silence. "I don't know why I left; why does anyone leave? Why did you leave?"

"So, you've been talking to Mad Dog, I hear?"

I wasn't ready for the question to be thrown back at me. I couldn't tell him about Mary, but his proposition was clear: "you tell me about why you left, and I'll tell you some of my story." I so wanted him to talk to me, but don't you see, I couldn't tell him about Mary or he wouldn't speak to me again. He would hate me for descending so low—the very person who had put his life in jeopardy.

"Yes, you know I did. He told me about the South and some of what went on there." I paused and blew my nose. "I don't know half of what I do or *why*."

"Yes, I suppose it's that way, isn't it?" The smile was greater as his words shook me. We were talking about vague generalities because we weren't trusting each other. But couldn't he see that I wanted to be able to tell him all? I wanted him to trust me, but I couldn't tell him what he asked, because what I'd done was so heinous. There was no admitting it.

Soon the moment passed and we were climbing the steep hill back again. I felt an overwhelming sense of defeat. I had failed. I want so much to be close to T-Rx— like Mad Dog is—but when my opportunity presented itself, I was not up to the occasion. I could have made something up and told it to him, but I didn't want it that way. I had endured too many lies as it was. There could be no more. There wasn't any room.

I tell you Fred, life on the outside can be very difficult. I wish that I had someone who I knew would accept me no matter what I did. Why, if it wasn't for you and your ear, I don't know what I'd do with these things that have happened to me. They seem to demand expression to someone. I'm sorry if it seems that I only write you when I'm in a jam, but the truth is that it is during difficult times when I feel the need to talk with you the most.

Things are getting rather tense as this project is nearing term. Keep in touch.

Sincerely,

L.

Seattle
December 1, 1969
Larry Cohen to Fred Abrams

Dear Fred,

I suppose that I can tell you now, because by the time that you get this letter the deed will have already happened.

Tomorrow we are scheduled to bomb the R.O.T.C. building at the University of Washington. The R.O.T.C. is a symbol of military encroachment upon the youth of this nation. They supply the army with young bodies who should be out enjoying themselves—instead of becoming permanently scarred through the vulgarity of killing Asians. I haven't said whether I'm for the move or not. Bombing seems a bit harsh to me, especially as it may involve the killing of people in the process. I don't like to see anyone killed. Maybe it's a mistake, but anyway, our group is going to be the one to do it. While several other groups are involved with another associated project, we have a guy who has assembled a bomb that is very powerful. It can be put into an ordinary brown paper shopping bag. The plan is to put the bag down and walk away. In two minutes the place is blown to atoms.

When they discussed it, the plan sounded so interesting and right, but now that I'm writing it down, it seems simply awful. We are going to be as bad as our enemy. We're making a war against war. But is that really a contradiction? Like they say: can you rape to promote chastity?

Two hours later: I couldn't write anymore on those ideas as I was disturbed at what was happening. I have talked to Mad Dog and he tells me that some acts of violence are *necessary*. I don't know if I buy that. But I suppose that people smarter than I am *do*. I hope to be able to write about it later in short doses when my time is more my own.

I should make one thing clear as to how I discovered that Mary is in Seattle. I was up on the roof, cleaning the gutters of our house (a must in the Seattle monsoon season) when I heard a familiar voice. At first I thought that the noise was in my head or that I was mistakenly interpreting other natural sounds, such as leaves rustling or something like that, for the voice of that dreaded woman. I attempted to drive the noises out of my head, but they persisted, so I gave up trying to expunge them and altered my activity of obstruction to one of recognition.

It was then I discovered that the noises were coming from inside a room that was only a few feet under me and to my left. I could have moved closer, but still wouldn't have been able to make out what was being said since the window was closed.

I moved down my ladder to a spot above the window and noticed that the curtains were closed. I attempted to lift the window, quietly from the outside, but was unsuccessful. Inside, I would catch some individual words, but nothing sustained.

My curiosity was aroused and I felt that I had a need to know what was being said. There was a strong sense that the person inside, Mary, was trying to depose my T-Rx and I wanted to be around to try and prevent this maneuver.

I could go up (back on the roof) and try something from there. But that was not a good idea unless I pounded my shoes to make noise below. I could go down and enter the house. But that might cause an unpleasant confrontation. Nothing seemed particularly hopeful to me. I searched my brain for some insight that would solve the dilemma, but none appeared.

In a shorter time than I would have imagined, Mary appeared at the bottom of the steps and was leaving. The question raced through my mind as to what I should do. Perhaps I could confront T-Rx directly, telling him that I knew that Mary had been there and describe my interest in the situation. This would be difficult, both because I didn't feel confident enough to approach Rx in such a way and because I wondered how much of my relationship with Mary was known to T-Rx.

I remember her saying that I was on her side once to Rx in an effort to name those in his group who supported her over him.

But since he seemed to think of me as a loyal follower, it seems apparent that he didn't believe that or has changed his mind if he ever did believe it.

The next morning 11:00.
No more is known except a briefing from Rx that the bombing will be delayed because of internal problems.

That evening 7:30
I talked with Mad Dog. "She's back, isn't she?" We'd just finished a ham sandwich, which was dinner. We were sipping a Dr. Pepper. We were sitting on the screen porch, which gave us a measure of privacy.

"How do you know?" he replied.

"I saw her leaving the house while I was cleaning the gutters."

"Did you hear what went on?"

"No, the windows were closed and they weren't talking loud enough."

"Well, our friend wants a large scale bombing followed by an extortion attempt on the city itself." As Mad Dog talked, he pursed his lips in an exaggerated fashion. One might take it as a symbol of kissing, but I knew it as one of disgust. I turned my head away to get my bearing.

I saw a feral cat in the backyard. I've always been partial to cats since my Tinkerbell (my companion in primary school). I turned back to Mad Dog, "We've heard a lot of proposals like that. They've all been unrealistic. Doesn't she have anything new?"

"Nothing new, except some force to back up her demands. She either wants us to join with her own group behind her, or to force us out of the scene." Mad Dog's voice was steady and carefully modulated.

"She wants us out of Seattle?"

"She wants us to merge. She wants to be the grand co-leader with T-Rx of the militant section of the anti-War movement. What is worse is that she has the muscle to back up her request."

"Do you mean the money factions against Rx in Frisco?" I reached out and touched Mad Dog's left hand. He was very tense.

His pursed lips began moving forward and back, almost spasmodically. He tried to gain control. Then he lit up a smoke.

"What can we do?" I asked, just realizing the full significance of the situation. Mary wanted to force Rx to become a national leader. Now she wants to be co-leader with him and stipulate that if he doesn't, he'll be destroyed by her thugs.

Trek could flee, but he would have to go the Midwest or the East, as he has old enemies in the South (who may still be pursuing him).

"I don't know. I wish I knew," said Mad Dog, putting his right hand atop mine. He finally smiled.

"If Rx organized his people into a *known group*, then he'd have more power than Mary," I said.

"You're right. Perhaps that's what needs to be done, except that it is contrary to what T-Rx stands for: unstructured resistance from that region that is neither in nor out of society: be like a gadfly that only wants to continue stinging random problems in order to raise consciousness. To become an organization, as he has said many times, means that you will necessarily become as evil as that which you are trying to change. Political structures are all evil. We can do the most good by being neither in nor out of it, but randomly highlighting evils within social institutions."

I didn't understand what he meant except that Rx didn't like the idea of forming an organization because there was something bad about organizations. I didn't pursue the topic, because I didn't want Mad Dog to know how dull I really am. I turned my attention back to the kitty cat. I blanched when I saw her hovering above a bird she'd just killed.

The next afternoon:
I was over at the Seattle Center, walking around the large fountain there and listening to the piped-in music and the water jets changing their angles in a simple choreography with the melodies. I was lost in a reverie when I felt a hand on my arm, and it was Mary.

"Hello," she said.

I didn't respond. "I have something that I want to show you." Her voice had lost none of its allurement for me. Why was it that I left my place at the fountain and went with her to a two-story apartment building and ventured with her inside and had a drink? It was as if she were a witch and she had a spell over me. I hated her, but yet her charms were more than I could withstand.

"I know that you've gone up in the world," she said, sitting next to me on the stone circle that circumscribed the fountain.

"Not really," I replied.

You always have been modest. But Larry, dear, my information says that you are now even more influential with T-Rx than Mad Dog."

"You think so?" I said, laughing, for nothing sounded more absurd to me in my life.

"I believe it. And I know that you can help me."

"Help you?" I echoed.

"Lawrence, you have always had a soft spot for me," she purred as she put her hand on my leg and slowly moved it toward my crotch. "What I want is what is good for us all. I want to create a coalition of protest forces. You see, they are all scattered around the country with no one to mobilize them. If we are to have any *real power* there must be a consolidation of our bases so that each confrontation can be negotiated." I moved my hand to lift hers into mine and away from my body. The fountain began playing Tijuana Brass. We were lightly splashed by the water.

"What does this have to do with me?"

She moved to me and kissed me on the cheek, "My dear, I want you for one of the chief lieutenant roles of this new group." I dropped her hand.

"I'm not interested." My reply was crisp.

"But Larr, you know that you have great leadership potential. As a man, you have the power to hypnotize others. With one of the large segments of our new coalition, I'm sure that we could make great strides in our effort to change this country's policies from war and repression to humane socialism."

I heard the words that she was saying, but it is only now that I fully understand what she meant. At the moment my eyes were fixed upon her jeans. They were hip-hugger, navy bell-bottoms that were smooth and accented her body in a more feminine way than the standard jean did. Her belt rode just on the pelvic girdle. There was something bewitching about those jeans and the smoothness of the lines. I wanted to stroke them.

"So you see," she continued, "if you can get Rx to come over to our side, and I know that you can, then I'm sure that there will be a high place for you in our organization."

By now I only heard words, and the connectives and referents were not registered in my head. She came close to me and put her hand on my shoulder. "We've always been close, haven't we Larry, darling?"

I smiled and put my hand on her leg to feel the navy jeans. "I've always made you happy, haven't I?" she smiled and ran her tongue over her top row of teeth as if she were about to have dessert.

My eyes were still focused upon her hips as she drew closer to me. "Now, you want to make us happy, don't you?" Then I felt a heavier sprinkling from the fountain. I was baptized into reality.

"No," I said absently. I didn't have anything particular in mind, but "no" seemed like the most positive thing that I could utter. We got up and started walking. I thought we were going back to The House, but we took a left turn just at the bottom of Queen Anne Hill. It was *her* place: a clapboard two story abode that was painted white. It was in very good condition (unlike the place where my crew was). We went in and sat on a leather sofa in the living room.

Mary put her hand against my face. "Do you want to *know* your lovely Mary again? You understand that since we last *made it* I've had to live as practically a nun. That's why I want you to be in our organization, partly so that I can have you around me. It's hard to find a man with your attributes." Then she kissed me. "You are a leader of people, Lawrence. You can make people follow you. I think that you will be a rising figure in the near future. Rx's power base will be in your hands in only a few years. Count on that; I know what I'm talking about. And then you and I will control it all to ourselves: together."

She moved her hand to touch me again, but I pushed it away. I wasn't angry with her, but just didn't want to be pressured. "Darling," she said as she began to unzip her trousers. As she did this, I looked up. I wanted to stare at the navy jeans and now they were disappearing! I became aware of talking in the hall. Several people seemed to be milling about. I became rigid.

"Don't mind them," she said, "they'll go away." My jaw dropped as the blue color was now entirely gone: a crinkled hump that could be anyone's dirty clothes. I stared into her eyes. There was an odd detachment that I felt at that instant. I've never been a violent man, but I felt at that moment that I could strangle her. That white, thin neck could so easily snap in my hands. The thought of it made me smile.

Mary thought that I was smiling at her and so continued in the process, but I was only thinking of how easily I could put an end to all the troubles that had faced Trek, Mad Dog, Hook, and myself: all in one simple maneuver. The spirits that reside within her could be released to roam about as they will in that netherworld where such evil resides.

She still had her shirt on, but was now trying to unbutton mine. Her lips pressed mine, but there was no joy anymore for me. The snowcapped jeans rose in a crumpled heap from the smooth, fake Persian carpet. They represented a mountain in the far distant past that now was so very remote from me.

"No," I repeated, this time with more force.

"But Larry—" she stated, but I wouldn't let her finish. There were loud voices in the hall. They were her friends. The jeans were no longer smooth. She noticed that I was sensible to the noises and yelled, "Go away, I'm busy." I took the interval to rise and re-button my top button.

She stood and brought me to her body. "I need you Larr; come to me, darling."

"No," I said once again. "No, no, NO, NO!" I shouted and pulled away. The motions were now quick. She saw what I was doing, and instead of trying to stop me, she ran back and tried to put on her jeans, but it was too late. I scurried to the front door. The noise of my pounding feet brought friends who had been in the hall just outside. They poured in with hoots and hollers.
I was gone.

The next morning:
Well, Fred, you are probably applauding my action. It wasn't anything laudable at all. I acted from instinct, not from principle. When I failed in San Francisco, it was because of things that I couldn't control. Well, the same thing happened yesterday, except that I am proud of the way it turned out. I am happy and can half-delude myself into imagining that I had something do with it. I don't think that I did. A strong repulsion fills me when I imagine

that she actually was trying to get to Rx through me. She thought that I would sell my good friend for her bag of tricks. Perhaps I had no active will to withstand her before, but I'd never do anything to hurt T-Rx and the group again.

I would go on, but there seems to be some commotion happening right now. I have to go now; things have changed. We're making a move and only Hook, T-Rx, and I are going out on this one.

Yours,

Larr

Missoula, Montana
December 17, 1969
Larry Cohen to Fred Abrams

Dear Fred,

We've been hitching since when I broke off the note and mailed it to you. (You know, before I write you I already have an envelope that is addressed and stamped. It makes for a fast mailing.)
It's hard getting rides after you get over the Pass[57] in Washington, because there are a lot of skiers, but they stop at the Pass. The eastern part of the state is desolate, but once we got to Spokane, the trip into Idaho was simple.

I think that I'd like to go back to Idaho someday: the scenery is beautiful.

There are not many towns in Montana. We've got three sleeping bags for four of us (Marcia and Mad Dog, T-Rx, and me) and we either take turns with them or double up. Everyone is pretty upset about things, so the comradery isn't much right now.

Next morning:
We've decided to get temporary jobs to earn some money. We'll never get across Montana at this rate, so we're doing casual labor to try and earn bus fare, not to mention eating money. Missoula is

---

[57] The "pass" is the Continental Divide that cuts the state in two. (I.B.)

a cow town. Because there are lots of cattle, beef is cheap (compared to San Francisco).

12/23
I never told you what happened back in Seattle. Well, we had our bombing, but we didn't bomb the R.O.T.C. building, but bombed the headquarters of the Worker's Liberation Front and Socialist Labor Party headquarters. We heard the blast from about a mile away. I wonder if anyone was killed. You can't send me any mail for a while, but we will be in Chicago sometime in the next week or two and can be reached in care of Lockely Henderson, 514 E. 57 St. #8, Chicago, Ill--I don't have a zip code.

1/10
The New Year came in, bringing up enough money to travel. Tomorrow we buy our tickets and wait until our final paychecks to pull out. I wonder if Mary was in the building when it exploded.
Larr

Minneapolis, Minnesota
February 1, 1970
Larry Cohen to Fred Abrams

Dear Fred,

As you can tell, we stayed a few days longer than we expected. The bus ride has been interesting. We are waiting in Minneapolis for a connection to Chicago. In the meantime, we've been venturing out to see a little of this mini-metropolis. It seems from my cursory view of the town that the main drag is Hennepin Avenue, where all the theaters are located. Mad Dog and I had some Chinese food at a place called the Nan King. The place is like a cafeteria in decor, but the food isn't bad.

I've been thinking about you a lot lately. You don't know how difficult it has been to write. My hands have been very cold lately (and don't say it's because of the weather). I find that I have needed to do a little drinking to steady myself, as I find it hard to stand the tension of being around T-Rx. He seems pressed by factors that he won't confide to anyone. There is no longer any of the calm rapport that he used to display. Now he is nervous and suspicious. Mad Dog thinks that he has been threatened by the many who want him to pay (the loan sharks, the radical groups who feel let down by him, and maybe his tail from the South). Perhaps it's the pressure that caused him to support the bombing of the other group in Seattle. Without his support, the less militant groups will not follow the radicals. Rx was a common mediator that held things together. When he left, it acted to serve notice to the other groups that he was breaking with the radical wing as represented by Mary's Worker's Front (who wanted to bomb the ROTC and try to take the University of Washington's president as hostage), he effectively smashed efforts to organize a large faction of dissidents.

This is similar to what he did when he left San Francisco, though more dramatic, of course. How many enemies he has been accumulating, no one knows, but I have been noticing that he is becoming paranoid about the most innocent situations. For example, we were in a public restroom and a group of three men came in, but before they could get inside, Rx was out the other door. He won't comment on it, but I'm sure that he thinks that someone is out to get him.

"It's natural," said Mad Dog. "You should have seen it when he was being hunted in the South. There are enough things to make it tough for a black and a white traveling together in Alabama—not to mention being followed by some goons who were trying to hurt us. He couldn't take the strain of it after a while, and so I got Marcia to agree to go to San Francisco with me."

I knew the story well—Mad Dog had told me about it before—but now we discussed it more and more. It was as if we were all suspended from T-Rx's emotional center. His anxiety was our own. Occasionally he would subside some, and then it was as if a tremendous burden were being lifted from our souls. I started several times to make a chart of all the times that Rx was in a situation of assassination, but I could never keep it up. You know I hinted that the reason we stayed was for more money. Well, that's only part of it.

Part of the problem was that Rx didn't want to travel. We had established ourselves in one spot in San Francisco and he wanted to stay where he was. Who were we to tell him that we had to move? What if he were murdered as a result? It would be our fault.

"But if he doesn't get moving," Mad Dog commented, "then he'll never get any better."

We all wanted Rx to get better. Even Captain Hook (who planned to join us in Chicago) gave up his regular work in order to help Trek. Hook had no scheduled gigs in Chi-town. His band stayed in Seattle. He was now a solo act. But no one was willing to buy. Seems his sound was different from what the Windy City wanted to blow their way.

"It's bad," Marcia said. We often were the first up in the morning and so had our cold coffee together. Sometimes I thought that Marcia and I were interchangeable in Mad Dog's mind. Though I loved Trek, it was rather a relationship of awe. With Marcia and Mad Dog, I felt that I had comrades.

"Yes, but what can we do?" It was near the end of January in Missoula. VERY COLD. "Mad Dog has been trying to get T-Rx to hit the road. But I'm afraid that the two of them aren't on the best of terms." We were in a diner. But it was not comfortable: a white guy and a black girl. The patrons were affronted. They reacted with their staring and their little unheard murmurings. Why couldn't they just let us be? I watched one guy, probably around sixty, who pointed with his index finger at us and shook his head. His booth-mate hit his fist on the pine-wood table. I wondered whether they were planning our demise.

I tried to keep my concentration. "Why is that?"

"I don't know," she said. "Mad Dog doesn't talk much with me anymore either. You are the only one who I can talk to. I tell you, I don't like what's happening. It's all so frightening to watch the people who you love change so much from the people you've always known them to be."

"But they aren't really any different," I said, trying to console. "It's just the stress that they are undergoing—all these changes and all." We decided to leave.

As we walked back to our VW van where we all slept, Marcia put her hand on my shoulder.

"I don't think I've ever given much thought to it, but you know, my whole personality is undergoing some kind of upheaval because of this." Marcia's hair was no longer in corn braids. It was like mine: generally unwashed and unkempt. I felt we were soulmates.

As we got closer to our van she said, "You mean, because you're upset."

"Yes, I guess it's the friction between the protest groups," I said.

"It's not just that. I mean, I have always partially understood myself, who I was, by Mad Dog's relation to T-Rx and my relation to Mad Dog. They were like fixed points that I always understood, but now they aren't the same and I have nothing to judge myself by. The whole society seems like it's falling apart: where do we turn?"

"I don't know," I said immediately. She was right, though. I had never thought of it before. Just look what's happening: the War, mores changing, all the old codes are being overturned—what can a person cling to, or are we meant to float about without anything that is fixed? I suppose you are my fixed point, Fred. But it's been so long since I've seen you that sometimes you don't seem real to me. You are this paper on which I'm writing. This paper is real (you notice that I always buy the same brand—what will happen if it, too, is discontinued?). My coffee cup was empty, so I waved to the waitress for another. Marcia is a beautiful woman. She is the only person that I can talk to in a relaxed way. "Maybe we can't turn to anyone," I ventured after the silence.

Marcia perhaps didn't hear me; at any rate, she didn't answer but sat staring into her coffee cup. I need to stop traveling, Fred. I'll never live in Montana.

Yours,
Larr

Corvallis, Ore.
January, 15, 1970
Fred Abrams to Larry Cohen

Dear Larry,

I was disturbed by your letter of Dec. 17. It sounds as if that band of yours is having a rather hard time of it. This business of bombing buildings can be very dangerous. I hope you know what you may be getting yourself in for. There are prison sentences for what you are doing, or being an accomplice to.

I read the account of what happened in Seattle, and no one was hurt. The action was attributed to an unknown extremist group, but knowing your friend, Mary, you can bet that the police will have a warrant out on T-Rx soon. It might be advisable for you to consider loosening your ties with this group. In case there is an investigation, it may go better on you if you are seen as a peripheral figure.

My studies are going fine, and I'm doing some work in the library in Corvallis this week and will return home on Sunday.
All the best to you and I hope that you don't get hurt.
I'm always around if you need me.

Your Friend,
Fred.

Chicago, Illinois
February 22, 1970
Larry Cohen to Fred Abrams

Dear Fred,

Glad to get your letter; it had be waiting for me when I arrived. You know, I suppose I'm happy that no one was hurt. But somehow I had hoped that Mary would be silenced once and for all. I don't condone murder, but somehow if I knew that she would never turn up again, things would be so much smoother.

There is no way that I can interact with her and feel satisfied about the encounter. Chicago is a cold place in the winter, especially if the place where you are hanging out doesn't have any heat. The only way to warm up is to keep all one's clothes on and to drink lots of warm liquids. The kitchen is the only room where there is any heat (from the stove). You should see it in the morning when Lockley (a fellow we've added here) wakes up and starts breakfast. Everyone moves for the stove--it's a dead run from where you were sleeping to the stove. After you have warmed up some, then there is the lottery for the john. It's all very coy. The only one who doesn't seem to be bothered by the cold is T-Rx. He has always been mysterious to me. For example, I saw him sitting in the living room alone one night when several of us had come back from a free film at Chicago State University. There were no lights on—only the glow from the street lights. He was sitting on an old sofa that was covered with a red toss-cover from Goldblatt's. He seemed to be staring at a silver neon light across the street that was flashing on and off: *Mexicana Cantina*.

"You look perfectly miserable," I said jokingly in an effort to get a conversation started. I had been stimulated by the film and I didn't want to let the feeling of euphoria that had captured me disappear.

"Did you like the movie?" he replied without looking at me. I didn't even know that he knew anything about my plans to see the movie with Hook and Marcia. "Yes, it was a queer one with horses galloping about—first in black and white, and then in color. Wasn't much of a story to it—mostly framing various natural venues." I started looking at the neon sign across the street. I noticed that the last three letters: the "i," the "n," and the final "a" in *Cantina* were out.

"Was Mad Dog with you?" he asked, turning his gaze at me. I thought this an odd query. If he knew that I had gone to the movie, I assumed that he must have known everyone who had gone. Also, what was strange about this question was that it was the first time that he had ever asked me where Mad Dog was. The tone of his voice showed me that he was concerned. There was no calm assurance that usually characterized his speech patterns.

I didn't know what to say, so I mumbled something about how I didn't know where he was, but that I was sure that he was all right.

"How?" T-Rx laughed, "How can you be sure?" At other times, this response would have been one of Rx's attempts at correcting a poorly constructed sentence. The normal sequence would be that one can't make statements about things to which he has no positive knowledge, or some such philosophical statement. But this time the tone was different. He was not being the pedagogue. Rather, the response had a snapping quality to it, displaying a marked impatience that bordered upon a cry—a cry that had such foreboding undertones that it struck a response of fright within me.

"I don't know," was all that I could manage.

Then his tone changed again. He sighed and motioned for me to sit down. You can imagine the disturbed condition that I was in, having just been so elated and now to experience this!

Perhaps I wouldn't have been sensitive to all that I felt was happening if my senses hadn't been sharpened by the film. It was a slow-moving artistic piece that heightened my sensibilities. Because of this, it seemed that every movement that I could see in the cold, dark room denoted something, and though the referent wasn't always clear, I could feel that it was there—hiding about me in the shadows. My gaze returned to *Mexicana Cant__* flashing on and off, again and again.

I should explain that we were sitting on the couch that was facing an ordinary double sash window with a broken window shade that hung part way down. The flashing sign from across the street irregularly lit up Trek's face, distorting the man I knew.

He lifted his hand, which emerged from the shadow, to his face. "So you like wild horses; does it remind you of Oregon?"

"No, not really," I replied, though there were wild horses near to where we lived. Still, I didn't want him to think me a country rube at that moment. Too many people think that Eugene is a part of the nineteenth century for that to be a joking subject with me.

"Where are you from?" I replied, before he could say anything else about Eugene.

"Where do you think?" he replied. He was smiling, but it made me uncomfortable.

"I wouldn't know."

"Pick a city."

"Atlanta," I said, offering the first city that came to mind.

"No, I'm not from the South," he said somberly. I realized that perhaps my response wasn't the most thoughtful considering his melancholy mood and all that had happened to him in the South. I decided to quickly add another city.

"Boston."

"No, I'm not from Boston either, though I've spent some time there. I'm from the east coast, but have traveled around quite a bit. My family never lived in one place more than a couple of years. My stay in San Francisco for almost four years was the longest time I've ever been in one spot in my life."

"I guess you sort of miss it?" I said, trying to hold up my end, but afraid of saying the wrong thing at any moment.

"Miss it? I don't think I'd use *that* phrase to describe what I feel. I was very happy while living there, but one must keep moving. You see, Larr, it is in the acquiring of creature comforts and attachments to certain external objects that a society gains a populace that is easy to control. They can be manipulated since they are frozen into particular lifestyles that are dictated by where they live and the types of obligations that can be imposed by the environment."

As T-Rx talked, I felt I was in the presence of his greatness once again. He wasn't concentrating, but merely speaking words that had been said countless times before by him to others. But still, despite the heaviness of his soul and his subsequent inattention, there was a presence of something that inspired awe within me. Here was a man who had lived by what he believed. He did not become entrapped by the snares of society, nor did he wallow in solipsistic isolation. Instead, he held the two alternatives in opposition to each other. This opposition created a tremendous tension which was now threatening to break him, and was already having an effect upon Mad Dog.

We must keep moving, he said—this seems true in once sense since time moves forward, but why must the past be blasted so that its comfort is lost entirely? Maybe I misunderstood him (I frequently do). In fact, it wasn't until I heard him talking that I realized that I finally hadn't an inkling of what he stood for. This after having been told so many times by himself and Mad Dog in word and deed their personal worldview. But now I heard the words of someone who was longing for some kind of relief. But what was oppressing him? Why the split with Mad Dog? These questions continued to haunt me even after I got up and left him sitting in the cold room, staring out of the window into the lifeless blackness punctuated by flashing: *Mexicana Cant__*.

2:45 a.m. that night:
Mad Dog just came in. I could hear him staggering down the hall. He must be drunk again. I don't know if I told you, but he no longer sleeps with Marcia.

T-Rx: The History of a Radical Leader 160

2/24/70
Today I visited the Museum of Science and Industry. It's really an interesting place. I went with Hook and Marcia. We walked through a model of the human heart that was ten feet tall! We also toured a real German submarine. They have countless interactive exhibits. I always like playing with such gadgets. There was one machine in which you could play tic-tac-toe with a machine. The machine always wins or ties. I played five games with it and tied once and lost four times. There is something disturbing about getting beaten by a machine.

2/28/70
Today it was very warm for mid-winter—maybe 40 degrees. I spent the day by myself, walking in Washington Park. There are times when I feel very lonely. Being with these people sometimes increases my loneliness. I can only escape from loneliness through movies. Chicago State has free movies once a week. It's only a twenty-minute bus ride down Cottage Grove to the end of the line at 95th street.

      Ever since Mad Dog has begun drinking excessively, I have been unable to admit any drugs of any kind into my body—aspirin or anything. I'm sickened and afraid of what's happening to this man. He is killing himself. Why doesn't he pull out of it, or leave? Something is going to happen to him. He can't continue like this. I can't take it. Maybe I should do something. I don't know. What could I do? How do I know anything? I have enough trouble taking care of myself, let alone getting out of myself to do something for someone else. I know that this sounds terrible, Fred, but I'm taking days one at a time now. When I lay in bed at night, I feel a relief that I have gotten through another day. You know, this morning I was reading a comic book in the park about how it was in caveman days. You know, back then, everyone had to fight for his meat, and the savages would go days without any food. Then suddenly they'd kill a pig or something and gorge themselves. The average mortality age was something like thirty, since you had to be very quick afoot to stay alive. Sometimes I feel like that. There are just too many problems to cope with for me to be really happy.

You know, I was thinking about getting a part-time job. I don't need the money, but I would like to have something to do with my time. Now that we aren't protesting, this sitting around is for the birds. I'm on welfare, so there's a limit on what I can earn. But perhaps I could work four hours a day—say, mornings—so that I wouldn't have to make those monthly trips to the welfare office and fill out all those forms and sit in that dirty waiting room to change my status.

3/1/70
Marcia is very upset about Mad Dog. She isn't his woman any longer, but she still cares very much what happens to him. Even she doesn't seem to know why he is going off the deep end like he is. T-Rx continues to be restless, too. He asks me more and more questions about Mad Dog. You know that Rx used to be always on the move. Well now, he just vegetates and takes long walks. He isn't in to any social protests or anything. Just walking and thinking. This situation is getting very oppressive. It can't last too much longer.

3/2/70
Everyone is changed as a result of Rx and Dog. Hook isn't hustling dope anymore. Marcia isn't as happy and has gotten a job at the same place I work (*The Chicago Sun Times* and *The Chicago Daily News*). I feel suffocated where we are. If we could only get involved just like we were in Seattle, I'm sure things would begin to pick up. Well, I've been working on this letter for a while. I guess that I'll send it off.
Yours,
Larr

P.S. 3/3
Before I posted this letter, I had an unusual experience that I want to put in here. I was walking down the midway near the statue of Father Time when I saw none other than old Alf. He was with a couple other guys and he noticed me first. Alf has changed and was very friendly.

"What are you doing in Chicago?" asked Alf. His British accent had become Americanized.

"I was just about to ask you the same question," I replied.

"Well, I came here via New York."

"New York. Is that where you went after San Francisco?"

"No, I first went to Miami and then up to New York. I was working on a political campaign."

"Are you running for something?" I asked.

"Not me, but I was selling my services as a worker for some of the Democratic candidates running for President."

"President, why that's still two years away."

"Yes, but everyone is starting early. There's Wallace, Jackson, Humphry (again) and some guy named McGovern." Alf was wearing a white collarless shirt, black Nehru jacket, and tight jeans.

"McGovern?"

"Yes, he's an anti-War man."

I'd never heard of McGovern. I thought that guy from Maine—Ed Muskie, I think they call him—had it all wrapped up. But then the election is still two and a half years away. I turned to Alf and looked down at him (he's several inches shorter than I am) and said, "With all this time left, don't you think the War will be a dead issue?"

"Hell, no, there are hundreds dying each week, and the issue will never be buried as long as there are boys in Southeast Asia who are dying every day."

I was taken by Alf's dedication. He was never really *for* something, always *against* things; trying to get an angle for himself. This new image was totally contrary to the man I had known. I was hesitant about accepting this transformation until he told me that he had other motives besides the completely altruistic.

"There's good money to be made in the politics game. Why, each of those candidates have millions to spend and they are lavish about giving money in large quantities within the proper state. That is, one that is strategic in the sequence of primaries."

This seemed very odd to me that people would be starting for the nomination two years in advance and spending large sums of money on staffs to promote their image. It makes me wonder how these men (who are supposedly senators and governors as well) can find time to fulfill the job that they were elected to manage. If they are spending all of their time on the stump, who is carrying on their duties back home—in their state or in Washington?

Alf's honest confession that he was profiting from this vulgar display of ambition and politicking seemed to be closer to the man who I had known in San Francisco. Alf, who always chewed gum, was working his lower jaw at a furious pace as we stood atop the large grassy plain that separated the flow of traffic between the University of Chicago and the high crime district that lay to the south and west. I thought that he looked rather like an advertising man who was willing to sell anything for a dollar. He could turn on a persuasiveness that was generated by a rough vulgarity that came across as honesty. If he was on your side (trying to make a favorable impression) then there was little one could do about going along with him. There was some intangible quality that made you want to kick yourself, but still go along with him. This had nothing to do with really being convinced or conned, but simply that everything seemed out in the open, and his aggressive nature seemed to be less repulsive for it.

But then he surprised me by suggesting that we go have a beer at a place on East 55th. I accepted, even though, as I have told you, I have given up alcohol and all forms of drugs. The bar was very ordinary: U-shaped where everyone sat on stools. The lighting was low. Then there were a dozen tables or so scattered evenly around the remaining space for people contemplating eating. We sat at the bar.

"So, what are you doing these days?" asked Alf.

This question surprised me as I lifted the pint glass to my mouth. It seemed that Alf must know what had been happening to me; though upon examination, I could not give any coherent explanation why this should be so.

"Nothing." The word starkly reminded me that I wasn't doing anything. My time was just being wasted. My life--whatever that is . . . anyway, I remembered my job. "I mean, I work some, but it is part-time putting out the afternoon editions of the *Daily News* and the *Sun Times*."

"Well, that's good work. It allows you some exercise."

"Yes exercise," I replied. It doesn't pay very well, I knew that, but that hadn't made any difference to me until now. Alf hadn't said anything negative, but suddenly I felt that there was something to be ashamed about working hard at a job that doesn't pay much. But I am working for the fun of it. No that's not right, not the fun, but the time that it uses up. I want some of my time scheduled so that I don't have to think so much about myself. That's destructive, and I can escape all of that on the job where I'm forced to direct my thoughts towards what I'm doing.

"The pay isn't very good," I suddenly blurted. I don't know why I said that, because I didn't want Alf to know much about me. The more that was secret the better. Somehow, I think that anything that he has on you, he might *use* against you in the future if he has the chance. Not that a little thing like the salary that I earned on a part-time job could make any difference (I didn't quote a figure, but used a descriptive term that could mean different things to different people: a small amount might be different for Howard Hughes than for a Chinese peasant). Besides, when I withhold information like that, he has as much control over me as if he were using everything that he could against me: he would be controlling me in both cases. "—But I like it. It gives me a chance to think," I said, stumbling for some rejoinder to what I imagined he might say.

Now he was forcing me to defend myself. I didn't want to do this, but what could I do?

Alf didn't respond, but smiled. It was a low, condescending smile that showed his contempt for me and everything that I stood for. Though it wasn't a large grin, it stung like a sneer, being all the more degrading to me since I'd imagine that to an impartial observer it would appear that he was simply being friendly with no malice at all. But his intent wasn't in the smile itself, which was innocent enough, but in what was behind that persona of friendship.

"You see, I don't have much time for work. What with the group and all, you know—the marches and political work."

"You mean T-Rx and the group are in Chicago?"

I didn't want to say this. I wasn't in complete control. He was taking advantage of me.

"Yes. For a short time."

"Well, where are you all? I'd like to see you again."

I knew that he'd say something like that. How I hated myself for not seeing that he wanted that all along. But perhaps I'm being too unkind to him. I don't know. All defense seemed worthless. I told him where we were and he said that he'd stop over and see us some time.

We finished our drinks, and just before we left he said something that made me see just how long it had been since I'd seen him. "Is Mary with you?" He didn't know about any of it: not the strife, power leverage, nor anything else that had passed. He was completely innocent. This man, who had been her lover, didn't know anything about *her* or *us*. To him we were now the same as before. Since he hadn't seen the changes, he couldn't know how embarrassing his question was.

"No, she's gone." The words were simple. I felt that I had some power over him now. I knew something that he didn't.

"That's too bad," he replied, and then we departed. I smiled to myself as I jaunted to my work.

Larr

Chicago
March 1, 1970
Larry Cohen to Fred Abrams

Dear Fred,

Alf has come and made several visits to see us. He brings newspapers, a commodity that I could have easily furnished if I had known that they would have been welcomed. It seems that his rift with the group is mended and we may move in with him soon.
T-Rx is getting excited about the political situation in Vietnam. He says that Nixon promised to get us out of the War in '68 and now he is simply escalating the conflict. The depression has seemingly lifted from him. He is more active than previously. Perhaps the return of Alf has had something to do with it? I am finding life with the group to be more and more removed from my own experience than ever before.

I don't know how long I will stay with them. Marcia feels the same way as I do. She may return to San Francisco. We spend quite a bit of our free time together, talking, though I am discrete about it so as not to offend Mad Dog—not that I think that I am doing anything wrong. No, Mad Dog has long since relinquished his "right" to her. No one sees him much anymore, and often he does not come home at night nor eat with us.

Next morning:
Last night Mad Dog and Alf were out together. I've decided to get another job. I went around this afternoon and got a few leads. I want to work with other people.

3/4/70
I found a job with a bookstore. It's right in Hyde Park in the basement of a church. They call it the Seminary Co-op. (I like the idea of "co-ops"—patrons buy a share of the bookstore for only $10 and get a share of the profits at the end of the year.) It is perfect. I work as a cashier and help put books on the counters as well as talk with the people who come in. I have wanted to get back to books for some time because I have felt that I could use a little more education. Someday I think that I will go back and actually finish high school. There are so many times when I wish I understood more about what is happening. For instance, you know all the times I have been so "politically" involved, but I haven't really understood *why* I was doing any of it. Around the group here, nobody questions you about *why* you think a particular way unless it is contrary to the group's way of thinking.

Everyone espouses the same things. The only discussion used to be when Rx would berate someone for making an imprecise statement, but then whoever understood what he was talking about anyway? I usually copied the words down on the back of an envelope (or later in the spiral notebook that I purchased for noting important things). I would look at the words later, but I rarely understood their meaning. Maybe I'm just dumb, but I think that I have a real sensitivity for certain observations that many other people don't have. Marcia finished high school, and I feel that I'm as perceptive as she is. I only have one term to go, so that I could do it at night—if I had a day job, or vice versa.

3/5/70
I just spent my first day on the job. It is great. I met several very interesting people who put me onto some pivotal writers who I will read as soon as I get a paycheck (I'm just about broke, as I have been lending money to the group for expenses).

I haven't spent much time together with the group lately. But on occasion, I have overheard fragments of conversation. For example, they mentioned T-Rx's name and said something about "going off of the deep end." I don't know whether this comment was directly about Rx or not.

You know, when we first got to Chicago everyone was tied to Rx and we all were attentive to his every quiver, but now it seems that all of us are moving away from him and his depression and branching off into other things. Marcia and I have jobs. Hook has started practicing some numbers on his guitar at a local community center. And Mad Dog has taken to Alf. When Alf first stopped by, I thought that he might not fit in again. But he was accepted right away by Rx, and Mad Dog hovered around him like he was the solution to all the problems.

T-Rx has slipped back into his somber state, but is having more people over than ever before. Mostly they are black leaders around the area who come to talk about local problems and possible solutions. I don't know what it is about this man, T-Rx, but wherever he goes he attracts the attention of dissidents who seem to think that he can solve their problems. Rx talks some highbrow language with them and they just keep coming back with other people, ready to swear by his power to heal them all with his magic recuperative powers.

If you want to know my opinion, this place isn't the real world. I am not so impressed with the "truth" that is here, because in reality all these *profundities* are in some other dream world: a world that seems to be real when you talk with the genii, but dissolves when entering a hard, uncaring society that would just as soon see you starve as become rich. There is no such thing as the *caring* that Rx talks about. People get jobs to feed themselves. That is the reality of existence. No crap about "fulfilling" oneself or escaping the "alienation" of proletariat labor. When you become very good at whatever you do, then the individual can begin acquiring various other comforts like a wife, a car, and a house. They make one feel secure that he is away from the day-to-day struggle for survival.

I think it is natural to want security of this kind. Only a few nuts like T-Rx can live without any money. But are they really living without any money? I say not. Right now, for example, Rx is living off the money that Marcia and I earn. We all live off the generosity of Lockley Henderson (the man on the lease who invited Trek and his crew to crash). If we crossed him, he could kick us out into the street.

Somebody has to do the work. Society isn't going to give us a ride. Rx says that he can't work to support a society that is unacceptable to him, but what is the difference if he works or not? Doesn't he still reap the benefits of that society? Doesn't he depend upon people who *do* work in the society? What is the difference in directly supporting the society through work and indirectly supporting the society through accepting handouts from others who *do* work?

I think it is the same thing. If he doesn't like it here, why doesn't he leave? What's keeping him here?

This might sound as if I'm mad, but really I'm not. I just don't understand why some things are the way they are. I've always respected T-Rx more than any other person I've ever known, but the society that he creates around himself isn't a stable one. I think that it's bound to fail because it isn't real. It isn't unlike the things I see in the bookstore under the category of *fiction*.

3/3/70
"I haven't seen much of you lately," I said to Mad Dog as I saw him approaching the house just at the same time that I was coming home from work.

"We haven't had our old talks," he replied.

"Why don't we take a walk now," I suggested.

"That's a better idea than what I was going to suggest, namely going over to Lou's place to have a few drinks."

As we walked, I said to Mad Dog, "You are hitting the bottle a little harder than I used to remember you doing."

He didn't answer at first but started scratching his nose. "Yes, I do take more alcohol into me, but that's because I have taken more of other things into me as well." This statement made me very uneasy. Somehow I felt as if he was directing his response to me.

"Certain people have shifty ways about them. You don't know if you can trust them because they do things behind your back."

This clarification convinced me that he was referring to my seeing Marcia, though we were not on intimate terms. Still, perhaps he felt that he had some kind of right over her. But isn't a woman free to associate with whomever she pleases? I felt that Mad Dog's anger at me was unjustified. Perhaps I could explain things to him, but first I had to make him spell out all his grievances so that I could attack the worst allegations.

"I don't know what you mean," I said.

"Don't you?" he said in a voice that intimated surprise (whether real or feigned, I don't know). We had gotten to the top of the Midway and the statue of Father Time. We sat on a bench there. Before us was the entire Midway and then Lake Michigan.

"Do you think that people have been working against you?" By people, of course, I'm sure he meant *myself*. If this was his charge, I was sure that I could defend myself.

"Yes, Larr, you are working against me. That's one way to put it. Not listening to me is another form of sabotage. Or listening to me and ignoring me and doing something else is a third. When someone is extremely shifty, you can't pin them down."

"Do you have someone specific in mind or are you talking about the group as a whole?"

"One person."

Why was he playing this cat and mouse game with me? Couldn't he come right out with his accusation? If he'd only confront me, I could tell him my side of the story.

"Does he or she know who they are?"

"*He* should."

"How can you leave anything to chance? I think you should come right out and tell him. Perhaps there is some misunderstanding."

"I don't think there is any misunderstanding."

This was unbearable. Maybe this was the method that Mad Dog was employing to try and get even with me. His form of retribution was very cruel indeed. I wanted to confess and throw myself at his abounding mercy, but though a movie script might call for such a display of emotion, I felt that I was being wronged.

Where was my fair trial where I am entitled to be confronted by my accuser? If Perry Mason were here, I'd demand that my charges be summarily dropped because of illegal procedures on the part of the prosecution. *Your honor, we object to this entire proceeding on the basis that it is incompetent and immaterial; the witnesses and accuser will not come forward. My client will not sit here and wait for these whispers to materialize into real people. We move for a dismissal.*

"Then the case is dismissed?"

"What?" answered Mad Dog.

"If you have no case, then the judge has no choice but to decline to hear the state's case."

"What in the hell has the state to do with anything? C'mon Larry, don't give me *the business*. I don't know what to do."

I blew my nose so hard that it made a loud honking noise. The effect was comical (considering that it was added to what had just preceded it).

We both laughed.

"Larry. I don't know what I'd do without you sometimes. You know just how to put things into perspective. Even if this person does turn against me, I can always count on *you* being on my side."

We parted after a stimulating discussion about Chicago and all it has to offer the poor wandering soul. When l was alone, I pondered over his statement, wondering whether he was being serious or sarcastic. There could be no resolution from the data that I had at my disposal. In such instances, a person can infinitely review the inconclusive evidence that he does have or toss the whole thing up in the air and call it a day.

Bed: As I lie in bed writing this now, I have visions of plots and subplots: of Mary and of Mike, of Alf and of Mad Dog. What a crazy day it was a couple of years ago when I went to San Francisco with my bus ticket ready for an exciting time only to find that the "excitement" that I was looking for wasn't real. It didn't fill my emptiness. When I think of all the intrigue around this place, I can't sleep. It is only when I enter the world of my job at the bookstore that I feel any sense of normalcy that allows me to relax and feel that everything is in order.

I hope that you are peaceful tonight.

Larry

Chicago
April 1, 1970
Larry Cohen to Fred Abrams

Dear Fred,

I bet you thought this would be another long letter, eh? Well, April Fools!
Lawrence

Chicago
April 28, 1970
Larry Cohen to Fred Abrams

Dear Fred,

I'm working now full time at the bookstore. It's really a very good job. I have read some interesting books, mostly dealing with knights and their quests. I think that such literature is very interesting. I love to think about times when men went out and hunted for the Holy Grail; the innumerable jousts and such. I have also met a very nice man who comes in twice a week and we talk about King Arthur and his knights. I don't know anything about literature, and I'm sure that people who know what they are talking about would say that what I'm reading is just junk, but even if it is, I don't care. I enjoy it. The store has been expanding and I have been building shelves for them. I have a very good design sense within my head for structural position. This allowed me to come onto the idea to stack two rows of books on one shelf, by using a half-shelf screen behind the rear one slightly raised so that you can partially see what's there. The shelf can pull forward so that you can pick up the volume behind. This allows the store to double its possible volume offerings in the same space.

4/26/70
I had intended on telling you more about the bookstore, but an incident last night has caused me to change my plan and relate what happened. We were sitting in the front room (T-Rx, Alf,

Hook, and I) when three guys and a girl from some college came in.

"We heard that you are a real leader in these parts," said the girl. She was maybe twenty. She wore the uniform: blue denim shirt with the three top buttons undone and Levis. Her hair was blonde straw, down to her waist. She had a stern look on her face.

"I don't know about that," said T-Rx.

"Are you coming to New York for the protest against the War next month?"

"I hadn't heard that there was one."

"Damn straight. We'll tell you all about it."

So they sat down and we all talked. Rx thought that the protest sounded interesting. They were from some dinky school in Ohio—Kent State, I think it is. They were having their own rally in a week or so. They were telling us about how campuses across the country were fed up with the War—especially with the new lottery system, which was taking people before they could go to college. Trek decided that we'd head to Ohio next.

"The contradictions are amazing," said the boy. We were on the porch of a restaurant/bar in Hyde Park. The local college kids had taken over the joint. "If you come from a city where the local board can fill their quotas with poor people, then you're safe, but anywhere else, it's off to Vietnam, baby!"

"Yes sir," said another college student. "Step right up every Harry, Dick and Tom,/ You're next stop is Vietnam,/You know war's a lot of fun/See the world through the barrel of a gun/Send a letter to mom and pop/that they can be the first ones on their block/To have their boy come home in a box!/Whoopee!"

Apparently, the college student was also a poet. His piece had been memorized by the group. They began singing this chant. With the refrain:

> Oh, I'm going to see Vietnam
> From a view six feet in the ground,
> I'm going to fight for Uncle Sam
> In order to kill the slant-eyed man
> Oh what do I care, I don't give a damn
> I gave it all up for South Vietnam.

Oh, I'm going to see Vietnam
From a view six feet in the ground
Kill 'em dead for tricky Dick
Keep on killing till it makes you sick.
Oh what do I care, I don't give a damn
Lay it down for that black shirt, Uncle Sam.

The evening was exciting as the singing brought out some booze and grass and though I didn't partake, I was still caught up in the mood until the offer came for us to go to Kent State to help them with their rally. We could use the event to try and drum up college support for the New York March.

"The situation is getting worse. We're getting deeper into this thing all the time," said the poet. Rx agreed and all seemed beautiful until I realized that for me to go, I would have to give up my job. I didn't like the idea.

For some time I have wondered how long I would stay with the group. Perhaps this is the time to terminate our arrangement? (I know that certain people look to me for something, at least that is what they've said.) But I have to live by my own principles and they dictate to me that my job is a more real existence than flying all over creation, stirring up trouble. I may not understand all the political philosophy that they espouse, but I do know that the people who come into the bookstore aren't bad people and these are the ones that T-Rx (and people like him) are trying to unsettle. Why unsettle them?

Everyone laughs at the middle class, but why? If it wasn't for them, freeloaders like Rx wouldn't be given a meal ticket, but would have to be working at a job to get his moolah. What's the alternative? Never have I heard anyone talk about what they would do to replace the system that they are trying to tear down. Shouldn't there be some kind of model that everyone agrees to before you go destroying what you already have? What are they against, anyway? I don't know. Is the Government the evil that must be exorcised, or is it the people in the Government? Or maybe it is merely the attitudes of the people in their respective posts?

I know that mine isn't a very intellectual way of approaching this matter, and if I had any education, I'd probably be *with them* (since it seems that college students are the most

active members of this group). It must be that when you are educated, certain things become plain that the regular people don't understand. Well, that's all right with me, for I'm happy at the bookstore, and I don't intend to leave.
Yours respectively,
Lawrence Cohen

Kent State, Ohio
April 29, 1970
Larry Cohen to Fred Abrams

Dear Fred,

Bet you wonder what I'm doing here after I said that I would stay at the bookstore. Well, I don't know exactly myself the reason why I came. Everyone was going and Mad Dog and I had a talk. I have a lot of sympathy for that man. I think that T-Rx has been treating him unfairly. A conversation that I had with him just before making my decision might illumine what I mean.

We were back again on the bench beneath Father Time looking out over the Midway and onto Lake Michigan. It was an isolated bubble just a few blocks south of Washington Park. We were alone. It was late afternoon.

"He's out to get me," said Mad Dog.

"Who is?" I responded.

"You know, I talked with you about it before, T-Rx. You said that I should confront him with what I felt, so I did." At that instant you can tell exactly how I felt, Fred. During that earlier conversation, I had thought that Mad Dog was referring to Marcia and me, while all the time he was talking about T-Rx and himself. Then a horrible thought entered my mind: what if I had offered him the wrong advice?

This consideration made me shiver. A human soul was at stake. Out of my egotism, I had imagined that his problem had consisted of one thing—it was all about *me*! But now I know that it was more than that. I should have been more open with him about what I was asking. Instead, I meddled blindly (because I wanted to save myself from personal embarrassment!). There is nothing so despicable than someone who hurts another from an ignorance that *should* have been avoided, *could* have been avoided but *wasn't* due to self-interest—or really, more precisely, *cowardice.*

That is the short of it. I was scared of what he would think of me if I confronted him with something that I was probably feeling guilty about, i.e. seeing Marcia (even though I shouldn't feel guilty about it, which makes me wonder whether it is wrong because I feel guilty, or whether wrongness is measured by some other scale?). I had been seeing Marcia. We talked together. We supported each other. We weren't lovers, but sometimes that part of it can be rather trivial. Intellectual and emotional connections are a far bigger part of the picture.

I know people who are so hard that they can steal and feel nothing, yet isn't that a wrong? Feeling can have nothing to do with real wrongness, but then how does one cope with it? How can someone escape the neurotic fears and tension of guilt?

"Okay," I replied, being able to say nothing more. The late afternoon sun caused a shadow caused by Father Time to engulf us. It made me shiver a bit.

"I told him," continued Mad Dog, hardly waiting for my response, "that I didn't think we should go to Ohio or New York. There were too many risks. 'If you don't like the risks, then get out,' replied Rx to me. We were in that Greek restaurant down 57th almost across from Powell's bookstore. We were splitting a side order of spanakopita with that strong coffee they put in those small cups. I looked up to make my point, 'But Trek, you know that people are after your hide in the West and South. If you show up in any of those places you're risking getting badly beaten—up or worse.'

"'A person can't spend his time worrying about what might happen to them. That is the hold that the established order has over its subjects. They use it to constrain the general populace,' replied Trek. Then he got within an inch of my face—*me,* who has been with him forever, and said, 'I'm surprised that you are getting soft this way. I had always thought of you as stronger than that.'

"'I'm just the same as I've always been. I just don't like it here in Chicago,' was my reply. Then Trek sat back and ate one of the spinach rolls. He took on that Buddhist-like air of contemplation. Then he leaned slightly forward, 'We almost gave up the ghost in the South. Then those money-goons and the fanatics almost took us down in San Francisco. They followed us to Seattle. You've always been there with me, Mad Dog. We've almost died together a dozen times: what's changing now?'

"'*You're* changing, Trek. You aren't the same—none of us is the same. It would be strange if we were.'

"I took the last of the spinach and cheese rolls and washed them down with the strong coffee.

"'You're *the one who's changing,* Mad Dog. I know you can't see it, but that's because of your alcoholism.'

"What are you talking about?"

"'You know as well as I do, you come back to our place day after day, when you bother to come in at all, staggering about because you have swilled yourself with liquor. You are becoming a slave to it.' Trek's face was like stone. I replied to him, 'I am not.' Trek responded, 'You are and I'll tell you something else: Alcoholics aren't good security risks.'

"'What do you mean by that?'

"'I'll tell you. You become more attached to the bottle than you are to any of us and then you'll sell us out to our enemies.'

"'Ah, so you admit to having enemies?'

"'Of course I do, I'd be a fool if I didn't. It's just that I don't believe in crawling in a hole because of them, that's all. I will continue my work. I will continue—'

"Now it was my turn to get into *his* face. 'Who has been telling you all this about me?'

"'No one. I can see for myself.' I repeated my question—'Is it Hook, or Larry, or Alf or Marcia?'

"'None of them,' was his reply.

"Then I turned to go. But Trek said, 'You can come with us if you like, but I think that it would be better if we made a clean break.' I didn't respond.

"That's it, Larry. He wants me to go."

I was shaken by his speech. Mad Dog had been a close friend to T-Rx for such a long time. I didn't understand how they could apparently just split up the way that they did so easily. The surface motive of Mad Dog's drinking hardly seemed like motive enough. T-Rx's behavior was brutal, but Trek wasn't that kind of man. Something just wasn't right, but I didn't understand what it was. Maybe things were happening that I didn't know about? But

I felt that somehow I had a responsibility to try and help put things back together if I could.

"What are you going to do?" I asked.

"I have half a mind to just get out as he suggests," began Mad Dog. I was going to offer a note of protest, but he interjected before I had my opportunity.

"But of course, I won't. Rx is in trouble, and he doesn't know it. I don't like his going to this Ohio gig, just as I didn't like his leaving Seattle. If we are to be effective, we have got to stay in one city, preferably a smaller one where our independent work can have greater effect. He always agreed with me on that, but his thinking has gotten mixed up of late. He's changing some of his basic ideas. I can't let him do that."

Those words rung it my head: *I can't let him do that because I don't know what he means or what stops he plans to take.* What I do know is that Mad Dog is planning to go to Kent State on his own and then to follow us on to New York.

Addendum:
Well, now we are in Ohio, staying with some "hip" people just off the campus of Kent State. This is only the third campus that I've ever been on, and I wonder what it is like for you to be attending college. I wonder if I could ever have made it.

4/30/70
This Cambodia bombing issue is really causing a stir around here. People are afraid of what will happen. I've been to a number of sessions listening to what is happening. It's like we're getting to a tipping point. (I'm also trying to locate Mad Dog). During these talks, I keep hearing the same things over and over again. The United States is supporting a corrupt government in South Vietnam and Cambodia and that the Communists are only acting for the good of the people. They say that our government is quashing a popular revolution (much like our own revolution in 1776) and that such a stance is hypocritical. Also, it is being bantered about that the Vietnamese have the right of self-determination. They had an election when the French left in the 50s and the North won. Now we are trying to overturn the will of the people as demonstrated via the election box. Don't we stand for democracy? Why prop up a regressionist government just

because they agree to "be on our side."? I don't really understand these issues very well (owing to my lack of education, I'm sure), but I did get up the nerve to talk in one of the groups, and I'll relate to you some of the naïve things that I said.

"I have a question," I interjected through the clouds of marijuana smoke and incense. "You told everyone that every nation has a right to form a revolution to change its government, correct?"

"Hey, what is this?" asked one long-haired seated cross-legged on a pillow. He had a peace sign tattooed on his right shoulder.

"You're out of line, stranger," said another.

"There's free expression here, isn't there?" I asked.

"Certainly, were all for freedom," they all agreed, "but why are you disagreeing with what *we* have to say? We are saying the *legitimate* free thoughts. There are no others."

"I'm not stating an opinion, just asking questions."

"All right, go on," said Mr. Peace-tattoo.

"Well, since every government has the right to have a revolution or separate itself from another state, then doesn't South Vietnam have the right to separate itself from North Vietnam?"

"No. You see, North Vietnam is the legitimate government." Mr. Peace-sign made his right hand into the image of a gun and pretended to shoot me dead.

"Why?"

"1954 accords."

"Didn't they call for elections?" added a person in the corner who I couldn't see.

"Yes," said tattoo-man against me.

"And were elections held?"

"I don't know," said peace man.

"Well I'll tell you; they weren't. There could be no agreement as to the procedure so the countries were separated and each formed their own government: Diem in the South and Ho chi Minh in the North." The speaker was a stocky guy with a crew cut.
"Okay, so there are two countries. I still think that the conflicts between nations should be their business and not the business of its fascist neighbors."

My memory was triggered to Trek's questioning on the subject of fascism. I couldn't go there because I wanted to ask something else. "Well then, here's my question," I began to get back into the conversation. "Do countries have the right to invade others at will if they want to, such as South and North Vietnam?"

"Yes, I just said so," said peace-man.

"Even if they are separate countries as has just been clarified?"

"What do you want, a signed statement? I just told you so."

"Then what is the difference between the U.S. entering South Vietnam and the North Vietnamese?"

"Because we're imperialists."

"What's an imperialist?" I asked, since I couldn't discuss something that I didn't understand. There was general laughter at my ignorance.

"An imperialist," began the cross-legged guru in a condescending manner, "is a nation that enters another nation in an attempt to widen its scope of influence."

"You mean if one nation invades another nation to try and affect the way it will be."

"That's right."

"Like the Germans did in World War Two?"

"Correct." There was some general crowd assent.

"Like the Russians did at the end of the War?" I asked again.

"Ah, well, not exactly, but what does this have to do with Vietnam?"

"I'm just trying to get the principle straight in my mind. An imperialist nation is one that invades another to control them. What should a neutral nation do when it sees imperialism? Intervene as we all did against Hitler?"

The guru on the floor was getting smug now. He leaned back and laughed. "Now you're catching on."

"So when, by your very admission North Vietnam is imperialistic because it is invading South Vietnam, then the United States ought to come to its aid because it is the duty of other nations to help the victims of imperialism?"

The one on the floor screwed up his face. He didn't like my question. He thought that I was out of place and got up, yelling, "If you think that I'm going over to Vietnam to fight for some two-bit government, then you are out of your fuckin head! I'm not going to die for any slanty-eyed Asian."

T-Rx: The History of a Radical Leader 180

There was general cheering and everyone broke into an anti-war song, which I can't remember except for a line in the chorus that went: *I ain't goin' to take no gun/ screwin' girls is much more fun.*

11:30 p.m.

Just saw Mad Dog. Things are very disoriented. I didn't find him, but he found me and in the oddest circumstances. I was walking back from one of these discussions when I heard a hissing noise. I turned around and saw a hand out of the shadows beckoning me. The body that was presumably attached to the hand was partially behind a dense bush. I didn't like it— thinking that someone might be trying to get me for asking the wrong types of questions earlier in the day. But then I heard my name. "Larry, it's me."

The whispering sounded familiar, so I made my way into the shadow. To my surprise, I found Mad Dog hiding behind the bush. "What are you doing?" I asked. "I've been looking all over for you."

"So have some *other* people."

"I don't understand."

"T-Rx is out after me."

"Trek? I don't believe it."

Mad Dog was talking nonsense, I was certain of it. But there was a frantic nature to his voice that assured me that he was very serious in what he was saying.

"It's true. I've been fingered by that traitor, Alf. Rx has got a fellow named Locke, whose purpose it is to extinguish me."

This news completely disoriented me (as it still does, which is why I just had to write it down in my notebook—though this required leaving the bush for a moment.) I had to write it down so I could refer to it later—you know my memory needs help to keep it accurate.

But the question still rocked my worldview: why would Rx want Mad Dog dead?

The question had no logical answer. "Why, Mad Dog? Why?" I then went back into Mad Dog's lair. It was Mad Dog who started talking first.

"I don't know about any of this. You never know when the schism becomes irrevocable. I suppose I just haven't allowed myself to accept it. . ." His tone dropped off as his head sagged down and he closed his eyes. Then, suddenly, he grabbed my shoulder and looked at me pleadingly. "He's not going to destroy everything that we've worked for; I won't let him." The words were spoken in a frenzy. I could feel the strength of his fingers as my shoulder throbbed with pain. He really meant what he was saying. I could not doubt his sincerity now. His condition made me afraid. I thought about how I felt when I heard that Mike was in trouble: the police, the running—memories that I had hoped were long since dead, were now only too real. It seemed that history was re-running itself before my eyes.

Mad Dog and Rx, just like Mike and me: friends betraying one another. But Mike and I really didn't split, it was just my failure to have a level head in a time of crisis. I was the one who caved. I didn't have the calm courage. I tried to do what I could, but that wasn't good enough. And now Mike's dead.

5/1/70: 1:00 am.
I've tried as hard as I can to sleep, but the attempt is useless. This place is intolerable for me. I've got to go.

9:00 am
It's going to be another day of demonstrations against Nixon's Cambodia policies. I hope that we are effective. I hear that other campuses across the country are doing the same thing. This is really something. It's so important, and to think that T-Rx has had something to do with this mobilization. There are firm plans to go to New York starting tomorrow. We will stay at Columbia University. I wonder if this is really the start of something big. The whole movement is just so incredible that one can become lost completely. I don't know what to say.

Nothing new about Mad Dog. He has gone underground. I wonder whether he has decided to leave or not.

Evening
I don't know what has happened. I know I won't have much time to write. All of them are out to assassinate Rx. The thought that worries me is whether Mad Dog is behind it.

5/5/70

Marcia and I are in Minneapolis. We read about the students who were killed at Kent State, but I'm sure that they weren't the prime target: T-Rx was. This was no random shooting incident, but a planned attack on T-Rx, by some group. They say that both he and Mad Dog have been flown to a special hospital in New York for treatment. They aren't too clear on the details.

I don't know who instigated this—maybe Alf or his henchman, the mysterious Mr. Locke? Was Locke a part of the Ohio National Guard? One bullet fired might have triggered shots by his cohorts—were they also in on it? Probably not.

I remember it all. The rally was set to begin at noon. On the way there, they were handing out leaflets that said the rally had been cancelled. But Trek said that was a ruse.

I was standing in front of a two-story building. I was near the back of the crowd but I could see the military men. There was a long line of them. They were wearing gas masks and carried rifles. They looked like they were ready for combat.

Then there was a chant of "Pigs off Campus" and canisters of tear gas being thrown by both sides. There was confusion and running. I didn't follow the crowd over the hill or to the athletic field. I wasn't alone.

But most of the people went that way or over to the Commons. I didn't want any part of it. I wanted safety and was in a small group of about six people who wanted out. We didn't know what to do. Then we heard a single shot from one source followed by rounds of shooting from a different direction.

I heard the shots. Then I saw Hook running toward me. The next thing I know, he tells me that someone is shooting at Rx, and he's been hit. Further, that we had better flee for our lives. I turned to Marcia. She had followed my path. Marcia and I turned to go, but Hook went back for the rest of the group.

As the haze of shock wears away, I wonder if we should have stayed around to try and help Rx or not. I don't know what we could have done. We have no specialized medical training.
I don't know what we will do *now*. The group is split-up for good. I'm sure of that.

You know, I'm beginning to like coffee quite a bit. I think that I'll come back out west, maybe to Oregon or perhaps Washington.—Larry

Tacoma, Washington
August 6, 1970
Larry Cohen to Fred Abrams

Dear Fred,

I have a job working in an auto garage here in Tacoma. You know, the people I work with are the nicest people that I've ever known. Marcia left to return to San Francisco where she had a number of friends. She and I just wouldn't have worked out; I know that now. With Trek gone, another chapter in my life has passed. I sometimes wonder whether there was something that I could have done to help. But thoughts like that don't move anyone forward. I've got to move on. And so I have.

The people that I work with are very genuine people with no pretensions or phony admiration for being educated. I can enjoy the things that I like and not feel ashamed of it. I'm dating a girl named Jan. Can you believe it! She's just the kind of girl that I've been looking for: uncomplicated and not one to take life too seriously.

I'm tired of asking so many complicated questions. It's time for me to enjoy myself because, after all, what is life all about if not to be happy?

Sometimes on the weekends I go to the Tacoma Cubs minor league baseball games. I think that life will be comfortable here. I haven't heard a word from any of the group nor do I desire to. The only one that knows where I am is Marcia, and I'm sure that she wouldn't say anything. If you are ever over this way, come up for a visit. I'd be glad to have you.

Best ever, and drop me a letter sometime (my address is on the envelope).

Your friend,
Larry

Part Two

The Diary of Mary Taylor: May 25, 1969

Dearest Diary (or however you wish me to address you): blank page of white coldness, I have tried to court you before, but with always the same result—nothing. However, I haven't learned a thing from the experience, as is evident from my continuance, eh? *How now, my dear, but why aren't you in college?* What an impudent diary! You had better hold your tongue; you know that your entire existence is in my control. If I choose to stop writing, you are only another pad of paper. You must cower with due respect that one in my position can command.

Indeed! My affairs are my own business and what I tell to you is my right (or more precisely that prerogative) which I have condescended to share with you. No more idle questioning about the fate of dear Macalester College. It is what it is: one of the most heavily endowed private colleges of its size in these fifty states (thanks to *Reader's Digest* money from a grateful alum). But let the drums beat a roll, and heralds blow their trumpets, for Sam Stern is now a relic of the past. No more fawning about such paltry legacies, my dear Faustus, for whither does it fly?

May 27, 1969
I fly to San Francisco so that my heart, never given completely to anyone (not even Sam), may find a new home, Tony Bennett. If the lesson of love's infiniteness (or is it lover's infiniteness? *Les mêmes* perhaps?) is that between words and deeds, the former shall always outdistance the latter. Then there is the bustle of the

hippie haven of love and flowers. Shall San Francisco become the home of this Ferdinand the Bull?

May 28, 1969
A real cool cat. Oh yes, I have met someone that has eyes for me. What a compliment to a woman for a man to look at her with eyes that say that he wants to carnally know her. Such beasts these men are. They have straw for brains. Amazons unite and kill these plebeians.

I have heard a name. Just a whisper at first, but now it portends things greater: "Rex." 'The king' in Greek. I must visit the king of the city and accept the proverbial keys, if such a cesspool as San Francisco has such implements, though one can't imagine why? There could be no gates, since the barbarians avoid this corrupt, lascivious den with firm resolve. So what am I doing here? I have joined the foreign legion *to forget*, but what am I to forget? I suppose that I have forgotten.

June 1, 1969
Most beloved book upon whose virgin whiteness I now deflower with the blackness of learning and truth, let the vileness that is *male* cease to spread throughout all creation so that the earth might not be the only such infected planet.

"But the blacks and the women of this country are in the same position," said one pompous long-haired male.

"I don't know about that," replied another, who was a copy of the first: long hair to the shoulders, blue shirt with button-down collar, and bell-bottom jeans. These iconoclastic individuals wore the uniform of the times. They are all interchangeable.

A third in the group was a young black man with a medium "fro." He put in, "I think all whites have privilege that is denied to blacks. You haven't been there, so you know nothing about it."

"What do you mean?" replied the first again. "Do you think that because you are black that you have it any worse than a woman who is white?"

"When were you ever stared at because of your color?"

"When were you ever stared at because of these milk glands that you yourself have bared and devoured with savage appetite?"

"That isn't fair," said the young black man.

"Of course it isn't. What is fair in this life? Do you think Sam cares whether life is fair or not?"

"Sam? You mean Uncle Sam?" The original interlocutor started pulling at his aspiring moustache.

"Yes, of course, Uncle Sam Stern. Some say that the heart of this country resides in Minneapolis."

"I don't follow you."

"Of course, that's because you are an angry canine," replied the second white copy.

"That isn't my real name."

"It isn't? Well, you could have fooled me. I thought that perhaps it was given to you by your slave master and that you still use it to tell women how lucky they are with their lot in life," put the first copy.

"You certainly have quite a bit of hostility, don't you?"

"Yes, don't you?"

June 6, 1969

Making love with a Negro man was a first for me. You know, a person spends so many years protecting herself from the male jackals. It's all about a state of being: virginity. But when that's gone, then there's an attitude change—and a good thing too, Sam. You were a crud, but at least I was freed from that illusion.

Somewhere in the cold environs of the land of ten thousand lakes is a man who has something not his. It is something that he stole as part of a contest that is run on the principle of breaking the spirit of a whole generation of women.

How can a woman get on in this world dominated by men? I don't know how to describe the ingenious manners in which this wholesale prostitution of a whole segment of the population occurred, but it has, through subtle political maneuvering and generations of brainwashing. Only now are women of the world finally becoming aware of the horrible atrocities that have been lavished upon them by power-seeking men.

Women have always stood for what is highest in people-kind. *Les femmes,* (perhaps) a more suitable substitution for the sexist name 'woman,' must now arise. We must learn the tricks that our captors have been using on us for generations. We must become free.

June 8, 1969

Again I see the Negro with the moderate afro hair. His name is Mad Dog. I find that black men can be just as oppressive as white men. I thought that perhaps they wouldn't be since they must know the cruel results of oppression, but now that things are loosening up for them, they would just as soon leave the rest of us in bondage.

Once free, no one remembers anyone. I learn daily of a man who seems different from others, his name is T-Rx. It sounds like a dinosaur. Perhaps he is one. Only then will I be able to talk with a man who isn't a tyrant. I must find a man who lived during the great gynarchies of old, when the earth mother ruled with feminine justice over men and women equally. Is it a return to the age of the dinosaurs that I must allow myself to be transported to. Back to Mesozoic grandeur, I will return to find a time before the Fall.

Now gracious amazon, what shall you do with this slave named Stern?

"Put him to death," she commanded.

"Yes, your highness, but how shall we do it?"

"Smear his body with honey and let the ants eat him alive. It is the only way to deal with such perversity. My punishments must be stern or they won't be obeyed."

June 7, 1969

A pamphlet a day keeps the doctor away. I must have handed out more than a thousand leaflets today about the War in Vietnam. I can see several sides to this issue. It is true that we are imperialistic aggressors that have no business being where we are, but on the other hand, it kills thousands of men. That's an upside for the women of the world.

June 13, 1969

I have met with Him. I'm not sure whether He is the prescription (Rx) that will cure me from my anxiety about being someone, but this person is no ordinary man. T-Rx, ancient Greek medicine man—do you think he knew Hippocrates or Galen? He is a shaman who is ruthlessly impartial in his bitterness. I believe that he hates the problems that I do *as much as* I do (if that were possible for a man to do). He is a misfit, a woman-in-spirit born into a man's body. I want him in every way, but as yet he wishes to keep our relationship on the spiritual level. This man understands me.

June 14, 1969

I don't think that I wish to remain any longer with Mad Dog. He is not a man who can get outside his personal problems; namely that he is of the wrong sex. All that he can talk about is that he is black. Why must people advertise what they are? *Mon Dieu!* My private journal: please let me sink quietly into the sunset as the camera rises on the truck and the streets of the western set that are seen in third-person-omniscient. Oh, John Ford—you silent man, where have all the cowboys gone? Well, they are wearing black skins and walking around with macho problems worse than some of the sickly whites, yellows, reds, and purples. These are atmospheric effects that defy maestro Turner, academy or no academy.

Enough of this private babbling. I can save that for my letters or the envelopes that I rip open along with the checks from home every month.

Oh, Daddy dear, how can I thank you for your overwhelming generosity for keeping you daughter dear supplied with what you never had as a youth growing up in such hard times? Hard Times, ah yea, the notes ring dear. Depression days here I come, back with John Wayne and John Ford and the rising camera taking pictures of that paycheck that keeps me in bad habits.

June 15, 1969

"What's your name again?"

"Larr." This is a retiring lad. He has some acne on his reddish-colored skin. Probably of Scottish descent. Doesn't really comb his curly hair. I wonder whether that is a metaphor of who he is? We were in the condemned warehouse that this group calls 'home.' They don't really have rooms, but they have a common area and then in a semi-circular pattern they have constructed little private areas with pieces of wood or other debris they have found on the street to mark off their own space.

"Larr, what a queer name."

"Watch it." Mr. curly hair lifted his shoulders as if in affront.

"Watch what?"

"Calling me a queer."

"Who called you a queer?"

"You did; I heard you."

"Boy, are you stupid, defensive, or endowed with a wry sense of humor? I said that your name is queer. I never said anything about you as a person."

"A person is their name."

"How's that?"

"I said a person is his name. There is no difference between the *name* and *personality,* for one expresses the other. If I pronounce your name properly, that is, the way in which you do, then I will say something about what you are as a person in the inflection that I use. Others may use different inflections, but then they are reflecting their opinion of you in the different usage." The boy gestured with his hands as if he were talking to an audience instead of a person he's just met.

"I think I get it, you're saying that when I'm characterizing your name as queer, that I'm asserting that you're queer?"

"Yes." The boy smiled. He must have deep inferiority issues.

I don't mind admitting, dear diary, that I found this confounded nominalism to be the mark of either a poorly-educated mind or someone who is playing the Noël Coward light bantering act. I decided not to underrate this curly redhead and so I replied, "What if I say my name several times with a different accent each time?"

"That depends on whether you were serious or not. If you were serious, then you'd have a multiple personality, but if you were joking it would simply be another form of humor. We all tell jokes from time to time where we are the butt of the humor." Then the head of Larr[d] began nodding. He felt very assured at what he took to be either intelligence or clever repartee.

This conversation really happened, Diary! I'm telling you no lie; why would I lie to you when I share such secret feelings with you? There now, now that you believe me, let me continue. I responded with what might be aptly termed as a horrendous belly laugh that I felt coming for what seemed like the longest and most awkward of moments, but once it burst from that suppressed reservoir it exploded, and reverberated about the corners of the spacious common room and echoed against those aged red brick walls even to the wood-beamed ceiling.

Then this Larr[d] began to laugh, too. It was at that moment that I knew that he was no Noël Coward. This was a simple, small-town boy. I made a mental note to treat him with gentleness. He was not a door to power, but he was not the enemy either. It was like I met a child in a man's body. I like children. I will leave this one alone.

6/24/69

Today the world is bright sunshine. I will reflect on what has so often become of poor little me. I have been a victim of a male dominated society which is at war with its female citizens, who are in perpetual retreat. No one believes in anything. This might be a good thing, for then there will be no stupid dogmas to color the communal vision with false images of lies pretending to be true.

What worries me is the low level of intelligence that is generally exhibited among people who supposedly are devoted to change. For example, the den of the most influential member of the protest movement in San Francisco, T-Rx, is filled with second-class minds. Only their leader is of truly worthy material. As evidence of this opinion, I wish to offer a conversation which I had in said group. As result of this interchange, I came away with the impression that this cadre is little more than a collection of intellectual dwarfs.

We were in the largest space of the common room. It is a place that is defined by a collection of carpets picked up on garbage day around the city. They are put together so that they form a square. There is no continuity in their patterns or their pile. Only their composition together in an approximation of a square gives them continuity. They are a break from the concrete floor of this old warehouse that is now housing radical anti-War squatters.

On one side was a white guy with long hair. He has a Jewish nose, but I think he's really Italian. He fancies himself as a soft-rock singer and goes by his stage name: Captain Hook.

Hook was standing in the center of the carpeted square and asked of those present, "What do you think about the march?"

"Sounds like quite an idea, eh?" replied a girl who was just above the height of a dwarf. She had hair that was dyed red and green. They said her name was Alice and that she, also, came from Minnesota. She had the hots for a thin, Norwegian guy with short, really blonde hair and expression that showed that he was eternally "out to lunch." The guy was the *babble-express*. His group name was "The Prophet." (I wonder what the Moslem members of the peace movement might think about *that*?)

"It should be on a grand scale," replied an outsider, who no one looked at. He had very tawny-blonde, Michael Caine hair. His accent was also British. I later found out his name was 'Alf.'

"What will it accomplish?" asked yours truly.

"Accomplish! Why, it will help bring an end to the War in Vietnam," replied Hook with enthusiasm.

"How's that, Mister Hook?" queried Alf.

"Well, by showing the government how committed the people of this country are. The government is only given leave to operate by the people, and when the people make known their feelings about a particular subject, then government officials *must* listen."

There was general agreement to this ludicrous statement. How can they expect a state that is built upon powerful special-interest groups to do anything when confronted by random demonstrations of peaceful people carrying placards? What is needed is *organization*. If various local movements were linked together through a national network, then the dissidents would control some real power. As it stands now, they will be ineffectual because there is no coordination in their efforts.

A demonstration is an act like anything else. It cannot be a disorganized expression carried out by teens and those in their twenties carrying homemade placards. No. To be effective, marches have to be choreographed by a leader who is attuned to all the nuances that might affect the total effect.

On the local front, I have decided to move in with the den of stupid people, because there is nothing better to do with my time. They live on a low level, but I will supplement my meager meals with them by partaking in restaurants on my own. I've opened a bank account, as I've a comfortable surplus just now.

Oh, by the way, dear diary, drugs are cheaper in the land of happy flowers.

6/25/1969

I'm very depressed today. Things aren't working out the way that I'd like them to. Whatever I try, I keep getting screwed up by this male-dominated society. Why won't they leave me alone? Why are they all on the prowl for a woman 24 hours a day?

This Larr reminds me of a child. He sits by the water all day and watches the ripples flow. I don't see how he can stand it. Doesn't he see the garbage that abounds in that bay? The very thought makes me want to retch.

6/30/1969

Let me talk about my relationship with T-Rx. He is a possible candidate for the position of national leader, as I've described. He seems to be well-connected with groups of all description, from the violent radical to the pacifist singers of "Kumbaya."

First, a description of him alone. The man is of medium height: 5 foot 11 inches—or so. He is thin—perhaps 160 pounds. But he is wiry; I've seen him show surprising strength. I'm told he is an effective fighter, using surprise to keep his opponent off-balance.

His complexion is sallow and he has long, curly hair that he pulls back with a red rubber band into a ponytail. He also has an odd habit: at times he consciously inhales sharply and then looks up to the sky. This is a peculiar ritual about which I'm totally baffled.

Nonetheless, Rx seems to be a committed man, who lives idealistically toward non-involvement with the government. He is always for the rights of the underprivileged and has a great amount of energy for protest work. But his major drawback is that he has no personal vision.

"Trek," I began as we sat together on the lawn of the Court Building. "This march can be a big thing, you know."

"Can it?" he replied, almost smiling.

"Yes," I replied, "I want to help if I can."

He was silent for a long while and then replied, "What can I do you for?"

Now, coming from anyone else I would take such a comment as an insult, but from T-Rx it was a sincere question. He was giving me the questionnaire that has a blank for "useful skills and previous experience."

"My favorite subject has always been economics," I told him truthfully. I have had quite a bit of experience with financial matters. Anyway, I know that the heart of any operation is its financial structure and if I were to influence this future messiah, it must be through some tangible means such as financing—for without a strong financial base no aspiring political figure has a chance with promoting his particular cause (you know, it takes almost a million dollars to back a successful Broadway Musical).

"We don't really have a financial sector," he said.

"What do you do with your money?"

"We don't take in money, really. I mean, the local groups handle it themselves."

"But how do you know that it is being distributed equitably?"

"I don't."

"But doesn't that disturb you?" His attitude dismayed me. How could he allow himself to be the head of an organization of which he didn't have complete control? He was the organizer of this march and yet he held his coalition together more loosely than the Articles of the Confederation held these 13 colonies together one sunny eighteenth century day. Didn't he know that his following might be rife with internal disorder unless he created strict regulations that might order them? Why, with no idea of what one hand is doing, he is leaving himself open for anyone or any group to throw his entire operation into chaos! The principle is simple: a leader is responsible for what goes on in his sphere of command.

To insure responsibility, a leader must maintain tight control over his group or else he won't be able to manage what goes on beneath him—though he *will be* responsible for such outcomes.

This T-Rx seems to think that it is some kind of virtue to not be interested in organization, but I'll tell you, it's folly. He gave me the sole office of handling what little money they had and doing with it what I thought best. I accepted this position with great enthusiasm. I don't know what I'll do with the position, but I do know that I am now in a leveraged situation in which I can control this leader of the people.

July 1, 1969

I have been in contact with the Young Socialists League, and they want to join our March. But they want some of the issues that they consider important to be represented in the March, such as the imperialistic, capitalistic nature of our country as it stands. A few other groups that also seem allied to these causes are connected with Stalinist Factions. They want to lend support if they are given leave to respond to any intimidation by the police. All they want do is protect us as we march. I don't see why Trek will deny their requests.

Also, I have a lead on a big source of money: a feminist group of rich housewives who want a part of this event. They are willing to put up ten thousand dollars to be in the demonstration and conduct themselves according to their own philosophy (which I'm not familiar with, but I suspect is some kind of sensationalism for them).

What I need is a large donor of money. I don't know what I'd do with it, but if the larger vision rolls out, then money is what we'll need. I have been giving some thought to my plan to organize some kind of cohesive national unit. The idea is still fresh in my head, but I have these collections of impulses which might set out the structure for such an organization.

7/3/69

Tomorrow is the big day. I have to meet with a couple of groups that want to be in our demonstration. I don't think I'll go through Rx, since he was so disagreeable the last time that I came in with some people. He's hung up on the idea that this is a decentralized effort: a kind of show of the people who spontaneously come together for a common cause—such as ending the War in Vietnam. The notion is that if it is a groundswell of people getting to their feet with little organization, then it somehow shows the *will of the people.*

How stupid! Sometimes I think that he has a too-limited vision to be the man that I want him to be. What drives me forward is the deep feeling within me that I've got to succeed. All day I've been thinking about my life and how I haven't done anything. That's why I left college. I wasn't accomplishing anything there. The main purpose of my college was a group of boys trying to seduce a smaller group of girls. I fell for the bit. I admit it. I thought that what I wanted was a home in Edina with two cats and a child and a half—but how wrong I was. The bow of that vessel toward my future turned out to be the stern: what I took for my voyage to the future was really just my vision of the past. Such pain cannot be endured more than once. Each time it has to become less. I will not fall for any more *lines* from that species of three-legged creatures again.

Success. Yes, that's the ticket—to make a name for myself. How sweet the feeling of power is. When I see these yahoos on television being treated with so much respect and living in such absolute luxury, I could just scream. Here am I (much more deserving than any of them) and because I am unknown I'm sitting here in front of a blank sheet of paper hammering out letters that fit into some coherent pattern—for what? If I become famous, then these words will be invaluable. I can sell them for a dollar a word. Just think of all the money that I've made so far on this thing!

But all that is *potential* money, *potential* grandeur based on possibilities that are as remote as my inventing the light bulb. No, chances are I will sit the bulk of my life in the shadows of large steel and glass structures. How many thousands of people want to become powerful and are doing something about it? But what am I doing about it? I just play around with these small-time people who have empty heads and as much imagination as a corpse.

If only I had a few hundred thousand, then I could get control of a sizeable group. After putting the principal into a municipal bond or mutual fund to bring me 8%-10% interest, I'd have thirty or forty thousand each year guaranteed with which to operate. I could get a loan off of my principal and raise a small army to do my bidding. Within a matter of a few years, I could be the most powerful person in the United States.

Dreams, all dreams, but they could happen—though the chance of me ever getting more than the 500 dollars-a-month check from my father are rather slim. How I hate these checks. I hate all that they stand for. Sometimes I feel like using the money to hire a killer to take care of my old man so that I can net all of his money. But I don't want a cent of it. I despise him and all his money and the system that gave it to him. He thinks he can control me with his green bank roll. Well, he may have had influence over me in the past, but no more. I have had such a hard time separating what I think from what he wanted me to do that I often times don't really know what my own mind is.

I can only sigh when I think of the worms he put squiggling in his hook as he fished for more money. If he hadn't hated those worms, then I probably wouldn't despise him as I do.

Worms, all! My father, the troller of bottom fish, and all his unhealthy catch have caused the acne scars that are on my temple. I used to obsess on the way he made his money—and yet I lived on it, and I still do!

> Now I lay me down to sleep,
> Hope my thoughts don't turn to the creep
> Or clots of blots so full of worms.
> Leave this tread, the tire is growing thin,
> And live in a coffee can that is round

(This is a line of poetry that I heard once in the Twin Cities).[58]

It is my guess that there should be four regional groups: West, Mid-West, South, and East. Each region should have a leader who would preside over the local organizations within each state. The leaders of each region would sit on a national council that was headed by a central committee and a president. I think that T-Rx would be a candidate for president, or at least West Coast Leader. This organization must be built up a little at a time.

7/5/69

"Did you like that?" I asked him.

"Yes, I suppose so."

"What kind of answer is that?" was my reply.

"An honest one."

"Don't you know that there is no honesty among lovers and worms?"

"What do worms have to do with it?"

---

[58] I could not find the source of these lines that I could verify. One person in the English Department at Georgetown University thought they came from an obscure poet named Michael Boylan.

"I was just quoting a poem." Of course he didn't get it. How could he?

We sat up and put on our clothes. There was a lazy quality about him that I found rather distracting. I longed to see him excited about something—anything. Why was life such a bore to him? Was this a type of ennui, or something else? I couldn't tell, but I needed to ask him. "Your March was a great success."

"Was it?"

"Of course it was."

"I didn't include your all of your people."

"I know," I said rather testily.

"Doesn't that make you angry?"

"I can take it." I didn't like his attitude. He thought he could put on his little Buddhist act—or whatever it was—and win me over. That's just another power play. And I'm not going to be anybody's bitch. I do what I want, when I want. Period.

"That's not what I asked you." I looked at my one-night-stand. His hair was disarrayed. The rubber band was gone. We were in the most private of makeshift cubicles. But this only afforded visual privacy. And I was acutely aware of that.

"Yes, I suppose that it made me a little perturbed."

"I thought so."

"What do you mean by that?"

I wanted to tell him how he'd missed a large opportunity to get support from a group that had been working separately with the anti-War groups for some time. (Let's call them ABC investment group—a capital investment company [not their real name]). It was a chance for big bucks. They wanted *in* to this group of committed young people. They thought that this student protest thing was only a fad, but they wanted to play on their camaraderie.

Their angle was toward making contact with this large group of soon-to-be middle-aged people who, after the long-term struggle, they might target for a marketing place for these wannabe activists. They were also interested in conventional marketing schemes within the mainstream capitalist economy as well. It was their vision of the *revolution road.*

I didn't know quite how to play them, but I'd gotten support from The Worker's Liberation Front. They were a conventional leftist group (whose mission is part conviction and part profit-marketing). I thought I might end up on top with them.

It would take a large contribution from some loan makers (or at least a promise of a contribution) in the Bay Area to move forward with my plan. I felt rather good, so that no amount of blubbering from T-Rx would put me off my guard.

"You're such a pushy woman," he said as he got dressed.

"Thank you," I replied.

"That wasn't meant as a compliment," he retorted. I could tell that he was getting a little testy. I ran my fingers through my hair to get out the snarls.

"Oh, I'm sorry then." I don't know why I said that.

"No need to be sorry; that's your nature."

I looked up at him and grimaced.

"Oh really?" I retorted with an edge to my voice.

Trek twisted his head with both hands in feigned ignorance. This was an odd approach for him to make.

I didn't understand him. Was he trying to alienate me? Or was this merely his form of blunt honesty: he said whatever he felt in the moment without regard for what someone else might feel around him. No matter. I was immune to his barbs. No amount of needling on his part could make me hate him.

Even if there wasn't anything personal between us, he was still an integral part of my plan. This man had so many contacts that it would take quite a while to duplicate the work that he has amassed in such a long period.

The conversation changed to other things of a more mundane nature as we walked through the streets of San Francisco. There had been something strange about that day that I couldn't elucidate precisely; it was if someone had been watching us. I wondered whether Rx was being bugged by the FBI? Whatever he was or not, the residual feeling gave me a very uneasy sensation. We had walked up Nob Hill near Grace Cathedral when we stopped in a little park that was set up for children. We sat down on a bench.

"What's next?" I asked.

"Nothing," was the reply as his voice lingered over the vowels. This man was always pronouncing words in the most peculiar way. He would emphasize certain syllables or vowels or consonant clusters as if his new way of pronouncing the word acquired a unique meaning. Perhaps he thought he was a poet? I don't know. But the sound came out (nu th—eeeeenng).

"Oh-eee," I said, trying to mock him, but he apparently didn't catch my meaning because he continued to move his eyes about as if he were looking for something. After an unbearable silence, I became interested in his encore. Then he inhaled sharply. I wondered whether this was a voluntary or involuntary act.

If there were to be an organization, then it must have something to do.

"Shall we have another protest next month?"

"Maybe we'll have one *today*." Trek didn't smile, but merely tilted his head. His unkempt curly hair met his bare shoulder in an uneven distribution with the bulk draping down his back.

"C'mon, Rx, you know what I mean. Another *big* protest, like we just had. Shall we plan another?"

"Would you like to organize it?" Trek lifted up his chin.

I couldn't detect whether this was a serious rejoinder, or merely banter. He hated organizing things; this I knew. He was at his best when he was in the position of a leader. But what an odd leader. He didn't go after taking control in the conventional way of Eisenhower or Patton. Instead, he was like a Zen master who would sit on his mat, contemplating nothingness.

I'm not sure whether this is a permanent problem. Can a Buddhist really lead a rebellion? I'm not too up on Buddhism (I skipped the Comparative Religion Class at Macalester) but I think they're about *desire* or something like that. I don't know about Trek, but I *thirst* for power to actualize who I really am. I'm a *woman leader*. I'm a leader of people who happens to be a woman. Get used to it—those of you who carry a "Y" chromosome. "X X" can rule the world! Those who tell you any different are slave masters.

Trek claims to know nothing about the political decisions that have to be made when large groups of people are melded together for the purpose of changing our government. I decided to take him at his word. "I could help you in a more positive way, if you'd let me. You don't know what I just did, do you?" The view from Nob Hill is great. It's a tony neighborhood, but it still has active trolley tracks running down to the hinterlands.

"I'm sure that you probably had a multiplicity of private meanings associated with the demonstration, as did the thousands who helped, but the public meaning is clear: it was a voice against the War from the People." Trek lifted his hand to the sky and dropped his jaw after delivering his messianic words.

After a significant pause where I allowed Moses[59] to return to Earth I inquired, "Well, how has the money been going?"

"I'll talk about that later with you."

I didn't want to pursue the money angle because I wanted to keep some kind of reserve power base in case I needed it. I have a profound fear that this man is not the loyal type. He's just another wormy blot as far as loyalty goes. I need something rather more tangible to keep him in my plans.

7/8/69

I spend most of my time within the little chicken shell that Rx calls home. He has been very cold since we last talked, and I haven't had the opportunity to get him alone. Last night I had a dream that I was leading a demonstration in Washington D.C. It was being covered by C.B.S. news, and I was being interviewed by Walter Cronkite. Thousands of my loyal supporters were screaming slogans in the background. It was a grand occasion. I had the country on its knees. Ah, what bliss of supreme happiness to be where all aspire to be, but few achieve.

Such a life of powerful ease it would be. What marvelous wonders might come to pass if I should be that leader and so bring to fruition to all their wishes, at last.

We were all crowded in the shell, talking, when Rx came in and the conversation turned to the group of socialists that had been turned away by him. These feminists might have brought him a tidy sum, but he had rejected them out of ignorant pride. Trek asked me why I had brought them, and I told him. Then he broke into some kind of tirade about the precise etymology of several

---

[59] Of Course, T-Rx's name on his birth certificate was "Nehemiah Moses." He changed his name when he was marching in the South in the mid-1960s. It is unclear whether Mary knew this when she made her comment.

terms, missing the entire meaning of what I had been trying to communicate.

I wonder whether this was an indication of an inferior mind or a malicious one? He tried to make me seem ridiculous when, in fact, he was the only one who was ridiculous since he ignored what I was saying for some verbal nit-picking.

I don't understand why T-Rx is so hostile to me. Perhaps it is the thing that I had with Mad Dog, I don't know. Those two seem to be growing apart. I think that Mad Dog is becoming afraid that he will lose some of his influence now that Trek has broadened his power base—a move that didn't include Mad Dog. It's my guess that Mad Dog will try and acquire a base of his own to insure his continued presence in Rx's organization.

I have made such attempts to broaden the influence that I have beyond our tight shell-cell prison. The most receptive group to date has been the Workers Liberation Front. I met a woman named Tara, who had heard about Rx and wanted to meet him. Unfortunately when I took her to our shell, he wasn't there.

She wanted do know whether we were Stalinist, Leninist, or Maoist, but I replied that our leader had a new philosophy that was attuned to his unique worldview.

She scrunched up her nose. And I couldn't blame her. What I like about her group (even though they are somewhat hokey in their use of traditional Russian propaganda phrases), is that they have organizational links in several cities such as Los Angeles, Seattle, Chicago, and St Louis. This means that if we can form a partnership, my skeleton organization is already in the making. I must cultivate this part of their organization as my power base so that I can maneuver in a more advantageous position.

You know, diary, dear, there are certain people in our cell who must go. Hook is one of them. This kind of person is fully corrupt. People like him feed their bodies with hard drugs and live in a world of popular culture. He has a band that is very local. They play at small bars and the like for nickels and dimes. All their values are related to the reinforcement that they get from speaking to their friends who tell them they are conforming to the norms of the popular culture ideal.

When I look at Hook, I think about so many lives being wasted. Their political consciousness is next to nothing as the only reason they march against the War is because it is another role within the popular culture mold of what an attractive thing marching is. It has a pleasure value—everything they do has a pleasure value that can be measured in sexual terms or some kind of drug induced state of euphoria.

Hook is the only one in the cell who exhibits such unusual behavior (unusual only in relation to the rest of the people in our cell, who are more serious and sober). I would just like to see how long such a feeble-minded person as Hook could last in a serious organization like the W.L.F. (Workers Liberation Front), an organization that is only local, being a splinter group of the Young Democrats of the United States. Tara introduced me to this organization, which is headed by a guy named Ché (after the famous revolutionary). They both belong also to the W.L.F. These groups are serious and discipline their members who step out of line. I don't think that Hook would last a month with them. He'd be best advised to have his life insurance paid up. Death to the blot!

7/9/69

Trek seems to be definitely estranged from me. He isn't responding to anything that I do. I don't know how to handle this.

7/8/69

Mad Dog, who has considerable support at San Francisco State, has been making moves to consolidate his people. I found this out from Alf, a relatively new member of the shell, who is a very useful person. You can't trust Alf except when it is to his advantage. I like a man like that. He lays it right out for you to see, so there is no illusion or false pretenses.

He thinks that the group is splitting three ways: Rx's faction, Mad Dog's faction, and my faction. He thinks that my group will be the strongest so he wants to align himself with the winner.

If our group were larger and I had more immediate power, then I'd move to purge Mad Dog in any manner possible. I have talked to Alf about this and he thinks that he can put some pressure on Mad Dog so that he gets the impression that he isn't safe in San Francisco (from unknown and unnamed threats). We won't let on who it is from, but if anything, he will assume it is from Trek, since they are very far apart these days.

I haven't had any luck with the money. It just never materialized, but I must maintain that it *has* in order to maintain my position of power with T-Rx. I am in a delicate position. 'Opportunity' is the operative term. It's the key to success. Without it, I'm history.

I must make my own opportunities by putting pressure on every member of the group. There is no time to lose. If I am to be a success, then I must act quickly before someone else does, and I lose my chance.

7/9/69

Little Larr is a child. Come and sing my little Larr.

> Won't you play,
> Won't you stare,
> Out at the bay?

> Life is a ripple without a care,
> In the bay, on a lazy day,
> You will sing, you will dance,
> You who live without a care,
> Come and soothe me, my little Larr.

"He isn't altered," said the child, Larr.

"But Larr, you can see it for yourself. Trek is acting distant."

"Ah, goo-gooo-gah," cried the child, wanting mommy to burp him. So I did, taking him in my lap while the hand tapped his baby back.

"What's wrong, little one?" I asked.

But there was no response, only a cooing from the little child. His eyes were fixated upon the bay that he took as paradise when it was really floating garbage. Babies don't know much about garbage. After all, they constantly poop in their nappies.

"I want to make Rx a leader, and you can help me," I said.

"Yes," he gurgled.

Then I comforted him and showed him the motherly attention that he had lacked for so many years.

7/12/69
I had to tell Rx that I got more money than I ever expected. He wants me to give it back, but I told him that it was impossible. T-Rx doesn't want to talk any more. Alf has started the rumor that Mad Dog was going to split with Rx. This led to a long meeting between the two where presumably the differences that had been popping up were being ameliorated. Such a situation couldn't be allowed to continue, so I tried to apply some more pressure.

I know that as long as Mad Dog is with Rx, he will speak against me and I will not be able to persuade Trek to my point of view. If I can get Mad Dog out of the way, then I can get to Rx through my own persuasion and through baby Larr, who Trek dotes on. I will have both of them in the position where they can be used as I desire. Who knows, the stupid Larr might be valuable on the local level?

There has got to be some kind of leverage that can be used to get Mad Dog out of San Francisco. But how? I must discuss this with Alf and Ché.

7/15/69
My busy head has been spinning and grinning at a pace that is so furious that only the real Commander Cody would be able to tell the difference. But to the problem of Mad Dog, I have found (completely by accident, as one of the members of the Worker's Liberation Front in St. Louis had been alerted about the need to get some information that could be used as a possible blackmail on Mad Dog) that there is an outstanding warrant for Duvall Jackson, alias Mad Dog Jackson, in Huntsville Alabama for attempted murder. Since there is no statute of limitations for murder warrants or attempted murder warrants, it is still good. Now, all that I have to do is let this information leak in the right places and Mad Dog will be gone. The advantages of a multi-city organization are working already.

Tara has been working on this since the beginning of the month, and only now have we found such a delightful piece of information.

7/17/69

The beautiful piece of news has proven to be false. The warrant had been issued, but then the charges had been dropped soon afterwards. However, this has caused some commotion. There are plans for something big in Seattle, and I hear that Hook is going to see what it is all about. Meanwhile, I have made some contacts with the organization in Los Angeles and they are perfectly willing to combine forces with the U.L.A. in San Francisco and Santa Barbara, an event that Ché has been organizing.

Yesterday I had the following conversation with T-Rx. We were sitting just outside the shell on city-installed benches. From our vantage point we could see just how dilapidated our condemned structure really was. It metaphorically reminded me of our country, it was firmly built by a bunch of white males on the model of Athenian Greece: white male landholders could get their way. This model gave us sexism, slavery, and genocide against indigenous peoples.

Time and progress made such a model a crumbling, condemned shell. And that's what this cell calls 'home.' I turned to our curly long hair. "I have gotten together several groups that would be willing to give you their support if you would organize a large demonstration in Los Angeles or Berkeley against R.O.T.C. recruiting. Are you interested?"

"So you've been putting together a statewide organization?"

"No, I wouldn't call it an *organization*, as such."

"What *would* you call it?"

"Listen, you made a big splash with your San Francisco March. Why don't you do it again while people still remember?"

"What for?" Trek started doing things with his hands in the air at the same time that he was audibly inhaling air through his teeth so that it made a hissing sound. Was it some sort of Buddhist Tai Chi? This diversion must not be allowed to sidetrack us.

Besides that, his reply 'What for,' is rather meaningless. Why do we do anything? It is because we believe it's *right*, and because it makes us feel good to do something important. Doesn't he want an end to the War? Doesn't he care about the millions of people across this country who don't have adequate food? What about the illiterate and victims of discrimination? All these pressing social problems that can only be met by people who are humanely interested in bettering the lot of all the working and oppressed peoples in this country—and they have a solution.

People everywhere are alienated from their *real* selves. Unless they can find this *real self* through creative self-expression, then they will live a life of frustration and bitter meaninglessness. Each of us has potential, which she should develop. We have a *duty* to do so. But millions are being thwarted by a repressive capitalistic system which creates inauthentic people. Anything that can be done to oppose such a tyrannical force should be excised to bring fulfillment to the masses.

Here I am, offering the opportunity to this man to become a great national leader in the Struggle, and all he does is ask *why*.

"Why do you eat?" I responded. The question seemed so ridiculous that I didn't see how he could answer it. If someone asked if the Pentagon killed people, no one would do anything except laugh since the statement was so tautological.

"Does General Motors make cars?" I quickly added.

"No, they make robots," was his reply.

We both laughed. I put my hand on his arm tenderly. "I believe in you, T-Rx. I think that you could make a difference in the way that this country is being run. You have so much to offer, that I think you owe it to yourself and to others to use what you have." I put my hand on his back to rub it, but he withdrew it.

"I can't have it that way."

"I understand," I said, thinking he was speaking about my physical advances. "We don't have to be close in that way, but rather be as consort battleships side-by-side working to destroy our foe."

"What makes you think that your organization will be any better than what you are trying to destroy?" he asked.

"Can it get any worse?"

"Yes. There are governments that I think you'd find worse. There are always trade-offs. You may trade moral fiber for material gain, or affluence for peace of mind, or stability for loss of freedom. The list is endless. The more order we experience, the less freedom we have to move outside that prescribed framework." He stopped moving his hands but he hissed once again.

"That's what I want to do; destroy the framework." Then we were interrupted by a girl who was trying to roller skate past us on the sidewalk. She couldn't be more than 11. She wore a wide skirt and had red hair, which she had in pigtails. The sight was comical. It seemed that she was always about to fall down and skin her knee. But somehow she was able to retain her balance.

Then Trek grabbed me by the shoulders and turned me around. "You haven't understood a word that I've said, have you? It's the same thing. Your framework will be just as bad and corrupt in its own way as our own government is now."

"What a reactionary!" I said, scrunching up my face.

"Perhaps, but I want to shy away from any order as much as is possible. Certainly everyone must accept something. But I try to keep myself as free as possible while still staying within the society. I'm not interested in power or movements; I'm interested in working with small groups of people in little ways, not in big ways. I'm a revolutionary who has nothing to propose. I want to shake up the established order now and again because it is only outside of our comfort-zone-daily-order that we are able to reflect upon *what* we are and *where* we really feel like going."

"That's a bunch of crap, and you know it," I said, standing up. "I'm a little sick of your messianic attitude. You're no better than the rest of us. You are just a phony. If you don't do anything about the appalling national cesspool, then you're as guilty as all the rest of them." I turned and started to walk away. Then I turned to give him my zinger. "And may you all rot in hell together."

"I didn't know you were the religious type, Mary."

This was more than I could stand. This man was trying to make me look ridiculous. He wasn't listening to a word that I was saying. How can someone tolerate being around someone who has no sensitivity?

7/23/69

The sun is rising. I haven't been to sleep all night; I've been alone. My head has been full of thoughts. The ideas pound against my skull. My future fame had seemed so secure to me, but now as I sit watching the sun hang on the horizon, I am not so sure. My vision was dwindling just as surely as the sun would, too, after its peak at noon.

Everything had been presented to me so easily. It had been so certain: the magical organization for social change that would make a difference. All the struggles of my youth would not be in vain. I will sit back and laugh on these days of pain and suffering.

I open my back door and lean over my fire escape. I'm on the third floor of a three-story building. My Castro District flat has a view of Haight Ashbury just past Corona Heights Park. I'm also situated near the Dogpatch where Trek's condemned shell exists.

Then I hear a noise from below. There is a man from a second floor flat who is also on the fire escape. He's dressed in a cheap Robert Hall suit with a skinny necktie. He's trying to study some notes and is in distress. He's probably some insurance bookkeeper who's trying desperately not to make a mistake. Peon! What does his job matter? Does he know that living above him is a woman who may change history? Does he understand my true greatness? Does anyone yet recognize me when they see me in the street? Why am I not flocked by admirers who beg me for the privilege of touching my garments? Power flows through me. It resides in an inviolable place within. With every sigh, I can feel potency rippling in my muscles.

I am an Amazon: the true race of women. I dominate men and use them as thralls. When I think of their puny minds that I encountered in college, I must laugh to stop myself from becoming ill. Their small, pointed minds have such limited parameters. They can spend a lifetime thinking about some silly irrelevant piece of data, like that man below me with his trivial balance sheets—or whatever it was he was sweating over. While, on the other hand, I might run for Congress and rule this country.

Why is it that the priorities of this country are so fucked up? Is this whole country anally repressive? Has the male-imposed pressure caused a case of national constipation? It is time for an enema! I will flush out the bowels of this hemorrhoid-ridden country. It is a time for *new vision* that will bring new revisions: broad horizons for change. Only then will we hear the holy flush as the country (as we know it) goes down the sewers.

The sun is rising, and I stand here thinking of how I have accomplished nothing in twenty-plus years. Those first thirty years are key. That's why they say, "Don't trust anyone over thirty." Did not Alexander the Great conquer much of the known world in that time period? —yes, Alex the *grape* did, and made wine to intoxicate the masses, but he is just a cheap imitation of the eternal earth mother who begot the sun and all of the planets.

Course upon worthless course I took at dear Macalester for no purpose except to sleep with a worm who didn't deserve the purity that I brought to him. He didn't understand what it meant to *feel*; they never do. How could I give him such power over me?

Just look at me and what I will do, and how a simple worm caused me to trip and fall to the ground. But my place is not on the ground under foot. I am exceptional. For *me* there is no right or wrong except *whatever brings me power* or whatever denies it. The capable shall rise. The common and coarse shall rule until the pure-blooded aristocracy goes mad like the czars of Russia. Within the sun is so much energy: constant energy that fills us all with a sense of tremendous awe. The sun is a child of the great earth mother and should not be confused with the real source of power, *Gaia*, the earth.

All around me is city; desolate concrete that is barren, whose fecundity was lost when men raped her and made her captive. How long shall the real source of power remain in servile bondage? It will be as long as man remains worshipping the sun and ignoring the earth.

7/24/69

Tara and I were talking when Alf came into our space. I think that Alf is a rather quaint fellow who believes he is out for himself. But this is not the case or he would not allow himself to be manipulated by the likes of me.

"I have a joke," said Alf.

"I have one for you first," said Tara, her eyes sparkling.

"Alright, tell yours first."

"There was a man who was dying of a heart ailment and his heart suddenly stopped beating. The man was pronounced dead, but minutes later he was revived by an energetic lab technician. Upon being revived, the man was questioned about what it was like being dead. The man smiled. 'Did you see heaven?' asked the doctor. The patient nodded his head. 'Well, tell us about it, then. Tell us about God.' The patient sat up and cleared his throat. 'Well, first of all, she's black.'"

Alf laughed, though I could tell he didn't think the joke was funny. He laughed because he was weak. I didn't even smile at this fascist, racist demonstration of feeble mindedness. How insect-like are men?

T-Rx: The History of a Radical Leader 210

7/25/69
I have made some contacts with our new organization in Portland. They will be planning a series of marches in cooperation with a student group at Reed College. There must be a way that I can get rid of Mad Dog. I'm certain that he is the stumbling block between myself and my control of T-Rx. I have Larry in complete control. And since Larry is so close to Rx, I will be able to control Trek, by extension, soon. With no one near to him supporting his stand against me, Rx will have to relinquish his non-rational opposition to me.

Ché came to me and we talked about options we had to rid ourselves of Mad Dog. We were in the Presidio situated on a little hill overlooking a green that could be used for various activities. At present, some teenage boys were playing Frisbee. They were hamming it up and trying to make acrobatic catches. "Of course, the easiest thing to do is kill him."

"Kill him?"

"Yes, it doesn't cost very much money. You hire a gun and it's done in a few days. Neat, clean, and no one will know. It's perfectly safe."

I didn't like the idea of simply killing someone. I don't know if my reaction had anything to do with the relationship that I once had with Mad Dog, but the thought of hiring a killer seemed very fascist to me.

"I don't like that," I said.

"Why?

I didn't have a rational explanation for him. How could I tell Ché that I didn't want Mad Dog killed because I once was intimate with him? Was this any reason? Hadn't I slept with many men? That didn't make much difference to me about them. But somehow concerning Mad Dog, it did. Perhaps because it was at the beginning when I wasn't used to the numbing mechanics of it all. Sex still held some pleasure and meaning to me—I don't know; the subject made me very tired. All that I knew was that I wasn't ready to go that far—not yet.

"It's simple," I began, lighting a cigarette. The activity bought me some time. After a few puffs I continued. "If we kill Mad Dog now, T-Rx will know that we did it and we'll so harden him against us that he'll never come around."

"Who cares?"

"Do I have to explain everything to you?" My action wasn't out of fear, but out of caution. I knew that I didn't want to act hastily right now. "T-Rx is our key to becoming a national organization."

"We already are national," Ché began, smoothing back his slick, thin, black hair. A Frisbee came down near us. Ché got up and tossed it in another direction. A teenaged boy who had been running it down stopped in his tracks. Ché hardened his expression. He seemed to be daring the boy to complain. The boy understood and ran quickly away.

"Do you call five cities national? The farthest east we go is St. Louis. And you know what kind of operation they run there."

"If you're talking about that information that didn't stand up, then I say: they just made a mistake." Ché broke into a broad smile.

"A mistake!" I was livid. "Do you know what that mistake could have cost us?"

"All right, lay off." Ché's smile vanished.

I had Ché where I wanted him. I can control anyone.

"We need another plan," I said.

"How about *threats* on his life?" was his counter-offer.

"Do you have a percentage of the killing business? Because you're beginning to sound like a salesman who gets a commission on each sale."

"Listen, Mary, I know that the only sure way to take care of anybody is to make strong decisions, and nothing is more final than death."

"No, what we need is some way to get T-Rx to rid himself of Mad Dog."

"How do you propose we do that?" Ché's smile was returning.

"I don't know, but we have to plant mistrust between them. That is something that I want you to do. It has to appear that one of them is selling the other one out to some third force. You have to either find a third force that dislikes one or both of them, or create one. Once you've done this, we will have them distrusting each other. Then we will have them at our disposal."

Ché dutifully obeyed. I didn't discuss any specifics with him. In order to be effective I must keep some things secret from everyone. Not only do I have to arrange my schemes with T-Rx, but I have to consolidate my support in California among the WLF. This will require some traveling around. It can't be avoided, and I've saved quite a bit from my allowance checks to do as much traveling as I'll need to do.

7/26/69
My trip plans will have to be delayed. I've just found out that Mad Dog has been meeting with the Black Student Unions in San Francisco. They are arranging something with the Black Panthers, I think. If only our group had a better intelligence network.

7/30/69
I still have the same the financial story available: Trek believes that I handle large sums of money in his name. He is trying to get me to divest myself of these funds, but I claim that I won't.

Tara has strengthened our position in Los Angeles.

Back here, it seems that Mad Dog is not spending much time at the old headquarters (the shell). I wonder what is in the air? I hope that they aren't planning a counter attack against us. Maybe I'll work on Larry tonight.

8/3/69
Mad Dog has left town. Larry has left town. Marcia has left town. Hook has left town. Either there has been some kind of purge that I'm unfamiliar with or some large scale operation is being planned.

How stupid I was to believe that T-Rx really didn't want to unite with me because he didn't like large groups! He was planning something big all along.

I know that I was stupid to try and win him (like other men) in bed. This isn't the *way* with Rx. He will sleep with you and yawn. This man is so cold that he cares for nothing but his own pleasures and power lust. What a blot on the title worm. Even a worm can be trusted to always be worm-like, but this creature changes so that he is warm at one instant and at the next he has carved your name into the wall destined for the morgue. How loathsome the species of men are. If I were Wonder Woman, I'd rid the planet of the male sex. Perhaps I'd join forces with the other super women of the planet and purify what is here so that decent people can survive.

When I think of all the hours that I spent in high school, lying on my bed and dreaming about Mr. Right. Then all of a sudden I was in college and the bed that I was lying on wasn't my own. It was *his*. He had won the prize, and I fully expected the typical Edina rewards for such—a home and all the rest. Maybe I didn't really want that. I'm happy the way I am now, but the dreams have changed. No longer am I agape at some man in the way that my mother is still in awe of Daddy. No, I see men as rather feeble animals who depend upon illusions to exist. They go about seducing. That's all that they are good at. The woman has to be unwilling at first so that the man can charm her into dropping her pants when he blows his whistle. Wrong from the start!

And now, what is there left to do but die? Power and death are the only sensations that continue to amaze this tired, frazzled, misused soul. But what's the use of ending one's life? Another triumph for T-Rx? How he'd laugh. No, that's wrong, he wouldn't laugh, but he'd say to himself that he was right all along about that girl. He'd say that she wasn't stable from the start. How sympathetic he'd be about my *type of person*. What a pity that this WOMAN didn't have the strength to continue. She always wanted to be a man. A man—ha! What a disgrace. How could I give anyone the satisfaction that they had won over me?

I still have men who support me. Though, in general, men repulse me. Men may adore me, but they leave me to fend for myself. It is, dear diary, at times like this that the hand is inclined to attempt the beautiful drawing that will signify what words cannot. But, alas, my hand was never meant for graphic art. The effort only frustrates the already despondent soul who wants to howl: holy, holy, holy.

Where am I? Right now, what am I doing? Well, to give you an answer, impetuous book, I'll tell you what I have told myself many times before (sometimes I think you mean to torment me with your hollow prating). I am one of three or four people with considerable influence in the W.L.F. We are constantly expanding, but at present, we are nothing but a small operation. Why, our members could be counted on one hand of a cripple's fingers. All that I really have is potential. There are opportunities here and there which I can realize by my mobility and time. I have both because of monthly checks.

But what of the future of the W.L.F.? I don't know. That's an honest answer, little liber book. I don't think that there is much expansion in that organization because of the extreme positions that they take on key issues such as nationalization of all industry in the United States. That will never fly. That's Ruskie talk.

No, T-Rx is my key to success. With him in my pocket, I can weld several splinter groups such as the W.L.F. into a grand scheme, which might be a third political force in this country. George Wallace showed in 1968 how the country is not satisfied with the normal political means. I believe that the trend is just beginning for splinter groups to make inroads into the traditional political machinery. The liberals will form three or four camps and the conservatives several of their own so that any party that can control 15% of the electorate can be a major factor. They can play kingmaker. The opportunity is there. It only takes someone with a grand vision to see such a plain reality. And yet there are so few of us who can really see. There are so few who can confront the future with noble designs. Someone is needed to lead. The vacuum of power exists. Will I be the one to fill it—or at least influence the one who does?

8/6/69
The Exodus has begun for the north. Everyone in Rx's cell has taken to the hills. I knew that something must be happening, but my dear Alf (impotent fool that he is) has been unable to fulfill the task for me. I think that I will have to make the trip to Seattle and try my luck at getting Rx into my fold.

8/7/69
I have just been talking to a student at the University of Wisconsin, in Madison, who says that they have quite a bit of activist support, but no one to lead them. He used to head the chapter of the S.D.S.[60] there, but now that group has broken up into several groups. I think I'll send Alf there to try and coordinate them for some big project, like a bombing. There is nothing like a common project to unite people who are in disagreement. I learned this from Rx.

---

[60] S.D.S. is Students for a Democratic Society. It was a semi-radical group for social/political justice.

8/8/69
I'm very excited that things may start to develop in a way that I couldn't have hoped for even a week ago. Now T-Rx has to join me when he sees how big I have become.

8/9/69
Perhaps I can work on Larry. I have taken the train from L.A. where I have been with Tara, who has moved into a position of prominence due to her successful instigation of a strike that raised the wages of non-union factory workers. I suggested to Ché that we should become active in the grape farmers strike, but he said that the United Farm Workers weren't interested in any political organizations at the present. I suppose that they don't want to go the way of the I.W.W.

Larry, dear Larr. There are times when I think that he is a pure, innocent child of nature. How can such a fellow be living amidst all the dope and rip-offs of the sub-culture in which we call home and still retain such a purity about him that makes this sewer seem only illusory? It is as if he doesn't live on the same low level as the rest of us. Could it be that he is mentally unstable and can't see the complexities that make the world of pastels transform into the nightmare of Jackson Pollock?

There is no order. I know this to be a fact. What we arrange for ourselves is designed to promote an action. Actions that benefit us are the only important items that need concern us. If I can successfully use this rosebud, then what is the loss if in the process the bud is lost forever? What counts is the *greatness* that I can achieve. People who worry about trivial matters such as petty morality deserve the low standing that they have in society. The herd values will not keep me away from my appointed mission: to be the Amazon Queen. It will all be for the best, because I have dared to become great. The measure of my greatness will be whether I can successfully keep beyond the trivialities that govern lesser beings. I must be able to play both ends against the middle. While I work for Rx's support I must be able to destroy him so that when the time comes, he also will be under my control.

8/10/69

I'm in bed—I have been for a while, but though I've been removed from the sewer for a tick, I still know that this city stinks. I can't imagine what T-Rx wants to do in a city that only has a shining space-age phallic building to make its claim to fame. Seattle is filled with provincial people who think that everything in Seattle is the greatest of anywhere. Their favorite conversation topic is how Seattle is such a great city.

I have forgotten to mention to you, dear diary, a ploy that I have instigated against T-Rx, who I'm now convinced will be won over only through pressure tactics. Rx thinks that I control a sizeable portion of money in his name from the March. I have told him that that a man named Peter Rossi has an IOU that he is anxious to collect. It is difficult to estimate the reaction that this piece of information had. The memory isn't crystal clear, but as I recall, Rx began to get very nervous.

"You can't do this," Rx said. We were at the Seattle Center near the merry-go-round.

"Don't you think so? Just watch me."

"But why are you doing this to me?"

"I'm not doing anything to you. *You* are doing it to yourself." Rx was getting agitated. He walked back toward a concession stand where they were selling cotton candy. For a moment it struck me as ironic that the elusive man was now framed by pink spun sugar. Perhaps that's all Rx has been all along?

Then Rx walked back to me. "But do you know what he'll do to me when he finds out I have no money?"

"He'll probably hurt you."

"And you're going to let him do that?" Rx's voice was flat. All of a sudden he didn't seem so agitated. I'm sure he had moved into his *protection zone*. He wasn't going to show me his real gut-wrenching discord. I had him, and I knew it.

"It isn't only me."

"What do you mean?"

"Your close friends, Larry and Mad Dog, are in on it too."

"You mean *everyone* is against me?"

I didn't answer, but laughed at him. The sight of the man who I had held in such reverence was now a broken, pathetic weakling in the presence of the Amazon Queen. I walked over to the big circular fountain. I sat down and crossed my arms and legs.

T-Rx followed and sat next to me. Then he said in even tones, hiding his inner torment, "You should help me."

"Why should I?" I asked, lifting my chin against this loser.

"Well, for starters, I was the one who took you in when we were in San Francisco. I gave you your start, took you under my wing. I gave you friendship. Then this is how you repay me?"

"Emotional man, I cannot remember feeling *anything* for you. Oh—wait, yes I remember an insignificant tryst that we had, if that's what you are talking about. Ha, you took that seriously? Ha, ha, ha, my little man, *you* don't know much about the reality of the world, do you?"

He didn't like being laughed at. But he was too scared to make any response. He lifted his right hand to his lips and began chewing on a hang nail. This showed me that he was going down for the third time. Then he looked me in the eye. "What do you want?"

"I want to lead your West Coast operations."

"What can you do?"

"I can bring in the feminists. I am viewed by many as a female leader: the Amazon Queen. You can bring me on as an equal."

"Of course, everyone in the Movement is an equal."

"Not quite. *You* make all the decisions. That's got to change. If you want me to make the money goon go away, you need to yield power to me. I have a vision."

Rx shrugged his shoulders. "I've never had a thing about being *the* leader. I think that each person should have his own say and go his own way." He looked down at his gnawed hang nail and then back to me. "If there is some sort of ceremonial thing I can do that will satisfy you, let me know. I'd like to get this goon off my back. It's inefficient to executing our purpose."

I nodded. The Amazon Queen had taken control. And it was all a bluff.

8/12/69

I have boon. I was approached by a Mr. Moran who wishes to buy into the organization that T-Rx and I have been starting. He said that he would give us money in return for a certain say in some of our activities.

I'm not sure whether this would be a good thing or not. Certain things that he said bothered me.

"You know that we don't care for these 'kiddie' movements, but we can see that you have some support within the working class."

"We're just starting; we haven't had the time—"

"Yes, I was speaking in relative terms, of course." Moran was a corpulent guy of medium height in his mid-thirties. He wore a Fu-Manchu moustache. It was probably a prop for his *shtick*.

This interchange bothered me because, in a real sense, we are a movement of young people. Most of our members are under twenty-five. And to be honest, we haven't got too many in our outer team who are over thirty. (I separate our skeleton inner team of a dozen or so and the outer team of people with day jobs, but who can be called upon to march with us and donate to the cause.)

What made me most uncomfortable with Mr. Moran is that he had an angle he wasn't exposing. He thought he could turn my head with flattery (big mistake on his part).

8/14/69

Trying out my new persona with T-Rx. It was a short interview. I have dropped the love approach and now am the person who can (he thinks) have him killed at my whim. The new watchword is *money*.

I'm not sure whether I can get to him to follow through with his commitments to me, but in case I can't, I'm pursuing a backup via high school students in Seattle. I've met some interesting students in a meeting I held at Garfield High School. I have found significant black discontent in this white city, which thinks it's liberal-minded because it has a black basketball coach and a glib mayor. I think that Seattle could be the center of some of the largest race riots in the country. There are two large communities that can be mobilized: the Asians and the blacks. The first group will be somewhat difficult, because they have a higher per capita income. I'm sure that Kip McRae, my new coordinator out here, can get some action in very little time. I told Kip that if he could establish a chapter of a thousand or so, he could begin making big money from the leverage that we will control once we can get some of our people placed in local positions in county and state government.

The Black Panthers here were not happy about our appearance. They claim we were splitting up the community and making their voice less effective. I told them where they could stick it and began working on some groups at the University of Washington.

The University of Washington has one of the largest minority enrollments in the country for a flagship public university. But they have only cared about numbers and haven't given much consideration about anything else, so they have thousands of minorities here that aren't really fitting in and have become frustrated.

They are victims of white racism and they want some blood. I'm not sure that we want this group as a part of the W.L.F. (Workers Liberation Front), but perhaps we can enlist the B.S.U. (Black Student Union) to be an affiliate of ours—a sort of ally, I don't know.

They afford great potential for political muscle if we ever need to flex it.

8/16/69
Diary, I'm tired. My brain has been searching for every way to develop this potential hotbed of Seattle into something really big, but so far all I've gotten are a lot of promises and people who want to "think things over." I don't know, maybe I push too hard? But don't all the real leaders push hard? Isn't that what it takes to get to the top?

When I'm tired like this, I don't feel enmity towards anyone. I don't want to cause trouble. I just want to be recognized for what I am.

8/17/69
There was a knocking at my door. "What are you doing here?"

"I thought that I'd come for a chat," he said, pushing his way inside of my one-bedroom apartment at the top of Queen Anne Hill, just spitting distance from Seattle Pacific College.

"Get out."

"That's no way to treat an ex-bedmate."

I tried to spit at Mad Dog, but I only slobbered on my own face.

Mad Dog walked into my common room and looked around. Then he pivoted back so he was facing me. "Lay off Rx."

"I thought that you and Rx were finished." I approached my intruder. I wasn't going to be bullied.

"You'd like that, wouldn't you?" Mad Dog gave me his *intent* look.

"I have no preference. Many of my best friends are homosexuals."

He grabbed me by the throat so that I couldn't breathe. "Now you listen good, slut. I know who you are and what you are trying to do. I know that you spent a month in a mental hospital because you're nuts. I know it, and I wouldn't mind telling anyone about it either. But what I *do* want to tell you is this: I'm not about to let a guy like T-Rx become entrapped by anyone like you. It won't happen, do you understand? I'll kill you first."

Now diary, you know me to be a perfectly level-headed person, not at all prone to violence. Why, I couldn't seriously injure someone even if I hated them intensely, as I do that black bastard. But he was holding me by the neck, choking me, and at the same time charging me with mental incompetency. Now, I ask you, diary, could I be so open about a problem (putting it voluntarily into my own diary) if I was really one of its victims?

I tell you that I am the type of person who wouldn't deal with it directly if there were any shrewd of truth in it. Why, if such a ludicrous event were so, I'd be the last to talk about openly, especially in these pages! It's only a red herring, dear diary, and nothing to hiss at.

8/18/69

A representative of Richard Moran has met with me this morning. Moran wants to become a backer of our movement in return for some influence in our Los Angeles chapter. He has offered five thousand dollars, and I have accepted.

This is a good omen. What we've needed for a long time is real money. I almost hit some in San Francisco, but the deal fell through, though T-Rx doesn't know it. Indeed, it is one of my "holds" over my errant leader. Moran's man has assured me that we will be given regular payments. He has even volunteered several men who I've agreed will be given prominent posts in our organization. My letter is off to Tara even now. We're growing bigger. Today it's Los Angeles. Tomorrow? T-Rx.

8/23/69
One of the big issues on the south side of Seattle is the Panther *free lunch program*. It has given them a foothold not only in the black community, but among liberal whites as well. They are gaining some respectability that they lacked only a few years ago when Cleaver, Newton, and Seale were shooting up California. What we need to do, if we are to reach the same constituency, is to either unite with the Panthers or force them out of Seattle. I think that it would be unwise to make a power move at present, so a coalition is the best answer.

Now, the next question is how to make a coalition seem attractive to them. The only way that we can do that is to show them concrete advantages to making such a pact. Now, the only real selling point that the W.L.F. has is that it represents a segment of white workers who might have similar interests to this black group. If they feel that white support is worth courting, then we may be able to strike up a deal.

9/1/69
I had this conversation with Roy Wise, a black activist who has a number of friends who rank in the organization of the Panthers. We met in a little Italian restaurant one block off Seattle Center: *Tony's*. Like the name, the restaurant is run by a wop named *Tony*. Tony likes to cozy up to patrons. At one time he aspired to be an opera singer, so he puts on opera records and occasionally joins in.

Just after being seated by Tony, Roy folded his hands on the table and asked, "How can you help us?"

"We can offer support on two fronts. First the workers— white factory workers who are members and second, the college students who are disenchanted with the S.D.S. and Yippies. They want an organization that will actually have some political power."

"What are you proposing?"

"A coalition in Seattle between our two groups. We will help each other with our respective goals, thus adding strength to both of our groups."

"How committed are you to black revolution?"

"We are committed to some revolution, if necessary to oust this fascist government that is now in power."

"Would you agree to the public execution of a few top government officials?"

"If it came to that. Sure." Tony brought some bread sticks. Wise was looking at me rather skeptically.

"Why should we trust you?" he asked, picking up two breadsticks at once.

"Because we need you, and you need us."

"We don't need anyone."

"Well, you must need something. Even the Democratic party is always looking to expand their influence."

"We don't need honkys like you."

"Do you have everything that you want?"

"Enough for us, lady."

"Well, then I guess I'm wasting your time. I thought that perhaps we could help each other out, but I suppose that I was mistaken. Sorry to have called you over here." I made a move to get up and leave. Roy raised his hand to check my departure.

"Not at all. Say, you don't know much about things, do you?" asked Roy, chomping through his third bread stick.

"What do you mean?"

"If you want to sell someone on something, then you have to come up with a commodity that he wants." Tony brought over the beer that Roy ordered. I had an iced tea.

I didn't respond. Was he hitting on me?

"Now, if you had hard support that the Panthers could count on, then maybe we'd have something to talk about."

"I have the support."

"Where? All you have is words."

"Do you know of a man named T-Rx?"

"The singing group?"

"No, the activist."

Ron was laughing. He took off his glasses to give them a wipe on his sleeve. When he'd finished his task, he lit a cigarette. "Yeah, I know who you mean. Is he the dude from San Francisco?"

"Yes, what about him?"

"I have his support," I said, leaning forward.

"You do?" Ron took a long drag and held it in his lungs for a moment.

"Yes."

"Well, if you can translate that into people, it'd help." Tony brought over my caprèse salad and Ron's salami and pesto bruschetta.

I took a bite and then looked up. "How do three hundred souls grab you?"

"If you have three hundred in this city, then I'd say we'd be ready to talk."

"You have my number."

We finished our light fare in just a few minutes. Ron was either on a tight time table or he wanted to give that impression. I was only a half-hour walk to my place so I set out. The interview went better than I expected. I think that I can consolidate support on this front if I can only find out what T-Rx is planning for Seattle.

9/25/69

I left town for Minnesota. It was my father's birthday and if I want continued financial support from him, it is a good idea to keep the old man happy. He has his strange habits, and one of them is having both of his children present for each of his birthdays. He must really value the natal day. I wonder why?

I don't know how someone can be so vain about himself.

9/27/69

I tried to contact L.A., but with little success.

10/2/69

I have found out that there is a bombing being planned for the R.O.T.C. building at the University of Washington. This is something that the Panthers might be interested in. I will have to feel them out.

Soon it will be time to contact T-Rx again. This next time, I will be very persuasive. He may not want me as his plaything, but he *will* want me as his equal when I offer him either destruction or union.

10/3/69

My perseverance, what a glorious thing! I got a letter from Tara telling me that Moran's men have come through with the money. I think that I have made a very smart move. Our organization, which was only about two hundred or so when I began, is now almost two thousand. This is incredible growth. And if I can count the Panthers, the figure will be much larger. There is nothing now that can hold me back from my goal. I will accomplish all for which I have set out. Things are too good not to go all the way now.

10/10/69

I bumped into Roy at an event in Ballard. Roy liked the idea of bombing the R.O.T.C., but he wasn't interested in giving Panther support. He said that if we came through well on our Project, then the Panthers would join us, for sure. Personally, I think that we may be so big by that time that we may not need the Panthers. His response to this was, "We'll wait and see. You can count on us as being with you, *informally,* for now. But don't you ever get the idea that you can get along in Seattle without our help, because we could destroy you in a week."

"What queer talk for allies," I responded.

"Yeah, *allies,*" he repeated as he walked away.

I think that there is much support to be garnered in the suburbs. I have some meetings that I will attend in Bellevue and Redmond to try and garner support. In Seattle, I think that the best approach is not to annex organizations, but to make them affiliates, in the same manner as we are trying with the Panthers.

10/27/69

What hard work building an organization is. The War is a dormant issue just now. What we need to change this is to tap the strong middle class discontent about the War (principally centered around the Draft) and use it in our organization as a central principle. These businessmen don't want their sons and daughters being affected by some War that isn't to our national interest. I don't see how this approach can fail to work.

I don't know why I keep thinking about Rx. It isn't love or admiration anymore. He represents something; maybe it's success? I don't know. In fact, there isn't much that I know about myself just now except that I want to be a leader and command the respect of those under me. This is my goal.

My goal, what does it mean? Questions like this aren't important to me, though they haunt me at those rare moments when I'm doing nothing. It is at those times when the dread comes. There is nothing that can be done then except to become busy.

Business activity and goals fill those blank spaces of time. It is the scheduling of one's time that I find to be the most challenging problem that I must face. What is one to do when confronted with nothingness? This is beginning to sound like total crap.

11/2/69

Diary, I sit here thinking about the field that I can see from my window. In the field there are children playing. I remember that when I was a child, I only liked playing with one other child, preferring recreation in couples to team sports. Now, I think of myself a potential leader of many and muse to others. It is ironical the child that I *was* should grow up to become an organizer of the masses, when I am still basically a person who is uncomfortable in groups.

I have knowledge of Rx's activities, but am doing nothing so that I can wait for my opportunity. I have come to him before with no success. My plan now must be different. Pressure. This is my selling point. I have the pressure point of knowing what he is doing. I also hold an imaginary threat of money through a "supposed" IOU that I took out in his name.

With this in hand, perhaps I can convince him that he needs my organization to be able to successfully complete what he has planned. The Panthers are not committing themselves either way, but I have some soft support with the University of Washington's Black Student Union and some other student groups in the suburban high schools.

With these in my portfolio, I think that I can bluff my way past Rx. The way that he accepted the money story makes me think that he won't be that difficult to convince.

One final note, I may try one last fling at Larry Cohen. I'm not sure of the utility of the method of pressure through him, but I may be able to disorient him sufficiently so that he will either leave or act erratically.

Besides, I have always had mixed feelings about Master Larry. He seems so unnatural in this setting of drugs and political intimidation. I wish he would leave before it destroys him.

11/4/69
They say that in the Roman calendar, November was the ninth month. I wonder if that meant that the ages of those great Roman statesmen were inflated?

Did Cicero really live to be 63? Is he to be *trusted*? After all, he was over 30!

I have reason to be happy. Our California organization promises to develop the way that I knew that it could, and I have already thought about establishing chapters in New York and Chicago. This network will take a minimum of two years to establish, but I think that we can be very effective (on a moderate scale) for the 1972 elections. Wallace had the outside force in '68, but we'll be the force in '72.

11/9/69
I just rented a house from which my organization can carry on our activities. It is close to the University, but not too far away from T-Rx. I am becoming confident that when things materialize, all will work out.

There is a guy who hangs around here a lot who has been reading Pindaric odes. I think that it would be very good if I had someone who would write odes praising me. This may sound somewhat vain, but I think that my accomplishments are of a greater order than those of those silly athletes. Why not an Olympic Ode #15—to Mary?

11/25/69
I've just returned from New York where I had talks with some students at City College, Brooklyn and some representatives of the independent printers. I told them about the printers we already had in our organization in Los Angeles.

"We don't want any union," they said.

"Why not?" I asked.

"Because we have seen what the union has done to other groups of printers. They take their salaries and give them little in return. Look, the printing industry is on a shoestring now. We can't get much more than cost of living raises, so why do we need to organize for that? If we're organized, then we will lose money that we will never see again. Besides, unions can tell you how to think—especially the small ones. You act according to their edicts and everything will be fine, but once you step out of line, whammo, that's it for you.

"You lose your job and get blacklisted elsewhere. You are then *down and out.* No count of 'ten.' Unions may be fine for auto workers, but we're doing just fine, thank you."

"I can appreciate your concern, but you know we're not a union. Our printers in Los Angeles (and there are a substantial number of them) aren't organized. In fact, you can use your chapter of the Workers Liberation Front to fight attempts to organize you."

They seemed to like this tack. I felt proud of myself for my pivot. If they had expressed the opposite sentiment, then I would have offered the opposite solution. The only way to become big is to be all things to all people.

We talked to some longshoremen who wanted to be able to lobby in a way that their union wouldn't.

"We are sympathetic to unionism," I told them. "We are a friend of the working man. In San Francisco, we represent over a hundred union men."

The key to organization is finding the right people and delegating authority. I haven't gotten anything firm on any of these people, but I am very hopeful.

A follow-up visit in February might win some real support.

12/1/69
I think that it is the time to make my move toward T-Rx. I have sent someone to see him and arrange a meeting.

12/9/69
Tomorrow is the day that I meet with T-Rx. Everything has worked as planned—I have enough apparent power, I think, to force T-Rx to either go along with me or give up his bombing plan of the R.O.T.C. building. I can't imagine him not carrying through

with his plan, which he has worked on for months, so I will soon have a partner. Rx is too vain to give something up when his reputation is on the line.

I don't expect T-Rx to like me, but just to work with me. I want him to consider me as an ally. We can do great things. All that it will take is imagination. The time is ripe. I have made every preparation. Victory is at hand.

12/12/69

Rx wasn't as enthusiastic as I'd hoped he'd be. He just sat there and listened.

"Is that all?" he asked.

"Need there be more?" I responded.

"No, I guess not. But I thought that you might have had more. You always seem to be very thorough."

Mad Dog, who had been present, left the room.

Later, I tracked Mad Dog down. He was walking with Rx and I asked, "What do you say, Trek?"

"Do you expect an answer?" We were out on West Prospect Street headed down to Mercer.

"Well, I did come here with a proposition."

"You came here to tell me that I had to do things with you or not at all."

"That's one way of rephrasing what I said."

Rx laughed and changed his direction back to their little duplex.

I put myself between the boys and grabbed each of their arms.

No one changed his pace, but Rx said, "Mary, Mary Taylor, you are a persistent one, aren't you?"

I didn't respond.

"You've been at me for months despite countless rejections. What I'm interested in, is why? I'm not some kind of God. There are countless other organizers who have more influence and power than I have. Why have I been singled out among the others to be the recipient of your unflagging attention?"

"Just lucky, I suppose."

"Yes, I suppose so. Well, Mary, I can't give you an answer just now. You have been very persuasive and I need some time to think things over, if you don't mind."

And so that is how I left it. No commitment. T-Rx departed alongside his sidekick, Mad Dog.

As I sit in my chair here in the house I just rented, I think back on all the effort that I have expended in the last months and naturally ask myself whether the pain and sacrifice was worth it after all? What a question. How does one judge whether a particular course is a good one? Such a query is based upon the construction of hypothetical alternatives. But in the very construction of these alternatives, the decision has been made. It is within the framing of the scenario that I am really saying to myself, "yes or no?" For if it is "yes," then I will construct an inferior story about what I have. And if it is "no," then the opposite will transpire.

Sometimes things seem to be unreal. How can I, Mary Taylor, a simple former college student who hasn't had any excitement in her life, really be in a position to control the political fates of a major political leader, such as T-Rx, and bring an entire scheme to its knees? Oh yes, what full-bodied taste this has! Oh Cicero, even you would succumb to me, for I exceed Philippics in craftiness.

"Jug, jug," goes my tune as happy euphoria threatens to make me swoon to the jaded melody of Scipioi somnium. Oh sweet delirium, rest my powers omnium so that they resterium might mellow with imperium *magister artis ingeniique largitor venter*.[61] Or however it is supposed to go (I got a C- in Latin).

Just let me relax in the knowledge that pax is in good hands, *my* hands, since Rx is finally on my list of causes won. It is a rare moment, dear Diary, liber liberty, that I can let myself relax in something that I fully deserve, but which (up until now) has been most cruelly denied to my most magnificent and honorable person by forces and personae who preferred to wait for me in the shadows, lighting matches and whispering obscenities. But now the V-2 rocket is on the launching pad, Herr von Braun, and the evil will be expunged with one mighty blast! I shall be the queen.

---

[61] *Magister artis ingeniique largitor venter*—literally "the belly is the teacher of art and the bestower of genius." It is often cited as "necessity is the mother of invention."

The Amazon Wonder Woman who, riding on her red carpet, removes all pollution from the surface of this fair planet.

12/14/69
A bomb.

12/15/ 69
Bombs. Bombs. Bombs. They are gone. They tried to kill me, and they are gone. So stupid. How could this happen to me? How could I have been so naïve to believe that Trek could be trusted?

Why would I think that they would act honorably? How could I have expected dirt to transform? No longer is the epithet "bitch" or "cad" appropriate, but we must descend in the alphabet to "Z"— the rest of the letters don't matter, but you can't get any lower than z: zebra, zombie, zipper, all the same, they sing the shame of the lowest of the low.

12/24/69
Peace on earth to zlotys. Poles of the world unite! For one large Zombie has violated my zonal rights of the sacred zodiac. The consequences of this will be felt. I'm at a loss to write them down. I can't write (only zooids are real to me and ought to be imprisoned in the zoo). Yes, to the zoo with them.

12/25
I have written the zookeeper today so that these zoo chores might be zoostered with a zootoxin. The zookeeper will know what to do with them. Ha! He will find them and bring them to justice.

1/15/70
It has been awhile, little book, that I have privileged your pages with the scribblings of this demented mind. Seattle has been lost. I have finally accepted this. The Zulus have taken care of that. They are still free, as the zookeeper hasn't found them yet. I think that it is a menace that they are allowed outside of their cages. But they should be found soon, because the publicity of my statement has reached everywhere. Even the post office displays the pretty wares of my advertising campaign to track down these dangerous animals.

But Seattle is not the world. I should never have followed them there, searching after the dangerous Sasquatch. The treasures of the queen city were not to fall to me because of the dangerous panthers. They wooed me and deserted as quickly as they had come, and without even a tip of the hat or a twist of their paw.

1/22/70
Zounds. What fire hath brought St. Elmo? Another foray from the son of Prometheus? Must I yield to these zooans? Moran, Zoran, dastardly t-s-deal.

1/30/70
Turning and turning the widening zenith, the zeolite will not hold. The Zeus does not hear; the zero and Zeno's paradoxes[62] have been solved. My path has zig-zagged from disaster to Zen Buddhism. They say that when the z-curity deposits have all been exhausted, that the world will become the universal zeitgeist: zein. This simple protein is not some corny joke that I'm playing, but an ancient le-z-end, de-z-ended to us from the original zenana of the earth mother, Gaia.

2/25/70
Back in San Francisco, I'm awaiting the final collapse of what once seemed to be a promising empire. In hours I will know if San Francisco is gone, too. First Seattle, then Mr. Richard Zoran betrays me in Los Angeles, causing Tara and Ché to leave me, and now my old base of San Francisco is deserting me.

    In February, I would have been going to New York to line up my eager prospects. They all wanted me—just months before. I had union and non-union support alike. The blacks and whites, students and working-class: everyone clamored for me to be their leader. Then, as if my empire were made of cards, the queen of spades was pulled away and all came a-tumbling down.

---

[62] Zeno, of Elea, was an ancient philosopher in the tradition of Parmenides. Zeno offered three logical paradoxes concerning how the empirical sensation that motion exists is actually false.

Perhaps I was stupid or simply unwise. But I still don't see my serious mistake, which has landed me in the mire that I'm in. Was it pride, stupidity, ambition, or cupidity—which of the seven deadly sins did I commit? Was it that I was a woman?

The surf—will it blunder and beat me dead? Or the winds sing a dirge over my head? Swish, Swish, the sound of the water at the dock by the bay. I sit on Larry's dock. How many times I have sat with him. And yet for all his simplicity, I wish he were here with me now.

He had an uncomplicated way with everything that I took to be so unsophisticated. How many pretentions come with sophistication? When one is naked, how little can one hide the real defects of the body?

But where were my mistakes? How could I have known that Zoran would have only been out to organize the non-union people in Los Angeles? How could I have foreseen that this would cause terrific dissension that would destroy the fabric of our movement there? None of this was my doing. I acted in good faith and expected others to do the same.

And now what is left? My organization is dissolved and I am left alone with my checks from my father. I could go back to school, I suppose, but that doesn't seem like a world that I could return to now that all this has happened to me. College is a place for the naïve. They go and read dusty books about theoretical problems that never have had a practical impact on anyone. Even "political science" is based upon textbooks and not upon the canvassing of voters and practice in the political process. Talk and talk: it's the verbiage (that baggage) that is garbage to anyone who is ready to really act.

If I was beyond all that long ago, how could I accept such trivia now? Sometimes I can sit and think about my fate, just as I'm doing—knowing that even as I try to decide my destiny, the *final decision* is being made for me. Sometimes I can sit and watch the water slowly lap against the pilings and wonder what it is all about. But at other times, I am struck by a blind rage at the unfairness of my situation.

How can I accept a world in which there are people making decisions that affect me who are inferior to myself? Those stupid dolts who are in the legislatures and in Congress are mental midgets. All that they have is money and power. Well, I have more intelligence and will have money someday, but I have no power. I am superior to all of them. Yet I must be lorded over by some fat, old hippos who have collected IOUs of fear to get them where they are. They succeed with shoddy politics, and yet when I try something not half as bad as they have done, I'm not only struck down, but crushed.

When I retaliate, nothing results. My letter to the police did nothing. T-Rx is still out there and doing all the things that make him happy. The world is not governed by rules. Everything is chance. If I succeed, it is due to a fickle turn of the wheel of fortune and nothing else.

The sun is very hot, and I am scared.

3/4/70
I've gotten a wire from Alf. He has found T-Rx.

3/6/70
I'm in Chicago, and I've got an appointment to meet Alf. I haven't heard from him in a long time. I thought that he'd departed for parts unknown. I've lost everything, but there is still a chance that I can get lucky in Chicago.

I don't know why I follow him when he has rejected me so many times and is the man who has caused my downfall, but now that there is nothing left, I don't know where to go, except to him.

3/8/70
It seems that they are holding up on the South Side. An idea is hatching in my head. It is an idea that is too terrible to write down just now. I think that it will mean an end to the terrible headaches that I have been having.

3/14/70
"Why did you call me?"

I met Alf in a little coffee shop they call *The Reynolds Club* at the University of Chicago on east 57th street. It's a typical hang out with coffee, tea, small sandwiches, and used books to buy. We were seated at a table that was unbalanced. I thought about folding a napkin to make the table stable, but I decided against it.

"You wanted to know where Rx is right now, correct?" he said.

T-Rx: The History of a Radical Leader 234

"You know that I do."

"Well, what are you going to do now that you've found him?"

"I don't have an address."

"Well, you remember the business arrangement that we made over the phone?"

"You bastard," I replied as I put my hand on the salt shaker in the center of the table. I briefly fanaticized about throwing it against that arrogant British forehead.

"Now, Mary, that isn't very nice. You of all people should appreciate a person out for a little profit." Alf chuckled. God, I hate this bugger.

"Yes, I will pay you. I don't know what came over me, Alf. You don't know what stress—I've been having such terrible headaches lately."

"Have you tried aspirin?"

"Valium would be more like it, dear fellow, but nothing works."

"That's too bad."

"Yes, it is."

I sat there waiting for him to continue, but he was waiting for his payment. So I got out my checkbook and wrote him his amount.

"Here," I said, thrusting out my hand. "Now tell me the news."

"I'll give you a house number and phone number. The rest is up to you—when this check clears."

"Alf," I began, but then realized that he was only being careful. There was nothing to stop me from stopping the check once I had my information. I began to remember the feeling that I had always had about Alf. He was so dependable because you always knew that he was out for himself and could be purchased for a price. There was never any ambiguity in his character. Somehow that gave me a sense of calm.

A pimply-faced young college student stumbled near us, but caught himself in time before knocking over our table. We both laughed.

Then I leaned forward. "I have some *other* business for you."

"I'm listening."

"No, later. After this all sorts out—meaning the two numbers I just bought."

"That's fine with me," he said. "Afterwards." Then he left. He didn't even finish his tea.

Alf called me only two and a half hours after he left. "About that *other* business?"

"I want to hire you."

"Hire me?" he said without much surprise.

"Yes, I want you to follow Rx and Mad Dog."

"But why? What do you have in mind?"

"I don't know yet." I told him the truth.

"Do you want them dead?"

Then I paused a moment. "Yes, of course." I cleared my throat. "I mean, don't take me the wrong way. What I want in the best of all possible worlds is not the same as what I'd be willing to do in *this* world."

"So you want *me* to do it?"

"No. You don't understand. I just want you to follow them. I might hate them with all of my mind and soul, but I don't want to be the agent of their deaths." Again, I cleared my throat. "Not just *yet*, anyway. I need time to think. You are not going to be a hired killer, but I do want you to keep a close surveillance over their activities."

"How much?"

"$150 a week."

"Three hundred."

"That's absurd. I can't afford that."

"Well, you'll have to. That's my price."

"Now listen, Alf."

We dickered over the price and I finally got him to come down to $250. I live day-to-day. I'm staying in a flop down on South Campus–just past the Midway. I purchased the new pepper-spray product because it's not very safe where I am. I do all of this to maximize my cash reserves so that I can act when I have to. I hope I haven't just made a mistake by paying Alf such an outrageous sum.

He knows that if they were willing to bomb my place in Seattle, then they won't think twice about doing the same to me here in Chicago. I'm paying some insect top money to keep close to someone that I can't stand.

I don't know whether that is entirely accurate. I don't know what I feel towards T-Rx. What has he been to me? He was a man unlike other men. I suppose it is that simple. He seems authentic because he sticks to his eccentricities. There could be no clichés applied to Trek. He is so unique that each micro-epithet that is applied to him seems to somehow illumine a part of his character.

The man is a mass of contradictions, as we all are to some extent, except in him what is human is magnified to heroic proportions. This man is larger than life. I would swear beyond a doubt that the type of superman that I wanted to be was only some kind of projection of the person that I believe him to be.

I know he is great. There never has been any doubt in me about that. Why is this so? What are the objective criteria by which I can make such a unilateral unequivocal statement? There are none. The only "data" that exist are the reactions he elicits from the people closest to him. It is these people who are so stuck by the aura of this being that they must hover about him like moths to a light. Inside that man is some attribute that makes people want to devote their whole souls to him. What it is or how it works is a mystery to me. But I feel the results.

Oh, crystal ball, which has properly observed so little and advised me so poorly in my short life, I indite you to lend me the wisdom that I might transcend the verbal cells that can so constrain me. Please allow me to create a *new being* which can soar within a private world of my own making. I wish to rid myself of the imprisoning influence of this man. What a pack of lies this whole confession has been.

I have said nothing that is true, and diary I did promise to be true to you above all others.

4/1/70
I have no answers. There is no self-understanding. All is a joke. From now on, all that I will do is report what happens and nothing more.

4/2/70

Alf said, "It's true. Mad Dog and T-Rx have split apart. It's serious. I don't think that they will ever get back together."

"But why? What happened?"

"I don't know exactly. From what I have been able to determine, Mad Dog wants T-Rx to return to San Francisco. He was against leaving all along. Mad Dog thinks that T-Rx is abandoning his ideals for an existence of drifting. I think that attitude makes Mad Dog upset since he had given so much of his own life to the work that they carried on in San Francisco."

Alf has upgraded his outfit. He's now wearing ties with white button-down collars and tan polyester suits, cut full (perhaps to hide a gun?). The little man has re-packaged himself.

"So because Rx doesn't want to go back to San Francisco, they are apart? That seems a little far-fetched."

"Listen, I can only tell you what I hear: nothing more and nothing less." Alf was bouncing by putting his weight on the balls of his feet and then lifting and dropping his heels. It gave an impression of impatience.

"What an admirable journalist you are, Alf."

"Anything else that you want?"

"Yes, some good information."

"If you don't like the job I'm doing, then fire me."

Alf talks with such a flip manner. He isn't the servile worm that he used to be. I don't know what's changed him. Something about him is different, but it is naturally not something that I can ascertain.

4/3/70

I have moved closer to T-Rx. I now live near the baseball park. I have found a basement that someone is letting by the week. It is the cheapest way to live. My diet is getting very bad. I've had to cut down smoking because it's too expensive. One of my Dad's checks is late. I hope that it comes soon, because I'm in a bad way.

4/7/70

Still no check.

4/8/70
The people who I'm renting from have sensed that I am short of money and have offered me a job to do for money. They want me to strip and re-varnish some furniture.

4/11/70
Never have I had such an odious job in my life. I actually own a scraper. But it's seen better days and didn't do the job efficiently. The table took me a very long time to do, though the chairs went slightly faster. Per hour I'm earning about forty-five cents. That's under minimum wage. That's where I've been living lately.

4/13/70
After I've all done, my dad's check finally comes. I have half a mind to write him a scathing letter demanding that in the future he be more prompt, but I'm afraid that such an action wouldn't be politically wise for it might result in my losing any future checks.
There is at least one career job that I know that I never want, and that is being a furniture restorer. We have had a few hot days and I have been constantly sweating. I have no access to a shower so the best thing I can do to wash myself is fill the work sink in the basement and use my wash cloth. I don't know why the days must be so humid and uncomfortable. Some day they should have universal air conditioning—just like the movie theaters.

4/24
I don't know how long that I can sit waiting for those zebras to make some kind of move. I am running out of patience and out of money. I've managed to save a little dough in case they decide to move. Perhaps this whole thing is a mistaken journey? How does one determine whether she is on the wrong track in her life pursuits?
I see people all about me caught up in a long work cycle and not having time to think about anything that is important. They go to work so they can eat in the morning. But they are still half-asleep. And they get home so late in the afternoon that they are tired and must relax. By the time that they have had their dinner, it's bedtime.

Thus, the cycle may repeat itself. Why should life be so aimless? How can people exist without some plan for themselves? A master dream that they are striving to fulfill?

Perhaps that is my trouble in a nutshell? I have no such guideline for myself. But is that what I really want?

Will it be best for me to just drift as I have? Should I just go back to school? Certainly not. I must be a person in my own right. But what other options are open for me?

I could get married; yuck. I could get a regular job and become an eight-hour-a-day-zombie like those around me. But that would be committing an emotional suicide.

There must be something else. There must be some way that I can find personal fulfillment. I just haven't got a clue where that might be.

In the last few days I have dreamed about my thoughts when I was a little girl and how I had wanted to play the flute and take dancing lessons. I did play the flute for five years, but then I gave it up so that I could concentrate on my high school studies in an effort to get into a good college so that I could secure for myself a good future. After all, the television advertisements had said that in order to be happy, one should go to college. College was pictured as being the key to future happiness. The high school dropout was pictured as a dirty, unhappy boy pitching pennies against a wall, while the college student wore expensive Brook Brother's suits and carried a briefcase. The message was clear and I believed it—but where did it get me?

What is the value of all this knowledge printed on the pages of dead trees? We have successfully defoliated part of our country, but to what end? Does Mankind really have that much to say that is important?

Are all those dead white men essential to our fulfillment? I'm white, but I'm not dead, and I'm not a male.

The only thing I can really do anything about is make noise about the fuckin' United States involvement in the Vietnam War. This bus gives a ride forward to various unremarkable stops. None of these capture my imagination. Nothing exciting is here.

I did like San Francisco. But now I'm at Kent State in rural Ohio. It's a pinpoint on the World map. What a drag

4/30/70

I have found a place to stay with some girls in a dorm. This place is really hopping. I would never have believed it was possible to get so many committed people together at once. This is better than San Francisco State. The students here are really committed.

"So what are you planning to do?" I asked a girl who seemed as if she were a young eighteen. We were on the third floor of this girl's dormitory. It was a "modern" building, probably constructed in the early 60s. The walls were light green and the carpet was dark blue. It certainly had an institutional look to it—not like the faux-historical sleeping quarters at Macalester.

"Strike," she said, lifting up her little chin.

"You mean leave your classes and all?" (This would have been unthinkable at Macalester.)

"Damn straight." She ran her fingers through her long blonde hair that hadn't been combed for a while.

"But won't that mean getting lower grades?"

"You must be kidding." A couple of other girls had been listening to me, the foreigner. They now moved forward, surrounding me. They began snicker. They were laughing at me because I was so concerned about irrelevant "traditional" things such as grades and what this might do to their futures.

"But won't this mean that you will have to give up your careers and any hopes of success that you might have?" I was partly the devil's advocate, but I even surprised myself at my conservative views now that I was no longer an active revolutionary myself.

"We might never have any future if this War continues. Do you realize that we are the greatest war criminals in the history of Humankind? How can anybody just sit down and let this happen?"

"I'm no radical," said another. "I voted for Nixon and peace in '68 and that 'peace plan' of his never materialized. What happened? He was supposed to be winding down the War, but instead he has escalated it. He has had two years and nothing has changed except that we still have the same attitude that we will win this War because America has never lost a war. What a pigheaded attitude! If we made a mistake, it only weighs the heavier in continuing in it."

In my mind rang the response, *do you weigh the worth and honor of a king on a scale of common ounces?* But I said nothing. In a way I felt that the people who were demonstrating were undermining me in some way and so were my enemies. All of these suburban kiddies who were nurtured upon milk and Walter Cronkite were now ready to lay it down to attempt to change the federal government. It is a futile task. I feel sorry for them, but more than that, I resent what they are trying to do. The United States *is* imperialistic—so what? Isn't every other country on this earth? We are no better and no worse than everybody else. We don't want to lose face, but the Russians acted the same way in Hungary and Czechoslovakia. Why are we expected to live up to a moral scale that no one else follows—or ever has followed?

These self-righteous kids have glaring immoralities in their private lives that don't seem to matter, but they are ever so pious about the public morality. Hypocrites! What an easy task it is, searching for the speck in the national vision, when personal logs fester in the eyes of the critics and create internal pus that threatens to make us all blind to the real private evils that we accept so easily.

Behind all this idealism, I sense that there is some self-interest. It is extremely hard to believe that they don't think they will get a piece of the action somehow. Those student leaders are looking to run for the senate someday. Power is the name of the game to them and they love every minute of it, but in the end that is all that there is for them. It is an empty realm of false gods. If they dedicate their lives to it, they will perish like rotten wood upon the pyre.

5/1/70

Alf came to see me. It was noon. We were standing near the Pagoda, which is just off Taylor Hall. We were alone. Nobody was near us to overhear.

"There is going to be a demonstration," he said, leaning against one of the Pagoda posts. He was wearing a dark tan polyester suit with a red shirt and no tie.

"What else is new?" I said.

"There may be some violence." Alf took out a cigarette and lit it.

"What do you want me to do about it?" I stood my ground about six feet away.

"Mad Dog."

"What about Mad Dog?" I clenched my fists together.

"Shall take care of him?" Alf started fidgeting with his fingernails.

"No, I have decided that I no longer need your services. Finish out the week and you're through." I pivoted to turn, but stopped.

"But what about the terrible things they did to you? Don't you want your revenge?" Alf gave a big smile.

"The words are all hollow now. It's time that I started putting some things together. I want to get away from all of it."

Alf looked visibly upset. He wanted to kill Mad Dog, I could tell. He didn't want it only for me. He had some skin in the game.

"It's interesting how quickly some people can change," he said with hesitation.   There was a bitterness in his words, but then I saw a calm return, as if he had somehow resolved what was bothering him.

My dear fellow, Alf, shuffled away in defeat. The entire scene stuck in my mind. The first thing that I thought of was that he would try to kill Mad Dog himself. If this was true, then I had to warn Mad Dog somehow. For as much as I detested him, I could not just allow him to be murdered.

Late evening.
I made a phone contact to Marcia. She told me that she didn't see much of Mad Dog these days. According to the few details that she was willing to give me (and believe me, she begrudged each one) Mad Dog was not with the group any longer, and she didn't know how long she would be either.

"Someone's out to kill Mad Dog," I said.

"Who?"

"I don't know," I said, recognizing that she wouldn't believe me if I told her.

"Why are you saying this?"

"I want to help."

"That's good comedy," was the reply.

"Listen, I don't have to take your verbal abuse. Mad Dog is in danger. If you care for him, tell him. Otherwise, don't do anything, but know that you were warned." This conversation didn't satisfy my desire to warn Mad Dog because I felt that I was sufficiently alienated from Marcia to where she wouldn't report anything that I said.

5/2/70
I have decided that in order to stop the murder of Mad Dog, I must find him myself. Marcia said that he wasn't around, but Alf had told me otherwise. His information didn't tell me *where* Mad Dog could be found, just that he was in town. I started circulating in an effort to get information, but by afternoon (the time of this writing) I couldn't locate him. All the talk is about the strike. The students are intoxicated with the possibilities of their possessing great power. Such an atmosphere is very volatile. Anything can happen.

Evening:
I still haven't found Mad Dog. I am frantic that something is going to happen. I was approached by two students (who I didn't know) telling me to stop asking questions. They weren't locals. I think that there are a number of out of state people hanging around. I don't like this.

5/3/70
A preliminary demonstration is planned this afternoon. I have to find Mad Dog. Also, something tells me that there is too much pushing for student power. I can't find Alf for more information.

5/4/70
Gone. How quickly it can all change. I've got to find out where they went. All of those deaths. What a bloody mess. Not all the shots came from the National Guard. Not all the casualties were students. They say T-Rx and Mad Dog were hit.

5/6/70
I've found Alf by accident. I will follow him.

T-Rx: The History of a Radical Leader 244

5/9/70

New York. T-Rx and Mad Dog were transferred from Kent, Ohio to a special unit at Mount Sinai Medical Center. I don't know the extent of their injuries, but I *do* know that they were shot by the thug employed by Alf. The assassin also tried to kill me, but Alf mistakenly got in the way. Imagine, him saving me! The very man who despised me was my savior.

5/11/70

At the student demonstration there was an assassin out to kill T-Rx, Mad Dog, and me. But why was he out after us? I can see how he might have wanted me, but Mad Dog and T-Rx? That doesn't make any sense. Sure, the National Guard killed at least 4. I've heard that there are almost a dozen non-fatal gunshot victims.

There were shots from the general area of the National Guard, but not *by* them. Those are the shots that worry me. Were they from the same angle of the troopers by a sniper positioned from behind? Or was there a plant among the troopers? None of the details seem to go together. All I know is that I want to protect T-Rx and Mad Dog from a follow-up attempt at their New York hospital.

I feel partially responsible; I must try.

5/15/70

By the strangest bit of luck I ran into Mad Dog at the bus station in Manhattan. He was just about to board. He told me that I should travel to Baltimore. His information is that T-Rx would be going there after he left the hospital. He had thought that T-Rx had hired a man named Locke. Mad Dog had thought that Locke might be a hit man aiming to kill him, Mad Dog. Now he says he knows that Locke was only an alias for T-Rx. The man Locke and T-Rx were one and the same.

"But are they near each other?"

"Who?

"Alf and T-Rx." Mad Dog was standing at the door of the bus, holding the right door panel in his hand so that it would not shut and leave him behind. Mad Dog wasn't wearing his headband that had been his sartorial stand-by. He was without it.

"I'm not sure, but I don't think that Alf is alone. I have a feeling that there is more behind this than is obvious just now.

Listen, I can't stay here talking with you. Thanks for the warning in Ohio. If you want to find T-Rx, try Baltimore—near Johns Hopkins around 29th street. That's where I'm going, but I can't keep contact with you. It's too dangerous. I'm wanted by the police, you know."

With that, he departed. I wonder if I'll ever see him again. As I lay here late at night in my hotel room, I think about the past year and wonder what happened to me.

Why am I here and not dating some guy who wears an argyle sweater and blue jeans? I breathe deeply and wish that I could go back to all of that, but know that I can't. It just wouldn't be real for me anymore (if it ever was).

When you come right down to it, my life has been only an empty set of spaces. I have always been too concerned with where I was going and trying to get there before anyone else. I know that I should see a therapist of some kind to get my problems resolved. I am much calmer now, but my life isn't a bed of delight. There are the moments of loneliness when I want to die. It is at these times, when I want to lose myself. I think that there is no relief from these episodes of uneasiness. I have tried alcohol, drugs, and sex and nothing works.

Right now it seems that I am through with another act in the play. Guilt, or some force I can't understand, feeds me so that I am reduced to nothing. It's time for the curtain to rise on the next act.

T-Rx. Who is he anyway? Is he some kind of mental case? I wonder if he thinks that he is a god of sorts?

He is always being so cryptic. What is the purpose of this if not merely to create an aura around him so that others may swoon with reverential wonder?

I have thought about this man for such a long time that I cease to be objective about him. I wonder what he's going to do now. I don't know what drives him, and he is so mysterious. All that I do know is that he has affected others in the same way that he has myself. There must be something about that man that mesmerizes, but what it is, I'll never know.

6/15/70
I stopped in Baltimore for a week. At first I tried looking up Mad Dog and Trek somewhere on 29th street. I did locate where they

were staying, but they were out when I was there. Someone at the row house said they were downtown working on some sort of economics project. I don't know—sounds to be outside their wheelhouse: jobs for poverty blacks.

While in Baltimore, I have taken several trips to Washington D.C. and have visited my state's senator and my district's congressman. I'm back to associating with Minnesota. I wonder whether a letter from my father might land a job for me. They are hiring staff replacements all the time, and the summer is a good time to look. With the midterm elections in the fall, I often wonder whether students are really more concerned than they used to be. It is an odd question, I know, but the thought is interesting as it implies that a new breed of young person is emerging: one who will be more politically active at an earlier age. Since the draft age is now universally eighteen, then I suppose they will have to lower the age a person can be president to twenty-five.

6/17/70
I have decided that I should go back home and talk to my father about a career in Washington, D.C. I have made the necessary applications, but I am sure that what is needed is a letter to the right person to get me the job.

6/19/70
I am writing this on the plane. At thirty-five thousand feet, any mind is clearer than it is at sea level.

I told Tony that I couldn't spend much time in Washington, but the city seemed to draw me. He got *his* job through a contact and advised me that it would the best course for landing a job there.

The Washington life is so exciting: one has the opportunity of meeting the people who are making the decisions that affect the entire world! Some of the things that Tony has told me are unbelievable about the accessibility to power. I think that I would most like to meet Henry Kissinger. Some of those dinners that they hold provide the perfect atmosphere for meeting and socializing.

It's been so long since I've eaten on an airplane, I've forgotten what it was like: the little trays of what tastes like freeze-dried mystery food with a roll and a sweet to round things off. I wonder if this is what the astronauts eat? I note that they didn't offer *Tang* as a beverage choice.

6/20/70
It has been such a long time since I first renounced Edina, Minnesota. This place is no better to me than when I first left it. There are so many things about this town that I despise. It is really amazing to me that I was able to last as long as I did without any serious consequences. I have had to tell myself several times in the short while since I've been here that there is a purpose in it all and that I haven't changed. My father thinks that I've become the perfect daughter and my mother is happy that I don't hang around with that hippie crowd anymore. Myself, I wait for Washington. My life will be full soon.

9/21/70
I can't believe it. The AP wire service reported in the *Washington Post* today that Nehemiah Moses was found murdered in a rooming house in the Lakewood Heights neighborhood of Atlanta. He was killed with a gunshot to the head. The police have a suspect: Duvall Jackson. That's Mad Dog!

Of course, he didn't do it. Why would he? The two of them were probably still on their new theme: job training programs for unemployed urban blacks. They had tapped into some funding from the Great Society programs that Nixon hasn't cut yet. This was what they were doing in Baltimore: setting up a program with local people and then moving on when the locals had it under control.

Their next stop was Atlanta. That's where I think they told me Trek came from—either that or Alabama. I can't remember. How odd, if it is true that one begins and ends in the same place. And what happens in between?

I've got to remember my dad's birthday in 4 days.

10/15/70
I'm on another plane ride. Going back to Edina for my sister's wedding. It will be a big affair with 200 or more guests. I have nothing against my sister. She took her eyes off the argyle sweater prize. They tell me he's into banking and has a subtle sense of

humor. Well, I'd guess you'd have to have a subtle sense of humor if you went into banking.

My mind turned to T-Rx. I am profoundly moved by the principles that T-Rx stood for. At his funeral in San Francisco there were 1,000 people. He was iconic but none of us are really sure what he stood for. It's as if what counted in the end was his total presentation. He was an anti-leader. He wanted to lead from *behind.* Though we cannot set out his ideas in any clearly delineated form, the total presentation of his lived action still creates in me a strong visceral reaction. Somehow I feel that his principles were well-thought out, but for the life of me I couldn't put them onto some list.

I have no hero worship of this man, only a deep respect for his level-headedness and plain-talking demeanor. I am sorry for all the trouble I have caused him, especially concerning the Seattle incident. But the only one left to take that rap is Mad Dog, and I will never testify against him. He supported Rx all the way. They were brothers. And now they say Mad Dog killed him. No way.

I have not forsaken the ideals that I have always held. But now when I examine the path I'm on (working for the U.S. Government in the Commerce Department), I don't think I'll be able to fulfill them this way. I wish that I could have located Mad Dog in Baltimore—would that have made a difference? No, it wouldn't have because that whole quest seemed so futile to me then. After Kent State it was over for me.

Afterward to Mary's Section

Mary Taylor (not her real name) worked in the Commerce department and lived in Foggy Bottom a couple of blocks away from George Washington University Hospital. Because of the way of the world, Mary had to enter that shabby habitat of men. This was a dilemma of many twentieth-century women. How can she get on in an environment which is tailored for men? Men have gained power over business and government. The entire established order is operated by men. Women have, traditionally, been offered a place by the fireside, tending an indefinite string of babies, or else they adopt the status of an outcast. This latter type was often termed an "old maid" or a "slut." It is interesting to note that these radical alternatives were not the only ones open to men.

They had oppressed women to the status of slaves through the biological fact of the consequences of propagation. The tools for this are found in the major religions which rigidly adhere to moral codes which cling to pagan, mythic elements of a virgin-worship cult. Such feelings run deep. Biological actions are seen to have ethical significance, when all they are, at most, are modes of personal expression.

Women have fought long and hard for control of their own bodies (something that men have always had). Mary's struggle is, in part, Women's struggle against an entrenched moral bigotry that tells women that they aren't fully people.

Mary's anger isn't directed at T-Rx as much as it is against the society that has put her where she is. She knows that *the neat little pattern* that her father has set out for her won't allow her to become a complete person, so she has to strike out on her own. Of course, she has no "blueprint" by which to follow in her wanderings. What is she to do? She is like so many other young people: lost without any direction. They search for some purpose that will make their lives meaningful. They are tired of all the old adages of an established order that looks upon women from the beginning as inferior.

For Mary, there is nowhere to go. Feminism and feminist groups seem to her to be a collection of lesbians who only want to fight among themselves about issues that men want them to fight about. What examples has she to follow when the women leaders that she sees always point to the fact of their second-class status and thus reinforce this conception in their minds?

What Mary wants is no thoughts about affirmative action, or quotas for hiring women—in equality there need be no quotas, because women are *not* viewed as dirt. The only direction for Mary to go is forward: doing what she thinks at the moment to be the best for her. She must not sell herself to the male-dominated establishment, but work for a change in consciousness in this segregated community.

I see Mary's struggle as important from the way that it exemplifies the struggle of women in the United States even today. Oh sure, there have been "advancements." But when you scratch a typical male you see the same regressionist blue blood of unjustified, privileged *authority*. Women are constantly thwarted by men and forced to feel submissive, even while they are being crushed by such a hierarchy.

Mary stayed true to herself throughout the section that we have. It is impossible to say that were she now as a major public figure what her lot might be. Mary worked in the civil service until her death on September 25, 1980. Her apartment—so close to George Washington University Hospital—was not close enough to save her when she put a 35 mm pistol into her mouth and pulled the trigger. She was 32 years old.

(I.B.)

Part Three:

Deposition taken by the Atlanta Police on Duvall "Mad Dog" Jackson[63]

September 24, 1970
18:00 hours

Q: **Where** were you in the afternoon of September 20th?

A: Well, in the morning I was working with the SUCCESS group that Trek and I were forming in Atlanta.

Q: It doesn't seem like you have very much "success" now does it?

A: That's a smart-ass thing to say. We used the model that we'd established in Baltimore for job training targeting poor people. That program has been running independently for three months and has been placing fifty people a week into jobs.

Q: Baltimore's a big city. Fifty people a week is a drop in the bucket.

A: Tell that to the fifty people who have gotten a job that can move them off welfare and into a nice apartment.

Q: Off of welfare? Those sorts of people don't want to move off of welfare. It's a free lunch, and I'm the one paying for it.

A: Then you should be happy that SUCCESS is lightening your load.

---

[63] This material was obtained under the Freedom of Information Act (I.C.).

Q: A bunch of crap, if you ask me.

(Prisoner is silent. He drinks a glass of water.)

Q: Let's cut to the quick. You know why we're here. You killed your buddy Nehemiah Moses at or around 4:30 pm on September 20th 1970 at 2070 Meador Ave, SE, apartment #3 at Momma Bea's, a rooming house.

A: I didn't kill him.

Q: The landlady, Momma Bea, heard some commotion and climbed the steps to the third floor and found you standing above Nehemiah Moses. He was bleeding from a shot to the head. His blood was on your hands and the gun was on the floor. Later forensic examination showed that your fingerprints were on the gun. Do you confirm or deny this?

A: This is circumstantial. You don't know how it all went down.

Q: All right. Why don't you tell me?

(Prisoner is agitated. He starts scratching his left arm.)

A: We had a meeting. You can confirm that if you want to. It was with the local office of Health, Education, and Welfare. It was about funding for our SUCCESS project. The meeting was at 2:00 pm. but he didn't show up. That's not like Trek. He was always 5 or 10 minutes early. I tried to make do without him. The meeting ran until a little after 3. Then I went out and caught a bus to his place.

Q: You knew where he lived?

A: Of course I did. We had been in Atlanta for over a month.

Q: But you lived in different locations. Isn't that rather different than the way you used to be when you did your radical travels together?

A: Yes. I was staying with a relative.

Q: So, you didn't stay with him as you usually did because there had been a falling out between the two of you?

A: No way. I was staying with a relative and he got a free room from someone who supported our SUCCESS project. You might call him a liberal-minded patron.

Q: What was his name?

A: I'm not sure. I think it was someone who owned a peanut farm around Plains, but I could be wrong about that.

Q: A peanut farm?

A: Yes.

Q: And you think I'm going to believe that a Georgia peanut farmer gives a rat's ass about helping poor black trash get jobs?

A: Please, don't talk about these unfortunates that way. It's degrading.

Q: And you're lecturing me? I'm a cop and you're a bad guy.

A: Is that the way you see it? Sounds like the philosophy of a police state. I thought that the Constitution made us equal.

(There is a break when the interrogator leaves the room for a conference lasting 45 minutes.)

The Resumed Testimony:

Q: What do you know about T-Rx?

A: Where do I begin? I lived with the man for so many years. We've been through so much together.

Q: When you say *live together*, what do you mean?

A: We shared the same quarters, okay? We weren't queer or anything, if that's what you mean.

Q: When did this relationship begin?

A: In Alabama around '65, I guess. The March at Selma. You may have heard of it.

Q: Can you give us some of the details of your activities?

A: We just both worked in the Civil Rights movement there.

Q: What happened then?

A: After a while we went north to San Francisco. We stayed there until 1969.

Q: Was it then that you were involved with the bombing incident?

A: No. Trek and I had nothing to do with that.

Q: You did it; now admit it.

A: No, we didn't.

Q: We have a statement from a Mary Taylor.

A: She won't testify to that in court.

Q: What makes you so sure?

A: I know, because we didn't do it. We had a little tiff at the time. She was trying to get our attention.

Q: I wouldn't be so sure, Jackson. (Prisoner is offered and accepts a cigarette.)

Q: Now, we want some more details of your activities in San Francisco. Could you detail to us your activities there?

A: It's a long story. We started in San Francisco because we thought that it would afford us the most liberal setting for doing what we wanted to do.

Q: And what was it you wanted to do?

A: I don't know if I can give you a simple answer to that one.

Q: Take your time; we have all night.

A: Can I have a cigarette?

Q: Give him a smoke. (Questioner motions to stenographer)

A: We started working in the Civil Rights movements in the middle sixties in the South: Georgia and Alabama. I don't remember just how I met T-Rx. He must have been at a rally at the same time that I was. I don't know. But from the first moments that I saw him I knew that he was a man of vision and perception. He was different than a lot of the bleeding heart liberals who came to Selma and Birmingham. T-Rx was very hard. He acted not out of a sense that he was helping the blacks of the South as a morally righteous white boy, but he was doing what needed to be done. He didn't identify himself as either inside the establishment or outside of it. I think that T-Rx was a natural-born fence-sitter. (Laughter on prisoner's part.)

It was shortly after one of the demonstrations that I talked with him. We were all moving in a group around town in Birmingham and I went into a bar with him. He told me a lot about language—that was his pet fascination. You see, T-Rx believed that communication was the main barrier between people.

He thought that English and not Political Science was the most volatile of the classes being taught. It was his contention that the people in the United States were beginning to express themselves so imprecisely that in a short time they will cease to be able to communicate—except in vague, ambiguous speech. This, he believed, was the route toward combat: when we cannot discourse in civil speech, the outcome would be violence.

The disadvantage from this was that Rx lived for reading more on linguistics. He wasn't a man interested much in talking about art or baseball—his idea of relaxation was to read an essay in philology. Though T-Rx never had extensive schooling, he studied quite a bit about the roots of the English language. He knew some Middle English and Anglo-Saxon as well as smatterings of Latin. I think that he studied some of the theories of spellings. He was quite interested in how words happened to change. Once he told me all about some process in which a word started in Gothic and went to West Germanic to successive stages of Anglo-Saxon and finally to Middle and Modern English. Every word has a history that mirrors the history of the society in which it evolved. In English, we have had a history of people who have been sloppy speakers. Our inflectional endings dropped from the words because of analogy, which comes about when people don't care enough to distinguish their datives from their nominatives.

I can't say I understand a very great amount of what he was trying to tell me, but I did remember some of it. He talked about it often enough to me.

Q: This is all fine and good, but could you get to more important details?

A: Important! You don't know anything about T-Rx, do you? His whole name, itself, is a joke that he derived. There are no vowels in his name. Every English word has a vowel in it except T-Rx's name. Even the consonant combination is significant in some way, though I don't know enough about it to tell it to you. But it was things like this that Rx really considered important. He couldn't care less for certain endeavors by others in academic fields. What he was interested in was language and how we say various things to each other. It was from this concern that he became political. For language is a social thing. We talk or write from one person to another. In this way, language requires more than one person. This is analogous to political and economic problems. In politics, the problems begin when more than one person happens to inhabit the earth. If there were only one person, then things would be just dandy, but when an extra person has to be accounted for, the trouble begins.

Look at Adam in the Garden of Eden. If he had stayed by himself all would have been fine, but the minute someone else was brought in there, the system began to stall. The rights and responsibilities of more than one person require some kind of system of ethics and politics under morality. Human actions become coherent only in their own perspective and the extreme purity of a theocracy must fall to the sordid reality of power and imperialism. Throughout the Holy Books there are records of the close tie between language and politics. The Tower of Babel recorded how man cannot be united in a political or linguistic venture on this earth. Time and time again we have recorded violations against the "Word of God."

The Word is of utmost importance. We must never forget just what the *Word* is and what it stands for. For when we do, this country is bound to crumble.

(The prisoner is reprimanded for seditious talk.)

A: I'm so sorry for the prophecy, but you know it to be true yourselves, or you would have laughed at me instead of (garbled words).

(Prisoner is allowed a towel to wash the side of his face)

A: So beautiful. You have such finesse.

Q: When did this Nehemiah Moses become interested in overthrowing the United States of America?

A: Never.

Q: Did you engage in any anti-American activity in San Francisco?

A: No.

Q: Did you not organize multiple sit-ins and protests around the city?

A: We were involved in some.

Q: You organized them, you mean.

A. We were involved in some.

Q: Don't you call this activity anti-American?

A: No.

Q: Why not? You were always trying to subvert authority.

A: The authority to govern in our country is from the consent of the people. You say that we were against authority. This is true when you refer to authority that is not in accord with the Constitution. Authority that is wielded contrary to the Constitution and the Declaration of Independence is un-American, we abhor. We stood up for America. We supported the people of the United States who are the sovereign power in a democracy.

Q: Let the record show that you have not answered my question.

A: When we worked to organize our San Francisco Peace March don't you think that we had the consent of the people? What about the tens of thousands of people who joined us in a peaceful demonstration? You do understand that petitioning the government is a right under the first Amendment of the Constitution. We even got a signed permit to march from the mayor of San Francisco. You say that we are against the United States: what about the housewives and businessmen who came out and marched with us? Are they anarchists, too?

We weren't all just young kids. There was your entire middle class out there, marching in force, trying to tell their government that they were wrong. We were telling the government to stop killing our men in Vietnam. We were exercising a right that we have guaranteed us under the Constitution: the right to petition our government.

Q: That doesn't include the right to bomb or use violence.

A: You can't prove that.

Q: You don't think so? Then you admit that you did it?

A: I admit nothing. I merely said that you couldn't prove that we ever used violent means to achieve our ends.

Q: Then how was your friend murdered? By passive means?

A: The goons who did that deserve to be brought to jail, not me.

Q: We've got who we need.

A: Oh you have, have you? What about Alf McTaggart and Jason Davies?

(There is a general disturbance and the meeting is quickly ended at 23:54 hours/ 11: 54 p.m.)

Continuation of the interview with Duvall Jackson, September 25, 1970
07:00 hours

Q: You have your lawyer with you, is that correct?

A: Yes.

Q; Let the record show that the defendant Duvall Jackson is being represented by counsel during questioning. Now, you mentioned two names at the end of your last questioning, is that not correct?

A: How come I didn't have counsel last time?
(Prisoner is told by his counsel to shut-up and answer the question): I don't know.

Q: Just to refresh your memory, I will read you what you said: "Oh you have, have you? What about Alf McTaggart and Jason Davies?" Now, what relationship did you have with these two men?

A: Relationship? I didn't have any relationship with either one of them.

Q: How did you know about them?

A: One was in our group in San Francisco for a short time. I knew him through his being there and the girl he went around with. The other person I never met, but found out about in the year or so that I was moving around with T-Rx.

Q: You mean when you were following him?

A: Yes.

Q: Then you admit to stalking him for the express purpose of murdering him?

A: No.

Q: But you just agreed to it.

A: No I didn't. What I agreed to was that I followed him; not that I murdered him. I never agreed to that.

Q: But you do agree to having stalked him for the purpose of murdering him?

A: No, I never wanted to murder him. I followed him in the same way that the disciples followed Jesus or the brothers followed Dr. King. We saw a man who inspired us to be the best we could be. Why would someone murder that?

Q: But why would you go all around the country staying near to this man if you didn't want him dead? You didn't maintain friendly contact with him, did you?

A: T-Rx and I were not talking to each other near the end due to an argument that we had, but I didn't want to kill him. (Defendant's lawyer tells him to stop.)

Q: So you two had an argument, oh? That sounds like a motive good enough to kill a man.

A: It might have been for some, but not for me. (Defendant's lawyer taps defendant on the shoulder and then exits the room.)

Q: Let the record show that the defendant admits to having followed T-Rx around the country after *first* having a bitter argument with him. Now can you tell us something about this argument?

A: Yes, but first I need to give you some background information so that you will understand what I will tell you.

Q: Fine, but please be brief.

A: You mean I don't get all the time I require? Let me talk to my lawyer.

Q: When he returns you may talk with him.

A: All right, I might as well talk now. If I insist on talking to him, I'll only be thought of as uncooperative and suffer the resulting (garbled) as a consequence. You have to understand that where we lived in San Francisco was ideal for our purposes. We paid a low rent and could get all that we needed to eat from friendly produce men who gave us food in return for some small services we'd do for them.

Q: You mean extortion?

A: Well, if you call unloading trucks extortion. I swear, you are always trying to find something wrong with me, aren't you? You take whatever I say and twist it away from my initial meaning.

Q: I serve the public's good. I must protect it.

A: And am I not a part of that public?

Q: No, you are a prisoner.

A: Accused and not convicted. There's a difference.

Q: Only in degree, *boy*, only in degree.

(Prisoner refuses to talk until his lawyer returns. Interrogator leaves the room. After one-half hour the interrogator and lawyer return together. The last question is repeated.)

A: Well, as I was beginning to tell you, we lived in San Francisco in perfect conditions for the activities that we wanted to do.

Q: Didn't you work?

A: I told you we did some light work in return for our food, but we didn't have full-time jobs.

Q: And you lived off the state, eh?

A: No, we never took any welfare. T-Rx didn't believe in becoming wards of the state. He thought that such dependence might result in a loss of our freedom to operate in the way that we knew we had to. We lived from our meager work and the contributions that some of the people who lived with us made. Also, there were people interested in what we were doing and wanted us to continue. They also contributed so that we were never in need of any cash. We never had more than twenty together at one time, but we were comfortable. The people who lived with us would stay from four to six months usually, and then they would move on.

Q: If it was so great where you were, why didn't they stay?

A: Rx wasn't trying to build an army. He liked the idea of people, from all over the United States, who filtered into San Francisco, going back to wherever they came from but in a state of higher political awareness and sensitive to the problems of communication that plague our society.

Q: Kind of a training school in activism, eh?

A: In communication. It was a training school in communication. (Pause as the deputy prosecutor takes over the questioning)

Q: What exactly did you do at this training school of yours?

A: I'm sorry; I must have given the wrong impression somewhere. We didn't operate a school in any usual sense. I was merely responding to a joke that the other man made.

Q: He wasn't joking.

A: Sorry, but I didn't see how anyone could have proposed such an idea seriously.

Q: What did you do to the people who came to see you, then?

A: You have to understand, we weren't that organized. In fact, it was our intention to never organize ourselves.

Q: You mean you were anarchists?
(Prisoner turns to his attorney who has fallen asleep)

A: No. Don't you understand? How could a grammarian ever be an anarchist? A man who believes so strongly in the existence of publicly acknowledged rules of speech could never align himself to anarchy. You don't understand T-Rx at all.

Q: Nehemiah Moses.

A: Whatever. But that's not the point, is it? You asked me about attitudes and then you go and badger me. This isn't about getting the truth, is it? (Prisoner looks to his lawyer who has fallen back to sleep.)

Q: Answer the question.

A: T-Rx could never repudiate that which reinforced his life: rules. No, T-Rx loved rules. He would spend hours upon hours reading about Grimm's Law. This is a man who became enraptured over the thought of why certain changes in language came about. Do you seriously believe that such a man could set up a school in anarchy?

Q: No, I don't. If this man is exactly as you say he was, then I don't believe that he would have engaged in the things he did *in fact* do: violent acts against the Constitution of the United States.

A: Rx wasn't a violent man.

Q: No, if your description is correct, then I would find more plausible to believe that this self-made scholar would hide himself away in some turret at a university, somewhere in the library never to surface except for a learned article now and again. That's what I would think about this Moses, if he was really the man who you say he was. But frankly, I don't believe a word of it. I think the whole thing is just a collection of lies. Now what do you have to say to that?
(The prisoner doesn't answer. He is directed to answer, but stubbornly refuses. The questioning is postponed until the prisoner can be convinced that it is in his best interests to continue)
Questioning Resumed: 9/25 1700 hrs.

Q: Now, Mr. Jackson, we were discussing your activities in San Francisco. Can you tell us what happened to the people who came there from all parts of the country?

A: Nothing. Can I have a smoke?
(The prisoner is given a cigarette)

Q: What do you mean, nothing?

A: Just that. We didn't run a center of any kind that was organized like a school with a curriculum. There were no degrees given in how to be conscious of political communication.

Q: What attracted people to your group for, then?

A: I don't know. Reputation, perhaps, or maybe there were some people who simply felt lost and needed a sense of direction. I suppose there are as many reasons why people came as there are people who went.

Q: What are some of the activities, unscheduled, if you will, that went on in you group?

A: They would do things connected with the community. People volunteered in various projects that needed people who would work for free or at a very low cost: like tutoring the illiterate, work at drug centers for addicts, work at shelters for battered women, work for enrolling new voters—stuff like that. We were committed to helping the community so that we might know what issues most affected them. We were there to help.

  T-Rx and I were models for them. When we worked, they worked; when we got involved they usually got involved (though they were never under any compulsion to do so). We were very tolerant of anyone except the intolerant.

Q: Mr. Jackson, you make your organization sound as if it should have been funded by the Boy Scouts. It appears to have been such a high spirited organization dedicated to the principle of making us all better citizens. But isn't it a fact that you organized strikes that crippled a major college? Didn't you work with dissident farm workers? Didn't you form alliances with queers who are sexually perverted? For this last group you constantly struck city hall to change city ordinances and generally made a public nuisance of yourselves. Do you call *that* civic minded?

A: I never said that we were trying to make people better citizens. To do so would have forced us to commit ourselves to a stance we might not have been able to support. But we tried to fulfill our civic duty to the people of San Francisco so long as we were there.

Q: So you admit to being against the United States?

A: I admit nothing. We weren't working against this country. We saw ourselves as operating on the fringes of society. We sought to help the marginalized that everyone else wrote off. It was our only objective place. It was from there that we could deliver our messages. It was there that we could communicate to others—free from a self-interested motive. You see, all the political groups in this country have some kind of motive of self-gain. They attempt to tear down certain institutions for the sole purpose of placing themselves in the place of the deposed institutions. We never have had any pretentions to power. We had no interest in becoming leaders of some new society. The only thing that we wanted to do was exist on the level of the private man who is acting by himself. The few people who lived and worked with us did so because they wanted to help. We didn't intend to be anything more—in San Francisco or elsewhere.

Q: How sweet. I suppose you think that we should be giving you a medal instead of trying you for murder. (No response. Jackson's lawyer whispers in his ear) What do you think of that? (No response) Oh, well, perhaps we are right in taking in a murderer. It's all that we can do as policemen.
        Don't like the joke? Maybe you don't get it. (No response). Well, let's see, I think we should nail this down. Now, am I correct in assuming that you just went about your normal activities of demonstrating and begging food, no matter who was around?

A: We didn't beg.

Q: Work then, whatever you did. Am I correct that you took these neophytes along with you and showed them the techniques of planning and executing a successful demonstration?

A: There were no classes—

Q: I'm not talking about classes. Did you show them techniques of protest?

A: Not directly.

Q: Didn't they go with you?

A: Yes.

Q: Could they see what you were doing?

A: Yes.

Q: If they asked a question, did you answer them, even if the question was about the things that they were doing, namely demonstrating?

A: Yes.

Q: Thank you. Let the record show that Mr. Jackson has admitted that he and his associates instructed willing participants in the tactics of urban warfare.

A: Not warfare.

Q: Correct that to read urban resistance. Now, what I'd like to know next is to ask you *why*, if your existence in San Francisco was so idyllic, did you move away?

A: That's a very complicated issue.

Q: Well, suppose you begin and I'll cut you off when I want clarification.

A: It all began with the San Francisco March.

Q: You mean the Anti-War March of July 4, 1969?

A: Yes, the Peace March. Well, it began as an effort that Rx organized between some State people and a couple splinter groups.

Q: Who does State refer to?

A: San Francisco State College.

Q: Who were the splinter groups?

A: I can't remember really. I think they were fifty or so—Panthers and a few Yippies.

Q: Black Panthers?

A: Yes. At any rate the entire thing began mushrooming so that it was getting bigger than any of the organizers had planned. More and more groups wanted in. Now T-Rx didn't like doing things on a large scale, and he tried to get out of the planning business. But his reputation was such that the groups that were already committed threatened to revolt unless he stayed in the planning phase.

Q: Why was this?

A: People trusted T-Rx. When you get together so many divergent groups with different aims into one project, the risk that is that one group will convey its will upon the entire group. When that happens, there can be retaliations and sub-conflict can result, perhaps even open warfare between the groups.

Q: Warfare among peace freaks? (laughing)

A: People trusted T-Rx. They were right to put their trust in T-Rx, but that trust was a tremendous burden to him. He wanted to get out, but once he had been thrust into the leadership position, there was little that he could do to get out since such an action would trigger a tremendous discord within the city. Not only would the March be canceled, but violence and senseless destruction might result as well. T-Rx was in a predicament. He came to me to talk about it several times, and each time I suggested that we abdicate, but he was too insistent about the awful consequences that might follow.

Q: Didn't the consequences bother you?

A: Of course they did, but what bothered me more was the possible destruction of a man who I so highly respected and liked.

Q: What a change a few years makes.

A: Ha. You're partially right, but in a way that you wouldn't understand.

T-Rx: The History of a Radical Leader 270

(Another officer): What do you mean by that?

Q: That's enough, Wilson. I have an interrogation to conduct. I will run it in my own manner. Now, Jackson, tell me more about your conversations with Moses during this period.

A: Well, he was always on edge, which was unusual because, by nature, he was a much calmer person than how he was acting.

Q: When you say 'on edge' what do you mean? Did he become violent?

A: No, he was never violent. Well, hardly ever violent. I suppose you might describe it in terms of his verbal responses to the rest of us. He would snap answers and act sullen when he was by himself. T-Rx had a nervous habit of sucking air through his teeth so that it would make a sound. He would often joke about it, saying that when he would do this he was taking back all the evil things he had said that he regretted. You know, when you think about it, it almost was like the opposite of talking. He was pulling air back into his mouth and making a sound while talking is pushing air out of the mouth, making noise.
　　　　Anyway, when he was on edge (as in the time I'm just describing), he would sit by himself and alternately suck air in and sigh it out. It's difficult to describe, but you know those paired actions create one of the most plaintive sights that I have ever witnessed.

Q: This is all very touching, but could you please tell us why Moses was acting in this bizarre manner?

A: I have already told you. Perhaps you didn't listen. (Prisoner is reprimanded for being insolent)

A: T-Rx was depressed. He was forced into a leadership position that he didn't want.

Q: But he chose it.

A: No, he didn't. He chose to organize three small groups of people together into a demonstration of two hundred at the most. The alteration of the projected increased the size to over one hundred fold. This changed the nature of T-Rx's task. It wasn't merely transformed by a degree, but in kind. The task was one in which he wasn't enthusiastic.

You can see how a person of this temperament might take to such a task in a negative rather than a positive light. As I said before, I had encouraged him to leave and let someone else do the work, but Rx was too responsible to be liable for the results that might follow.

Q: And it was this pressure that made him leave California?

A: Partly. You see, there were two minor irritants as well. The press was nosing around, trying to get some story. Now, T-Rx wasn't averse to people making a living, even at the distinguished profession of journalism. But when the pursuance of such a career came in the way of his personal liberty, then he ceased to look on these guardians of our society as anything but nuisances.

I think that you gentlemen might be able to appreciate his position. Being as often times you must have been in uncomfortable places in which the prodding of the press made your jobs as police only that much more displeasing. Such was the situation of my friend T-Rx. He became slightly paranoid about the press being around. This led him to being more secretive than I've ever known him before. I can't say I was entirely sympathetic at the time. I felt that the press offered him an excellent opportunity to communicate some of the things that he thought were important. If part of our aim was to promote the most healthy, authentic communication, then what better way could we do it than through the written word (newspapers) and spoken word (radio and television)? Certainly the written word is as good as the spoken. I used to say to him that if he had such a prejudice against the printed page, then he ought to be consistent and not read those linguistic journals that he was addicted to (browsing in his spare hours).

Q: You were approached for news coverage?

A: Yes.

Q: By whom?

A: I don't remember all of their names.

Q: I mean who did they work for? Were they local or national?

A: Both, though there was more national pressure than local. The local papers had known about T-Rx for quite a while and weren't so taken by his flamboyant style.

Q: And was this pressure that you mention responsible for the interview in *Newsday Magazine* and *The New York Times* in that year?

A: Rx said that there was a difference between popular news and scholarly journals. The first was an instrument of power. Rx didn't want any power and felt that any notoriety that he might receive would only force him into more situations in which he might have to assume power. You see, Rx wasn't offering any counter plans. He didn't want to tear down and start over with himself at the helm. He only wanted to criticize and work on the level of the individual. The scholarly journal, he said, did just that. He claimed that it was designed for such a small audience. Its appeal was to the individual. There is no power base in scholarly journals.

Q: So you say that his behavior changed as a result of this "pressure" from the national media.

A: Yes.

Q: What were the manifestations of this changed behavior?

A: Well, he would go out alone more than usual and not tell anyone where he was going. He would bring strange people by and then act erratically by being friendly to them one minute and throwing them out the next. He used to be an open person with me, and at this time he became very closed off. He wouldn't even discuss what he was going to eat that day. When you know someone very well, then you can just feel the strain that he is under and you want to help. But with T-Rx, the more he felt the effects of his position, the more withdrawn and unpredictable he became. I would categorize it as some kind of mental illness, but of course, those terms were never used around the place. T-Rx was revered as an unmaterialistic man in a material age. This made him a holy man, and one does not criticize a holy man.

Q: You speak with some bitterness.

A: No, not bitterness. I just feel that it would have been better for us to have stayed in San Francisco. It was there that T-Rx had roots. San Francisco was the ideal town for him. It is such a tolerant town. I've never been anywhere that allows more people to adopt an idiosyncratic lifestyle and not persecute them for it. I believe that if T-Rx had remained in San Francisco, he would be alive today.
(Long pause as questioner gets some coffee. Prisoner is offered and accepted another cigarette)

Q: You mentioned two minor causes for his leaving the city. What was the second one?

A: I should reiterate that the major cause was his exalted position that occurred as a result of the 4th of July March. When the March was over, he could no longer step back into anonymity. The left-wing wouldn't allow that. They saw in T-Rx a man who would be all things to them. The Panthers thought that he was a white who would promote their cause, or at most one who could be manipulated so that their power might he increased. The Socialists saw him as a budding Joseph Hansen or Gerry Healy. Others saw him as the next Malcolm X. It was unbelievable the way that T-Rx attracted people. I don't know the reason for it. Perhaps it was the way he eschewed power. People don't like a person leading them who is fully enjoying the fruits of his own leadership. They want a person who they feel is their servant. A servant, it must he remembered, is someone who is pressed into service and acts against his own will. Rx gave that impression to others. He was their servant. He didn't seek power and position and so it was handed to him—even forced upon him. I think the surest way to power is to deny the aspiration for it.

Q: You mean this was all a ploy?

A: No, not in T-Rx's case. I was just formulating the principle. I'm still trying to work all this out for myself, you see.

Q: Let's get back to this second minor cause.

A: Well, there was this other member of our group, Mary.

Q: Mary Taylor?

A: Yes.

Q: Was she with you in San Francisco?

A: Yes, she had just gotten out of school. I think she had left after a year or something. I don't remember exactly. Anyway, she became infatuated with T-Rx and wanted him to become a national figure.

Q: And this affected T-Rx? Sounds strange, were they lovers or something?

A: What makes you say that? How would I know such a thing?

Q: You say that you were very close to Moses. Surely someone that close would know whether he was sleeping with a girl or not.

A: I know that they didn't sleep together.

Q: All right, stop picking hairs, did they have sexual relations?

A: I don't know.

Q: Don't you?

A: No sir.

Q: All right, we'll leave it at that. But tell me, why do you think that she had an influence on T-Rx's leaving Francisco?

A: I would characterize it as one small factor that contributed to his decision to leave. You have to understand how it was. T-Rx was a victim of his own good intentions. He wanted to stage a protest march on a small scale. It began as only that, but then things went out of proportion. He was into something that was bigger than he was. T-Rx was no longer in control, and he didn't like it. Around the periphery were the press and Mary. The press was troublesome because it destroyed his privacy. Mary was dangerous because she fed the fear that he would be pushed into something that he didn't want to be: a great political figure.

Q: He didn't want power (laughing).

A: No (whisper).

Q; What was that?

A: I said 'no.' If you haven't listened to what I have said, then you aren't as perceptive as that other goon who was questioning me. T-Rx was a man who wanted to do things in a small way. He wanted to control the events that he was involved with: nothing tremendous—just simple, humble action at the level of one person on his own with a few friends. There was something romantic in this vision, I know, but there was more than that. He believed that true communication only occurred at the personal level where men grappled with the strange meaning of nouns and adjectives. It was at this level that the language evolved, it was at this level that political change came about.

Q: What is all this language mumbo-jumbo?

A: You have only to look to history to bear me out.

Q: Could you be a little more specific as to how this has to do with Nehemiah Moses?

A: The normal word order is subject-verb-object. Now that sounds simple, eh? But it's not! There is a book here on how our language is sexist and how it contributes to racial unrest. This is a possible outcome but the people who put forth these claims are stupid jackasses who have never studied the history of this language or have any linguistic understanding whatsoever. They step beyond their expertise. When I think about all the people who talk about language as if they knew what they were saying, it makes me want to become mute and only move my hands in wild gyrations so that I might only be understood in the crudest manner. For so is the imprecise word usage and ignorance of almost everyone.

Q: That sounds as if it were memorized.

A: It almost is.

Q: This is the propaganda that you fed your students?

A: We had no students. I've told you that already. But this is a truism from the mouth of T-Rx. And many of us revere its truth.

Q: You speak of him as if he were a god. That's certainly different than your tone just a minute ago.

A: It's never been absent. If you didn't perceive it, then that says more about your perception than any change in attitude on my part. My dear fellow, let me assure you that there was never a time in the string of moments when I knew T-Rx that I didn't consider him a very worthwhile man who brought much good just by his very presence on this earth. He may have been misguided in certain respects, but that never altered my basic awe of him.

(Pause as the questioner gets more coffee. Prisoner is offered and accepts a cigarette.)

Q: Let's take it from the time you left San Francisco. You had decided on somewhere, or did you merely take off and go where you pleased?
A: We didn't really have a plan. We just headed north.

Q: How did it work? Who decided on Seattle? Was it you or Moses?

A: Neither.

Q: Would you mind explaining that?

A: It didn't work that way. You see, T-Rx was getting restless. He wanted to alleviate the constant pressure cooker that he felt we were in, to expand nationally. In San Francisco, everyone wanted him to step forward as a national leader. He was their superstar. If he stayed there, they might have nominated him for public office: senator, governor, or even President of the United States.

This was the plan of Mary. But T-Rx would have none of it. For him the only answer was to escape somewhere. This is where I agreed with him—to a point. I thought that he should leave as well; but only for a short time. I was convinced that our home was and always should be San Francisco. I talked with him about it but as I think back on it, I can say that though my thoughts at the time were crystal clear, we weren't in real dialogue together. He had shut himself off. I just assumed he agreed with me. What he agreed with was that he should leave the city. But I suppose that his ideas about returning weren't as firm as mine.

Q: So you just left?

A: No we decided that we should leave, but it took us a while discussing where we should go. You see, I thought that it should be somewhere on the West Coast since I was convinced that we would be coming back shortly and there would be no other real alternative to us since hitchhiking across the country would be too grueling for us and our monetary resources were rather limited. There was no real group decision. In fact, most of the people in the group probably didn't know what was happening. I imagine that they were surprised at the news when they heard it (laughing).

Q: Fine. You've told us quite a bit about why you left. But how did you choose Seattle?

A: Hook.

Q: What?

A: Captain Hook. He was a member of our group. He had been based in Seattle. He had a small band and had some gigs already lined up that paid pretty well. He was willing to rent a house for us, so why not? He told us marvelous things about the Queen city. We had everything that we needed. It would be perfect. The decision was no more mysterious than that. It was almost entirely random. We had a nice opportunity for the things that we needed and so we took it. You have to understand that I thought of this respite as sort of an extended vacation. I thought that we'd stay until the year was out and then return home, with T-Rx rested and ready to resume his schedule.

Q: Let me get this straight, you weren't forced out of the city in any way, but went of your own accord?

A: Yes.

Q: Did you know that we have testimony from a women's action coalition who said that they expelled you from San Francisco because you weren't on board with them?

A: What do you want me to do about it? Jump up and down?

Q: Does that mean 'yes' or 'no'?

A: That means that you are an idiot and it is difficult to talk to such stupid people as you.

(The prisoner was instructed in forceful terms not to be impolite)

Q: Now, comment please on why were you run out of town?

A: We were not run out of town. (Prisoner spits on the floor)

(The prisoner was reminded again to be respectful)

A: Now, that's better. I haven't been roughed up in a long while. Thanks for the unconstitutional rough house. If my lawyer weren't a drunk, he'd be able to document your treatment of me. I'm pretty certain that the stenographer (while taking my words) did not record (inaudible).

Q: Shut-up. He will come in directly. You aren't his only client, you know. If you had money you could pay for one yourself. Be thankful for what you've got at the taxpayer's expense.

A: They pay your salary, too, don't they?

Q: Was Rx, I mean Moses, run out of town by dissident groups?

A: You know, if my body was more resilient to physical abuse I would continue answering these questions in the way that they should be answered. But you will have a cooperative boy, here, yes, sir. I will cooperate better than anyone. Is that what you want?

Q: Jackson.

A: You want my full answer?

Q: No.

A: Well then.

Q: What?

A: That's your answer. You said it.

Q: Don't get smart again.

A: I told you why T-Rx left. You don't have to believe it, but that's the way it is.

Q: Listen Jackson, I've had all I can take of your smart aleck comments. You get your black ass in line with our inquiry or you will wish you had. I'll keep you up all night for all that I care, and no more cigarettes.

A: I've spent so many pleasant nights in your pleasant jail already. Do you really think that another frightens me?

(The prisoner is taken to his quarters)

Continuation of the interview with Duvall Jackson September 26, 1970: 02:25.

Q: Now, Jackson, I hope that we find you ready to be more cooperative than you were last time.

A: Can I talk with my lawyer?

Q: Certainly.

A: Alone?

Q: You've had plenty of time for that earlier. Let the record show that Prisoner Jackson has requested and received different counsel. He has been given ample opportunity to meet privately with counsel before questioning.

Now, what we want to know is a little more about the alleged bombing incident in Seattle, Washington on December 14, 1969.

A: What do you want to know?

Q: How many people were in on the incident?

A: How should I know?

Q: Well, you were in on it for starters. I think you'd know who did it.

A: Hey, now; where did you get such crazy ideas? I wasn't in on any bombing. I know that one occurred from reading the newspapers, but I'm not in any position to talk about something that I wasn't involved in.

Q: Are you expecting us to believe that you knew nothing about the bombing?

A: I told you; I read about it in the papers. That's all.

Q: But you have admitted in questioning that you knew Mary Taylor and that she was once a member of your group, is that not correct?

A: Yes.

Q: And is it not correct that there was considerable friction between Ms. Taylor and Nehemiah Moses?

A: What do you mean by friction?

Q: Did they like each other or not?

A: I think that she liked him very much.

Q: And did he like her?

A: Now, to that I couldn't say. How can I speak for what another man thought or felt? I mean, anything that I might say would be pure conjecture on my part, wouldn't it?

Q: You say that you were very good friends with the deceased?

A: Yes.

Q: But at the same time you would have us believe that you didn't know whether he liked or disliked someone as pivotal as Mary Taylor?

A: What makes you think that she was important?

Q: She did head a splinter group called the Workers Liberation Front, which was gaining influence at the time--considerably more influence and organization than your own following had in that period, I might add.

A: We weren't looking for a power base.

Q. But you did realize that Mary had one?

A: Yes, I suppose so, but what difference does that make?

Q: You have also said that Mary tried to pressure Nehemiah Moses to organize, and that she was a contributing factor to his leaving San Francisco.

A: An incidental factor. You will remember that I said that she was only a minor cause. The principal cause was his disdain for power.

Q: Quite so, a disdain that brought him to a city for escape. And such an escape it was; he attended meetings all around town, drumming up support for his cause.

A: We never had a single cause.

Q: He went to these meetings to do one thing: to obtain support from other groups in the area. Now, there is only one reason that a person would want to build up the support of radical groups, and that is to accomplish some task. This is logically deducible from the evidence. To argue with such a conclusion is mere stupidity. Now, Mr. Jackson, I will ask you again, why did Moses wish to bomb Ms. Taylor? Was it because they represented rival factions and Moses wanted to eliminate the competition?

A: You've got it wrong. Rx was not trying to build any base of support. Look, I'll concede one point: that T-Rx and Mary Taylor broke apart for ideological reasons. Mary favored a highly organized approach. She wanted to create this super organization and become a dominant force in American politics, but T-Rx would have none of it. He wanted to stay small. He needed to do things his own way. Since he believed that mass communications dulled personal intercourse, it would be hypocritical for him to organize any group whatever. He couldn't become big, because the erosion that he had detected had occurred because of "bigness" itself. T-Rx didn't have anything that he was trying to sell. He wasn't an activist, really. I suppose I'm even more of an activist than he was—you see, he just wanted to make people think. He was like Socrates: his grand purpose was to make people question themselves and to be able to communicate their feelings constructively to others.

Q: How touching, but if I'm to make anything from the garbage that you just said—

A: It's not garbage! (Prisoner is visibly angry and is reprimanded; the interview is paused while the interrogator gets coffee. The prisoner is offered and accepts a cigarette)

Q: Now, let's continue. I don't understand how I'm to get any constructive information out of you because of your clearly hostile attitude. You obviously don't want to tell us anything, do you? (Prisoner is silent)

Q: No answer, ha, I wouldn't think so. If you were smart, you'd listen to your lawyer. Spill your story, and things will go much easier on you in court. This whole justice business is connected, you know. If you're nice to us, they'll be nice to you.

A: What do you want?

Q: The inciting incident.

A: There was none.

Q: You mean Moses bombed Taylor for no reason?

A: He didn't bomb her.

Q: Who did, did you?

A: No.

Q: Well, who was responsible? Listen, we know that things travel fast in the subculture that you live in. You pass information faster than the wire services.

A: You have to understand that we left Seattle before the bombing occurred. We would have no contacts. I couldn't hear any rumors because we were gone.

Q: You left the day of the bombing, not before. We have statements that will prove that. But what we're really interested in is why it all happened. Now, you say that Taylor broke from Moses because they had different ideas on how their radical message should be conveyed? Now it seems to me that Mary's approach, in order to be effective, must consolidate and annex all the splinter groups she meets within a given area. Could it be that Nehemiah's anarchist influence was making her job more difficult and so an open warfare resulted?

A: I don't know. You seem to know more about this than I do.

Q: C'mon, Jackson. Don't treat me as if I was some kind of thick-headed cop. I have been to college and I know the subtle things in life probably better than you or your dead friend. Show me some respect and don't feed me these illogical responses to intelligent questions. Moses and Taylor hated each other. There could only be room for one, so it became a question of who would strike first, isn't that right?

A: Look, you are so sure that T-Rx did it, why do you even ask me any questions? I have told you what I know about the bombing. Rx didn't do it. Perhaps Mary bombed herself and tried to pin it on T-Rx; did you ever consider that?

Q: Yes, we've thought of them all, but none of them ever really removes the blame from Nehemiah Moses and his group. I don't know what makes you so reticent to talk, I mean, he's dead. No one could put any responsibility on you. All we want to know is, who helped Moses do it?

A: It would be so easy to affix blame to a dead man, wouldn't it?

Q: Yes.

A: But what would I do then? I'm accused of murder. I will probably be found guilty due to an unfair system of "justice." So if I lie now, what good will it do me? All I have is the truth. That will be the only solace that I will have, sitting there in prison. I will know that I am right, and that everything you have been saying about T-Rx is a pack of lies. But you see, gentlemen, if I start lying now, then I will have nothing to strengthen me within those dark walls when I'm railroaded by a pack of lies. All I have is the truth, and I have to cling to it.

Q: Well, now that you've decided to tell us the truth, perhaps you'd like to enlighten us on just what Moses was doing in Seattle if not trying to drum-up support?

A: He was there for a rest, as I told you earlier. T-Rx had been under tremendous stress and I'm not sure how much more he could handle. It's true that he attended political meetings, but he didn't have any grand design in mind. T-Rx wasn't that orderly. He would think of something that he felt needed doing and then go do it immediately. This is not the behavior of a person scheming to gain political power at all costs. This is not the kind of man who would sleep dreaming of some grand design. No, it is a man who is used to living around a certain type of person.

   He would naturally stay around that same type of person wherever he went. You, for instance—if you went to a city where you were a stranger—might try and locate other policemen so that you might have common ground with someone--or if you see yourself as a tennis player, you might go to a tennis club, because the people there are familiar. It is a natural human response to the unknown.

Q: You say that the only reason that Moses frequented radical meetings was that he was used to that type of person, and he went there just to be comfortable.

A: That's essentially right.

Q: Is there anything wrong with it?

A: No.

T-Rx: The History of a Radical Leader 286

Q: Well, there's plenty. Nehemiah Moses was a known agitator. You have said as much yourself, whether you want to admit it on a small level or on a larger one. The fact still remains that he caused trouble. Now if you accept this, as you must since you have stated the same thing in so many words, then you have to also accept that Moses' presence in those meetings stirred things up—whether he intended it or not. He incited people wherever he went. Now you may claim that it was simply his natural instincts to act the way he did. This is what you've been telling me just now—but to that I respond that his natural instincts must have been directed toward inciting people to violence (which is against the law). He is responsible for his conduct and any of his accomplices are also responsible.

No response? Well, you have that privilege not to incriminate yourself, though your silence speaks louder against you than you ever could. Let us proceed. You left Seattle for whatever reason you had. Where did you go then?

A: Missoula, Montana.

Q What did you do there?

A: We worked in various odd jobs.

Q: Did you stir up any radical activity?

A: No.

Q: You mean that you didn't even go to any meetings?

A: No.

Q: But I thought that wherever you went, you sought out the radicals because it was only with them that you felt comfortable.

A: We didn't associate with any radicals.

Q: So what you told me just moments before was a lie, wasn't it?

A: No.

Q: Explain yourself.

A: I can't; things were different.

Q: How were they different?

A: I wasn't close to T-Rx or the others at that time.

Q: Why was that?

A: I'd rather not go into it.

Q: Was it because you were feeling bad about the bombing in Seattle?

A: No.

Q: Wasn't that the real reason? Weren't you experiencing a power struggle at that time? Maybe you had different opinions about the bombing—whether it would be successful or whether it was the best tactic to use?

A: No.

Q: Didn't you get into a fight with Moses because you didn't think he was handling the operation in the way that you wanted it to be?

A: Stop it.

Q: Didn't that result in an open rift between you two where you vowed to depose him as leader of the group?

A: No, you've got it all wrong.

Q: Have I? I don't think so. I think that you became so upset by his opposing you that you planned revenge.

T-Rx: The History of a Radical Leader 288

(The prisoner, obviously shaken, puts his head in his hands and sighs heavily)

Q: Come now, Jackson, answer me, wasn't it then that you planned to kill Nehemiah Moses? Didn't you dream of killing your friend T-Rx?

(The prisoner's sighs turn to violent sobs; he is on the point of hysteria)

Q: Answer me!! Talk to me, you lousy killer. Tell me how you did it. Tell me how you killed him.

(The prisoner attempts to get up, but is forcefully restrained by the guards)

Q: Jackson, you weak excuse for a man, can't you face up to it? Can't you admit your murder?

(The prisoner looks up and grasps his right arm with his left hand. Both hands are held in tight fists. There is great strain in the prisoner's face, but he is no longer crying.)

A: What do you want?

Q: Your confession.

A: What do you want me to confess to?

Q: The murder of Nehemiah Moses.

A: I will confess to anything else, the Great Train Robbery, the Assassination of President Kennedy—anything, but I won't admit to doing that.

(Prisoner is speaking in a barely audible voice)

Q: Repeat that Jackson.

A: I didn't think he should have gone to Seattle. I thought that he was associating with the wrong types of people. They were people who wanted to use him for their own designs. He tried to escape that kind of pressure in San Francisco, but he only got more of it in Seattle. They wanted him to be their king. T-Rx was the new messiah. He listened to their prating, but I knew that he couldn't accept any of it. There was trouble starting between the whites and blacks over influence at the University of Washington.

I think that he wanted to stay and alleviate the bloodshed if he could. The bombing? I don't know who did it, but I do know that Mary Taylor was stirring up a lot of hatred on both sides. She was playing one side against the other. I think that one of them did it. Rx tried to stop it, but was unsuccessful. He got blamed by her, but he was only trying to be a peacemaker. It wasn't his fault.

(The prisoner drops his arm and falls forward; his right arm is bloody where he had torn the skin with his fingernails while talking. A staff member is called to administer first aid.)

Q: Now, suppose we go back to that trip that you took. Where did you go after Missoula?

A: Minneapolis.

Q: How long did you stay?

A: I don't know; a couple of weeks.

Q: Then you went to Chicago?

A: Yes.

Q: Would you describe your relations with Nehemiah as cordial at this time?

A: No.

Q: Were you hostile?

A: We just weren't speaking to each other.

Q: Why was that?

A: Do we have to go into that?

Q: Yes.

A: Couldn't we wait until morning? I'm tired.

Q: We're all tired. The sooner you finish the sooner you will be permitted to sleep. Now, tell us what the primary disagreement was.

A: I thought that he was betraying everything that we had worked for.

Q: What do you mean?

A: We were running just like we had some years earlier in the South. We made a vow then that we would never run again. We said that we would live our life in one place.

Q: So you didn't like moving around?

A: Yes, but not for itself, but for what it did to Rx. He was a broken man in Chicago. I think that he thought that his way of life was over. He could not go back to it. People who had special interests in T-Rx would make sure of that. He tried to help in any way that he could, but Seattle was a failure. I knew that it would be. He needed a rest and only got more headaches. Now he was running away from all of it. He was changing, and I couldn't give him the lip service that he sought because I felt that it might have ultimately made his condition worse. I cared for him too much for that.

Q: So because you were his friend, you avoided him and made everyone think that you hated him.

A: Who said that I hated him?

Q: We have our sources.

A: They lie.

Q: Then you didn't hate him?

A: No.

Q: You put on a pretty good show. Open hostility, drunkenness, loud behavior—it would appear that *you* were the broken man and not Moses.

A: What happened to me is my business.

Q: Correction, it's our business too.

A: This has nothing to do with anything.

Q: I think it does. Why did you suddenly befriend Alf McTaggart?

A: What do you mean?

Q: In Chicago. Do you pretend not to know that he was working with a man named Locke and that Locke was tied to a Jason Davies, a known underworld figure?

A: So that's why you're interested in all of this? Underworld, eh, pretty big feather in your cap if you can put one of them in jail. There's nothing in a small man like myself. Ha, you say that Alf was working for a man named Locke? Didn't you know that Locke and McTaggart are one and the same?

Q: How do you know this?

A: Locke and Alf were on the trail of Rx, only I didn't know it. Alf kept telling me about this fellow Locke who was going to kill me in Ohio, but it was Alf who took the shot at me. I was wounded superficially. Don't you see, McTaggart was trying to kill *both* of us.

Q: But how do you know that it was McTaggart's plan to fabricate the existence of another killer?

A: By simple deduction. Locke was supposed to have killed me in my room, so I was notified by Alf that I should be sure to come to the demonstration. This was supposed to be for my protection. Then I saw a couple policemen who weren't policemen. One was Alf dressed for the part. I didn't make the other guy. We were recognized and one of them fired at both of us. I got the better of it.

Q: Which one shot you?

A: I can't be sure. They were moving about.

Q: When was this?

A: This was just as the demonstration was to occur.

Q: You mean to say that McTaggart was disguised as a policeman?

A: Yes. Him and a confederate. Both of them stood out to me. They didn't walk-the-walk convincingly enough.

Q: But why?

A: I don't know. I had been told that this fellow Locke was out to kill me. I thought at first that Alf and Locke were working together; one would hang about my room while the other was roaming the streets for me. But what seemed strange to me was the fact that Alf had been working for Mary.

Q: Mary?

A: Yes, Mary Taylor. She had been tracking T-Rx and me since Chicago. She told me that she hired Alf to keep tabs on us. That is why it seemed rather strange that he should fire at the person who was paying him—or used to pay him, I should say, since he had been sacked by her.

Q: Then it's your guess that he was mad at her?

A: No, I don't know exactly what I thought at the time. I was confused at why he was firing at us, but then I guessed it. Mary came to me telling me that someone was out to get me. She had heard this from Alf. Alf had called me telling me the same thing. For some reason, Alf didn't want me around my hotel room. The only reason I can think of is that T-Rx was planning to see me there and Alf didn't want that to happen.

Q: Why?

A: Well, if someone wanted to murder T-Rx, then his best bet would be to get Trek alone. It was to the killer's advantage to isolate T-Rx, and what better circumstances than when Rx and I were arguing? The day of the demonstration would also be ideal, since there would be so much confusion. I think that the plan was worked out down to the last detail.

Q: But this still doesn't explain why someone would want to kill you and Taylor.

A: I know. That bothered me for a long time, too. You see, I don't think that it could have been mere chance that Alf was trying to get the message to me. I don't see myself as the hunted man. And I don't think it was an accident that the name of T-Rx was often linked to this man Locke as the instigator of my death warrant.

Q: You were told that T-Rx wanted you dead.

A: Yes.

Q: Did he?

A: Of course not. That's just the point. It was a ploy that they were using to further split us apart. I never really believed it, myself, but it was confusing for a while.

Q: That could be another motive for you, you know.

A: You're missing the point again. Listen. I have told you about all of these planned occurrences, but what I haven't told you about was the accident.

Q: Accident?

A: Yes, the happenstance encounter with Alf. T-Rx and I were heading toward the demonstration. He hadn't planned on running into us. When he saw us that afternoon, it was a complete surprise to him.

Q: Why do you say that?

A: His actions. If he had been ready, then he would have had ample opportunity to have killed us in a sophisticated manner. All would have been very simple. In our walk that day we had been in situations numerous times when we would have afforded a sniper to have had several good shots at us with no trouble at all. For example, it would have been much easier for him to have killed us when we were isolated in town. The entire episode was too ad hoc.

Q: So you think that because he merely wounded you that he hadn't been planning to kill you?

A: Yes, he had had so many opportunities earlier, which, if he had been out to kill me, it would have been very easy.

Q: I'd agree with you there.

A. His face also showed surprise. It was as if our recognizing him constituted a threat of some kind. We weren't supposed to see him there. He was there for a purpose, but it wasn't to kill me or Mary.

Q: Where was this? Was this near the site of the demonstration?

A: About fifty yards away.

Q: What connection do you think there was?

A: Why T-Rx, of course. He had been the target all along.

Q: T-Rx?

A: It fits very well, especially since you just now associated the names of Locke to Jason Davies. I think this connection brought the synergy to Ohio. Davies was on the trail of Rx all around the country—ever since the South. *He* was after T-Rx. I didn't find this out until I reached Baltimore, shortly before his fatal trip to Atlanta. That was the end of our sojourn in the South. If Locke was the same as Alf, then he was working for Davies in the hunt for T-Rx.

Q: It's a nice theory except for one thing. We have found evidence linking McTaggart to Richard Moran, a mobster from Los Angeles. From a letter and a decoded Western Union telegram, we have been able to determine that McTaggart was being hired to kill Mary Taylor and not you at all.

A: I don't understand. You mean Alf was working for Mary, but at the same time taking money to kill her?

Q: That's what it looks like. Your friend Alf was playing one against the other, getting money from both hands. When he met you that day, he was not in the midst of an operation concerned with killing you.

A: But if that is so, then isn't she still in danger? Won't someone try and kill her now?

Q: Apparently not. She hasn't reported anything for some time. She's working in Washington D.C. for the government and seems to be doing very well. Perhaps her position has bought her protection; I don't know.

A: But couldn't there have been some mistake? Alf was hired to scare her or something less than murder. I have too much respect for his talents to believe that he couldn't have killed us all if he had really wanted to do so.

Q: There was no mistake. McTaggart was hired to take care of Mary.

T-Rx: The History of a Radical Leader 296

(There is a break while the interrogator is given some coffee; prisoner is offered and accepts a cigarette.)

A: But couldn't McTaggart have been working for both Davies and Moran?

Q: There is that theoretical possibility, but then so could you. Speculation isn't a policeman's work. Facts are. The facts indicate that McTaggart was working for Moran and Locke for Davies.

A: But Locke is the same as Davies.

Q You haven't given me any sound proof to back that up.

A: All right, what about the time we were in Warrenville, New Jersey, and I saw Alf leaving the hotel. When I checked the register, the only recognizable name written was that of Locke?

Q: That doesn't prove anything.

A: Don't you see—the night clerk knew everyone but two or three faces and all of them had been there before except this Locke or Alf. It all fits.

Q: Try putting that evidence before a jury and see how far it gets you. It's just too loose. I think that you might be trying to construct a smoke screen so that we might stop thinking about you as the prime murder suspect.

A: You mean that in your thorough investigation you didn't uncover the fact that there had been several people following T-Rx around the country?

Q: No, we know that. We know that Davies and Locke were following T-Rx, as well as you. But you see, *you* were found in Moses' room. It was *you* who was with the body when it was still warm. Now you claim that both of you were hit on the way to the demonstration at Kent State, and that you took your comrade back to your room. Neither Locke nor Davies were in town at the time.

A: Where were they, Mexico?

Q: No, smart man. Davies was in Texas and McTaggart hasn't been heard of since.

A: So he has gone into hiding, has he?

Q: Who said anything about Alf? I said McTaggart hasn't been heard of since.

A: Then you know where Alf is?

Q: Well, no. Not exactly. He could have been brought for attempted murder, except Miss Taylor wouldn't press charges against him.

A: Wouldn't press charges! And I was wondering why she hasn't been the target of Moran? Why, he has her exactly where he wants her. Why should he kill her? They are probably making deals right now—and *not* with all our lily white government agencies.

Q: Be quiet, black man.

A: So it's a racial slur contest, is it? C'mon now, you can do better than that. After all I'm not only black, but I'm an evil radical, don't you remember?

Q: Jackson, be quiet.

A: That would be a good one, wouldn't it? But you and your fat-bellied pig policemen can't even follow up the good leads that I have just given you.

Q: Jackson!

A: You know that Alf was involved in this, and you don't want to do anything about it because you can't find him. You've got me, so I'm a convenient guinea pig—the pigs recruit another pig.

(The prisoner is taken away)

T-Rx: The History of a Radical Leader 298

A: (As he leaves) You know it's true. You know I'm innocent. Alf has bought Mary off—that is, Moran or Alf's superiors have. He tried to kill both of us. I was wounded superficially, but T-Rx was hit harder. They sent us both to Mt. Sinai in New York. Alf killed T-Rx. For all I know, they paid you off. This whole investigation stinks. It's a fake, do you hear me!? I'm being scapegoated for that Judas—I'm the scapegoat for this whole rotten society. I'm innocent!

Epilogue

On September 20, 1970, Nehemiah Moses, also known as T-Rx, was found shot to death in his Atlanta hotel room[64] by the rooming house manager, Bea Dixon, who had been trying to elicit rent payment from Moses for the room for three days. Because of this financial interest she paid special attention to his comings and goings. The time was 4:00 p.m. (about an hour before the manager planned to confront her tenant about money once again). She noticed a man later identified as Duvall "Mad Dog" Jackson go up the stairs to room #3. This seemed suspicious to the landlady. She didn't rent rooms to black people. So she decided to stop what she was doing in order to follow Jackson up the stairs (though this required that she take off her apron and stabilize what she had been working on in the kitchen). In her sworn testimony she admitted that these tasks might have taken as much as 5 minutes.

When Mrs. Dixon ascended the stairs, she noticed that #3 was open. She quickened her pace. When she arrived at the open door of T-Rx's room, her court testimony asserted that she could see Jackson hovered over the body of her tenant: Nehemiah Moses. There was blood on the floor. She turned around and descended the stairs at a quick rate and phoned the police.

Within ten minutes the men in blue arrived. They entered the room and saw T-Rx lying on the floor dead with an apparent

---

[64] The location was a rooming house in the Lakewood Heights section of Atlanta: 2070 Meador Avenue, S.E. The name of the establishment was *Momma Bea's*. T-Rx's room was apartment #3. It was on the second floor. It was a single room with a shared toilet down the hall. (I.B.)

gunshot to the head. Jackson had vacated the scene. Since Mrs. Dixon did not hear him descending the stairs, she assumed that he had climbed through the window and down the fire escape.

Jackson ran to an associate of the SUCCESS Project who had accompanied him to Momma Bea's rooming house.[65] The two immediately left the scene. Later that day, Duvall Jackson was arrested by the police at the SUCCESS storefront. He did not resist arrest. When asked why he fled the scene he told the officers, "I was afraid that Alf was still about and would kill me, as well. That's why I went out the window and that's why I high-tailed out of there with Pierce."

Jackson was tried on November 20th and pleaded innocent against the advice of his lawyer. After a four-day trial, Jackson was found guilty of first degree murder and sentenced to life imprisonment.

Jackson was sent to a maximum security prison: Georgia State Prison, in Reidsville. He was incarcerated for two years when an anonymous donor hired an attorney to review his case. With the help of this new lawyer, additional evidence was found that cast doubt on his conviction.

The corpse was exhumed and a thorough autopsy was performed (3/10/73). There had only been a casual report written by a student intern in the medical examiner's office for the first

---

[65] The SUCCESS Project was begun by T-Rx and Mad Dog in Baltimore. It was a pivot by T-Rx away from *protesting against* something to being an advocacy group *for* something. In this case it was a job training program that targeted young, unemployed African-Americans (both male and female). The program was geared to last for 3-6 months and included job placement. After two months in Baltimore, they got a federal grant and a staff to start. (The program ran for three years and trained and procured employment for 850 people.) Then the pair went down to Atlanta to try the same thing. Apparently, there was a feud between the two and they stayed in separate living quarters. On the day of T-Rx's death, Mad Dog Jackson was accompanied by Pierce Rowman who was local person (who would have been the director had the program grant ever been approved).

trial. Now there was a thorough autopsy performed by the medical examiner himself.

The re-examination showed that there were two bullet wounds to the head fired at point blank range. By comparing the entrance and exit wounds, it was the opinion that the murderer was firing upward. This would imply that the killer was smaller than his victim.

However, Duvall (Mad Dog) Jackson was a full three inches taller than T-Rx. If he had been the killer, the entrance and exit wounds would have showed a downward slant. The medical examiner concluded that Jackson couldn't have committed the crime unless he was standing on knees (which wouldn't have made the angle right either). From the wounds it was shown that there was no way that Jackson could have fired the pistol (one bullet in the wall [cited and photographed in the original investigation] confirmed that Mad Dog couldn't have raised T-Rx up on anything either to give the effect of a shorter man having committed the crime).

This data gave some confirmation to what Mad Dog contended about Alf who, incidentally, was several inches shorter than T-Rx.[66] The appellate court overturned Duvall (Mad Dog) Jackson's conviction after Jackson had spent 30 months in prison. The district attorney for Atlanta decided not to re-try the case. Therefore, the judge set a release date of 7/4/73. However, tragically, on the day before he would have been a free man, Mad Dog was murdered in his cell, presumably by another inmate.

A final ironic note should also be added to the story. The obituary that T-Rx was given in New York City's largest newspaper was only 50 words. Just a year before, T-Rx had been front page news. National magazines had printed stories on him. He was frequently mentioned in news broadcasts. But his death was, oddly enough, ignored by the mainstream media. Not a single national magazine had a story about it. It didn't make the network nightly news in any way.

Big stories of the day included: (a) "Five Easy Pieces" and "Tora, Tora, Tora" are hits at the movie box office; (b) The Soviet Union's space probe made it to the Moon and collected rocks; and

---

[66] We know Alf's relative height from an examination of several photographs that were in an envelope at the end of Mary Taylor's diary.

(c) Jim Morrison of the *Doors* singing group was found *not guilty of lewd behavior at a concert.*

The *New York Times* said in an obscure corner of their general obituaries: "Yesterday, student activist T-Rex was found murdered in his Atlanta hotel room. Rex was active in the anti-War movement and the civil rights marches of the middle and late sixties."

In San Francisco, some 1,000 people showed up to commemorate his burial-ashes being dispersed into San Francisco Bay—just off the Presidio.

How quickly our country forgets its gadflies. I wonder if T-Rx, grammarian that he was, would have found it significant that the largest newspaper in the country, *The New York Times*, couldn't spell his name correctly in their insignificant back page obituary?

Iris Brooke

Other Novels by Michael Boylan

Rainbow Curve (2014) Fans of baseball's history will appreciate this compelling tale about race, politics, and corrupting power and one's man's courage to stand-up. *De Anima #1*

The Extinction of Desire (2007) What would you do if you suddenly became rich? *De Anima #2*

To the Promised Land (2015) Are there limits to forgiveness: personal, corporate, and political? *De Anima #3*

Maya (2018) Follow the fate of an Irish-American family through three generations in the U.S.A. It's the story of immigrants, and a story of History. *De Anima #4.*

Naked Reverse (2016) There is a backdoor to the ivory tower. Find out what happens to one college professor who escapes. *Archē #1*

Georgia: Part One (2106), *Part Two* (2017), and *Part Three* (2017) A novel told in three parts. Explore racial identity through a murder mystery set in the early 20th century. *Archē #2, 3, 4*

The Long Fall of the Ball from the Wall (forthcoming) A novel set in the investigation of the JFK assassination that connects this event to larger social phenomena. *Archē #6*